P9-CLB-749

THE SECOND
FOUNDATION TRILOGY

Foundation's Fear
by Gregory Benford

Foundation and Chaos
by Greg Bear

Foundation's Triumph
by David Brin

By Isaac Asimov

Gold: The Final Science Fiction Collection
Magic: The Final Fantasy Collection

Isaac Asimov's History of I-Botics

Isaac Asimov's I-Bots: Time Was
by Steve Perry and Gary A. Braunbeck

Published by HarperPrism

THE SECOND
FOUNDATION TRILOGY

Foundation and Chaos

GREG BEAR

HarperPrism
A Division of HarperCollinsPublishers

HarperPrism
A Division of HarperCollins*Publishers*
10 East 53rd Street, New York, NY 10022-5299

This book contains an excerpt of *Foundation's Triumph* by David Brin. This excerpt has been set for this edition only and may not reflect the final content of the hardcover edition.

This is a work of fiction. The characters, incidents, and dialogues are products of the author's imagination and are not to be construed as real. Any resemblance to actual events or persons, living or dead, is entirely coincidental.

ISBN 0-06-105640-5

A hardcover edition of this book was published in 1998 by HarperPrism.

Cover Illustration © 1997 by Jean Targete

First paperback printing: May 1999

Printed in the United States of America

Visit HarperPrism on the World Wide Web at
http://www.harperprism.com

00 01 02 ❖ 10 9 8 7 6 5

For Isaac and Janet

ACKNOWLEDGMENTS

Special thanks to Janet Asimov, Gregory Benford, David Brin, Jennifer Brehl, David Barber, and Joe Miller. And also to the millions of fans of Isaac Asimov, who will keep his universes and characters alive for a very long time indeed.

The centuries recede, and the legend of Hari Seldon grows: the brilliant man, wise man, sad man who charted the course of the human future in the old Empire. But revisionist views prosper, and cannot always be easily dismissed. To understand Seldon, we are sometimes tempted to refer to apocrypha, myths, even fairy tales from those distant times. We are frustrated by the contradictions of incomplete documents and what amount to hagiographies.

This we know without reference to the revisionists: that Seldon was brilliant, Seldon was key. But Seldon was neither saint nor divinely inspired prophet, and of course, he did not act alone. The most pervasive myths involve . . .

—Encyclopedia Galactica,
117th Edition, 1054 F.E.

1.

◆

Hari Seldon stood in slippered feet and a thick green scholar's robe on the enclosed parapet of an upperside maintenance tower, looking from an altitude of two hundred meters over the dark aluminum and steel surface of Trantor. The sky was quite clear over this Sector tonight, only a few vague clouds scudding before nacreous billows and sheets of stars like ghostly fire.

Beneath this spectacle, and beyond the ranks of gently curving domes, obscured and softened by night, lay a naked ocean, its floating aluminum covers pulled aside across hundreds of thousands of hectares. The revealed sea glowed faintly, as if in response to the sky. He could not remember the name of this sea: Peace, or Dream, or Sleep. All the hidden oceans of Trantor had such ancient names, nursery names to soothe. The heart of the Empire needed soothing as much as Hari; soothing, not sooth.

Warm sweet air swirled around his head and shoulders from a vent in the wall behind him. Hari had discovered that the air here was the purest of any in Streeling, perhaps because it was drawn directly from outside. The temperature beyond the plastic window registered at two degrees, a chill he would well remember from his one misadventure upperside, decades before.

He had spent so much of his life enclosed, insulated from the chill as well as the freshness, the newness, much as the numbers and equations of psychohistory insulated him from the harsh reality of individual lives. *How can the surgeon work efficiently and still feel the pain of the carved flesh?*

In a real sense, the patient was already dead. Trantor, the political center of the Galaxy, had died decades, perhaps centuries before, and was only now obviously falling to rot. While Hari's brief personal flame of self would flicker out long before the Empire's embers powdered to ash, through the equations of the Project he could see clearly the rigor of morbidity, the stiffening face of the Empire's corpse.

This awful vision had made him perversely famous, and his theories known throughout Trantor, and in many parts of the Galaxy. He was called "Raven" Seldon, harbinger of nightmare doom.

The rot would last five more centuries, a simple and rapid deflation on the time-scales of Hari's broadest equations . . . Social skin collapsing, then melting away over the steel bones of Trantor's Sectors and municipalities . . .

How many human tales would fill that collapse! An empire, unlike a corpse, continues to feel pain after death. On the scale of the most minute and least reliable equations, sparkling within the displays of his powerful Prime Radiant, Hari could almost imagine a million billion faces blurred together in an immense calculus to fill the area beneath the Empire's declining curve.

Acceleration of decay marked by the loci of every human story, almost as many as the points on a plane . . . Beyond understanding, without psychohistory.

It was his hope to foster a rebirth of something better and more durable than the Empire, and he was close to success . . . according to the equations.

Yet still his most frequent emotion these days was cold regret. To live in a bright and youthful period, the Empire at its most glorious, stable and prosperous—that would be worth all his eminence and accomplishment!

To have returned to him the company of his adopted son Raych, and Dors, mysterious and lovely Dors Venabili, who harbored within tailored flesh and secret steel the passion and devotion of any ten heroes . . . For their return alone he would multiply geometrically the signs of his own decay, aching limbs and balky bowels and blurred eyesight.

This night, however, Hari was close to peace. His bones did not ache much. He did not feel the worms of grief so sharply. He could actually relax and look forward to an end to this labor.

The pressures pushing him were coming to a hard center. His trial would begin within a month. He knew its outcome with reasonable certainty. This was the Cusp Time. All that he had lived and worked for would be realized soon, his plans moving on to their next step—and to his exit. Conclusions within growth, stops within the flow.

He had an appointment soon to meet with young Gaal Dornick, a significant figure in his plans. Mathematically, Dornick was far from being a stranger; yet they had not met before.

And Hari believed he had seen Daneel once again, though he was not sure. Daneel would not have wanted him to be sure; but perhaps Daneel wanted him to suspect.

So much of what passed for history on Trantor now reeked of misery. In statecraft, after all, confusion *was* misery—and sometimes misery was a necessity. Hari knew that Daneel still had-much work to do, in secret; but Hari would never—*could* never—tell any other human. Daneel had made sure of that. And for that reason Hari could never speak the complete truth about Dors, the true tale of the odd and virtually perfect relationship he had had with a woman who was not a woman, not even human, yet friend and lover.

Hari, in his weariness, resisted but could not suppress a sentimental sadness. Age was tainted and the old were haunted by the loss of lovers and friends. How grand it would be if he could visit with Daneel again! Easy to see, in his mind's eye, how that visit would go: after the joy of reunion, Hari would vent some of his anger at the restrictions and demands Daneel had placed upon him. The best of friends, the most compelling of taskmasters.

Hari blinked and focused on the view beyond the window. He was far too prone these days to drift off into reverie.

The ocean's beautiful glow was itself decay; a riot of bioluminescent algae run rampant for almost four years now, killing off the crops of the oxygen farms, making the air slightly stale even in the chill of upperside. No threat of suffocation yet, but for how much longer?

The Emperor's adjutants and protectors and spokesmen had announced imminent victory over the beautiful plague of algae only a few days before, seeding the ocean with tailored phages to control the bloom. The ocean did seem darker tonight, but perhaps the uncharacteristically clear sky dimmed it by comparison.

Death can be both harsh and lovely, Hari thought. Sleep, Dream, Peace.

Halfway across the Galaxy, Lodovik Trema traveled in the depths of an Imperial astrophysical survey vessel, the ship's only passenger. He sat alone in the comfort of the officers' lounge, watching a lightly plotted entertainment with apparent enjoyment. The ship's crew, carefully selected from the citizen class, had stocked up on such entertainments by the thousands before launching on their missions, which might take them away from civilized ports for months. Their officers and captain, more often than not from the baronial aristocratic families, chose from a variety of less populist bookfilms.

Lodovik Trema in appearance was forty or forty-five, stout but not corpulent, with a pleasantly ugly face and great strong sausage-fingered hands. One eye seemed fixed skyward, and his large lips turned down as if he were perpetually inclined toward pessimism or at best bland neutrality. Where he had hair, he wore it in a short, even cut; his forehead was high and innocent of wrinkles, which gave his face a younger aspect belied by the lines around his mouth and eyes.

Though Lodovik represented the highest Imperial authority, he had come to be well liked by the captain and crew; his dry statements of purpose or fact seemed to conceal a gentle and observant wit, and he never said too much, though sometimes he could be accused of saying too little.

Outside the ship's hull, the geometric fistula of hyperspace through which the ship navigated during its Jumps was beyond complete visualization, even for the ship's computers. Both humans and machines, slaves of status space-time, simply bided their personal times until the pre-set emergence.

Lodovik had always preferred the quicker—though sometimes no less harrowing—networks of wormholes, but those connections had been neglected dangerously, and in the past few decades many had collapsed like unshored subway tunnels, in some cases sucking in transit stations and waiting passengers . . . They were seldom used now.

Captain Kartas Tolk entered the lounge and stood for a moment behind Lodovik's seat. The rest of the crew busily tended the machines that watched the machines that kept the ship whole during the Jumps.

Tolk was tall, his head capped by woolly white-blond hair,

with ashy brown skin and a patrician air not uncommon for native-born Sarossans. Lodovik glanced over his shoulder and nodded a greeting. "Two more hours, after our last Jump," Captain Tolk said. "We should be on schedule."

"Good," said Lodovik. "I'm eager to get to work. Where will we land?"

"At Sarossa Major, the capital. That's where the records you seek are stored. Then, as ordered, we remove as many favored families on the Emperor's list as we can. The ship will be very crowded."

"I can imagine."

"We have perhaps seven days before the shock front hits the outskirts of the system. Then, only eight hours before it engulfs Sarossa."

"Too close for comfort."

"The close shave of Imperial incompetence and misdirection," Tolk said, with no attempt to conceal his bitterness. "Imperial scientists knew that the Kale's star was coring two years ago."

"The information provided by Sarossan scientists was far from accurate," Lodovik said.

Tolk shrugged; no sense denying it. Blame enough for all to share. Kale's star had gone supernova last year; its explosion had been observed by telepresence nine months later, and in the time since . . . Much politicking, reallocation of scant resources, then, this pitifully inadequate mission.

The captain had the misfortune of being sent to watch his planet die, saving little but Imperial records and a few privileged families.

"In the best days," Tolk said, "the Imperial Navy could have constructed shields to save at least a third of the planet's population. We could have marshaled fleets of immigration ships to evacuate millions, even billions . . . Sufficient to rebuild, to keep a world's character intact. A glorious world, if I may say so, even now."

"So I've heard," Lodovik said softly. "We will do our best, dear Captain, though that can be only a dry and hollow satisfaction."

Tolk's lips twisted. "I do not blame you, personally," he said. "You have been sympathetic and honest and, above all, efficient. Quite different from the usual in the Commission offices. The crew regards you as a friend among scoundrels."

Lodovik shook his head in warning. "Even simple complaints against the Empire can be dangerous," he said. "Best not to trust me too much."

The ship shuddered slightly and a small bell rang in the room. Tolk closed his eyes and gripped the back of the chair automatically. Lodovik simply faced forward.

"The last Jump," the captain said. He looked at Lodovik. "I trust you well enough, councilor, but I trust my skills more. Neither the Emperor nor Linge Chen can afford to lose men of my qualifications. I still know how to repair parts of our drives should they fail. Few captains on any ship can boast of that now."

Lodovik nodded; simple truth, but not very good armor. "The craft of best using and not abusing essential human resources may also be a lost art, Captain. Fair warning."

Tolk made a wry face. "Point taken." He turned to leave, then heard something unusual. He glanced over his shoulder at Lodovik. "Did you feel something?"

The ship suddenly vibrated again, this time with a high-pitched tensile grind that set their teeth on edge. Lodovik frowned. "I felt *that*. What was it?"

The captain cocked his head, listening to a remote voice buzzing in his ear. "Some instability, an irregularity in the last Jump," he said. "Not unknown as we draw close to a stellar mass. Perhaps you should return to your cabin."

Lodovik shut down the lounge projectors and rose. He smiled at Captain Tolk and clapped him on the shoulder. "Of any in the Emperor's service, I would be most willing to entrust you to steer us through the shoals. I need to study our options now anyway. Triage, Captain Tolk. Maximization of what we can take with us, compared to what can be stored in underground vaults."

Tolk's face darkened, and he lowered his eyes. "My own family library, at Alos Quad, is—"

The ship's alarms blared like huge animals in pain. Tolk raised his arms in instinctive self-protection, covering his face—

Lodovik dropped to the floor and doubled himself up with amazing dexterity—

The ship spun like a top in a fractional dimension it was never meant to navigate—

And with a sickening blur of distressed momenta and a sound like a dying behemoth, it made an unscheduled and asymmetric Jump.

The ship reappeared in the empty vastness of status geometry—normal, unstretched space. Ship's gravity failed simultaneously.

Tolk floated a few centimeters above the floor. Lodovik uncurled and grabbed for an arm of the couch he had occupied just a few moments before. "We're out of hyperspace," he said.

"No question," Tolk said. "But in the name of procreation, *where*?"

Lodovik knew in an instant what the captain could not. They were being flooded with an interstellar tidal wave of neutrinos. He had never, in his centuries of existence, experienced such an onslaught. To the intricate and super sensitive pathways of his positronic brain, the neutrinos felt like a thin cloud of buzzing insects; yet they passed through the ship and its human crew like so many bits of nothing. A single neutrino, the most elusive of particles, could slip through a light-year of solid lead without being blocked. Very rarely indeed did they react with matter. Within the heart of the Kale's supernova, however, immense quantities of matter had been compressed into neutronium, producing a neutrino for every proton, more than enough to blow away the outer shells just a year before.

"We're in the shock front," Lodovik said.

"How do you know?" Tolk asked.

"Neutrino flux."

"How—" The captain's skin grayed, its ashen sheen growing even more prominent. "You're assuming, of course. It's a logical assumption."

Lodovik nodded, though he assumed nothing. The captain and crew would be dead within an hour.

Even this far from Kale's star, the expanding sphere of neutrinos would be strong enough to transmute a few thousandths of a percent of the atoms within the ship and their bodies. Neutrons would be converted to protons in sufficient numbers to subtly alter organic chemistries, causing poisons to build, nervous signals to meet untimely dead ends.

There were no effective shields against neutrino flux.

"Captain, this is no time for deception," Lodovik said. "I'm not hazarding a guess. I'm not human; I can feel the effects directly."

The captain stared at him, uncomprehending.

"I am a robot, Captain. I will survive for a time, but that is no blessing. I am deeply programmed to try to protect humans from harm, but there is nothing I can do to assist you. Every human on this ship is going to die."

Tolk grimaced and shook his head, as if he could not believe his ears. "We're going crazy, all of us," he said.

"Not yet," Lodovik said. "Captain, please accompany me to the bridge. We may yet be able to save something."

2.

Linge Chen might have been the most powerful man in the Galaxy, in appearance as well as fact, if he had merely willed it. Instead, he settled for something a mere shade less, and wore a far more comfortable rank and uniform—that of the Chief

Commissioner of the Commission of Public Safety.

The ancient and aristocratic Chens had survived through thousands of years to produce Linge by exercising caution, diplomacy, and by being useful to many Emperors. Chen had no wish to supplant the present Emperor or any of his myriad ministers, councilors, and "advisors," or to be any more of a target for young hotheads than he needed to be. His present visibility was already too high for his taste, but at least he was a target more of derision than of hatred.

He had spent the last of these early-morning hours looking over reports from the governors of seven troubled star systems. Three had declared war on their neighbors, ignoring threats of Imperial intervention, and Chen had used the Emperor's seal to move a dozen vessels into those systems as safeguard. Fully a thousand other systems were showing severe unrest, yet with recent breakdowns and degradations, the Imperial communications systems could only handle about a tenth of the information sent from the twenty-five million worlds supposedly under their authority.

The total flux of information, sent in real time and unprocessed by experts on Trantor's companion worlds and space stations, would have increased Trantor's temperature by tens of degrees. It was because of their considerable skill and intuition borne of thousands of years of experience that the Palace—that is, Chen and his fellow Commissioners—could keep a kind of balance with just the minimal, boiled-down stock from the vast Galactic stew.

He now allowed himself a few minutes of personal exploration, essential to his sanity. But even that was far from frivolous amusement. It was with an expression of curious intrigue that he sat before his informer and asked about "Raven" Seldon. The informer, a hollow, elongated ovoid arranged horizontally on his desk, gleamed its natural eggshell white for an instant, then brought up all the various murmurings and documents from around Trantor and key outlying worlds. A few small filmbook articles appeared in the center of the display, a piece from an offworld mathematical journal, an interview with the student newspaper at Seldon's sacrosanct Streeling University, bulletins from the Imperial Library . . . Mentioning nothing about psychohistory. The infamous Seldon was remarkably quiet this week, perhaps in anticipation of his trial. None of his colleagues in the Project had had much to say, either. Just as well.

Chen closed that search and leaned back in the chair, contemplating which crisis to respond to next. He had thousands of problems to deal with daily, most of which he fed to his selected councilors and their assistants, but he was taking a personal interest in the response to a supernova explosion near four relatively loyal Imperial worlds, including beautiful and productive Sarossa.

He had sent his most reliable and ingenious councilor to oversee what little rescuing could be done at Sarossa. His brows furrowed at the thought of the inadequacy of this response . . . And what political dangers the Commission, and Trantor, might face if nothing at all could be accomplished. Empire after all was a matter of *quid pro quo*; if there was no *quo* then there might as well be no *quid*.

Public Safety was more than just a political catchphrase; in this endless painful age of decay, an aristocratic official such as Chen still had an important function. The public image of the Commissioners seemed to be one of irresponsible luxury, but Chen took his duties very seriously. He harked back to a better time, when the Empire could and did look after its many children, the citizens of its far reaches, with established peacemaking, policing, financial and technical aid, and rescue.

Chen felt a presence at his elbow and his hair stood on end. He turned with a sudden flash of irritation (or was it fear?) to see his chief personal secretary, small and mild Kreen. Kreen's usually pleasant face was almost bloodless and he did not seem to want to convey his message.

"Sorry," Chen said. "You startled me. I was enjoying a relatively peaceful moment on this infernal device. What is it, Kreen?"

"My apologies . . . for the grief we must all feel . . . I did not want this news to come to you through your machine." Kreen was naturally suspicious of the informer, which could do so many of his own functions so quickly and anonymously.

"Yes, damn it, what is it?"

"The Imperial survey ship *Spear of Glory*, Your Honor . . ." Kreen swallowed. His people, from the small southern hemisphere Lavrenti Sector, had worked as servants to the Imperial courts for thousands of years. It was in his blood to feel his master's pain. Sometimes Kreen seemed less a human being than a shadow . . . though a very useful shadow.

"Yes? What is it—blown to smithereens?"

Kreen's face crinkled with anticipated distress. "No! Your Honor . . . That is, we do not know. It is a day overdue, and there are no communications, not even an emergency beacon."

Chen listened with a sinking heart and a twist in his stomach. Lodovik Trema . . .

And of course a fine captain and crew.

Chen opened and closed his mouth. He needed more information desperately, but of course Kreen would have given him all that there was, so there was no more.

"And Sarossa?"

"The shock front is less than five days from Sarossa, Your Honor."

"I know that. Have any other ships been dispatched?"

"Yes, sire. Four much smaller ships have been deflected from the missions to save Kisk, Purna, and Transdal."

"Sky, no!" Chen stood and fumed. "I wasn't consulted. They must not reduce those rescue forces . . . they're at minimum already."

"Commissioner, the representative from Sarossa was received by the Emperor just two hours ago . . . without our knowledge. He convinced the Emperor and Farad Sinter that—"

"Sinter is a fool. Three worlds neglected for one, an Imperial favorite! He'll get his Emperor killed someday." But then Chen calmed himself, closing his eyes, focusing inward, drawing on six decades of special training to set his mind calmly and quickly to finding the best path through this morass.

To lose Lodovik, ugly, faithful, and supremely resourceful Lodovik . . .

Let the opposing force pull you down, gather its energy for the spring back.

"Can you get me a summary or an actual recording of these meetings, Kreen?"

"Yes, sire. They will not yet be subject to review and interdiction by the court historians. There is commonly a backlog of two days on these rewritings, sire."

"Good. When an inquiry is held, and questions asked, we will leak Sinter's words to the public . . . I think the lowest and most popular journals will serve us best. Perhaps the *All-World Tongue*, or the *Big Ear*."

Kreen smiled. "I myself am fond of *The Emperor's Eyes*."

"Even better. No authentication required . . . just more rumors among an uneducated and unhappy population." He shook his head sadly. "Even if we bring down Sinter, it will be small recompense for losing Lodovik. What chance he might survive?"

Kreen shrugged; that was well outside his limited expertise.

So few in the Imperial Sector understood the vagaries of hyperdrive and Jump science. There was one, however. An old ship's captain turned trader and occasional smuggler, who specialized in sending goods and passengers along the quickest and quietest routes . . . A bright and unscrupulous rogue, some said, but a man who had been of service to Chen in the past.

"Get me an *immediate* audience with Mors Planch."

"Yes, Your Honor."

Kreen bustled out of the room.

Linge Chen took a deep breath. His time at the display was over. He had to return to his office and meet in person with Sector generals and planetary representatives from Trantor's food allies for the rest of the day.

He would have much preferred focusing all his thoughts on the loss of Lodovik and how to convert Sinter's foolishness to his own best interests, but not even such a tragedy, or such an opportunity, could interfere with his present duties.

Ah, the glamour of power!

3.

◆━

Privy Councilor Farad Sinter had overstepped his bounds so many times in the past three years that the boy Emperor Klayus referred to him as "my pillar of prying ambition," a typically ill-worded phrase that today, at least, carried no overtone of admiration or affection.

Sinter stood before the Emperor, hands clasped in unconvincing submission. Klayus I, barely seventeen years of age, regarded him with something less than anger and more than irritation. In his all-too-recent childhood, he had been called down too many times in private by his tutors, all selected and controlled by Commissioner Chen; he had become a sometimes sly, underhanded young man, more intelligent than most gave him credit for, though still subject to the occasional extreme outburst. Early on, he had learned one of the major rules of leadership and statecraft in a competitive and hypocritical government: He never let anyone know what he was really thinking.

"Sinter, why are you looking for young men and women in the Dahl Sector?" the Emperor asked.

Sinter had taken pains for this effort to be concealed. Somebody was playing political games, and that somebody would pay.

"Sire, I have heard of this search. I believe they are being sought as part of the genetic reconciliation project."

"Yes, Sinter, a project you began five years ago. You think I'm too young to remember?"

"No, your Highness."

"I do have some influence in this Palace, Sinter. My word is not completely ignored!"

"Of course not, your Highness."

"Spare me the obsequious titles. Why are you hunting down children younger than I am, and disrupting loyal families and neighborhoods?"

"It is essential to understand the limits of human evolution on Trantor, Your Highness."

Klayus lifted his hand. "My tutors tell me evolution is a long, slow process of genetic accretions, Sinter. What do you expect to learn from a few invasions of privacy and attempted kidnappings?"

"Pardon my even hoping to act as one of your tutors, Your Highness, but—"

"I hate being lectured to," Klayus said in a low growl that broke halfway through.

"But, if I may continue, with your permission, sire, humans have lived on Trantor for twelve thousand years. We have already seen the development of populations with particular physical and even mental characteristics—the stocky, dark people of Dahl, sire, or the menials of Lavrenti. There is evidence, sire, that certain extraordinary traits have occurred in certain individuals in the last century . . . Scientific evidence, as well as hearsay, of—"

"Psychic powers, Sinter?" Klayus tittered behind spread fingers and lifted his eyes to the ceiling. A few projected birds flew down and circled them, making as if to peck at Sinter. The Emperor had rigged nearly all of his chambers to reveal his moods with such projections, and Sinter did not like them in the least.

"Of a kind, Your Highness."

"Extraordinary persuasion. So I've heard. Perhaps the tumbling of dice in games of chance, or the ability to render women susceptible to our charms? I'd like that very much, Sinter. My assigned women are growing tired of my attentions." His expression grew peevish. "I can tell."

I hardly blame them, Sinter thought. *An oversexed partner of few charms and little wit . . .*

"It is a matter of some curiosity and perhaps importance, Highness."

"Meanwhile, you cause unrest in Sectors that are already unhappy. Sinter, it's a foolish liberty—or rather, a foolish breach of liberty. I am supposed to guarantee my subjects' freedom from being strapped to the horrid little hobbyhorses of my ministers and advisors, or even my own. Well, my hobbyhorses are relatively comfortable mounts . . . but this, but *you*, Sinter!"

For a moment, Sinter thought the Emperor was actually going to show a spine, some Imperial fortitude, and forbid this activity, and he felt a momentary chill. It was because Sinter was so good at finding attractive women for young Klayus, and replacing them when he or they grew bored, that Klayus put up with so many of his peccadilloes.

But the Emperor's eyes grew heavy-lidded, and his energy and irritation appeared to dissipate. Sinter hid his relief. Klayus the Young was, after all, relenting once more.

"Please don't be so obvious, my good man," Klayus said. "Slow down. What you need to know will come to you in good time, don't you think? I'm sure you have all of our interests at heart. Now, about this woman Tyreshia . . ."

Farad Sinter listened to Klayus's request with apparent interest, but in fact had switched on his recorder and would pay attention in more detail later. He could hardly believe his fortune. The Emperor had not forbidden these actions! He could indeed redirect and slow the less fruitful investigations; and he could also continue.

In fact, it was not humans, exceptional or otherwise, that he was after. Sinter sought evidence for the most extraordinary and long-lived conspiracy in human history . . .

A conspiracy he had traced back to the time of Cleon I, and probably long before that.

A myth, a legend, a real entity, coming and going like a wraith in Trantor's history. The Mycogenians had called him Danee. He was one of the mysterious Eternals, and Sinter was determined to find out more, however he might risk his reputation.

Talk of the Eternals was regarded with as little respect— less, actually—as talk of ghosts. Many on Trantor, an ancient world filled to overflowing with extinct lives, believed in ghosts. Only a select few paid attention to stories of the Eternals.

The Emperor talked on about the woman he was interested in, and Sinter appeared to listen attentively, but his thoughts were far away . . . Years away.

Sinter imagined himself being credited with saving the Empire. He savored energizing visions of sitting on an Imperial throne, or even better, of replacing Linge Chen on the Commission of Public Safety.

"Farad!" The Emperor's voice was sharp.

Sinter's recorder instantly fed him the last five seconds of conversation.

"Yes, your Highness. Tyreshia is indeed a beautiful woman, reputedly very high-spirited, and ambitious."

"Ambitious women like me, don't they, Farad?" The boy's tone softened. Klayus's mother had been ambitious, and successful, until she had fallen into Linge Chen's bad graces. She had tried to work her wiles on the Chief Commissioner in the presence of one of his wives. Chen was extremely loyal to his wives.

Strange that a weak boy like Klayus would enjoy strong women; invariably they grew bored with him. After a time, not even the most ambitious could hide their boredom. Once they learned who was really in power, ultimately . . .

Neither Sinter nor Linge Chen cared much for sex. Power was so much more rewarding.

4.

The greatest engineering feat in the history of Trantor had failed ten years before, and the echoes of that failure still plagued the important and crowded and troublesome Dahl Sector. Four million Dahlite engineers and heatsink workers, supplemented by an additional ten million laborers and even a smuggled force of the banned tiktoks, had worked for twenty years to drive the deepest heatsink yet attempted—over two hundred kilometers—into the crust of Trantor. The difference in temperature at the proposed depth and the surface would have generated sufficient energy to power one-fifth of Trantor's needs for the next fifty years . . .

But while ambitions were high, ability was not. The engineers had shown themselves to be less than inspired, the project management had been plagued by corruption and scandal at all levels, the Dahlite workers had revolted and for two years the project had been delayed. Finally, when completed, it had simply . . . failed.

The collapse of the shaft and its associated sodium and water towers had killed a hundred thousand Dahlites, seven thousand of them civilians living immediately above the shaft, beneath the oldest of Dahl's domes. The closest subsidiary sinks had also been threatened, and only by heroic intervention had further disaster been avoided—personal courage stepping in where leadership and design skill had collapsed miserably.

Ever since, Dahl had been under a political cloud, a scapegoat Sector on a world that was still capable of placing some trust in its leaders. In truth, Linge Chen had investigated and prosecuted all the corrupt officials and incompetent designers and conniving contractors. He had seen to it that tens of thousands were tried and sent to the Rikerian Prison, or put to hard labor in the worst depths of the heatsinks themselves.

But the economic effects had not been mitigated. Dahl could no longer meet its quota of Imperially mandated power; other Sectors tried to take up the slack, and what favor Dahl had ever had in the Palace declined to a wretched minimum. Near starvation had followed.

It was in this world that Klia Asgar had been born and raised, in the miserable shanty quarters once reserved for workers. Her father had lost his job a year before her birth, and spent the years of her childhood alternately dreaming of a return to prosperity . . . and drinking himself silly with yeasty, foulsmelling Dahlite liquor. Her mother had died when Klia was four; she had raised herself from that time on, and did remarkably well, considering that so many cards had been stacked against her from before her birth.

Klia was of moderate height for a Dahlite female, slender and wiry, with thin strong fingers on long hands. Her hair was short and black, and she possessed the family trait of finely furred cheeks that gave her a somewhat softer aspect than her hard, chiseled features would have otherwise conveyed.

She was quick to learn, quick in motion, and, surprisingly, she was also quick to smile and quick to express sentiment. In her private moments she dreamed of vague and indefinite improvements that might be possible in another world, another life, but they were just dreams. All too often, she dreamed of a strong alliance with some resourceful and handsome, bushymustached male, no more than five years her senior . . .

No such male entered her life. She was no great beauty, and the esteem and affection of others was the one area where she refused to exercise her surprising abilities to charm and persuade. If the male entered without prodding, well and good; but she would not apply any major push to get him. She believed she naturally deserved better.

In another age, another time, long forgotten, Klia Asgar would have been called a romantic, an idealist. In Dahl, in the year G.E. 12067, she was simply regarded as a stubborn but naïve girl of sixteen. Her father told her so whenever he was sober enough to express himself at all.

Klia was thankful for small favors. Her father was neither brutal nor demanding. When sober, he took care of his own few needs, leaving her free to do whatever she wanted: work in the black market, smuggle from the outside luxuries to the less savory (and Imperially oppressed) elements of the unemployed . . . Whatever she could do to survive. They rarely even saw each other, and they had not lived in the same apartment for two years. Not since that argument and the thing she had done in anger.

This day, she stood on a promenade overlooking the Distributor's Market, the most ragged and disreputable retail district in Dahl, waiting for an unnamed man in dusty green to pick up a package. The pieced squares of sky in the overarching dome showed great flickering gaps that cast shadows on the crowds, now thinning as the evening and home hours approached for the first shift of workers. Men and women shopped for their night's sparse supper, bartering more often than using credits. Dahl was developing its own economy; in fifty years, Klia thought, it might go independent, pushing out a weak and vacillating Palace-mandated economy for something more fundamental and native. But that, too, was little more than a dream . . .

Imperial trade monitors stood on the outskirts of the market, men and women with eyes and cameras constantly watching, recording the crowds. Where money and political oversight were concerned, creativity seemed to flourish; in every other endeavor, Klia thought, Trantor was intellectually bankrupt.

She saw a man who met the description standing between two of the omnipresent trade monitors. He wore a baggy, dusty green suit and cloak. The monitors seemed prepared to ignore him, much as they ignored Klia when she ventured into the market. She watched this with narrowed eyes, wondering whether he had bribed them, or whether he had other, less common ways of not attracting attention.

If he could do what she did, he would be a person to reckon with, perhaps partner with, in business—unless his skills were stronger than her own. In which case, she would have to avoid him like a fatal rash. But Klia had never met anyone stronger than she.

She lifted one arm, as she had been instructed. He quickly spotted her and walked with a light, almost mincing step in her direction.

They met on the stairs leading from the promenade to the market and the taxi square. Close-up, the man in dusty green had a plain and unremarkable face not improved much by a thin and unconvincing mustache. Klia was conventional enough to enjoy a good mustache on a man; this one did not impress her in the least.

Then he looked squarely at her and smiled. The corners of the mustache lifted and his teeth shone brilliant white behind smooth, babylike lips.

"You have what I need," he told her. No question; declaration.

"I hope so. It's what I was told to bring."

"That," the man said, pointing to her small parcel, "is of no consequence." Still, he extended a handful of credits and took the package with a thin smile. "*You* are what I seek. Let's find a quiet place to talk."

Klia drew back cautiously. She did not doubt she could take care of herself; she always had. Still, she never walked into any situation unprepared. "How quiet?" she asked.

"Just where we don't have to listen to the street noises," the man said. He lifted stiff-fingered hands.

There were few such places around the market. They walked several streets away and found a small coco-ice stall.

The man bought her a red coco-ice, which she accepted despite her distaste for the popular Dahlite delicacy. He bought himself a small dark stimulk, which he licked with quiet dignity as they sat at a tiny triangular table.

A square of sky above them darkened so severely that she could barely see his face. His lips seemed to glow around the stimulk.

"I'm looking for young men and women eager to see other parts of Trantor," the man said.

Klia grimaced. "I've heard enough recruiters to last me a lifetime." She started to rise.

The man reached out and took her arm. Without words, she tried to compel him to move it. "For your own good," he said, and did not react. She tried harder.

"Let me go," she ordered.

As if stung, the hand withdrew. It seemed to take a few seconds for the man to compose himself. "Of course. But this is a good time to listen."

Klia watched the man curiously. She hadn't compelled him; he had obeyed more like a servant reacting to his mistress than to a young girl he was trying to collar in a public place. Klia focused with more intensity on the man. His surface was not particularly attractive, but she encountered unexpected reserves, a central stillness, a peculiar metallic sweetness. His emotions did not *taste* the same as others.

"I only listen to people who are interesting," Klia said. She was starting to sound a little too arrogant. She fancied herself a more dignified sort of woman, not a street braggart.

"I see," the man said. He finished his stimulk and deftly tossed the stick into a receptacle. The proprietress walked to the receptacle, removed five sticks—a meager show for the day— and took them back to the rear of the stall to clean. "Well, is survival interesting?"

She nodded. "As a general topic."

"Then listen closely." He leaned forward earnestly. "I know what you are and what you can do."

"What am I?" Klia asked.

He looked skyward, just as the square immediately above flickered back to full brightness. His skin was unusually sallow, as if he wore makeup against some skin condition, though she could not detect the pockmarks of brain fever. Klia's cheeks themselves showed deep pocks, beneath the fur. "You had a bout of fever as a child, didn't you?" he asked.

"Most do. It's typical on Trantor."

"Not just here, young friend. On all human worlds. Brain fever is the ever-present companion of intelligent youth, too common to be noticed, too innocuous to be cured. But in you, it was no easy childhood illness. It nearly killed you."

Klia's mother had nursed her through the rough time, then had died just months later, in an accident in the sinks. She hardly remembered her mother, but her father had told her all about the illness. "What about it?"

His eyes were pale, and she suddenly realized they were not looking directly at her face, but at some irrelevant point to the right of her forehead. "I can't see well now. I make my way around by feeling the people, where they are, how they move and sound; in a place without people I am in some distress. I prefer crowds for that reason. You . . . do not. Crowds irritate you. Trantor is a crowded world. It confines you."

Klia blinked, uncertain whether it was polite to keep staring at his dead eyes. Not that she cared overmuch for politeness in a situation such as this.

"I'm just a runner and sometimes a swapper," she said. "No one pays much attention to me."

"I can feel you working on me, Klia. You want me to leave you alone. I disturb you, mostly because what I am saying has a certain truthful resonance—am I right?"

Klia's eyes narrowed. She did not want to be special or even memorable to this blind man in dusty green.

She closed her eyes and concentrated: *Forget me.* The man

cocked his head to one side, as if experiencing a muscle cramp. His mind had such an odd flavor! She had never experienced a mind like it.

And she would have sworn he was lying about being blind . . . but none of that was important in the face of her failure to persuade him.

"You've done well for yourself, for a child," he said in a low voice. "Too well. People are looking for those who succeed where they should fail. Palace Specials, secret police, not at all friendly."

The man stood and arranged his coat and brushed crumbs from the seat of his pants. "These chairs are filthy," he murmured. "Your effort to make me forget was exceptionally powerful, perhaps the most powerful I've experienced, but you lack certain skills . . . I will remember, because I *must* remember. There are a surprising number of those with your skills on Trantor now; perhaps one or two thousand. I've been told, no matter by whom, that most of you are marked by a particularly strong reaction to brain fever. Those who hunt for you are mistaken. They believe it passed you by."

The man smiled in her general direction. "I'm boring you," he said. "I find it painful to be where I'm not wanted. I'll go." He turned, seemed to feel for somebody to guide him, and took a step away from the table.

"No," Klia said, her voice catching. "Stay for a minute. I want to ask you something."

He stopped with a small tremor. Suddenly, he seemed very vulnerable. *He thinks I can hurt him. And maybe I can!* She wanted to understand his strange flavor—clean and strangely compelling, as if within this man, behind flimsy masks of deception, lurked a basic honesty and decency she had never encountered before.

"I'm not bored," she said. "Not yet."

The man in dusty green sat down again and put his hand on the table. He took a deep breath. *He doesn't need to breathe,*

Klia thought, but put away the absurdity quickly.

"A man and a woman have been searching for your kind for a number of years, and many have joined their group. I hope they live well where the man and woman will send them; I, for one, am unwilling to take the risk."

"Who are they?"

"They say one is Wanda Seldon Palver, the granddaughter of Hari Seldon."

Klia did not know the name. She shrugged.

"You can go to them, if you want—" the man continued, but she made a sour face and interrupted.

"They sound *connected*," she said, using the word in its derogatory meaning of close to the Palace and the Commissioners and other government officials.

"Oh, yes, Seldon was once a First Minister, and they say his granddaughter has gotten him out of a number of tough scrapes, legal and otherwise."

"He's an outlaw?"

"No, a visionary."

Klia pursed her lips and frowned again. In Dahl, visionaries were a dime a dozen—street-corner crazies, out of work, out of the grind, most driven insane by their work in the heatsinks.

The man in dusty green observed her reaction closely. "Not for you? Now, however, another man is searching for your type—"

"What type?" Klia asked nervously. She needed more time to think, to understand. "I'm still confused." She felt out his defenses lightly, hoping not to intrude in a way he would notice.

The man flinched as if poked. "I am a friend, not an enemy to be lightly manipulated. I know there's risk even talking to you. I know what you could do to me if you put your mind to it. Somebody else in a position of power thinks your kind is monstrous. But he doesn't understand at all. He seems to think you are all robots."

Klia laughed. "Like tiktoks?" she asked. The worker machines had fallen out of favor long before her birth, banned because of frequent and unexplained mechanical revolts, and the public distaste for them still lingered.

"No. Like robots out of history and legend. Eternals." He pointed west, in the general direction of the Imperial Sector, the Palace. "It's madness, but it's Imperial madness, not easy to overcome. Best if you leave, and I know the best place to go . . . on Trantor. Not far from here. I can help you make arrangements."

"No thank you," she said. There was too much uncertainty here for Klia to put herself in the hands of this stranger, however compelling parts of his story might seem. His words and what she sensed did not add up.

"Then take this." The man thrust a small display card into her hand and stood once more. "You *will* call. This is not in question. It is only a matter of time."

He stared at her directly, his eyes bright, fully capable.

"We all have our secrets," he said, and turned to leave.

5.

◆

Lodovik stood alone on the bridge of the *Spear of Glory*, peering through the broad forward-facing port at what might have been a scene of exceptional beauty, had he been human. Beauty was not an easy concept for a robot to grasp, however; he could see what lay outside the ship, and understand that a human would think it interesting, but for him, the closest analog to beauty was successful service, perfect performance of duty. He would in some sense *enjoy* notifying a human that a beautiful view was available through this port; but his foremost duty would be to inform the human that this view was in fact caused by forces that were very dangerous . . .

And in this duty he had no chance of succeeding, for the humans on *Spear of Glory* were already dead. Captain Tolk had died last, his mind gone, his body a wreck. In the last few hours of rational thought left to him, Tolk had instructed Lodovik on the actions that might be taken to bring the ship to its final destination: repair of the hyperdrive units, reprogramming of the ship's navigational system, preserving ship's power for maximum survival time.

Tolk's last coherent words to Lodovik had been a question. "How long can you live . . . I mean, function?"

Lodovik had told him, "A century, without refueling."

Tolk had then succumbed to the painful, murmurous half sleep that preceded his death.

Two hundred human deaths weighed on Lodovik's positronic brain like a drain on his power supplies; it slowed him somewhat. That effect would pass. He was not responsible for the deaths. He simply could not prevent them. But this in itself was sufficient to make him feel *weary*.

As for the view—

Sarossa itself was a dim star, still a hundred billion kilometers distant; but the shock front revealed its extended spoor like a vast, ghostly fireworks display.

The streams of high-energy particles had met the solar wind from the Sarossan system, creating huge, dim auroras like waving banners. He could make out faint traces red and green in the murky luminosity; switching his eyes to the ultraviolet, he could see even more colors as the diffuse clouds of the explosion's outer shells advanced through the outlying regions of the system's cometary dust and ice and gas.

There was so little time to act, nothing he could do . . .

And worse still, Lodovik could feel his brain changing. The neutrinos and other radiation had overwhelmed the ship's armor of energy fields, and had done more than just kill the humans; they had somehow, he believed, interfered with his own positronic circuitry. He had not yet finished his autodiagnosis sequence—that might take days more—but he feared the worst.

If his primary functions were affected, he would have to destroy himself. In ages past, he would have merely gone into a dormant mode until a human or another robot repaired him; but he could not afford to have his robotic nature discovered.

Whatever happened to him, there seemed little chance of discovery. *Spear of Glory* was hopelessly lost, less than a microbe in an ocean. He had never managed to trace the malfunction or make repairs, despite the captain's instructions. Being jerked rapidly into and out of hyperspace had burned out all the circuitry for faster-than-light communication. The ship had automatically broadcast a distress signal, but surrounded by the shock front's extreme radiation, there was little chance the signal would ever be heard.

Lodovik's secret was secure enough. But his usefulness to Daneel, and to humanity, was over.

For a robot, duty was everything, self nothing; yet in his present circumstance, he could look through the port at the effects of the shock front and speculate for no particular reason about physical processes. While not completely stopping his constant processing of problems associated with his long-term mission, he could drift in the middle of the bridge, his immediate needs and work reduced to nothing.

For humans, this could be called a time of introspection. Introspection without the target of duty was more than novel; it was disturbing. Lodovik would have avoided the opportunity and this sensation if he could have.

A robot, above all else, was uncomfortable with internal change. Ages past, during the robotic renaissance, on the almost-forgotten worlds of Aurora and Solaria, robots had been built with inhibitions that went beyond the Three Laws. Robots, with a few exceptions, were not allowed to design and build other robots. While they could manage minor repairs to themselves, only a select few specialty units could repair robots that had been severely damaged.

Lodovik could not repair this malfunction in his own

brain, if it was a malfunction; the evidence was not yet clear. But a robot's brain, its essential programming, was even more off-limits to meddling than its body.

There was one place remaining in the Galaxy where a robot could be repaired, and where occasionally a robot could be manufactured. That was Eos, established by R. Daneel Olivaw ten thousand years ago, far from the boundaries of the expanding Empire. Lodovik had not been there for ninety years.

Still, a robot had a strong urge to self-preservation; that was implicit in the Third Law. With time to contemplate his condition, Lodovik wondered if he might in fact be found, then sent to Eos for repair . . .

None of these possibilities seemed likely. He resigned himself to the most probable fate: ten more years in this crippled ship, until his minifusion power reserves ran down, with nothing important to do, a Robinson Crusoe of robots, lacking even an island to explore and transform.

Lodovik could not feel a sense of horror at this fate. But he could imagine what a human would feel, and that in itself induced an echo of robotic unease.

To cap it all, he was hearing voices—or rather, a voice. It sounded human, but communicated only at odd intervals, in fragments. It even had a name, something like *Voldarr.* And it gave an impression of riding vast but tenuous webs of force, sailing through the deep vacuum between the stars—

Seeking out the plasma halos of living stars, reveling in the neutrino miasma of dead and dying stars, neutrinos intoxicating as hashish smoke. Fleeing from Trantor's boredom, I grow bored again—and I find, between the stars, a robot in dire straits! One of those the Eternal brought from outside to replace the many destroyed—Look, my friends, my boring friends who have no flesh and know no flesh, and tolerate no fleshly ideals—

One of your hated purgers!

The voice faded. Added to his distress over the death of the captain and crew of the *Spear of Glory* and his odd feedback of selfless unease, this mysterious voice—a clear sign of delusion and major malfunction—brought him as close as a robot could come to complete misery.

6.

◆

From his vantage in the tiny balcony apartment overlooking Streeling University, R. Daneel Olivaw could not feel human grief, lacking the human mental structures necessary for that bitter reassessment and reshaping of neuronal pathways; but, like Lodovik, he could feel a sharp and persistent unease, somewhere between guilt at failure and the warning signals of impending loss of function. The news that one of his most valued cohorts was missing distressed him at the very least in that way. He had lost so many to the tiktoks, guided by the alien meme-entities, it seemed so recently—decades, however, and his discomfort (and loneliness!) still burned.

He had seen the newsfilm in a store window the day before, of the loss of the *Spear of Glory* and the probable end to any hope of rescue for the citizens of several worlds.

In his present guise, he looked very much as he had twenty millennia before, in the time of his first and perhaps most influential relationship with a human, Elijah Bailey. Of medium height, slender, with brown hair, he appeared about thirty-five human years of age. He had made some small accessions to the changes in human physiology in that time; the fingernails on his pinkie fingers were now gone, and he was some six centimeters taller. Still, Bailey might have recognized him.

It was doubtful that Daneel would have recognized his ancient human friend, however; all but the most general of those memories had long since been stored in separate caches, and were not immediately accessible to the robot.

Daneel had undergone many transformations since that time, the most famous of them being Demerzel, First Minister to the Emperor Cleon I; Hari Seldon himself had succeeded him in that post. Now the time was approaching when Daneel would have to intensify his direct participation in Trantor's politics, a prospect he found distasteful. The loss of Lodovik would make his work all the more difficult.

He had never enjoyed public displays. He was far more content to operate in the background and let his thousands of cohorts act out public roles. He preferred, in any case, that his robots assert themselves in small ways here and there over time, at key locations, to effect changes that would in turn effect other changes, producing a cascade with (he hoped) the desired results.

In the centuries of his work he had seen a few failures and many successes, but with Lodovik he had hoped to insure his most important goal, the perfection of the Plan, Hari Seldon's Psychohistory Project, and the settlement of a First Foundation world.

Seldon's psychohistory had already given Daneel the tools necessary to see the Empire's future in bleak detail. Collapse, disintegration, wholesale destruction: chaos. There was nothing he could do to prevent that collapse. Perhaps had he acted ten thousand years ago, with then-impossible foresight, using the crude and piecemeal psychohistory then at his disposal, he might have put off this catastrophe. But Daneel could not allow the Empire's decline and fall to proceed without intervention, for too many humans would suffer and die—over thirty-eight billion on Trantor alone—and the First Law dictated that no human should be harmed or allowed to come to harm.

His duty for all of those twenty thousands of years had been to mitigate human failures and redirect human energies for the greater human good.

To do that, he had mired himself in history, and some of the changes he had effected had resulted in pain, harm, even death.

It was the Zeroth Law, first formulated by the remarkable robot Giskard Reventlov, that allowed him to continue functioning under these circumstances.

The Zeroth Law was not a simple concept, though it could be stated simply enough: some humans could be harmed, if by so doing one could prevent harm for the greater number.

The ends justify the means.

This dreadful implication had powered so much agony in human history, but it was no time to engage in that ancient internal debate.

What could he learn from the loss of Lodovik Trema? Nothing, it seemed; the universe sometimes decided things beyond the control of rational action. There was nothing so frustrating and difficult to encompass, for a robot, as a universe indifferent to humans.

Daneel could move anonymously from Sector to Sector, along with the migrating unemployed now pandemic on Trantor. He could maintain contact with his cohorts through a personal communicator or his portable informer, as well as through illegal hookups to the planet's many networks. Sometimes he dressed as a pitiful street beggar; he spent much of his time in a cramped, dirty apartment in the Trans-Imperial Sector, barely seventy kilometers from the Palace. Nobody wished to look at a figure so old, bent, filthy, and pitiful; in a way, Daneel had become a symbol of the misery he hoped to overcome.

No humans remembered a fictional character who had so enjoyed going out in disguise among the common people, the *lower classes*, a man of pure and impossibly discerning intellect, a *detective* much like Daneel's old friend Elijah Bailey. With Daneel's frequent memory dumps and adjustments, all that he remembered was a single name and an overall impression: Sherlock.

Daneel was one of the many robots who had become disguised Sherlocks among the masses; tens of thousands throughout the Galaxy, trying not just to solve a mystery, but to prevent further and greater crimes.

The leader of these dedicated servants, the first Eternal, brushed as much of the street's filth from his rags as he could manage, and left the cramped and empty General Habitation Project hovel in search of finer clothes.

7.

◆

"They've searched the entire apartment," Sonden Asgar moaned, rubbing his elbows and looking smaller and more frail than she had ever seen him before. Klia's respect for her father had not been high in the last few years, but she still felt a pang for his misery—and an abiding sense of guilt that strengthened a sense of responsibility. "They went through our records—imagine that! Private records! Some Imperial authority . . ."

"Why your records, Father?" Klia asked. The apartment was a shambles. She could imagine the investigators pulling up cabinets and throwing out the boxes and few dishes within, tugging up the worn carpets . . . She was glad she hadn't been here, and for more than one reason.

"Not *my* records!" Sonden shouted. "They were looking for *you*. School papers, bookfilms, and they took our family album. With all your mother's pictures. Why? What have you done now?"

Klia shook her head and upturned a stool to sit. "If they're looking for me, I can't stay," she said.

"Why, daughter? What could—"

"If I've done anything illegal, Father, it's not worth the attention of Imperial Specials. It must be something else . . ." She thought of the conversation with the man in dusty green, and frowned.

Sonden Asgar stood in the middle of the main room, three

meters square, hardly a room at all—more of a closet—and shivered like a frightened animal. "They were not kind," he said. "They grabbed me and shook me hard . . . They acted like thugs. I might as well have gotten mugged in Billibotton!"

"What did they say?" Klia asked softly.

"They asked where you were, how you had done in school, how you made your living. They asked whether you knew a Kindril Nashak. Who is that?"

"A man," she said, hiding her surprise. Kindril Nashak! He had been the kingpin in her greatest success so far, a deal that had put four hundred New Credits in her accounts with the Banker in Billibotton. But even that had been trivial—surely nothing worth their attention. Imperial Special police were supposed to seek out the Lords of the Underground, not clever girls with purely personal ambitions.

"A man!" her father said sharply. "Someone who's willing to take you off my hands, I hope!"

"I haven't been a burden to you for years," Klia said sourly. "I only dropped by to see how you were doing." *And to discover why any thought of you made my head itch.*

"I told them you're never here!" Sonden cried. "I said we hadn't seen each other in months. None of it makes sense! It will take days to clean this mess. The food! They spilled the entire cookery!"

"I'll help you pick up," Klia said. "Shouldn't take more than an hour."

She certainly hoped not. Other faces were making her head itch now: Friends, colleagues, anyone associated with Nashak. One thing she was sure of: She had suddenly become important, and not because she was a clever member of the black market community.

An hour later, with the mess largely taken care of and Sonden at least beginning to recover his calm, she kissed him on the top of the head and said good-bye, and she meant it.

She could not look at her father without her scalp seeming

to burn. *Nothing to do with the Guilt,* she told herself. *Something new.*

Hereafter, any contact with him would be extremely dangerous.

8.

Major Perl Namm of Special Investigations, Imperial Security, assigned to the Dahl Sector, had been waiting for two hours in the private Palace office of Imperial Councilor Farad Sinter. He adjusted his collar nervously. The desk of Farad Sinter was smooth and elegant, crafted from Karon wood from the Imperial Gardens, a gift from Klayus I. The top of the desk held only an inactive Imperial-class informer. A sun-and-spaceship plaque hovered to one side of the desk. The office's high ceiling was supported by beams of Trantorian basalt, with intricate floral patterns spun-carved by tuned blaster beams. The major looked up at these beams, and when he looked down again, Farad Sinter stood behind the desk, wearing an irritated frown.

"Yes?"

Major Namm, very blond and compact, was not used to private audiences at this social level, and in the Palace, as well. "Second report on the search for Klia Asgar, daughter of Sonden and Bethel Asgar. Survey of the father's apartment."

"What else did you learn?"

"Her early intelligence tests were normal, not exceptional. After the age of ten, however, those tests showed extraordinary jumps—then, by the age of twelve, they revealed that she was an idiot."

"Standard Imperial aptitude tests, I assume?"

"Yes, sir, adjusted for Dahlite . . . ah . . . needs."

Sinter walked across the room and poured himself a drink. He did not offer any to the major, who wouldn't have known what to do with fine wine anyway. No doubt his tastes were limited to the cruder forms of stimulk, or even the more direct stims favored in the military and police services. "There are no records of childhood illness, I presume," Sinter said.

"Two possible explanations for that, sir," the blond major said.

"Yes?"

"Hospitals in Dahl typically record only exceptional ill-nesses. And in those cases, if the exceptions might reflect badly on the hospital, they report nothing at all."

"So perhaps she never had brain fever at all . . . as a child, when almost everyone of any intelligence contracts brain fever."

"It's possible, sir, though unlikely. Only one out of a hun-dred normal children escape brain fever. Only idiots escape completely, sir. She may have avoided it for that reason."

Sinter smiled. The officer was stepping outside his exper-tise; the number was actually closer to one in thirty million nor-mals, though many claimed they had never had it. And that claim in itself was evocative, as if escaping conferred some added status.

"Major, are you at all curious about the Sectors you do not patrol?"

"No, sir. Why should I be?"

"Do you know the tallest structure on Trantor, above sea level, I mean?"

"No, sir."

"The most populated Sector?"

"No, sir."

"The largest planet in the known Galaxy?"

"No." The major frowned as if he were being mocked.

"Most people are ignorant of these things. They don't care to know; tell them and they forget. The larger vision is lost in the day-to-day minutiae, which they know well enough to get along. What about the basic principles of hyperdrive travel?"

"Sky, no . . . Pardon me. No sir."

"I'm ignorant of that myself. No curiosity at all about such things." He smiled pleasantly. "Have you ever wondered why Trantor seems so run-down nowadays?"

"Sometimes, sir. It *is* a nuisance."

"Have you thought to complain to your neighborhood council?"

"Not my place. There's so much to complain about, where to begin?"

"Of course. Yet you're known as a competent and perhaps even an exceptional officer."

"Thank you, sir."

Sinter looked down at the polished copperstone floor. "Are you curious why I am so interested in this woman, this girl?"

"No, sir." But the major thought it worth a small, conspiratorial wink.

Sinter's eyes widened. "You believe I'm interested in her *sexually*?"

The major straightened abruptly. "No sir, not my place to think anything of the sort."

"I would be frightened even to be in her *presence* for long, Major Namm."

"Yes, sir."

"She never had brain fever."

"We don't know that, sir. No records."

Sinter dismissed that with a shake of his head. "I *know* that she never had brain fever, or any other childhood disease. And not because she was an idiot. She was more than merely *immune*, Major."

"Yes, sir."

"And her powers can be extraordinary. And do you know how I know that? Because of Vara Liso. She first detected this girl in a Dahlite market a week ago. A prime candidate, she thought. I should send Vara Liso with you on your rounds now, just to refine the hunt."

The major said nothing, merely stood at parade rest, eyes

fixed on the opposite wall. His Adam's apple bobbed. Sinter could read the man well enough without seeing into his mind; the major did not much believe all this, and knew little or nothing of Vara Liso.

"Can you find her for me, without Vara Liso's aid?"

"With sufficient numbers of officers, we can find her in two or three days. My small crew, by itself, would probably take two or three weeks. Dahl is not in a cooperative mood right now, sir."

"No, I suppose not. Well, find her, but do not attempt to arrest her or attract her attention in any way. You would fail, as her kind has made so many others fail . . ."

"Yes, sir."

"Tell me what she does, whom she sees. When I give you the order, you will shoot her with a large-bore kinetic-energy gun, from a distance, in the head. Understood?"

"Yes, sir."

"As you have so faithfully done before."

"Yes, sir."

"Then you will bring her body to me. Not to the criminalists, but to me, my private chambers. Enough, Major."

"Sir." Major Namm departed.

Sinter did not much trust the competence of any police, in any Sector. They could be bribed easily enough, yet Sinter's extended police patrols had not yet managed to bring down one robot; all of their targeted individuals had been humans, after all. The robots had deceived them very cleverly.

But Klia Asgar . . . a young girl, in form at least. How did a robot manage to appear to grow? There were so many mysteries Sinter looked forward to solving.

Brain fever's effect on curiosity, and on civilization in general, was not the most interesting of those mysteries, not at all. No mystery at all. Sinter strongly suspected that robots had created the disease, perhaps millennia before, after their banishment from the worlds of humans—their goal to subtly reduce intellectual capacity, creating an Empire that so seldom rebelled against the Center . . .

His mind whirled at the implications. So many suspicions, so many theories!

With a small, intent smile, Sinter lost himself in speculation for several minutes, then went to the desktop informer to look up the name of the largest world in the Galaxy.

Sinter had never had brain fever, himself; had somehow escaped it, despite having an above-normal intelligence. He was eternally curious.

And completely human. Farad Sinter had x-ray images taken at least twice a year to prove that fact to himself.

The largest inhabited world in the Galaxy was Nak, a gas-giant circling a star in the Hallidon Province. It was four million kilometers wide.

Now he had other matters to consider. He stood before his desk—he never sat while working—and scrolled through the briefs supplied to him by the informer. There was a stink rising over reassignment of ships to Sarossa, following the probable loss of the *Spear of Glory*. He could almost smell Linge Chen behind the growing public indignation. Yet that had actually been Klayus's doing, almost entirely. Sinter had gone along to allow the boy some sense of purpose.

Chen was a very intelligent man.

Sinter wondered if Chen had ever had brain fever . . .

Lost in thought, he sat for five minutes as the briefs filed past, ignoring them. He had more than enough time to deal with Commissioner Chen.

9.

◆

Mors Planch, in his fifty years of service to the Empire (and to his own ends), had watched things go from bad to worse with grim calm. Not much upset him, on the surface; he was quiet and soft-spoken and used to carrying out extraordinary missions, but he never thought he would be called upon—by Linge Chen, no less—to do something so mundane as go looking for a lost starship. And a survey vessel, at that!

He stood on the steel balcony suspended above the Central Trantor spaceport docks, looking down the long rows of bullet-shaped bronze-and-ivory Imperial ships, all gleaming and brightly polished on the surface, and all run by crews who performed their duties more and more by ritual and rote, not even beginning to understand the mechanics and electronics, much less the physics, behind their miraculous Jumps from one end of the Galaxy to the other.

Spit and polish and a shadow of ignorance, like an eclipse at noon . . .

He smelled the perfumery on his lapel to put him in a better mood. The pleasant aromas of a thousand worlds had been programmed into the tiny button, an extraordinary antique given to him by Linge Chen seven years ago. Chen was a remarkable man, able to understand the emotions and needs of others, while having none of his own—other than the lust for power.

Planch knew his master well enough, and knew what he was capable of, but he did not have to like him. Still, Chen paid very well, and if the Empire was going to rank growth and bad seed, Planch had no qualms about avoiding the worst of the discomforts and misfortunes.

A tall, spidery woman with corn yellow hair seemed to appear by his elbow, towering over him by a good ten centimeters. He looked up and met her onyx eyes.

"Mors Planch?"

"Yes." He turned and extended his hand. The woman stepped back and shook her head; on her world, Huylen, physical contact was considered rude in simple greetings. "And you're Tritch, I presume?"

"Presumptuous of you," she said, "but accurate. I have three ships we can use, and I've chosen the best. Private, and fully licensed for travel anywhere the Empire might care to trade."

"You'll be carrying only me, and I'll need to inspect your hyperdrive, do some modifications."

"Oh?" Tritch's humor faded fast. "I don't even like experts doing such work. If it ain't broke, don't fix it."

"I'm more than an expert," Planch said. "And with what you're being paid, you could replace your whole ship three times over."

Tritch moved her head from side to side in a gesture Planch could not read. So many social customs and physical nuances! A quadrillion human beings could be remarkably difficult to encompass, especially at the Center, where so many of them crossed paths.

They walked toward the gate to the dock aisle where Tritch's ships were berthed. "You told me we were going on a search," she said. "You said it would be dangerous. For that amount of money, I accept great risks, but—"

"We're going into a supernova shock front," Planch said, keeping his eyes straight ahead.

"Oh." This news gave her pause, but only for a second. "Sarossa?"

He nodded. They took a pedway to the berth itself, sliding past three kilometers of other vessels, most of them Imperial, a few belonging to the Palace upper crust, the rest to licensed traders like Tritch.

"I turned down four requests from local folks to go there and rescue their families."

"As well you should have," Planch said. "I'm your job today, not them."

"How high up does this go?" Tritch asked with a sniff. "Or perhaps I should ask, how much influence do you have?"

"No influence at all. I do what I'm told, and don't talk much about my orders."

Tritch undulated in polite dubiousness, walked ahead to

the gangway, and ordered the ship's loading doors to open. The ship was a clean-looking craft, about two hundred years old, with self-repairing drives; but who knew if the self-repair units were in good working order? People trusted their machines too much these days, because by and large they had to.

Planch noted the ship's name: *Flower of Evil.* "When do we leave?"

"Now," Planch said.

"You know," Tritch said, "your name sounds familiar . . . Are you from Huylens?"

"Me?" He shook his head and laughed as they walked into the cavernous, almost empty hold. "I'm far too short for your kind, Tritch. But my people provided the seed colony that settled your world, a thousand years ago."

"That explains it!" Tritch said, and gave another sort of wriggle, signifying—he presumed—pleasure at their possible historical connection. Huylenians were a clannish bunch who loved depth history and genealogy. "I'm honored to have you aboard! What's your poison, Planch?" She indicated boxes filled with exotic liquors, constrained by a security field in one corner of the hold.

"For now, nothing," Planch said, but he looked over the labels appreciatively. Then he stopped, seeing a label on ten cases that made his pulse race. "Tight little spaces," he swore, "is that Trillian water of life?"

"Two hundred bottles," she said. "After we get our work done, you can have two bottles, on the house."

"You're generous, Tritch."

"More than you know, Planch." She winked. Planch inclined his head gallantly. He had forgotten how open and childlike Huylenians could be, just as he had forgotten many of their gestures. At the same time, they were among the toughest traders in the Galaxy.

The lock door closed, and Tritch led Planch into the engine room, to examine and tinker with her ship's most private parts.

10.

As evening fell beneath the domes and the light outside his office windows dimmed, Chen sat in his favorite chair and called up the Imperial Library's news service, the finest and most comprehensive in the Galaxy. Words and pictures flitted around him, all relating to the Sarossan disaster and the loss of the *Spear of Glory*. There was no sign of the ship, and not likely to be; the best experts said it was very likely swallowed by a discontinuity within its final Jump, a hazard associated with supernova explosions but rarely seen, for the simple reason that supernovas were rare on human time scales. In all the Galaxy, less than one or two occurred each year, more often than not in uninhabited regions.

Already the popular journals were calling on the Emperor (respectfully, of course) and on Councilor Sinter, more acerbically, to rethink the transfer of rescue ships. Chen smiled grimly; let Sinter chew on *that* for a while.

Of course, if he heard nothing from Mors Planch, he would need to replace Lodovik, and soon; he had four candidates, none of them as qualified as Lodovik, but all worthy of service in the Commission of Public Safety. He would choose one as his assistant, and put the other three in apprenticeship programs, saying that the Commission should never again be caught with no immediate backups for the loss of important personnel.

There were three Commissioners who owed Chen for a few choice and private favors, and Chen could use this as a pretense for putting loyal men and women into their offices.

He shut off the news-service report with a flick of his hand and stood, smoothing his robes. Then he went out on the balcony to enjoy the sunset. There was no real sun visible here, of course, but he had mandated the repair of the Imperial Sector dome displays on a regular basis, and the sunsets were as reliable here as they had been everywhere in Trantor in his youth. He watched the highly artistic interpretation with some satisfaction, then put away all these masks of pleasure and considered the future.

Chen rarely slept more than an hour a day, usually at noon, which gave him the entire evening to do his research and make preparations for the work of the next morning. During his hour of sleep, he usually dreamed for about thirty minutes, and this afternoon, he had dreamed of his childhood, for the first time in years. Dreams, in his experience, seldom directly reflected the day-to-day affairs of life, but they could point to personal problems and weaknesses. Chen had great respect for those mental processes below conscious awareness. He knew that was where much of his most important work was done.

He imagined himself the captain of his own personal starship, with many excellent crewmembers—representing subconscious thought processes. It was his task to keep them alert and on duty, and for that reason, Chen performed special mental exercises for at least twenty minutes each day.

He had a machine for that very purpose, designed for him by the greatest psychologist on Trantor—perhaps in the Galaxy. The psychologist had disappeared five years ago, after an Imperial Court scandal orchestrated by Farad Sinter.

So many interconnections, interweavings. Chen regarded his enemies as his most intimate associates, and sometimes even felt a kind of sorrowful affection for them, as they fell by the wayside, one by one, victims of their own peculiar limitations and blindness.

Or, in Sinter's case, of aggressive idiocy and madness.

11.

▶

Hari lived in simple quarters on the university grounds, in his third apartment since the death of Dors Venabili. He could not seem to find a place that felt like home; after a few months, or in this case ten years, he would grow dissatisfied with the feel of a place, no matter how bland and characterless the décor was, and move to another. Often he spent his nights in a room in the library, explaining that he needed to get to work very early the next morning—which he did, but that was not his main reason for staying.

Wherever he was, Hari felt so very *alone*.

He was not above using his rank in the university, and his standing in the Imperial Library, to get new housing assignments. He allowed himself a few eccentricities, as one might allow an old engine extra maintenance, hoping that he could finish his task without breaking down. Coming to the end was difficult; he had so many memories of the beginnings, and they were far more exciting, far more satisfying, then anything reality at this point in his life could generate . . .

For that reason, he was almost looking forward to the trial, to a chance to confront Linge Chen directly and force the Empire's hand, his last and grandest finesse. Then he would know. It would be finished.

When he had been First Minister to Cleon I, he had also taken advantage of his position, on rare occasions, to gather the information he most needed. One of the crucial problems of psychohistory then had been the notion of unexpected cultural and genetic variability, that is, how to factor in the possibility of extraordinary individuals.

At the time, he had not seriously considered the psychic powers of individuals such as his granddaughter, or her father, Raych; he had not known about such things, other than in the abstract, and he had not considered too rigorously the powers of Daneel in that regard.

All of them, of course, had peculiar talents for persuasion, and he had in the past few years made sure that psychohistory took into account these particular talents, on the level exercised by Wanda.

In the time of his First Ministry, however, he had been concerned with the more familiar historical and political problem of ruthless ambition, whether or not aided by personal charisma. There had been plenty of examples around the Empire to study, and he had examined these political episodes as best he could from afar . . .

But that had not been enough. With the blind and unshakable determination Hari could bring to bear when confronted with a psychohistorical problem, and against Dors' wishes, Hari had appealed to Cleon to bring to Trantor five individuals of just that political breed, the ruthless, charismatic tyrant. They had been removed from their worlds after either rebelling against or subverting Imperial authority, which happened on about one in a thousand worlds, every standard year. Most often they were secretly executed; sometimes they were exiled to lonely rocks to live out lives empty of further victims.

Hari had asked Cleon to allow him to interview the five tyrants, and perform certain reasonably non-intrusive psychological and medical procedures.

Hari could remember the day quite clearly, when Cleon had called him into his ornate private rooms and shaken the paper on which his request was written in Hari's face.

"You're asking me to bring these *vermin* to Trantor? To subvert legal procedures and even forestall executions, just so you can scratch a bump of *curiosity*?"

"It's a very important problem, Highness. I cannot predict anything if I do not have a complete understanding of such extraordinary individuals, and when and how they appear in human cultures."

"Huh! Why not study *me*, First Minister Seldon?"

Hari had smiled. "You do not fit the profile, Highness."

"I'm not a raving psychopath, am I? Well, at least you think I might be redeemable. But to bring some of these obscene monsters to my world . . . What would you do if they escaped, Hari?"

"Rely on your security forces to find them again, Highness."

The Emperor had sniffed. "You have a confidence in Imperial Security's abilities that I don't, I'm afraid. Such monsters as these are like cancers—their talent is for bringing together tumorous organizations and subverting all to their own ends! Truthfully, Hari, what do you hope to accomplish?"

"It's far more than simply being curious, my Emperor. These people can change the flow of human events just as earthquakes can change the beds of rivers."

"Not on Trantor, they can't."

"Actually, sire, just the other day—"

"I know about that, and we're having it fixed. But these men and women are aberrations, Hari!"

"Common enough in human history—"

"And well enough understood that we can profile them and eliminate them from all Imperial positions. Most of the time."

"Yes, sire, but not always. I need to fill in those gaps."

"Purely for psychohistory, Hari?"

"I will see if I can improve your profiles, Highness, and perhaps make tyrants even more rare among your worlds."

Cleon had considered for a few seconds, finger on chin, then had lifted his finger away from his face, twirled it in a small circle, and said, "All right, First Minister. We have our political excuse, if we need it. Five?"

"All I could study in the time allowed, sire."

"The very worst?"

"You are familiar with the names I've requested."

"I never met with any of them, nor did I personally give them their Imperial imprimaturs, Hari."

"I know, sire."

"I won't be blamed for them in your psychohistorical textbooks, will I?"

"Of course not!"

And so, Hari had had his way. The five tyrants had been brought to Trantor and installed in the highest security prison in the Imperial Sector, the Rikerian.

The first meetings had occurred in—

Hari was deep in this reverie when the apartment announced that his granddaughter was outside the front door and wished to see him. Hari was always glad to see his granddaughter, especially in the limited time they had left together— but now! When he was on the track of something important!

Even so, he had not seen Wanda in weeks. She and her husband, Stettin Palver, had been assembling a core group of mentalics from Trantor's eight hundred Sectors, and there had been no time for socializing. In weeks, as soon after the trial as possible, the mentalics would leave for Star's End, to begin the work of the proposed secret Second Foundation.

Hari got up and let his legs gather strength before he put on his robe and told the door to open. Wanda entered, bringing with her a draft of cold air and the smells of the halls outside— cooking yeast (and not delicacies from Mycogen, either!), ozone, something like fresh paint.

"Grandfather, have you heard? The Emperor is hunting us down!"

"Whom, Wanda? Hunting whom?"

"Mentalics! They've subverted one of our party and she's confessed to all sorts of incredible stories, lies, to save her own skin. How could that *boy* do this? It's totally illegal to hunt citizens and assassinate them!"

Hari held up his hands and implored her to slow down. "Tell me about it, from the beginning," he said.

"The beginning is a woman named Liso, Vara Liso. She was one of the people we'd picked out for the Second Foundation. I thought she was unstable to start with—Stettin agreed with me, but she was very skillful, very persuasive and sensitive. We thought we could use her to speed up our hunt for other mentalics, if we didn't trust her to go with us . . . on the flight."

"Yes, I met her at the last meeting," Hari said. "A small woman, nervous-looking."

"Like a little mouse, I thought," Wanda confirmed. "She went to the Palace last month, without our knowing—"

"Whom did she talk to?"

"Farad Sinter!" Wanda fairly spat out the name.

"And what did she tell him?"

"We don't know, but whatever it was, Sinter has secret police hunting for certain mentalics, and if he finds them, they die . . . Of a bullet in the head!"

"Ours? The ones chosen for the Project?"

"No, amazingly enough. There's no one-to-one correlation. But he *has* killed candidates we haven't yet approached."

"Without even taking them in for questioning?"

"No such amenities. Murder, pure and simple. Grandfather, we're never going to fill our quotas at this rate! Our type of person is not common!"

"I've never met Sinter personally," Hari mused, "though some of his people interviewed me last year. Wanted to know about Mycogenian legends, as I recall."

"They're tearing up Dahl now, looking for a young woman! We don't even know her name yet, but some of our people in Dahl have felt her . . . almost found her . . . An extraordinarily powerful talent. We're sure she must be the one they're looking for. I hope she can survive long enough for us to find her first."

Hari gestured for Wanda to sit at his small table and offered her a cup of tea. "Sinter seems to have no interest in me or in the Project, and I'm certain none of them know about our interest in mentalics. I wonder what he's up to?"

"It's madness!" Wanda said. "The Emperor won't rein him in, and Linge Chen does nothing!"

"Madness is its own end, and its own reward," Hari said softly. He had followed the popular discontent with Sinter's handling of the Sarossan problem. "Chen may know what he's doing—and in the meantime, we have to survive and keep the Project on track."

Even the seriousness of Wanda's news did not stop Hari

from being irritated by the intrusion. If anything, it made the intrusion worse. He wanted very badly simply to be left alone to think about the tyrants and his interviews. Something important lurked in those memories, though he could not pin it down . . . However, he asked Wanda to stay for dinner with him, to calm her and see if she knew anything more.

And in the course of their dinner, Hari suddenly put the memories and equations together, and had the link he sought. The link was his vague sensation that he had encountered Daneel. When? Where? Then came the suggestion, and he had little doubt the meeting had occurred, and that Daneel had told him something ridiculous and potentially damaging . . . About Farad Sinter.

"I'm going to request an audience," Hari said to Wanda, as they brought out dessert together. She set the cups of cold pudding on the table and added a coco-ice for herself, a taste she had acquired from her father, Raych.

"With who?" she asked. "Sinter?"

"Not him, not yet," Hari said. "With the Emperor."

"He's a *monster*, a terrible infant! Grandfather, I won't allow it."

Hari laughed sharply. "Dear Wanda, I've been wandering into the jaws of lions since long before you were born." He looked at her seriously for a moment, then asked, quietly, "Why, do you sense something going wrong?"

Wanda looked away, then turned back to him. "You know why we've continued looking for mentalics, Grandfather."

"Yes. You and Stettin have discovered that your abilities wax and wane, for unknown reasons. You're looking for a more stable core group whose opposed strengths and weaknesses will cancel each other out and produce a steady influence."

"I can't hear anybody very clearly the past few weeks, Grandfather. I don't know what could happen to you. I see nothing . . . a blank."

12.
◆

Vara Liso had not slept through the night in years, for fear of what she might hear while asleep or on the edge of sleep. It was at these times that she could feel her net spread out over her neighborhood like a cloud, and when it came back, reeling itself in as it were, stuck to it were the emotional colors and desires and worries of her fellow humans for kilometers around, like fish she could not help but consume.

When young, this unwanted talent for night-fishing had come only once or twice a month, and she had never been sure whether she was simply mad or really could learn what she seemed to learn, from parents and brother, from neighbors, from lovers, the few she had attracted, for there was something spooky about her manner and appearance even then.

Now, the net swept wide every single night, and she could no longer absorb what it brought back, nor could she discard the bits and pieces of other people's lives. She felt like a strip of insect-gathering paper left to hang in a garbage dump.

It was when she had been approached by other mentalics— that was what they called themselves, though she had never given her talent a name—that she realized what she could do might be valuable to some. And it was when she spent one night in training at Streeling University, with other mentalics, that she caught a bit of dream that shook her to her core.

It was a dream of *mechanical men*. Not tiktoks, those funny little worker machines that had so worried the workers of Trantor and other worlds in their heyday, now gone, not tiktoks, but robots who looked like men, who could move unnoticed among men.

And there were even mechanical *women*, so this dream showed, capable of amazing feats, capable even of *murder* and of provoking love.

Vara Liso thought about this dream for weeks before

requesting an audience with the Emperor. This half-mad request—how could she hope to have an audience with such a lofty personage!—had been answered, and she had met not with the Emperor, but with another, his self-anointed Voice of Imperial Conscience, Imperial Councilor Farad Sinter.

Sinter had received her with politeness, a little cool at first, but as she had expanded upon her evidence, he had begun to burrow down with his questions, digging underneath her confusion to find the gems of evidence she herself had missed. Farad Sinter had taken a dream fetched raw and alive from anonymous night and given it political authority, a logical weight and structure she herself could not have pieced together in a million years.

In her way, Vara Liso had come first to respect Sinter, then to admire him, and finally to love him. He was so like her in many ways, sensitive and nervous, tuned to frequencies of thought no others could see . . . or so he convinced her.

She wanted to become his lover, but Farad Sinter convinced her that such physical pursuits were beneath them. They had loftier intimacies to satisfy them.

So she went this morning to his complex of private rooms in the Palace, escorted as always by a frosty pair of female security guards, convinced she was going to deliver to him that which he most sought. Yet Vara Liso kept something to herself, something that did not fit somehow.

"Good morning, Vara!" Sinter greeted. He sat at a small breakfast table on wheels, still wearing an ornately quilted golden robe, and his small, piercing eyes crinkled with something like amused welcome. "What do you have for me today?"

"Nothing more, Farad." She slumped into a couch in front of him, tired and discouraged. "It's all so jumbled. I swear I get so cluttered!"

Sinter tsk-tsked and shook his finger at her. "Don't disparage your particular talent, lovely Vara."

Her eyes widened with hungry need, which Sinter pretended he had not seen. "Have you learned who started you on this? With his dream of mechanical men?"

"I don't know whether it was a man or a woman, and no, I still don't know. I remember faces of those in the dream, but recognize none of them. Have you caught *her*?"

Sinter shook his head. "Not yet. I haven't given up, though. Any other clues, other candidates?"

Vara Liso blushed slightly and shook her head. Soon enough she would have to reveal how this had all begun, that she had once worked to become part of a group of low-level mentalics, much weaker than she, and weaker by far than the young woman she had sensed just two weeks before, whose mind had blazed in the night. But they had treated her well, and she had kept this back from Sinter for two reasons: because quite clearly these people were not robots, and because she had at least some sense of honor and loyalty. She tried to guide his vision this much, that he would not go off searching for every little petty mental persuader; she was sure he was wrong there, though of course she would not tell him so.

She suspected Sinter would not react well to being told he was wrong, even in some small detail.

Sinter had sent her to Dahl because of an unexplained hunch that there were more candidates there than elsewhere on Trantor, and that was where Vara Liso had tossed and turned one night in a dingy hotel room, gathering in her web, and bringing back the biggest catch ever.

She had hated Dahl, with its miasma of resentment and neglect and anger. She hoped never to return.

"I think you'll have to return and help the Specials personally," Farad Sinter said lightly. "They're not having much luck."

She stared at him, and tears welled up in her eyes.

"Oh, Vara, so sensitive! It's not as bad as all that. We need you there, to help us find this particular needle in the straw. If she's as talented as you say, well . . ."

"I will go if you wish me to," she murmured. "I had hoped you would have enough to go on."

"Well, we don't. I don't. I doubt I'll be given much more time to come up with hard evidence."

She forced herself to brighten, and asked the first question that came into her head. "What will these robots do if they know we know?"

Sinter's face stiffened. "That is our greatest danger," he said darkly. He lowered his gaze for a few seconds. "Sometimes I think they will replace us with replicas of ourselves, and we will go on doing everything we have ever done, just as we used to do it. But without spirit, nothing inside." He dug for the ancient word that sounded so mysterious and alien when spoken. "No *soul*."

"I don't understand what that means," Vara said.

Sinter shook his head briskly. "Nor do I, but it would be terrible to lose it!"

For a moment, they enjoyed this grisly prospect together, savoring the sense of shared and secret danger.

13.

◆

"Your request to see me is a little odd," the Emperor said, "considering that Linge Chen's Commission is putting you on trial for treason next month." Klayus waggled his head from side to side and raised his eyebrows. "Don't you think it's unseemly for me to agree to a meeting?"

"Very," Hari said, hands folded, head bowed. "It bespeaks your independence, Highness."

"Yes, well I'm far more independent than anyone gives me credit for. In truth, I find the Commission convenient, because it does a lot of the uninteresting work of managing little details I care nothing for. Linge Chen is wise enough to let me handle my own affairs and projects without interference. So, why should I be interested in you? Other than your professorial eminence."

"I thought you might be interested in the future, Highness," Hari said.

Klayus snorted faintly. "Ah, yes, your eternal promise."

Hari followed the Emperor through a central circular chamber at least twelve meters in diameter and perhaps thirty meters high. Above, all the inhabited star systems of the Galaxy rotated across the dome, blinking in order of settlement, tens of millions of them. Hari glanced up and squinted at the immensity of humanity's reach. Klayus I ignored the display. His pinched lips and wide, yet somehow vacuous eyes disturbed Hari.

Klayus pushed open a huge door to his entertainment room. Silently, the door—more like the entrance to a vault—swung on its immense hinges, and insects, green and gold, crawled over the frame. Hari assumed they were projected, but would not have been surprised to discover they were real.

"I have very little interest in your future, Raven," the Emperor said lightly. "I do manage to keep informed. I won't stop the trial, and I won't second-guess Chen on this."

"I refer to your own immediate future, sire," Hari said. *I hope Daneel's message was not just a dream, a fancy! This could turn deadly, if so.*

The Emperor turned, smiling at this dramatic turn of phrase. "You're on record as saying the Empire is doomed. That sounds treasonous enough to me. On this, Chen and I agree."

"I say Trantor will be in ruins within five hundred years. But I've never predicted your future, sire."

The entertainment room was filled with hulking sculptures of giant creatures from around the Galaxy, all savagely carnivorous, all caught in poses of attack. Hari regarded them with little appreciation for the artistry. Art had never interested him much, and certainly not the more popular forms, except where he could abstract entertainment trends as indicators for social health.

"I've had my palm read," Klayus said, still smiling, "by a number of beautiful women. They all found it most attractive, and assured me my future was bright. No assassinations, Raven."

"You will not be assassinated, sire."

"Deposed? Exiled to Smyrmo? That's where they sent my heroic quintuple-great-grandfather. Smyrmo, hot and dry, where you can't go outside without protective clothing, where the rooms smell of sulfur and there are only cramped tunnels through the rock fit for vermin. His memoirs are quite good entertainment, Raven."

"No, sire. You will be ridiculed until you lose all stature, then you will be ignored, and Linge Chen will never even have to defer to you. He will soon enough declare a people's democracy and leave you only as a symbol, with declining revenues, until you can no longer even keep up appearances."

The Emperor stopped between two Gareth-lions, the largest carnivores on any mid-gravity world, life-size—about twenty meters from clawed feet to razor-barbed, prehensile snouts. He leaned on the canted ankle of one. "Psychohistory tells you this?"

"No, sire. Experience and logical deduction, without benefit of psychohistory. Have you ever heard of Joranum?"

The Emperor shrugged. "I don't think so. Person or place—or perhaps beast?"

"A man, who wanted to become Emperor, and who betrayed his hidden origins by subscribing to an ancient myth . . . About robots."

"Robots! Yes, I believe in them."

Hari was taken aback. "Not tiktoks, sire, but intelligent machines made in human form."

"Of course. I believe they existed once, and that we out-grew them. Put them aside like toys. The tiktok experiment was simply an anachronism. We don't need mechanical workers, much less mechanical intelligences."

Hari blinked slowly, and wondered if he had underestimated this young man. "Joranum believed"—(*Was led to believe, by Raych! he reminded himself*)—"that a robot had infiltrated the Palace. He claimed First Minister Demerzel was a robot."

"Ah, yes, I seem to remember something about that . . . not that long ago, was it? Though before I was born."

"Demerzel laughed at him, sire, and Joranum's political movement collapsed under the weight of ridicule."

"Yes, yes, I remember now. Demerzel resigned and Cleon the First filled his shoes with another's feet. With your feet. Correct, Raven?"

"Yes, sire."

"That's where you acquired the political skills you so ably exercise, isn't it?"

"My political skills are minimal, your Highness."

"I don't *think* so, Raven. You're alive, and yet Cleon the first was assassinated by . . . a *gardener* . . . who had strong connections to you, correct?"

"In a way, sire."

"Still alive, Raven. Very savvy indeed, perhaps with your own secret and embarrassing files to reveal at key moments to key players. Do you have a secret file on Linge Chen, Raven?"

Hari, despite himself, let out a chuckle. Klayus seemed amused by this reaction, rather than affronted. "No, Your Highness. Chen is politically very armored. His personal behavior is above reproach."

"Isn't it, now! Who, then? Who will disgrace me and bring me down?"

"You have an assistant, a member of your privy council, who believes in robots." *This is what Daneel wanted me to know.* For a moment, Hari felt a chill. What if Daneel no longer existed, or had left Trantor, and he was imagining all this? The strain of the last few months, his constant gnawing grief . . .

"So?"

"Robots currently existing on Trantor. He is hunting them down and *shooting* them. With kinetic weapons."

Wanda's information had nested so well with Daneel's: the link, the gnawing suspicion, had come together. But Hari wanted, desperately needed, to think over his interviews with the tyrants. Something was still missing!

"Really?" The Emperor's eyes gleamed. "He's found real robots?"

"No, sire. Humans. Your subjects. Citizens of Trantor, even one offworlder, from Helicon, oddly enough, my home world."

"How interesting! I did not know he was hunting for robots. Shall I bring him here and question him, in front of you, Raven?"

"That is of no matter to me, Your Highness."

"I assume you refer to Farad Sinter."

"Yes, sire."

"Shooting and killing subjects! I did not know that. Well, I doubt that, Raven, but if it's true, I shall stop that part . . . But as for hunting down robots, surely that gives him something harmless to do."

"Linge Chen will let out enough wire for Sinter to entangle himself thoroughly, then he will turn on the power . . . And there will be many sparks, my Emperor, as Sinter fries. You might get burned."

"Ah, I see—Chen will remind everybody of the forgotten Joranum, and of the disgrace of my allowing such a person to run around killing citizens." Klayus buried his chin in one hand and frowned. "An Emperor, killing citizens . . . or ignoring their unjust deaths. Very volatile. Highly inflammable. I see it clearly enough, and it's not an unlikely outcome. Yes." The Emperor's expression darkened and his eyes narrowed. "I had plans for tonight, Raven. You've spoiled them, I'm afraid. I doubt this is something I can dispose of in a meeting of a few minutes or less."

"No, Your Highness."

"And Sinter is in Mycogen today, not returning until after dinner. So you will stay with me, and perhaps give me some advice, then, after, Hari—may I call you Hari?"

"I would be honored, Your Highness."

"After, we will celebrate, and I will reward you for your services."

Hari showed nothing on his face, but this of all things was the last he wanted to do. The Emperor's amusements were known to a few, and Linge Chen kept that number small by careful bribing and not-so-subtle pressure. Hari did not want to be one of the number Chen had to pressure, especially now . . .

He had to survive long enough for the trial, and beyond, to see the Foundations established . . . One by edict, the other in secret.

But he could not just allow Sinter's odd madness to imperil Wanda and Stettin's future, and the future of all those who might yet go to Star's End. Who had to go! The equations demanded it!

14.

◄═══►

Lodovik, after five days alone, had lapsed into the robot equivalent of a coma. With nothing to do, no way to return to a position of usefulness, and no one to serve, he had no choice but to enter a time of stillness, or face serious damage to his circuits. In this robotic coma, his thoughts moved very slowly, and he conserved the few remaining mental explorations left to him; in this way he avoided shutting down completely. Complete shutdown could only be reversed by a human or a maintenance robot.

In the slowness of his thoughts, Lodovik tried to assess how he had changed. That he had changed was certain; he could sense the change in key patterns, in diagnostics. Part of the basic character of his positronic brain had been altered by the flux of radiation in the supernova shock front. And there was something else as well.

The hypership drifted light-days away from Sarossa, far from any communications that would pass through status geometry, unable to receive hyperwave radio; and yet Lodovik was certain that someone, something, had examined him, tinkered with his programs and processes.

From Daneel he had heard of the meme-entities, beings who encoded their thoughts not in matter, but in the fields and plasmas of the Galaxy itself, those intelligences who had occupied the data processors and networks of Trantor, who had taken revenge upon some of Daneel's robots before Lodovik's arrival on the Capital World of the Empire. They had fled Trantor over thirty years ago. Lodovik knew little more about them; Daneel had seemed reluctant to spell out details.

Perhaps one or more of the meme-entities had come to inspect the supernova, or to energize themselves in its violent brilliance. Perhaps they had come across the lost hypership and found only him, and had touched him.

Altered him.

Lodovik could no longer be certain he was functioning properly.

He slowed his thoughts even further, preparing for a long, cold century until extinction.

Tritch and her first mate, Trin, regarded Mors Planch's activities with some concern. He had buried himself with several mobile diagnostic machines deep in the hyperdrive, far enough from the active coils of solid helium and the anti-queried, posi-tunneled meter-cubed crystals of sodium chloride, common table salt, to avoid injury, but still—

Tritch had never allowed any work on a hyperdrive while

her ship was actually in transit. What Planch was doing fascinated and frightened her.

Tritch and Trin watched from the engine gallery, a small weighted balcony that looked down the fifteen-meter length of the drive core. The end of the core was darkness; Planch had suspended a light over the place he worked, surrounding him in a pale golden glow.

"You should tell us what you're doing," Tritch said nervously.

"Right now?" Planch asked, irritated.

"Yes, right now. It would ease my mind."

"What do you know about hyperphysics?"

"Only that you pull up the deep roots of all atoms within a ship, twist them widdershins, and plant them in a direction we don't normally go."

Planch laughed. "Very impressionistic, dear Tritch. I like it. But it doesn't butter any parsnips."

"What are *parsnips*?" Trin asked Tritch. She shook her head.

"Every traveling hypership leaves a permanent track in an obscure realm called Mire Space, named after Konner Mire. He was my teacher, forty years ago. It's not studied much anymore, because most hyperships get where they're going, and the Empire's actuaries believe it's more trouble than it's worth to track lost ships, since they're so few."

"One in a hundred million voyages," Trin said, as if to reassure herself.

Planch poked up from between two long pipes and pushed a mobile diagnostic machine away from the engine, allowing it to float free. "Every engine has an extension into Mire Space while a ship is in transit, which helps the ship avoid becoming random particles. Old techniques which I won't go into allow me to hook up a monitor to the engine and look at recent trails. With some luck, we can pick up a trail with a frayed end, like a sawed-off rope—and that will be our lost ship. Or rather, the track of its last Jump."

"Frayed end?" Tritch asked.

"An abrupt exit from hyperdrive status leaves a lot of ragged discontinuities, like a frayed end. A planned exit solves all those discontinuities, smoothes them over."

"If it's so simple, why doesn't everybody do this?" Tritch asked.

"Because it's a lost art, I said, remember?"

She huffed in disbelief.

"You asked," Planch said, his voice muffled and hollow in the engine bay. "There's a one-in-five chance of screwing it up and throwing us out of hyperspace, scattered over about a third of a light-year."

"You didn't mention that," Tritch said tightly.

"Now you know why."

Trin swore under her breath and glared accusingly at her captain.

He worked for several more minutes, then poked up again. Trin had left the balcony, but Tritch still stood there.

"Still good for a couple of bottles of Trillian?" he asked her.

"If you don't get us killed," she answered grimly.

He floated away from the cylinders and pushed the diagnostic machines toward the hatchway. "Good! Because I think I've found her."

15.

◆

Hari's legs hurt from standing so long. Klayus had finally stopped describing his beast statues and gone off, and Hari had found a divan and sat gingerly, blowing out his breath.

Here was his chance to see just how far things had gone to ruin, and how much further the Empire had to decay. He didn't relish the opportunity, but he had long since learned that the best way to get along in life was to find multiple uses for unpleasant experiences. He longed to get back to his Prime Radiant and lose himself in the equations. People! So many tiny and yet possibly disastrous disruptions, like being chewed by hungry insects . . .

Hari turned toward the still-open hatchway and tried to see the crawling insects, but the projectors had turned off at Klayus's exit. When he turned back, a small Lavrentian servant, a young male, stood beside him.

"The Emperor says I shall make you comfortable before your business engagement," the servant said, smiling pleasantly, his round, smooth face like a small lamp in the gloom of the statue room. "Are you hungry? There's to be an elaborate dinner later this evening, but you should probably eat something now, something light and delicious . . . Shall I prepare something for you?"

"Yes, please," Hari said. He had eaten Palace food often enough not to turn down a chance to have more, and to eat in semiprivacy was a luxury he had not hoped for. "My muscles ache, too. Could I have a masseur sent in?"

"Certainly!" The Lavrentian smiled broadly. "My name is Koas. I am assigned to you for your stay. You've been here before, haven't you?"

"Yes, the last time in the reign of Agis XIV," Hari said.

"I was here then!" Koas said. "Perhaps I or my parents served you."

"Perhaps," Hari said. "I remember being very well treated, and I'm afraid parts of this evening are not going to be pleasant. I'm sure you'll relax me and prepare me for the work to be done?"

"Our pleasure," Koas said, and bowed fluidly. "What shall I prepare for you, or do you require a menu? We will, of course, use only the finest offworld and Mycogenian ingredients."

"Farad Sinter is a connoisseur of Mycogenian delicacies, is he not?" Hari asked.

"Oh, no, sir," Koas said, lips turned down. "He is fond of

much simpler fare." Koas did not seem to approve of this.

Then he's in Mycogen to force a little information out of them, Hari thought. *Their myths about robots. The man may very well be obsessed!*

Koas did not specialize in bodyworks, so two female servants entered with a suspension couch. Hari lay on the couch and gave in to their skilled ministrations with a grateful sigh, and for a few minutes, at least, was almost glad he had come to the Palace and requested his audience with Klayus.

The masseuses began work on his legs, smoothing out the corded muscles and somehow removing a pain in his left knee that had been bothering him for weeks. They then worked on his arms, pushing and prodding with a surprising force, causing a delicious sort of pain that quickly melted into a liquid lassitude.

As they worked, Hari thought of the special privileges accorded to leaders and their associates, their families. There was, of course, the velvet trap of power, sufficient luxuries to attract reasonably competent and competitive individuals to an ungratefully demanding job (in Hari's opinion; of course, Cleon I had been remarkably sanguine about being an Emperor at times, and even Agis had tried to act the part, which had led to his downfall under Linge Chen's Commission).

For Klayus, there was luxury without much responsibility; that meant endless opportunities for distortions of the personality, which Hari had seen so often in history, among figurehead rulers of various systems . . .

As the masseuses caressed and pummeled and prodded, he lapsed back into his memories of the meetings with the tyrants. They had taken place more than a kilometer beneath the Hall of Justice and the Imperial Courts, in the Rikerian Prison, at the center of a labyrinth of precisely controlled security systems. During his decades on Trantor, Hari had come to love interior spaces, even small ones, but the Rikerian Prison had been designed to punish, to flatten the spirit.

He had had nightmares about those tiny confined spaces, on and off, for years after.

In a cell barely tall enough to stand in, with slick hard black walls and two holes in the floor, one for waste and one for food and water, and no chairs, he had interviewed Nikolo Pas of Sterrad, the butcher of fifty billion human beings.

Cleon had his bizarre sense of humor, forcing the interview to take place there and not in some neutral meeting area. Perhaps he had wanted Hari to understand the man's current plight, to put things in perspective, perhaps to pity him, at least feel something, and not reduce everything to equations and numbers, as Cleon felt was Hari's wont.

"I'm sorry I have nothing to offer in the way of hospitality," Nikolo had said as they faced each other in the tiny, dim space. Hari had responded with some dismissive pleasantry.

The man before him was more than six centimeters shorter than Hari, with pale blond, almost white hair, large dark eyes, a small pug nose, broad lips, and a short chin. He wore a thin gray shirt and shorts and sandals. "You've come to study the Monster," Nikolo continued. "The guards say you're the First Minister. Surely you're not here to pick up some political tips."

"No," Hari said.

"To observe Cleon's triumph and the restoration of dignity and order?"

"No."

"I never rebelled against Cleon. I never usurped the Emperor's authority."

"I understand. How do you explain what you did?" Hari asked, deciding to jump in with no further preliminaries. "What was your reasoning, your goal?"

"They tell everybody I butchered billions on four worlds within my system, the system I was chosen to preserve and protect."

"That's what the records tell. What happened, in your opinion? And I warn you—I have the accounts from thousands of witnesses and other records at my disposal."

"Why should I even bother talking with you, then?" Nikolo said.

"Because it's possible what you say can prevent more butchery, in the future. An explanation, an understanding, could help us all avoid similar situations."

"By killing a monster such as myself at birth?"

Hari did not answer.

"No, I see you're more subtle than that," Nikolo murmured. "By preventing the rise to power of one like myself."

"Perhaps," Hari said.

"What do I get out of it?"

"Nothing," Hari said.

"Nothing for Nikolo Pas . . . How about the right to kill myself?"

"Cleon would never allow that," Hari said.

"Just the right to inform Cleon's First Minister, to give him more understanding, and therefore more power . . ."

"I suppose you could look at it that way."

"Not in this hole," Nikolo had said. "I'll talk, but someplace clean and comfortable. That's my price. You wouldn't put *vermin* in a hole like this. And I have ever so much to tell you . . . about humans as well as machines, or about machines that *seem human* . . . past as well as future."

Hari had listened, trying to keep his face impassive. "I'm not sure I can get Cleon to—"

"Then you'll learn *nothing*, Hari Seldon. And I see by the look in your eyes . . . I've touched something that provokes a deep curiosity, haven't I?"

Hari twitched on the suspension couch and the masseuse working on his neck softly ordered him to lie still. *Why haven't I remembered this conversation before now?* Hari asked himself. *What else has been suppressed? And why?*

Then, tension spoiling all the masseuses' work, another question, *Daneel, what have you done to me?*

16.

◆

The bodies had been arranged in neat floating rows in the crew lounge, the largest space in the ship, and also the closest space to the emergency hatch amidships.

Mors Planch backed away from the entrance, wondering for a moment if he had come upon a scene of torture and piracy. All the bodies were connected by ropes to keep them in place. *Tended to, taken care of even in death.* The air in the weightless chamber smelled from the decay of several days. Yet he had to make a count, to see if there was any value in searching elsewhere in the ship.

Tritch kept well back from the hatchway. Her red-rimmed eyes stood out above the white handkerchief she held over her nose and mouth. "Who put them in there?" she asked, voice muffled.

"I don't know," Mors said grimly. He put on a breather mask and entered to make his count. Several minutes later he emerged, his face wan. "Nobody alive, but not everybody is in there." He pushed past her and expertly caromed down the corridor, toward the bridge. Reluctantly, Tritch followed, stopping briefly to pass an instruction to Trin.

"They all died within minutes of each other, I'm guessing," Planch told Tritch as she caught up with him. "Radiation poisoning from the shock front."

"The ship is heavily shielded," Tritch said.

"Not against neutrinos."

"Neutrinos can't hurt us . . . They're like ghosts."

Planch peered into the darkened officer's lounge, switched on his torch, played it around the furniture and walls, saw nobody. "Neutrinos in sufficient numbers are what blew away the outer shells of the supernova," he said tightly. "Under such conditions, in such hordes, they can play strange and deadly tricks with matter, particularly with people's bodies. Smell the ship?"

"I smell the dead, back there," Tritch said.

"No. Smell the ship *here*. What do you smell?"

She took the handkerchief away from her nose and sniffed. "Something burnt. Not flesh."

"Right," Planch said. "It's not a common smell, and I've only experienced it once before . . . in a ship caught in a neutrino surge, but not from a supernova. From a planet being broken up and swallowed by a wormhole. One of the transit-station disasters, thirty years ago. The ship was caught in the emerging jet of converted mass. I investigated, part of a salvage crew. Everybody aboard was dead. The ship smelled scorched, like this . . . Burnt metal."

"Pleasant work," Tritch said, putting the cloth back to her nose.

The hatch to the bridge was open. Planch held out his arm to keep Tritch back. She did not argue. The bridge was illuminated only by starlight from the open direct-view ports. He turned his torch on and shined it on the panels, the captain's chair, the displays. The displays were all blank. The ship was dead.

"We won't have much air soon," he told Tritch. "Keep your crew back."

"I already have," Tritch said. "I don't want to stay here any longer than I have to. We can't salvage anything if the ship can't be revived."

"No," Planch said. The bridge seemed empty, and cold enough to make his breath cloudy. He pushed in farther, flailing briefly against the cold stale air with one hand until he caught a stanchion and rotated. From that vantage, he aimed his beam into the opposite corner. There, he saw a form curled into a fetal ball.

He pulled himself along until he floated a meter from the form. What he had been told was true; this one was alive. The head turned, and he recognized the features of Councilor Lodovik Trema. But it was not Chief Commissioner Chen who had told him Trema would be alive.

When they had first sighted the hulk in deep space, drifting helplessly, he had communicated first with Chen, then with another, who had paid him even more handsomely than Chen: the tall man who had many faces and many names, and who had hired him so often before.

That man was never wrong, and he had not been wrong this time. *Where all others might be dead, one might still be alive . . . And he must not be returned to Chen. He must be reported dead.*

Lodovik Trema blinked slowly, calmly, at Planch. Planch held his fingers to his lips, and whispered, "You're still dead, sir. Don't move or make a sound." Then he spoke a coded phrase incorporating both numbers and words that the man of many faces had told him to use.

Tritch watched them from across the bridge. "What did you find?" she asked.

"The man I'm looking for," Planch said. "He lived a little longer. He must have arranged the others, then come here to die."

As he brought out Lodovik, Tritch tried to back away, but could not find a grip fast enough. The body, curled and lifeless, floated ahead of Planch, under Tritch's nose, and she nearly gagged with some reflex expectation.

"Don't worry," Planch said. "This one doesn't smell much. It's colder on the bridge."

Tritch could not believe they had come all this way just to retrieve a single body. Back aboard the *Flower of Evil*, with Lodovik safely stowed in a box in the hold, she passed Planch a bottle of Trillian water of life, and he poured himself a glass and lifted it in cheerless toast.

"The Chief Commissioner wanted to make sure. And now that we know he's dead, and all the others with him, I'm to take him back to his home world and see him decently buried, with full Imperial honors."

"And leave all the others? That seems a little bizarre."

Planch shrugged. "I don't question my orders."

"Which world is he from?"

"Madder Loss," Planch replied.

Tritch shook her head in disbelief. "A man in such high authority, from a planet of disgraced parasites?"

Planch inspected his glass and lifted one finger before finishing its contents. Then he poked glass and finger at Tritch. "I remind you of our contract," he said. "The death of this man could have political repercussions."

"I don't even know his name."

"People could guess from what little you do know, if you spread it around in the wrong places. And if you do, I'll find out."

"I keep my contracts, and I keep my mouth shut."

"And your crew?"

"You must have known we were trustworthy when you hired us," Tritch said softly, dangerously.

"Yes, well it's even more important now."

Tritch stood and lifted the bottle from the table between them. She corked it firmly. "You've insulted me, Mors Planch."

"An excess of caution, no insult intended."

"Nevertheless, an insult. And you ask me to go to a world that no self-respecting citizen willingly visits."

"They're citizens on Madder Loss, too."

She closed her eyes and shook her head. "How long do we stay?"

"Not long. You drop me there and leave at your own pleasure."

Tritch was finding this harder and harder to believe. "I will ask no more questions," she said, and tucked the bottle under her arm. Apparently Planch was no longer so attractive to her, and henceforth their relationship would be strictly professional.

Planch regretted this, but only slightly.

When he delivered Lodovik Trema to Madder Loss, he would be a very wealthy man, and he would never have to work for anyone again. He imagined buying his own luxury vessel—one that he could keep in tip-top condition, which was more than could be said for most Imperial ships.

As for the strange and tightly disciplined man in the hold, a man who could stay enclosed in a coffin for days without complaint or need . . .

The less he thought about *that*, the better.

Lodovik lay in the darkness, fully alert but quiescent, having heard the coded phrase that alerted him to Daneel's participation in his rescue. He was to cooperate fully with Mors Planch; eventually, he would be brought back to Trantor.

What would happen to him there, Lodovik did not know. Having performed three self-checks in the coffin-shaped box, he was reasonably certain that his positronic brain had been altered in subtle ways. The results of his self-checks were contradictory, however.

To keep himself from deteriorating through disuse, he activated his human emotional overlay and ran diagnostics on that, as well. It seemed intact; he could operate as a human in human society, and that provided some relief. However, the contact with Mors Planch on the bridge of the *Spear of Glory* had been too brief for him to try out these functions. Best to be kept isolated until a more thorough test could be performed.

Above all, he must not reveal himself to be a robot. For all the robots in Daneel's cadres, this was of paramount importance. It was essential that humans never learn the extent to which robots had infiltrated their societies.

Lodovik put his human overlay into the background and began a complete memory check. To do so, he had to shut down his control of external motion for twenty seconds. He could still see and hear, however.

It was at this moment that something bumped against the box. He heard fumbling outside, then the sound of metal scraping against metal. The seconds ticked by . . . five, seven, ten . . .

The lid of the box was pried open with a metallic groan. With his head turned to one side, half facing the wall of the box, he could only gather a blurry glimpse of one face peering in, and a fleeting impression of one other. Eighteen seconds . . . the memory check was almost complete.

"He certainly looks dead." A woman's voice.

The memory check ended, but he decided to remain still.

"His eyes are open." A male voice, not that of Mors Planch.

"Turn him over and look for identification," the woman said.

"Sky, no! You do it. It's your bounty."

The woman hesitated. "His skin is pink."

"Radiation burns."

"No, he looks healthy."

"He's dead," the man said. "He's been in this box for a day and a half. No air."

"He just doesn't look like a corpse." She reached in and pinched the tissue of his exposed hand. "Cool, but not cold."

Lodovik blanched his skin slowly, and dropped his external temperature to match the ambient. He felt inefficient and incompetent for not having done that earlier.

"He looks pale enough to me," the man remarked. Another hand touched his skin. "He's cold as ice. You're imagining things."

"Dead or whatever he may be, he's worth a fortune," the woman said.

"I know Mors Planch by reputation, Trin," the man said. "He won't just hand his prize over to you."

Lodovik, on his conveyance into the rescue ship, had heard the name "Trin" applied to a woman he gathered was second-in-command to the captain, Tritch. This could be a very serious situation.

"Take his picture," Trin said. "I'll get a message out this sleep and we'll learn if he's the one they want."

A camera was lifted over the box and silently recorded his image. Lodovik tried to model all the possible causes for this behavior, all the scenarios and their potential outcomes.

"Besides, Tritch has given her word to Planch," the man continued. "She's known to be honorable."

"If we succeed, we'll make ten times what Planch is paying Tritch," Trin said tightly. "We could buy our own ship and become free traders on the periphery. Never have to deal with Imperial taxes or inspections again. Maybe even go to work in a free system."

"Pretty rough territories, I hear," the man said.

"Freedom is always dangerous," Trin said. "All right. We're here. We've broken the seals on the box. We're committed. Make an incision in his scalp and let's get what we came for."

The man withdrew what sounded like a scalpel from his pocket. Lodovik activated his eyes and watched them in the dim light of the hold. The man swore under his breath and brought the scalpel down.

Lodovik could not allow himself to be cut. He would bleed from any superficial wound, but even an untrained eye would see that he was not human if the scalpel cut deep. Lodovik quickly calculated all the pluses and minuses of any particular action he might take, and arrived at the optimal, based on what he knew.

His arm shot up from the box. His hand wrapped around the wrist of the man with the scalpel. "Hello," Lodovik said, and rose to a sitting position.

The man seemed to have a fit. He jerked and shrieked and tried to pull his hand away, then shrieked again. His eyes rolled up to show nothing but white and foam appeared on his lips. For several seconds he twitched in Lodovik's grasp, as Lodovik appraised the situation from his new perspective.

Trin backed toward the hatchway. She looked terrified, but not as terrified as the man in his grip. Lodovik judged the man's condition and carefully removed the scalpel from his fingers, then released him. The man clutched his shoulder and gasped, his face turning a medically questionable pale green.

"Trin," the man groaned, twisting toward her. Then he collapsed. Lodovik climbed from the box and bent to examine him. The woman near the hatch seemed transfixed.

"Your friend is suffering a heart attack," Lodovik said, glancing at her. "Do you have a doctor or medical appliances on this ship?"

The first mate gave a small, birdlike cry and fled.

17.
◆

Klia Asgar approached her contact in Fleshplay, a tough though popular family and labor resort on the outskirts of Dahl, near the entertainment Sector of Little Kalgan. Here, acts and rides from Little Kalgan itself were tried on very tough customers before they were exported around Trantor.

Fleshplay was full of brilliantly illuminated signs climbing up the walls of buildings almost to the ceil of the dome, announcing new shows and performance teams, old favorites revived in the Stardust Theater, popular beverages, stimulk, even outlaw stims from offworld. Klia glanced at the pouring cascades of projected beverages with a dry and thirsty appreciation.

She had been standing in a store alcove for twenty minutes waiting for her contact, not daring to abandon her position even for the time it might take to get a drink at a nearby street-vendor stall.

Klia watched the crowds with more than just her eyes, and saw them in more than just surface detail. On the surface, all seemed well enough. Men, women, and children at this evening hour strolled by in what passed for leisure-time dress in Dahl, white blouses and black culottes with red stripes around the waist for the women, pink jumpsuits for prepubescent children, a more rakish cut of black worksuit for the men. A more than cursory examination showed the strain, however.

These were the higher citizen classes in Dahl, the more fortunate day-shift and managerial workers, functionally the equivalent of the omnipresent gray-clad bureaucrats in other Sectors, yet there was a grimness in their faces when they weren't actively responding to banter or forcing smiles. Their eyes seemed tired, a little glazed, from months of disappointment and extensive layoffs. Klia could read the colors of their internal moods as well, caught in brief flashes, since she was otherwise occupied: angry purples and bilious green murmurings hidden within the deep holes of their minds, not auras, but pits into which she could glimpse only from certain mental perspectives.

Nothing extraordinary in all this; Klia knew what the mood of Dahl was, and tried to ignore it as often as possible. Full immersion would not just distract her, but could even infect. She had to remain isolated from the general herd to keep her edge.

She recognized the boy as soon as he walked into view across the street. He was perhaps a year older than she, shorter and squat, with a pinched face marked by several small scars on his cheek and chin, gang marks from Billibotton's tougher streets. She had delivered goods and information to him several times in the last year, when better courier jobs were not to be had. Now, she realized she might be seeing even more of him, and she did not like it one bit. He was tough to convince . . .

Good jobs had become almost impossible to find in the

past few days. Klia was known to be marked; few trusted her. Her income had plummeted almost to nothing, and worse still, she had narrowly escaped being captured by a gang of thugs whose leader she had never seen before. There were new folks in town, with new allegiances, providing new dangers.

Klia still had confidence in her ability to worm her way out of any tight situation, but the effort was exhausting her. She longed for a quiet place with friends, but she had few friends—none willing to take her in the way things were.

It was enough to make her rethink her whole philosophy of life.

The pinch-faced boy caught sight of Klia when she wanted to be seen, then went through a deliberate masquerade of casually ignoring her. She did the same, but edged closer, looking around as if waiting for somebody else.

When they were within earshot, the boy said, "We're not interested in what you're carrying today. Why don't you just slink out of Dahl and plague someone else?"

Brusqueness and even rudeness meant little, she was so used to them. "We have a contract," Klia said casually. "I deliver, you pay. My day boss won't take it well if you—"

"Word here is your day boss is in the sinks," the boy said, staring at her boldly. "And so's every other day or night boss who used you. Even Kindril Nashak! Word is he's been threatened with Rikerian, held with no charges! A free warning, girlie. No more!"

The noose was closing. "What do I do with this?" Klia asked, lifting the thin box under her arm.

"I take nothing and pay nothing, that's the word. Now slink!"

Klia glanced at him for less than a second. The boy shook his head as if touched by a buzzing insect, then looked right through her. He would not report having seen her.

If everybody wanted her to vanish, and there was no longer any work or reason to stay, it really was time to vanish. The thought scared her; she had never been outside Dahl for more than a few hours. She had less than two weeks' living in credits, a lot of those black-market exchanges good only for local merchants—who might shun her business now anyway.

Klia walked up the street to a less prosperous neighborhood, known euphemistically as Softer Fleshplay, and ducked through a fractured plastic front into an abandoned food stall. There, among scattered old wrappers and broken sticks of furniture, she cut the security seal on her package and opened it, to see if it contained anything valuable outside Dahl.

Papers and a bookfilm. She leafed through them and examined the seal on the bookfilm; personal stuff, in code, nothing she could decipher or sell anywhere. She had known that before she opened the package. She was handling only cut-rate deliveries anyway, often enough backup deliveries, information too tricky to risk being sent where security eyes could intercept it, yet not so tricky anyone wanted to pay large sums for better couriers . . .

And once she had been the very best of couriers, one of the highest paid in Dahl, inheritor of a tradition thousands of years old, as convoluted and ornate with language and ritual as any religious commerce off Trantor. Sometimes, even official and public papers were handed to the Dahlite couriers by legitimate day bosses, just to ensure faster delivery now that other communications systems were so often stalled or subject to surveillance by the Commission.

For her, it had all come to nothing, in just a few days!

With a jerk, she realized she was crying, silently, but nevertheless crying.

She wiped her face and blew her nose on a reasonably clean if dusty wrapper, dropped the package in the litter, and took to the street again.

Once outside, she crossed the street and waited for a few minutes. Soon enough Klia saw her tail, the one she expected would be after her if the delivery failed. It was a small, thin girl only a few years younger than she, pretending to play in the streets, dressed in a scaled-down version of a black heatsink work jumper. Klia was too far away to exert any persuasion, or learn anything; but she did not need to.

The girl darted into the abandoned stall and emerged a few seconds later with the shredded wrappings and contents of the package.

Klia had tailed couriers at the very beginning, sometimes cleaning up after failed deliveries. Now, it was being done to her. This was the last slap in the face, the final insult.

The street traffic was increasing. With the darkening ceil, the lights on the marquees above the streets would become brighter and more frantic, the crowds would jam shoulder to shoulder, looking for a moment's relief from dreary lives. For a hunted person, such a crush could be fatal. Anything could happen in a crowd, and she would be hard-pressed to persuade, hide, make the masses forget, or even just get away quickly; she might be found and killed.

She thought of the man in dusty green. The memory of him did not make her scalp itch, but she would have to fall much lower before she gave up her independence and actually joined a *movement*, even if they claimed to be like her . . .

Perhaps especially if they were like her! The thought of being among people who could do what she did—

Suddenly, everyone around her made her scalp itch. With a moan, she pushed through the roiling crowds, looking for the entrance to a plunger, the large, ancient elevators that worked the levels in Dahl and most of the other Sectors of Trantor.

Vara Liso, exhausted and haggard, begged the stolid young major by her side to let her rest. "I've been here for hours," she groaned. Her head ached, her clothes were drenched in sweat, her vision blurred.

Major Namm plucked at his Imperial insignia absently,

chewing on his lower lip. Vara focused on him with a hatred she had seldom felt before—but she dared not hurt him.

"Nobody?" he asked in a gruff tone.

"I've found nobody for the last three days," she said. "You've scared them all away."

He stepped back from the edge of the balcony overlooking the crowded Trans-Dahl thoroughfare through Fleshplay. Throngs on foot passed below the balcony, while trains and robos on elevated rails and narrow slaveways rumbled a few meters above them, rattling the empty apartment. Vara had been surveying the crowds from that location for seven hours; dark was falling quickly and the bright street signs across the thoroughfare were beginning to give her a headache. She simply wanted to sleep.

"Councilor Sinter would appreciate some results," the young man said.

"Farad must have some concern for my health!" Vara shot back. "If I become ill or burn myself out, what will he do then? I'm all the ammunition he has in this little war of his!" Her tone surprised her. She was close to the limits of her endurance. But rather than keep the focus on Farad's need for her, she pushed the onus onto the major. "If you're responsible for my effectiveness being reduced . . . What will Councilor Sinter say then?"

The young man considered this possibility with little apparent emotion. "You're the one who has to answer to him. I'm just here to watch over you."

Vara Liso held back a sharp bolt of anger. *How close they come! They don't even know!*

"Well, take me to a place where I can rest," she demanded sharply. "*She's* not here. I don't know where she is. I haven't sensed her for three days!"

"Councilor Sinter is especially concerned that you should find her. You told us she was the strongest—"

"Other than me!" Vara shouted. "But I haven't felt her!"

The blond major seemed to get it through his head that she wasn't going to work anymore today.

"The councilor will be disappointed," he said, then bit his lower lip again.

Is everybody here an idiot? Vara raged inwardly, but realized anger, letting her exhaustion control her, would get her nowhere, and could even harm her chances of getting what she wanted from Sinter. "I need to be alone for a while, rest, not talk," she said hoarsely. "We can try again tomorrow, in another Sector. I need a smaller area to work in—a few blocks at most. We need more agents and better reports."

"Of course," the major said, matching her tone with a more reasonable approach of his own. "Our intelligence has been a little weak. We'll try it again tomorrow."

"Thank you," she said softly. The major walked through the empty apartment and stood by the door, holding it open for her. She was almost through the door when a sharp spike of what she could only call *envy* shot through her: the sudden awareness she was close to a fellow human with talents like her own. Her face went white, and she stammered, "N-n-not yet. She's here!"

"Where?" the major demanded, pushing her back to the window.

"Yes, yes, yes," Vara muttered as he propelled her. *They treat me like a despicable runt!* But the excitement of the chase was strong. She pointed a trembling finger and wiped her lips with the back of her other hand. "Down there! She's close!"

The agent peered down into the crowd, following the line of the small woman's finger. He saw a female figure, swift and almost colorless, dart through the crowds toward the entrance of a plunger.

Immediately, he used his comm to alert other agents on the street below.

"You're sure?" he demanded of Vara, but she could only point and rub her lips, the sensation was so great. She had to work hard to keep from trembling. She hated this sensation—had come to know it whenever she was around the others in Wanda and Stettin's group, but never as strongly as this. *Envy* like an ache in her chest, as if this *girl* could steal everything in life from her and leave only empty expectations and endless disappointment!

"Her!" she said. "Get her, *please!*"

Something made Klia's scalp feel as if it were on fire, and she cried out as she darted into the plunger cab. Two older men with heavy black-and-gray mustaches looked at her with mild concern.

Klia could not see over their shoulders. She jumped and caught a glimpse of two square-featured men running as fast as they could toward the open plunger doors. The doors started to close; the agents shouted for it to stop, and even flashed code blinkers to take control of the mechanism.

Klia dug into her pocket and produced a maintenance key, illegal but standard issue for couriers. The elevator doors hesitated, then stopped. She plunged her key into the control panel and shouted, "Emergency! Down now!"

The doors resumed closing. The two men could not make it and pounded on the outside, shouting for her to stop.

The older males gave her a wide berth. "Where would you like to get off?" she asked breathlessly, smiling.

"The next level, please," one of them said.

"Fine." She gave the plunger its instructions, then made the older males forget they had seen her or experienced anything out of the ordinary.

They stepped out onto the next level, and she quickly ordered the doors to close again. With a sigh, she leaned against the dirt-smeared wall. A scratchy mechanical voice said, "Emergency instructions. Which maintenance level?"

She reached out with all her strength and found spots of

trouble for many levels above and below. Her scalp still hurt. She had to get out of range of the teams sent to find her. There was only one likely direction—down.

"Bottom," she answered. "Zero."

Four kilometers beneath all the occupied levels—

The suburban rivers.

18.

◆

Tritch met Mors Planch in neutral territory, far from the hold but aft of the crew quarters, in a weightless service hallway. If she had hoped to have him at a disadvantage in weightless conditions, she had hoped in vain; Planch was as much at home weightless as in standard gravitation.

"Your corpse has some remarkable talents," she said as Planch pushed into view around the curve of the bulkhead.

"Your crew suffers some remarkable ethical lapses," Planch replied.

Tritch shrugged. "Ambition is a constant curse these days. I found Gela Andanch outside the hold, in very bad condition. He's stable now in the infirmary."

Planch nodded; Lodovik had not heard the man's name, and had just happened to run into Planch while carrying the limp body forward. Planch had taken Andanch and told Lodovik to return to the hold. Presumably, he was still there.

"What were they looking for?"

"Someone paid them off," Tritch said lightly. "I presume it was someone opposed to the party or parties paying you. If they delivered Lodovik Trema, they'd each get fifty times what I pay them in a standard year. That's a lot of money, even for Imperial corruption."

"What are you going to do with them?" Planch asked.

"I presume they would have taken the ship and put us out of action, maybe killed us. Trin is in my cabin now, drinking heavily—and not Trillian, either. When she's drunk enough, I might just toss her out of the hold over Trantor, and hope she burns up over the Palace." Tritch's eyelids fluttered slightly, and her lips grew tight. "She was a good first mate. My problem now is, what should I do with you?"

"I haven't betrayed you," Planch said.

"And you haven't told me the truth. Whatever Lodovik Trema is, he isn't human. Trin is babbling about simulacra, *robots*. Whoever paid her off told her she'd be looking for mechanical men. What do you know about robots?"

"He's not a robot," Planch said with a shake of his head and a smile. "Nobody makes robots anymore."

"In our nightmares," Tritch said. "Class B filmbooks. Tiktoks with mutated brains bent on mindless revenge. But Lodovik Trema . . . first councilor to the Chief Commissioner of Public Safety?"

"It's nonsense," Planch said shortly, as if this entire conversation was beneath his dignity.

"I looked it up, Mors." Tritch's face suddenly became sad, assuming a kind of limpness away from the draw of gravitation. "You were right. Neutrinos in sufficient numbers are deadly. And there's no shielding against neutrino flux."

"He's dying," Planch lied. "His condition in any case has to be kept secret."

Tritch shook her head. "I don't believe you. But I'm going to keep my word and drop you on Madder Loss." She mused for a moment. "Maybe I'll drop Trin and Andanch there with you, let you all work things out. Now go confer with your dead minister."

She turned and headed forward.

"What about getting back into my cabin?" Planch said.

"I'll send food and a cot back to the hold. If I let someone who consorts with a living corpse go forward, I'd have a mutiny on my hands. We'll be at Madder Loss in a day and a half."

Planch shuddered as she passed out of sight. He, too, didn't like associating with Lodovik Trema. Tritch was perfectly correct.

Nobody aboard the *Arrow of Destiny* could have survived. Nobody human.

Lodovik stood in the hold beside his box, hands folded, waiting for Planch to return. By his actions, Lodovik had apparently brought severe harm to a human being, and yet the expected difficulties of such a situation—decrease in mental frequency, critical reexamination, and under extreme circumstances, even complete shut-down—did not affect him much, if at all. Even allowing for the extended nature of his long-term mission for Daneel—and under the provisions of the Zeroth Law—there should have been deeply uncomfortable repercussions.

Yet there were none to speak of. Lodovik felt calm and fully functional. He did not feel contented—he had caused damage and was aware of that, quite clearly—but he experienced nothing like the near-paralyzing realization of having broken one of the Calvinian Three Laws.

Clearly, something within him had changed. He was trying to track down what that might be when Planch returned.

"We're stuck back here for the duration," Planch said matter-of-factly. "I had a very nice cabin, too. And the captain and I were . . ." He shook his head sadly, then his features sharpened. "Never mind. Something is very wrong with this whole scenario."

"What might that be?" Lodovik asked. He stretched and smiled. The human persona slid smoothly over all his other functions. "The box was cramped, but I've spent time in worse conditions. I emerged at the wrong moment, I suppose?"

"No supposing about it. The man suffered a heart attack."

"I'm very sorry. But they were up to no good, I'm afraid."

"Someone else wants you, alive or dead," Planch said. "I thought the Chief Commissioner of Public Safety was pretty much unassailable. Invincible."

"Nobody is invincible in this forsaken time," Lodovik said. "I apologize for causing you difficulties."

Planch stared hard at Lodovik. "Up until now I've ignored all my misapprehensions about this mission, about you. In Imperial politics, anything can happen—individuals can be worth entire solar systems. That's how centralized politics works."

"Surely you're not a diffusionist, Mors Planch?"

"No. There's no money and not much life in being a traitor to Linge Chen."

"You mean, to the Emperor."

Planch did not correct himself. "My curiosity has been piqued to dangerous levels, however. Curiosity is like neutrino flux—it can penetrate anything, and in sufficient quantity, it can kill. I'm aware of that . . . But my curiosity about you . . ." He clamped his jaw shut and looked away.

"I'm a middle-aged man with extraordinary good fortune, let's leave it at that," Lodovik said, making a wry face. "There are things neither you nor I can be told . . . and we would be best served by keeping our curiosities in check. Yes, I should be dead. I know that better than anybody. The reason I am not dead, however, has nothing to do with extraordinary superstitions about . . . what was it . . . robots? You can rest assured on that point, Mors Planch."

"This isn't the first I've heard about robots, you know," Planch said. "Murmurs about artificial humans sweep the worlds from time to time, like a dusty breeze. Thirty-five years ago, there was a massacre in a Seventh Octant system. Four planets were involved, quite prosperous worlds, united by a proud common culture, shaping up to be a real force in Imperial economics."

"I remember," Lodovik said. "The ruler claimed he had

positive proof that robots had infiltrated to the highest levels, and were fomenting rebellion. Very sad."

"Billions died," Mors Planch said.

Lodovik said, "I presume you will be paid well for your heroic rescue."

Planch's face went slack. "That's the trouble with this whole situation," he said. "The captain and crew don't like us. Honor is a sometimes thing with these people, and I should know . . . It's the same with my people, ancestral traits as it were. They'll take us where we want to go, but there's always a chance they'll talk out of turn in a spaceport somewhere . . . And there's nothing I can do about that. But it's all incredible enough, I suppose nobody will believe. I wouldn't myself.

"I've told Linge Chen you're dead. The rescue failed."

Lodovik drew his head back, pressing his chin into double folds of flesh. "And we go to Madder Loss?"

Planch nodded. A look of sadness crossed his face, but he said no more.

19.
◆

Linge Chen was preparing for the informal dinner party at the Emperor's private quarters when Kreen brought him the sealed message from Planch. In the green oceanic depths of his meditation and personal room, he put aside the straight razor and soap he was using to shave, took a deep breath as Kreen departed, and placed his thumb on the small gray parcel. The first seal, applied by the receiver and decoder, came open at this touch—confirming his unique identity through microanalysis of his skin chemistry, as well as the pattern of his thumbprint. The second seal, within the disk's message itself, he opened through a few words spoken in his voice, known only to himself. The message flowered before him.

Mors Planch stood within a ship, the background in soft focus for the moment, and said in low tones, "My lord Chief Commissioner Chen, I am within the *Spear of Glory*. The ship I have hired is the only one to have found the vessel so far, and I anticipate with some personal concern your deep disappointment at the news I bring. Your councilor is dead, along with the rest of the crew . . ."

Linge Chen's lips worked as he played back the rest of the message. Planch showed the grim details: the rows of bodies arranged within one chamber, the discovery of the body of Lodovik Trema on the bridge, curled and still. Planch confirmed Trema's identity by placing the Commissioner's own identifier on Trema's bracelet.

Linge Chen shut off the message before it could reveal the unnecessary details of what Planch would do next. The body would not be retrieved; the vessel's discovery would be forgotten. Linge Chen did not wish to be accused of favoritism or extravagance, not at this time, when he was hoping to bring down Farad Sinter on the same charge.

For a moment, he felt like a small boy. He had been so convinced that Lodovik Trema moved on a different and superior plane to the rest of humanity. He could never admit it to himself, much less any other, but he had *trusted* as well as admired Trema. His personal instincts, which had proved almost infallible, had told him that Trema would never betray him, never do anything not in Linge Chen's best interests. He had even invited Trema to join his family on special occasions, the only councilor (or Commissioner, for that matter) he had ever invited to do so.

Lodovik Trema had been a steady and pleasant presence on those occasions, playing solemnly and with his own kind of innocence with Linge Chen's children, extravagantly complimenting their mothers on their cooking, which was adequate at best. And Lodovik's advice . . .

Lodovik Trema had never given Chen bad advice. They had

risen together to this supreme pinnacle of responsibility over twenty-five years of, at first, inglorious and often painful service. They had weathered the end of Agis's reign and the first years of the junta, and Lodovik had proven invaluable in designing the Commission of Public Safety to moderate and eventually replace the junta's military rulers.

Ten minutes passed. Kreen knocked gently on the door to the chamber. "Yes," Chen said. "I'm almost done."

He picked up the razor and finished shaving his fine beard, leaving smooth, pallid skin behind. Then, as a measure of his emotion, he cut two small slices in his skin just in front of his left ear. Blood welled over the hairs and he patted it with a white towel, then dropped the towel into an incinerator, offering his own blood to the powers that be, unspecified.

In his youth in the Imperial Education Municipality of Runim, he had learned such rituals as part of the path to adulthood, following the Rules of Tua Chen. Tua Chen had been the most successful product of the secret plan among orthodox Ruellians to develop a select breed of Imperial administrators and bureaucrats, four thousand years before, known as the Shining Lights. In his late maturity, Tua Chen had devised two Books of Rules, based on Ruellian principles: one for the training of aristocratic administrators (and occasionally an Emperor), the other for the training of the Empire's hundreds of billions of bureaucrats, the Greys.

Linge Chen was reputedly a direct descendant of Tua Chen.

The Shining Light school in its modern form was rife with superstition and almost useless, but in its heyday it had trained administrators that were sent to the far corners of the Empire. And in return, from all over the Empire, each year, millions of candidate Greys came to Trantor to receive the Tua Chen training. The best assumed positions in the planet's infinitely layered bureaucracy, competing with the entrenched and resentful Trantor Greys; the rest, having completed their pilgrimage, returned to their homes, or took positions on frontier worlds.

Linge Chen was the most successful of all the students to come out of the school, and he had not succeeded by being overly observant of those damnably persuasive secret rituals. But for Lodovik Trema . . .

It was the very least he could do.

"Sire . . ." Kreen said. With some concern, he observed his master's small wounds, but he knew enough to say nothing.

"I'm done. Bring me my robe for Imperial presence, and also the sash of black."

"What shall I place on the sash, sire?"

"The name of Lodovik."

Kreen's face fell in anguish. "No hope, sire?"

Linge Chen shook his head abruptly and pushed past his small servant, into the wardrobe. Kreen stood very still in the lavatory for a few seconds, his grief genuine. Lodovik had always given Kreen the impression that the small Lavrentian was the equal of anybody within their acquaintance. Kreen treasured that evaluation, even though it had never been spoken.

Then, with a jerk, he roused himself and followed his master.

20.
◆

The private dining room was crowded with Palace staff, making last-minute arrangements. Hari looked up at the huge chandelier with its ten thousand gleaming round glass ornaments modeled after the Emperor's chosen Worlds of the Galactic Year, then around the hundred-meter-long hall, with its solid prime opal matrix columns and the famous deep green copperstone staircase, imported from the only system yet settled in the

Greater Magellanic Cloud—a failed colony, abandoned forty years ago, leaving only this gift as a reminder. His lips twitched at the sight of the staircase. As First Minister, he had cut off Imperial support for that vigorous world, lest it grow independent and too powerful . . .

So many things done to preserve the Center, so many necessary sins of power. He had made sure that no more far-flung colonies were established, and none had been.

The table was set with thirty plates along its midriff, and thirty high-backed ebon chairs, none yet occupied, for the guests had not yet arrived and, of course, the Emperor himself had not yet been seated.

Klayus I escorted Hari around the hall as if he were an honored guest rather than a last-minute annoyance. "'Raven,' I've been calling you that, haven't I? Do you mind? 'Raven' Seldon, such an evocative title! Harbinger of doom."

"Call me what you wish, Highness."

"A tough moniker to lift properly," Klayus said with a smile. Hari, never one to miss feminine beauty, caught sight of three dazzling women in the corner of his eye and automatically turned to face them. The women brushed past him as if he were a statue and approached the Emperor, seeming to work as a team. As they surrounded him and two leaned to whisper in his ears, Klayus's face reddened and he practically giggled with glee. "My extraordinary trio!" he greeted them, after listening for a few seconds. "Hari, you would not believe how accomplished these women are, or what they can do! They've entertained at my dinners before."

The women looked at Hari as one now, with mild interest, but they read the Emperor's attitude toward this old man with quick, deadly accuracy. Hari was not a powerful figure to be attracted to, merely a toy, less even than themselves. Hari thought that if they had suddenly grown fangs and spouted hair on their noses, they could not have become less attractive so quickly. With wisdom born more out of his long life and from many conversations on human nature with Dors than any equation, he quickly imagined their expert blandishments, warm skin, dulcet voices, masking primordial ammonia ice. Dors had frequently made wry observations of that human sex after which she was modeled, and she had seldom been wrong.

Klayus dismissed the women with a few soft words. As they departed, they strolled around the hall, and he bent over to confide to Hari, "They don't impress you, do they? Their kind make up a large portion of the women here. Beautiful as frozen moons. My Privy Councilor manages to search out others of higher quality, but . . . !" He sighed. "Fine stones are easier to procure than gems among females, for a man in my position."

"It was so with Cleon, as well, Highness," Hari said. "He made arrangements with three princess consorts throughout his youth, then, in his middle years, foreswore women entirely. He died without an heir, as you know."

"I've studied Cleon, of course," the Emperor said thoughtfully. "A solid man, not intelligent, but very capable. He liked you, didn't he?"

"I doubt any Emperor has ever liked a man such as myself, Highness."

"Oh, don't be so modest! You have great charms, really. You were married to that remarkable woman—"

"Dors Venabili," said a reedy voice behind them.

The Emperor turned gracefully, his robes swishing over the floor, and his face lit up. "Farad! How nice of you to come early."

The Privy Councilor bowed to his Emperor and glanced in passing at Hari. "When I heard of your visitor, I could not resist, Highness."

"You know my Privy Councilor, Farad Sinter, and Farad, this is the famous Hari Seldon."

"We've never met," Hari said. No one shook hands in the Emperor's company; too many weapons had been transferred

between conspirators and assassins in past centuries that way
for a simple handshake to be any other than a gross and even
dangerous breach of etiquette.

"I've heard much about your famous wife," Sinter said
with a smile. "A remarkable woman, as the Emperor says."

"Hari has come here to warn me about your activities,"
Klayus said with a small grin, glancing between them. "I did
not know all you've been up to, Farad."

"We've discussed my goals, Highness. What more does
Professor Seldon have to add, in the way of information?"

"He says you're hunting down mechanical men. Robots.
From what he says, you appear to be obsessed with them."

Hari stiffened. This was becoming a very dangerous situation, and he was beginning to feel a noose tighten. He almost
regretted having taken this direct approach with someone so
devious and unpredictable as Klayus. It would not be at all good
to be singled out and marked for reprisal by Farad Sinter . . .

"He's confused my goals, though perhaps the rumors have
misled him. There are many false rumors about our activities,
Highness." Sinter's smile dripped honey and bonhomie.

"This genetic study . . . most valuable, don't you think,
Hari? Has anyone explained it to you?"

"System-wide, and also the twelve nearest Central Stars,"
Sinter said.

"It has been explained in the journals of Imperial Science,"
Hari said.

"But shooting people!" Klayus continued. "Why, Farad? To
take samples?"

Hari could hardly believe what he was hearing. The
Emperor could just as easily have signed Hari's death warrant.
Instead, he seemed to be handing Hari's head to his Privy
Councilor . . . on a plate, for dinner!

"Those, those are lies of course," Sinter said slowly, eyes
heavy-lidded. "The Emperor's police would have reported such
indiscretions."

"I wonder," Klayus said, eyes twinkling merrily. "At any rate, Farad, Raven here has some excellent points to make about this robot search. Hari, explain to us the political difficulties that might ensue, should such charges ever become widely disseminated. Tell Farad about—"

"Jo-jo Joranum, yes, I know," Sinter said, his lips thinning and his cheeks going white. "A Mycogenian would-be usurper. Stupid and easily manipulated—by you, in part, am I correct, Professor Seldon?"

"His name was mentioned," the Emperor said, glancing off to one side as if beginning to be bored.

"Actually," Hari said, "Joranum was just a symptom of a larger myth, with consequences far worse on other worlds than Trantor." *A myth I have not thought about, not measured, not researched—all because of Daneel's prohibitions!* Even now, Hari realized he would have some difficulty discussing the topic. He coughed into his fist. Sinter offered a handkerchief, but Hari shook his head and produced his own. Accepting such an item could also be misconstrued. *And would it even be dangerous? Has Trantor and the Empire come to that?* Either way, Hari would not fall for such a simple set-up. "On the world of Sterrad. Nikolo Pas."

The Emperor stared at Hari blankly. "I'm not familiar with Nikolo Pas."

"A butcher, Highness," Sinter said. "Responsible for the death of millions."

"Billions, actually," Hari said. "In a vain search for artificial humans he claimed were infiltrating the empire."

The Emperor stared at Hari for several seconds, his face slack. "I should know about him, shouldn't I?"

"He died in Rikerian the year before you were born, Highness," Sinter said. "It is not a glorious moment in Imperial History."

Something in the atmosphere had changed. Klayus had a sour, even a disappointed look, as if he were anticipating an unpleasant duty. Hari glanced sideways at Sinter and saw that the Privy Councilor was studying his Emperor's expression with some concern. Then it was that Hari realized Klayus and Sinter had been playing with him. The Emperor already knew about the murders of citizens on Trantor. Yet neither Sinter nor any of his tutors had told him about Nikolo Pas, and this was upsetting him.

"I'm not supposed to be so ignorant," Klayus said. "I really should set up more time for personal study. Go on, Raven. What about Nikolo Pas?"

"In decades past, and every few centuries, Highness, there have been tides and even storms of psychological disturbance, centered on the myth of the Eternals."

Sinter visibly flinched. This gave Hari some satisfaction. He continued.

"The resurgence of that myth has almost invariably led to social unrest, and in a few extreme cases, genocide. I conducted an interview with Nikolo Pas when I served Cleon as First Minister, Highness. I spent several days speaking with him, an hour or two at a time, in his cell deep in Rikerian."

The memories seemed to fill Hari's mind now.

"What did Pas believe?" the Emperor asked. The servants were at their positions around the hall. All the arrangements had been completed, the dinner was being delayed; guests could not be allowed to enter until the Emperor had left, to make a more formal entrance later. Klayus did not seem concerned by this.

"Pas claimed to have captured an active artificial human. He claimed to have placed it . . ." Hari coughed again. In this context, he could hardly bring himself to use the word *robot*. He felt badly exposed and even handicapped, for the prohibition against discussion of Daneel's nature had spread to other areas of thought, memory, even will. "He claimed to have isolated the artificial human—"

"Robot. We could be here all night," Klayus said impatiently. That seemed to break some barrier, and Hari nodded.

"Robot. In very secure quarters. The robot deactivated itself—"

"How frightening, how noble!" Klayus exclaimed.

"Pas claimed his scientists dissected and analyzed the body. And yet the body, the inactive mechanical form, was removed from these extremely secure circumstances and vanished without a trace. This was the beginning of Nikolo Pas's crusade. The details are far too long and gruesome to be spoken of here, Highness, but I'm sure you can locate them in the Imperial Library."

Klayus's eyes were like marbles in the head of a wax figure, pointed in Hari's general direction. He rotated toward Sinter. "Your point seems obvious, Hari. Professor Seldon. May I call you Hari?"

The Emperor had already asked him that at their last meeting, but Hari did not let on. Once again, he replied, "I would be honored, Highness."

"The point being that these waves of misery inevitably begin when some high official gets a bug in his hat and begins futile investigations. And when the investigations get out of hand, they cost the Empire many lives and much of treasure. Superstitions. Myths. Always dangerous, like religions."

Sinter said nothing. Hari merely nodded. Both had beads of moisture on their foreheads. The Emperor seemed thoughtful and calm.

"I'm willing to vouch that my Privy Councilor has no such illusions, Hari. I hope I can reassure you of that."

"Yes, Highness."

"And you, Farad, you understand the depth of Hari's concern, that he comes here to relay these items of information about the state of bureaucratic and popular perceptions? The citizens! Like a sea of whispers. The Greys! The eternal manipulators of human destiny, the greatest power below the Palace! And the gentry—baronial and aristocratic, aloof, conspiratorial . . . So important and so often subject to fluctuating themes. Eh?"

Hari did not understand quite what the Emperor meant.

"No hard feelings against Hari, eh, Farad?"

"None, of course, sire." Sinter smiled sunnily at Hari.

"Still . . ." Klayus put his chin in one hand and tapped his lips with a finger. "Amazing story! I shall have to look into it. What if the butcher's notions were true? That would change everything. What then?"

Klayus turned to receive a message from the chief servant of the private dining chamber, an older and very somber Lavrentian. "My guests, including the Chief Commissioner, are waiting," the Emperor said. "Hari, some day you must dine at table with me, as no doubt you did with the unfortunate Cleon and the almost equally unfortunate Agis. However, since you are currently in disfavor with Linge Chen, tonight would not be a good time. My servants will see you off the Palace grounds. Both my Privy Councilor and I thank you, 'Raven!'"

Hari bowed from the waist and two burly servants, more likely disguised Palace Specials, took positions at his flanks. As he was being escorted out of the chamber, passing beneath the amazing chandelier, the main doors opened to his right, and Linge Chen entered. His eyes met Hari's, and Seldon felt a peculiar tremor of some emotion he could not identify. He despised Chen, yet the man was playing a very important role in the Plan.

They were intimately connected, both politically and historically, and it gave Hari no satisfaction to detect a certain sadness in the Commissioner's features, *As if he's lost a friend*, Hari thought.

Nearly all my friends and loved ones are dead, too, or just . . . gone. Vanished. And some I cannot even speak of!

Hari nodded cordially to Chen. The Chief Commissioner turned away as if Hari were of no importance whatsoever.

The two burly servants escorted him from the Palace, and Hari was left by a taxi stand to make his way back to the library and his far more comfortable, if far humbler, quarters.

In the taxi, pressed back into the cushions of the rear seat, Hari closed his eyes and took a deep breath. He might after all last no longer than the time it would take one of Sinter's police assassins to shoot him. What would he tell Wanda? Had he succeeded, or had he simply made things worse?

It was impossible to know just how intelligent the Emperor actually was, how much control he exerted or wished to exert over his councilors and ministers. Klayus I was apparently a master at the art of concealing his true character and emotions, not to mention his intentions.

Still, Hari had long since known that Klayus was doomed to a short reign. His chances of being assassinated or deposed by Chen in the next two years were as high as sixty percent, no matter what his character or intelligence, according to the near-term glosses distilled from the equations in his Prime Radiant.

In his apartment within the library, Hari took off his clothes and showered quickly, then donned a thin night robe and sat on the edge of his simple frame bed. He checked through his messages. All could be taken care of when he returned to his offices tomorrow.

There were no windows in this apartment, no real luxuries at all; it was a simple two-room rectangle with a ceiling barely higher than his head. In all of Trantor, this was the only place where he could feel comfortable, safe, relaxed.

The only room where such illusions could prevail.

21.

◆

Klia shivered in the vast hollow space and looked between her feet at the conjunction of two of Trantor's greatest rivers. Once, twelve thousand years ago, they had had names; now they were designated simply by numbers, but even those numbers hinted at greatness: One and Two. One worked its way across half of Sirta, the continent which supported some of the most populated Sectors, including the Imperial Palace, Streeling, and Dahl. Thousands of years ago, as Trantor's population grew and engineers contemplated accommodating additional billions, they had made the decision to cover over all the landmasses, to dig beneath the crust and burrow even into the shelves which lay beneath the ocean shores.

Those ancient engineers wisely decided against attempting to reroute and change the nature of Trantor's watersheds. To have the metal skin of their new structures support so much water on its rush to the sea was wasteful, so they lined deep channels where natural rivers once had flowed, and let the rains gather and flow into them. Where early Sectors laid claim to natural aquifers, the engineers—with the mandate of the legendary Emperor Kwan Shonam—created new porous materials for the basins to allow the aquifers to remain useful.

Klia could no more understand the intricacies of water on Trantor than any normal citizen. What she knew was that here, fifty meters below where she stood, in the roaring maelstrom where the two rivers mated, lay power. She appreciated power, but she was too young to adequately fear it; and besides, she had an arrogance born of her abilities. She could not *persuade* rivers of water to change, but human rivers . . . That was something else again.

Klia was cold and hungry and angry. She felt abused; *if they only knew!* She took deep breaths and contemplated the day when she could hunt down those who were now making her run and hide like a rat.

Then she sat on the grating of the maintenance walkway, calves crossed in an easy X, and brought her all-too-negative emotions under control. She had to find a place to sleep; here, it was too moist and cold and loud. She had to find food. There would be little of that below ground; she could wait for a maintenance tram to rumble past, flag it down, steal foodboxes and persuade the crew to forget . . . She smiled at that. She would be a ghost, a phantom, the phantom of the two rivers . . .

Some in Dahl believed that those who lived good lives became part of the great rivers and flowed to the covered seas, there to live in perfect communes far from the knowledge of Empire. Those who lived badly went into the heatsinks to sweat and work forever. She did not believe such things, but they were interesting to contemplate while her subconscious mind worked through her problems and presented solutions.

The tram kept popping back into her thoughts. She imagined it a big wormlike thing on many wheels, with comfortable and well-lighted compartments within. She could make friends with the maintenance workers. Perhaps one of them would be exceptional, a native Dahlite with a huge mustache, far more manly than her father or any of the furtive black marketeers; he would comfort her gently at first, forcing nothing, until she decided what she wanted, what her body wanted . . .

These romantic visions only made her more lonely. She felt very vulnerable. She pounded her fist on a rail and listened to the hollow boom be swallowed by the vaster roar. No time for such dreams! She would be inhuman, above all passions and needs; she would take swift vengeance and live to create fear and respect. Children would be told her name to make them behave . . .

Suddenly, her moist eyes dried and she simply laughed at her own ridiculous imaginings. The laughter rose high and clear and, wondrously, the river's rage did not swallow the sound: instead, the laughter echoed through the great vaults over the confluence, and returned to her, like the laughter of hundreds.

For the time being—barring the appearance of that large, gentle Dahlite maintenance worker—she was licked. She knew it. She would have to go back up into Dahl soon, and she would need a place to hide. If people were looking for those with her talents, she would pick the best party and cooperate— for a while.

She sighed at this necessity, but Klia knew she was not an

idiot. She would not languish with her dying dreams down there in the dark and wet, with no company but the great rivers.

22.
◀▶

Mors Planch listened to the sounds of a smooth, gentle landing from his pull-down emergency seat in the hold. Lodovik Trema sat beside him, eyes closed, face peacefully composed.

Planch knew something about Madder Loss that neither Tritch nor her crew understood. Fifty years ago, Madder Loss had been a promising jewel in the Emperor's black robe of Galactic space, a Renaissance World where intellect and philosophy and science burned very bright indeed. The vast city-continents of Madder Loss had bid fair to outshine Trantor, even then revealing its age. And for a time, Trantor had tolerated Madder Loss as a *grand dame* might for a while tolerate the presence of a beautiful young woman in the court, watching her beauty mature with more amusement than envy.

But then the beautiful young woman, half unconscious of her effect, begins to attract the attentions of the *grand dame's* paramours . . . and the tolerance turns into benign neglect, and finally comes the inexplicable cutting off of resources and the young woman finds herself a nonentity, shunned by the court, her name a blighted rumor.

Planch had visited Madder Loss thirty years before to gather information for Linge Chen. At that time Chen had served as First Grade Administrator of Second Octant trade. What Mors had seen then would have broken his younger heart if he hadn't been prepared and forewarned by Chen himself: beautiful spaceports standing empty, gleaming new domes and plexes showing a certain air of decay, the listless officials in their out-of-date Imperial uniforms adhering to rules without enthusiasm. Flourishing black markets, and even crowds of hungry women and children outside the spaceport fence. Madder Loss had opened his eyes to the ebbs and flows of history and economics, and had also planted that seed of personal rebellion that had just flowered. He had from that moment looked for a way to counteract the cold, loveless rationality of Linge Chen and his gentry cohorts, commanding their suffocating hordes of Greys, drawing their lines and cutting off the bright young flesh of the empire for some obscure sense of Trantor's place and pride . . . For political expedience.

Tritch came down to the hold and held out her register for him to place his code imprimatur upon. "Everything as agreed," she murmured, not looking at him, and staying far away from Lodovik.

Lodovik rose from his seat and stood by the large hatch. Slight whirring noises and a change in pressure revealed it would be opening soon.

"As agreed," Mors said, and marked the forms.

"May our world-lines never cross again," Tritch said lightly, then held out her index finger. He hooked his index finger around hers, in the ancient common greeting of their mutual ancestors, and they tugged at each other gently. "Now get out," she ordered, and the two of them quickly complied, stepping out into the stale air and ominous silence of a huge docking bay, devoid of any other ships.

"I'm to take you to the private dwelling of a doctor living in the country," Planch told Lodovik as they waited for transportation from the passenger terminal. Here, in a vast hall designed to hold tens of thousands, they stood alone. The lighted tiles of the ceil formed haphazard puzzle patterns, their condition far worse than any such yet seen on Trantor. The hall was cast in murky twilight, and there were times when Mors thought he might choke, the air was so stagnant.

They had encountered a single elderly Imperial official in

the dusty passport docket, and he had waved them through with a sniff and something that might once have been a sneer. His world did not care, why should he?

The hall was littered with broken-down tiktoks, like victims of some mechanical plague. The plague had been lack of replacement parts; Madder Loss had embraced the mechanical laborers and retained them long after Trantor and most other Imperial worlds shrugged them off. They were no longer even being collected for scrap.

Lodovik looked at Planch sympathetically. "This is not pleasant for you," he observed.

"No," Planch said with a sigh. "Look what the Empire has done—a waste."

"What do you mean?"

"Trantor did this because it feared it would lose its eminence. Squeezed the life out of an entire world."

Lodovik looked away. "Do you blame Linge Chen? Is that why you have double-crossed him?"

Planch paled. "I never said anything about Linge Chen."

"No," Lodovik said. Planch looked at the man with sudden misgivings. If Chen ever learned, there was no place in the Galaxy where he would be safe.

A rickety, lozenge-shaped ground taxi approached on large white wheels. The driver was an elderly woman dressed in faded red livery. Her dialect was almost too thick to understand, but Planch managed to communicate with her. She seemed relieved to have paying passengers—in Imperial credits!—and even happier to be getting out of the urban center.

"I know that you have done work for Chen in the past," Lodovik said as they lurched along a potholed expressway. Here, the expressways lay out in the open, rather than being routed below domes or underground, as they were on Trantor. The morning sunshine dazzled Planch, and the air was tinted pink, giving everything a warm, nostalgic glow. "I was privy to some of the arrangements."

"Of course," Planch said.

"Now you work for a man named Posit," Lodovik said.

Planch started in shock and looked particularly miserable. "I should shoot you right now and leave Madder Loss," he murmured.

"Well, you know the proper codes," Lodovik said. "That much is obvious. You became angry at Chen when he carried on the policies that strangled Madder Loss . . . and other Renaissance Worlds. Yet the squeezing, as you describe it, of the Renaissance Worlds was not Linge Chen's policy initially. It began under the First Ministry of Hari Seldon, who implemented the policy to increase stability in the Empire."

Planch grunted that he was well aware of the Seldon connection. "I don't approve of a lot of Imperial actions, and Chen knew that when I worked for him. But I don't work for him now."

"You have no need to worry," Lodovik said. "Chen will never know."

Planch squirmed in his cracked seat.

"Twenty minutes," the driver called back in a cheery voice.

The house was the most unusual Planch had ever seen—a single small building standing alone in a field covered with short green plants, forming a kind of living carpet beneath the warm sunshine. The outskirts of the city were ten kilometers away, and the nearest structure similar to this one was almost five kilometers distant. The land between consisted of low, rolling hills covered with planar bushy growths, purple or deep bluish green. The countryside seemed elegantly vivacious, quite gaudy in comparison with the crumbling, unkempt city.

The taxi let them out in a broad paved circle at the front of the dwelling. A single tall male figure stood beneath a cloth awning that flapped lazily in the warm, gentle breeze. He stepped forward and bowed toward Mors Planch.

"You've done your work well," the man said.

Planch returned the bow, then awkwardly spread one arm toward Lodovik, and said blandly, "He wasn't much trouble." He stepped back as if they might do something unexpected, start fighting or perhaps just burst into flames.

"You're free to go," the man said.

"I need release papers. You seem to be the contact I met on Trantor, but . . ."

The man gestured and a worn but fully functional tiktok came out of the house carrying a small satchel. "This will complete our agreement, for now. The bag also contains any papers you might need to go wherever you wish to go, safely, in the territories still controlled by the Empire."

"I want to get away from the empire, forever," Planch said.

"You will find some documents that will help you do that, as well," the man said.

Planch, despite his unease, seemed reluctant to return to the waiting taxi.

"What else can I offer you?" the man asked.

"An explanation. Who are you, what do you represent?"

"Nothing," the man said. "I regret to say you'll soon forget everything you saw here, and your role in rescuing my friend as well."

"Friend?"

"Yes," said the man. "We've known each other for thousands of years."

"You're not joking. Who are you?" Planch asked, despite a tingling surge of awe blended with real fear.

"Please go," the man said, and tipped his head slightly. Planch tipped his own head in synchrony, turned without another word, and walked back to the vehicle. The door opened with a shuddering groan to receive him.

Lodovik watched his rescuer depart. Then, using no human words whatsoever, but a high-frequency pulse-modulated sound signal and bursts of microwave, both exchanged greetings, and Lodovik was partially debriefed.

After, R. Daneel Olivaw said, in spoken words, "Let's do this on human time and in human ways, for the moment."

"Certainly," Lodovik said. "I am curious as to where I might be assigned next."

Daneel opened the door to the dwelling, and Lodovik entered before him. "You state that there is something different about you. Yet I examine your transmitted status profile and see nothing amiss."

"Yes," Lodovik said. "I have been examining my mental structure and programming since the accident, trying to pinpoint what that difference could be."

"Have you reached any conclusions?"

"I have. I am no longer compelled to obey the Three Laws."

Daneel received this declaration with no humanly observable reaction. The main room of the house contained two chairs, and in the walls, there were niches for three tiktoks, but to Lodovik, they looked like the niches once reserved for robots on Aurora, tens of thousands of years ago.

"If that is true, there will be grave difficulties, for I observe you are still functioning. You have not deactivated yourself."

"That would have been impossible under the circumstances, for I did not understand this new condition until after I had been rescued by Mors Planch. I caused harm, unwittingly, to a human being on the ship Planch had hired to find the *Spear of Glory*. I did not feel even a hint of the reaction I should have felt. I conclude that the neutrino flux has altered my positronic brain in an unanticipated fashion. Certain key elements in my logic circuits may have been transmuted."

"I see. Have you decided on what action you should take now?"

"I must either deactivate, and impose on you to destroy my remains, or I must be sent to Eos, if my continued existence will serve any purpose."

Daneel sat on one of the chairs, and Lodovik took the other. It no longer seemed at all appropriate to occupy the niches, which in any case were too narrow for their human-scale frames.

"Why did you travel all this way, rather than send an emissary?" Lodovik asked.

"I have all possible emissaries in key positions at the moment," Daneel said. "None could be spared; nor can I afford to lose you. I was already scheduled to be on Madder Loss as a jumping-off point for Eos. Normally I would have delayed my trip, since this is a very delicate time, and the accident has caused grave difficulties. It has even triggered a political struggle in the Imperial Palace that might directly involve Hari Seldon."

Though Lodovik had not worked directly on the Plan, he was well-informed about the psychohistorian.

They sat in silence for several seconds, then Daneel spoke again. "We will go to Eos. I can arrange a small ship for you. There is a mission you can perform for me once you return—"

"I am sorry, Daneel," Lodovik interrupted. "I must emphasize that I am not functioning properly. I should not be assigned any new missions until I have been repaired or reprogrammed, whichever is necessary."

"That can only be done on Eos," Daneel said.

"Yes, but there is a possibility I will no longer follow your instructions," Lodovik said.

"Please explain."

"Humans would call it a crisis of conscience. I have had many long and idle hours to sort through and reexamine all my brain's memory contents, and all of my working algorithms, from this new perspective. I must confess that I am a very confused robot at this moment, and my behavior is not predictable. I may even be a danger."

Daneel stood and stepped over to Lodovik's chair, then bent from the waist and placed his hand on Lodovik's shoulder. "What does your investigation and examination tell you?"

"That the Plan is wrong," Lodovik said. "I believe . . . I am coming to believe . . . My state of thinking is such that . . ." He pushed up from the chair, past Daneel, and went to a broad window looking out on fields of planar bushes. "This is a beautiful world. Mors Planch thinks it is beautiful, and as I spent time with him, I developed a deep respect for his judgment. He resents the changes imposed upon Madder Loss. He regards them as a kind of punishment for aspiring to greatness in the Empire. His resentment led him to betray Linge Chen."

"I have known about his distaste for the Empire and for Chen," Daneel said.

Lodovik continued, "Yet it was not the Empire or Linge Chen that decreed Madder Loss be subdued, not directly." He turned to Daneel, and his face bore traces of human emotion—sadness, regret, grief, even in the presence of a robot, where it was certainly not necessary. "It was you who decided the Renaissance Worlds must be controlled, and induced changes in the politics of Trantor to carry out their strangulation."

Daneel listened with his own human expression—a troubled sort of fascination. Mimicking human behaviors for so long had created reflex pathways in both robots that sometimes seemed easier to display than to suppress.

"I foresaw greater instability," Daneel began. "Centuries of human conflict around systems aspiring to replace the Empire and become centers of power. Not all such worlds could win; the struggle would cause untold suffering and destruction, on a scale never witnessed in human history. The empire will fall; we know that much. But all my efforts have been dedicated to mitigating the effects of that fall, to reduce human suffering to a minimum. The Zeroth Law—"

"The Zeroth Law is what concerns me."

"You have accepted its primacy for centuries now. Why does it concern you?"

"I believe the Zeroth Law may be a mutational function, spread between robots like a virus. I do not know how it

arose, but it may have been provoked by another mutation—
mentalic powers in robots."

"To question the Zeroth Law could lead us to conclude
that everything I have tried to accomplish is in error, and that
all the robots who follow me should be deactivated, myself
included."

"I am aware of the magnitude of my supposition."

Daneel said, "Apparently, something very interesting has
happened to you."

"Yes," Lodovik said, and his pleasant, plump face went
through a series of random and uncoordinated contortions.
"These questions and divisive thoughts may all be due to my
own alteration. I have followed your lead for thousands of
years . . . To feel doubts now . . ." His voice became a strained,
metallic squeak. "I am miserable, Daneel!"

Daneel considered the situation carefully, as if he were
walking through a minefield. "I regret the disturbance you feel.
You are not the first to disagree with the Plan. Others expressed
similar views—many more thousands of years ago. There were
many schisms among robots when the humans abandoned us.
The Giskardians—those like myself, who followed the ideas of
Giskard Reventlov—were opposed by others who insisted on a
strict interpretation of the Three Laws."

"I do not know of these events," Lodovik said, his voice
steadier.

"There has been no need to talk of them. Besides, these
robots may all be inactive now—I have not heard from them
for centuries."

"What happened to them?"

"I do not know," Daneel said. "They called themselves
Calvinians, after Susan Calvin." Every robot knew of Susan
Calvin—though no human remembered her now. "Before those
schisms there were far worse events. Unspeakable tasks that
humans set for robots, carried out by some of those who would
become Calvinians. These memories are in themselves disturbing."

"It gives me no satisfaction to cause you distress, R. Daneel," Lodovik said.

Daneel sat in the second chair again and folded his arms. Both robots were aware of this mimicry of human actions; both were used to the promptings of their human overlays, and did not regard these behaviors and gestures as particularly annoying. Sometimes, they were even reassuring, and Lodovik noticed that Daneel's posture in the chair, the inflection of his voice, and his facial expression all seemed to become more human as their conversation progressed. Neither wished to return to the much more rapid modes of microwave or high-frequency sound communication; this was a situation of complexity and subtlety, and the slower modes of human speech seemed much safer.

"You will return to Eos. We will see what can be done there," Daneel said. "I hope for your complete recovery."

"As do I," Lodovik said.

Planch sat without moving for most of the ride back to the spaceport. He looked through the front windscreen, over the shoulder of the driver, and tried to ignore her thickly accented chatter. Then, with a small shudder, he removed the tiny recorder from its hidden pocket in his jacket and stared at it. He could not make up his mind for several minutes whether to play back the recording or just throw it out the window.

"This all war verra rich, co' da flow fro' tha por', aaw the ships do come in har . . ." the elderly woman said, and glanced over her shoulder. Her eyes were pale blue, very alert, very wise. She smiled and her face wrinkled into a hundred river deltas. Planch nodded while only half hearing what she said.

"Now it be col' poverty, na ships, na work. I am har day in and ou' for my wi' and amusemen', na more tha' tha'!"

She did not seem especially resentful, merely stating facts, yet her words rankled. There were worlds in the stellar neighborhood where the accent of Madder Loss was considered comic, used by entertainers portraying simpletons or charlatans. Tritch herself had referred to Madder Loss as a planet of parasites. Few from outside came here anymore; few knew what had really happened.

Yet now, within this recorder, there might be proof of something extraordinary, a clue to the larger picture. His memory since yesterday seemed murky and full of gaps. He did not even know why he had brought the recorder—he had done nothing important since taking Lodovik Trema's body to the transfer terminal and handing it over to Imperial agents. And why this ride into the country—just to relive old, sometimes painful memories?

"We'ra here. Ya shou stay longer; there are still beautiful sigh's i' the countr', lovely hostels whar to stay." Her voice became sly, a little wheedling. "I coul' show ya places o' beautiful wimma, nat'ral farm garls, all verra poor an' lone."

"No, thank you," Planch said, though he was tempted. His last love had been a native of Madder Loss, thirty years before. He had had no taste for others since, yet he felt a hollow ache at the thought of leaving the planet without trying for another romance. He was somehow convinced that to stay, however, could be very dangerous.

He paid the woman and thanked her in her own accent, then stood beneath the huge balloon roof of the immigration and transfer authority area. The blue skies and distant fields showed through gaps where buildings had been torn down and not replaced.

He found a cool, secluded spot next to an empty restaurant and sat on a bench, holding the recorder display up to see how much it had captured.

Five hours.

For a few seconds, he simply sat and tapped the recorder against his chin, eyes heavy-lidded. Then, brows drawing in, fingers white where they gripped the tiny tube, he said, "Code: *unforgivable*. This is Planch, log in personal. Play back, all."

23.

The candidates for the Second Foundation did not meet in secret. Instead, they shared a plausible cover: they were a social club, interested in the history of certain games of chance, little different from other hobbyists around Trantor. Hobbies swept the planet with boring regularity, and even after their times had passed, small groups of adherents remained loyal.

The mentalic candidates who could form part of the proposed Star's End settlement met, with official approval, twice a week, in a social hall in one of the less fancy dormitories on the outskirts of Streeling University. In these run-down facilities, they were ignored by students who had come to Trantor from some of the less privileged worlds.

The hall was not equipped with listening devices; Wanda herself had persuaded a caretaker to tell her of the older buildings whose bugs were either inactive or had been removed.

Wanda stood beside her husband, Stettin Palver, in the crowded hall and waited for the 103 candidates to settle in to their seats. The sergeant-at-arms closed and locked the doors, and three sensitives stood watch to make sure they were not eavesdropped upon.

In this core group of mentalics—the only one Wanda knew of, perhaps the only one there had ever been—there was little need for calls to order or other formal, spoken signals; the group tended to come to order with little overt fuss. She thought ruefully that this had nothing to do with politeness. There had been a large number of fractious outbreaks in the community since the beginning, but disorder manifested itself in different ways with her people.

Stettin raised his hand. The group had already fallen quiet. They all faced front with deceptively placid expressions. Mentalics seldom exhibited their true emotions, certainly not in the presence of their peers.

Wanda felt little ripples of uncontrolled persuasion; they made her neck itch. She could pick out a few distinct strands in the welter, like smells from a rich stew: currents of social and sexual tension, focused concern, even uncoordinated attempts to override Stettin's dominance. In mentalics, not just the conscious mind exerted its persuasive effects. *My people*, she thought. *Heaven save me from my people!*

"We need the reports from our recruitment cells," Stettin said quietly. "Next, I'll give my report on mathematical and psychological training—to bring our candidates up to speed with the other groups preparing for the mission—then we'll discuss the attrition."

"We need to discuss the murders now!" said a young woman historian with thick black hair cut in a wide bowl. Her green eyes blazed at Stettin and Wanda.

Wanda deflected the woman's automatic whip of persuasion. Her neck itched fiercely.

The woman continued, voice calm but inner emotions raging. "Every recruit for the last three months—"

"There's a traitor among us!" interrupted a man from the back.

Stettin pressed his lips together grimly and held up his hand again. "We know who the so-called traitor is," he said softly. "Her name is Vara Liso."

The crowd instantly quieted. Wanda observed the waves of turmoil and calm with an intense but somehow distant interest. *This is how we are. Grandfather chose us because we are this way—didn't he?*

"Perhaps we know her name, now," the young historian said. "But what good does that do us? She is stronger than any of us here." She could barely be heard.

"No one can persuade her," said another voice, Wanda could not tell where in the crowd.

"She smells us out like a tracker!"

"We must assassinate her—"

"Persuade somebody to kill her!"

"Someone who is expendable—"

Stettin waited for the suggestions to stop. Again, the crowd became unnaturally quiet. Even the ripples of persuasion seemed to still. All their lives, these people had used their talents to make their way in life. Finally, they were among their own kind, among equals, and their "luck" was distressingly ineffectual here.

"Wanda has asked Professor Seldon for help," Stettin said. "And he has gone to the Emperor himself . . . but we do not yet know the outcome of his visit. We should plan for the possibility of failure. We may have to do something we've only tried once before."

"What?" several asked.

"A massed effort. Wanda and I once unwittingly pooled our talents, with some success . . . But only against a normal."

A judge, Wanda remembered. *When Grandfather got in trouble with young toughs.*

"I think it is possible that ten or twenty of us, trained to operate in unison, may be effective against this woman."

The crowd of candidates absorbed this for a few seconds.

"To kill her?" the black-haired historian asked.

"That may not be necessary," Wanda said. She and Stettin had argued this through early in the evening, with some heat. Stettin had maintained that killing Vara Liso was the only safe option. Wanda had maintained with equal force that murder could enervate their cause, drive them one against the other. The balance of so many persuaders was already delicate.

Even her own marriage was fraught with difficulties. Two persuaders, placed in proximity for years, intimate for hours on end, could find many unique ways to irritate and stymie each other.

"I will not kill another human being, much less one of my own kind," the young historian said firmly, eyes brimming with emotion at her own idealism. "No matter how much we may be endangered."

Stettin set his jaw. "That would be a last resort. We must begin training volunteers for such an effort. I have a list of those whose work puts them in places where they might encounter Liso . . ."

Wanda listened as Stettin read out the names. The named stepped forward like guilty children, and Stettin took them to a separate room.

"The rest of us have other matters to discuss," Wanda said, hoping to distract the remainder. "There are more travel questions to be answered—health questions, family and financial situations to be tied up, and, of course, training in the Seldon disciplines—"

The group calmed and focused on these matters with some relief, glad to be done with the problem of Liso, for the time being. Eager to look the other way.

They were all like children, Wanda thought, every one of them, and the group as a whole: no better than awkward adolescents, stumbling along through life with powers they have only now recognized, for the first time fully aware of weaknesses they have never had to confront before.

Weaknesses hidden by persuasion.

We are all cripples! She kept her face calm, but her insides churned at the coming conflicts, so many and so dangerous. *How could Hari have chosen such a strange and disorganized group to safeguard all of human history!*

Sometimes, Wanda felt as if she were wandering through a dream. Not even Stettin could reassure her at those times, and she was close to despair.

Of course, she never confessed that to Hari.

24.

◆

Klia Asgar emerged during the main sleep period, ten kilometers from where she had descended to the two rivers. The ceil above this neighborhood of Dahl glowed twilight blue-gray, and the streets were filled only with night laborers, about a third of the volume of waking maximum. Nobody challenged her.

Rather than simply contact the number on the card given to her by the man in dusty green, Klia persuaded a small-time security scrambler in south Dahl to break the card's code. The card then gave her an address and acted as a guide, glowing and humming faint directions as she took transit and taxi to Pentare, a small municipality in the shadow of Streeling. She bought an Imperial-grade filmbook reader, hooked it to a general communicator, and fed it material from public files, using data credits she had amassed on two small jobs months ago. She read up on Hari Seldon and his granddaughter, Wanda. Seldon, it seemed, was not a persuader, yet the man in dusty green had said that his granddaughter was. Where did she get her powers, then? Klia looked up Wanda Seldon Palver's father: Raych. A Dahlite.

This caused her a moment of both concern and wonder, and even momentary pride. She had always known Dahlites were special.

The woman's family connection with a Dahlite was not enough to dispel Klia's suspicions about people connected to the Palace.

Still, Hari Seldon predicted the end of the Empire, the destruction of Trantor; he had established quite a reputation as a doomsayer. That might put him in opposition to the Palace; there were even rumors that he was to be put on trial for treason.

Yet Klia had an instinctive dislike for such visionary twaddle. Too often visionaries were trying to organize their own small cadres of totally obedient acolytes, little personal empires in the middle of a unimaginably bigger and almost completely impersonal Galactic Empire.

She had heard of a spectacular incident just last year, in Temblar, on the equator. Fifty thousand followers of a schismatic Mycogenian had committed suicide, claiming to get messages telling them of Trantor's imminent destruction. The messages had supposedly come from nonhuman intelligences parasitizing Imperial defense and information platforms in orbit around Trantor.

Klia knew nothing about the defense platforms, but she was smart enough to see that Seldon was clearly akin to these fanatics, and would do someone like her no good at all.

As the man in dusty green had indicated . . .

At the card's direction, Klia took a small slideway from the transit platform to a pedwalk artery dubiously called Brommus Fair. This led halfway across a district where goods were housed before distribution to retail shops, agoras, and markets around Streeling and the Imperial Sector.

She approached a large warehouse that reached to the edge of the ceil, where it met its supporting wall; a less than desirable neighborhood, but clean and orderly. There were even fewer people about at this early-morning hour than there had been in south Dahl. Still, she kept her senses keenly tuned.

The card directed her to a small side door. She looked at the door for several tens of seconds, biting her lower lip. What she was about to do seemed to be a very big step, and possibly a dangerous one. Still, everything the man in dusty green had told her rang true.

And he had given her information about herself, her nature, that had bothered her—deeply affected her.

She was about to knock on the small, featureless door when it opened inward with an abrupt squeal. A large, dark figure bent low to step out and almost bumped into her. Klia jumped back.

"Sorry," the figure said, and emerged in the twilight beneath the glow of a small lantern high up on the warehouse wall. It was a man, a very big man, with broad shoulders and glossy black hair and a magnificent mustache. A Dahlite! "The main entrance is around the corner," the man said in a deep, velvety voice. "Besides, we're closed."

She had never seen any male so handsome, and so compellingly . . . she tried to find the word: *gentle*. Klia swallowed and forced herself to speak. "I was told to come here. A man gave me this. Wears green. He never told me his name." She held out the card.

The huge Dahlite—fully two heads taller than any Dahlite she had ever seen before—took the card in large but dexterous fingers. He pulled it close to his face and squinted. "That would be Kallusin," he grumbled. He lowered the card. Klia felt something brush against her like a light breeze, then depart. "He's at home now, I think, or somewhere he can't be reached. Can I help you?"

"He . . . said he would find a . . . safe place for me. I think that's what he meant."

"Yeah. All right." The big Dahlite turned and pushed the door open again. "You can wait inside until he comes."

She hesitated.

"It's all right," the giant said, and his voice almost compelled her full belief. "I certainly won't hurt you. You're a sister. My name is Brann. Come on in."

Brann shut the door behind them and rose to his full height. Despite his size, Klia did not feel afraid; he moved with a careful grace that could have been calculated not to alarm or offend, if it had not seemed so natural. He smiled down on her.

"Dahl?" he asked.

"Yes."

"Most of us are from Dahl. Some come from Misaro, a few more from Lavrenti."

She lifted her eyebrows.

"Whatever it is, it makes good servants," Brann said with a small grin. "How long have you known?"

"Since I was a child," Klia said. "How long have you been here?"

"Just a few months. Kallusin recruited me during the equinox. I left Dahl five years ago. I was too big to work in the heatsinks."

Klia looked around the large space they had entered and saw many tiers of industrial shelving covered with crates, lumbering old automated lift engines, belt delivery systems, all quiet now and shrouded in darkness.

"What is this?" Klia asked.

"Kallusin works for a man named Plussix. Plussix imports stuff from offworld and sells it here." Brann walked down an aisle, glanced over his shoulder, and said, "It'll be an hour before Kallusin gets here. He's a late sleeper. Want to see some of the treasure?"

"Sure," Klia said with a shrug. She walked slowly after the big man, arms folded against the warehouse's slight chill.

"There's stuff from a thousand worlds here," Brann said, his voice barely audible in the vast spaces. The warehouse was larger than she thought—huge portals with massive rolling doors led to even more cavernous chambers. "Out there, where it comes from, it's junk—and believe me, it wouldn't impress the Emperor, either. But the Greys here on Trantor just gotta have it. Every little apartment nook needs a dried stingweed frond from Giacond, or a pre-Empire trance box from Dessemer. Plussix buys it for nothing, saves it from conversion and cycling. Buys empty space on food ships from the nutrient allies or from free traders with Imperial dispensation. Brings it here. Makes twenty percent per shipload, a lot better than the Trantor Bourse. In thirty years, he's gotten very rich."

"I've never heard of Plussix."

"He doesn't sell any of it himself. The bureaucrats like to

have a story, and he's pretty much no story at all. I've never seen him myself, and I don't think Kallusin has, either."

"So he just hands it over to good story-tellers?"

Brann rumbled softly, and with some pleasure, Klia realized he was laughing. "Yeah," he said, glancing back at her appreciatively. He seemed to want to face away from her. She almost subconsciously tried to persuade him to turn around. She wanted to understand more clearly how he felt about her.

"Stop that," he said, and his shoulders tensed.

"Stop what?"

"Everybody around here tries that and I don't like it. Don't make me do anything. Just ask with words."

"I'm sorry," Klia said, and genuinely meant it. His tone was more than offended—he sounded as if some friend had just betrayed him!

"Yeah, well, it's natural, I suppose. I feel it, but it doesn't work on me. I said you're a sister. You don't know what that means?"

"I . . . suppose it means you're like me."

"I'm not like you, not exactly. You persuade. I make people feel comfortable and happy. I can't make them do anything, but they like being around me. I like being around them. It's mutual. So you don't need to persuade me. Just ask."

"I will," Klia said.

"But don't ask me to look directly at you," Brann said. "Not for a while. I have a very rough time with females. That's why I left Dahl, not just because I couldn't work in the heatsinks."

"I don't understand," Klia said.

"I'm shy for a reason," he said.

"I'd like to know."

"Of course you would," Brann said amiably. "You're a woman. I can feel you liking me. And I like women . . . a lot. I think they're beautiful. Enchanting. So I fall in love with them, really quickly. But what I do . . . the effect I have . . . after a while, it wears off, and the women see me for what I am: this big hulking guy with no prospects. So they wander off, and there I am. Alone."

"That must be very painful," Klia said, though she could not really understand why. She had been a loner for so long that the thought of being alone caused her no concern. She had no clear notion of what it felt like to be in love, either. Her dreams were more of continuing, satisfying sexuality, not necessarily of a deep emotional connection. "I like being alone, myself. I don't really care what others think about me."

"You're lucky," Brann said.

"So who tells the stories about these things, to sell them?" Klia wanted to get away from this topic. Brann's shyness and vulnerability were a little too attractive.

"Shopkeepers all over Trantor," Brann said. "The staff writes up reports on the treasures, we attach the reports to official forms from customs, we deliver to the agoras, and the Greys run to buy 'em. Haven't you ever seen an offworld antique store?"

"Never," Klia said.

"Well, if you're around long enough, maybe one of the guys will take you to one. Me, I only go out during sleeps, when there aren't many people."

Kallusin, the man in dusty green, sat himself behind a ridiculously large desk and folded his hands. The desktop was covered with pretty baubles from many different worlds, all of them useless as far as Klia could determine, but attractive—or perhaps just distracting.

Brann stood behind her. She kept her eyes on Kallusin, though she felt the urge to look at Brann. There was something about his abilities that the big Dahlite was not telling her. Fair enough. He did not know everything about Klia, either.

"Our persuaders are a very creepy crew, you know?" Kallusin said, and smiled. "Very talented and very creepy. They have to watch us and maintain tight discipline here, or else word will get out—and do you think people on Trantor will enjoy knowing that their kind exist? Lucky people, persuasive people. People who manage to get along . . . but you know something strange? None of them have made it into the Palace. They stay at a constant level of human accomplishment, and they stay out of politics. Does that make sense to you, Klia Asgar?"

"No," Klia said, and shook her head. "We should be in control, if everything you've said is true."

"Well, you seem to be self-limiting. You're content just to live your lives and leave higher matters to normal people. Why that should be, I don't know. But the Trader Plussix enjoys your company. You realize that you'll never meet Plussix, not in person, even after you join and swear an oath?"

"Fine with me," Klia said.

"Does that arouse your curiosity?"

"No," Klia said with a sniff. "What do I need to do?"

"First, promise you'll learn to control your talents in the presence of your fellow persuaders. You, especially, Klia Asgar. You're one of the strongest persuaders I've ever encountered. If you applied yourself, you could make all of us do handstands, but we'd know what had happened, and we'd have to kill you."

Klia felt a small shiver of dismay. She had never really tried to control herself; she had grown up with this ability, using it as naturally and casually as she did speech, perhaps more so, since she wasn't much for conversation. "All right," she said.

"In return, we protect you, hide you, give you useful work. And . . . you get to be interviewed by Trader Plussix."

"Oh, good," Klia said softly.

"Don't be afraid of him," Brann said in his soft rumble.

"I won't be."

"He's deformed," Kallusin said. "So I've surmised. Plussix tells us nothing, but . . ." His hand indicated the office, the warehouse, their living quarters, all with one sweep. "He provides all this for us. My theory, which I've even told Plussix himself, is that he's another peculiar kind of mentalic, not very good at persuading or greasing the social skids, but a type who enjoys being around those with your talents. But he never confirms or denies anything."

"Oh," Klia said. She wanted to get the ceremonies over and go to her quarters. She wanted to be alone and rest. She hadn't slept well in days. Rest—and food. Since her arrival at the warehouse, Brann had taken her to the employee cafeteria twice, and she had eaten huge meals, but she was still hungry.

She resisted the urge to look at Brann. She kept her eyes on Kallusin.

"I'm very glad you've joined us," he said, and pressed his baby-smooth lips together. He neither smiled nor frowned, but his eyes, though they did not move, seemed to sweep her for every important detail. "Thank you," he said, and turned to the window overlooking the largest chamber of the warehouse. Brann touched her shoulder, and she jerked, then followed the big man outside.

"When do I swear my oath?" she asked.

"You already have, by accepting our hospitality and not asking Kallusin if you could leave."

"That doesn't seem fair. I should know all the rules."

"There are no rules, except you stay around here, you don't use your talents on us or on outsiders . . . unless instructed to do so . . . and you don't tell anybody about us."

"Why not put that into an oath?"

"Why bother?" Brann said.

"And what about you? You keep making me want to look at you. Shouldn't you stop that?"

Brann shook his head solemnly. "I'm not doing a thing," he said.

"Don't tell me that! I'm no idiot."

"Believe whatever you want," Brann said. "If you want to look at me, it's just because you want to look at me." Then he added, in a low voice, "I don't mind. Not with you."

He walked ahead of her down a narrow industrial gray corridor lined with closed doors and illuminated by simple globes. Klia felt a flush of anger at his presumption. "Maybe you *should* mind!" she called ahead sharply. "Maybe you should *worry*! I'm not a very nice person!"

Brann shrugged and handed her the ID card that also served as a key to her room. "Enjoy your rest," he said. "We probably won't see each other for a while. I'm going with Kallusin to escort a shipment of goods to Mycogen. It might take us days to conclude the deal."

"Good," Klia said, and inserted the card. She pushed open the door to her room and entered swiftly, then slammed the door behind her.

For some seconds, she hardly saw the room, she was so angry with herself. She felt weak and taken advantage of. Swearing an oath without even hearing the oath! Plussix sounded monstrous.

Then the furniture and décor came into focus. It was spare, soft greens and grays with sunny yellow accents, not luxurious but not oppressive, either. There was a plain foam mattress, not too old, an armoire, a trunk, a tiny desk and chair, then another chair, not much larger but with more padding than the desk chair. There was a lamp in the ceiling and a lamp on the desk. A bookfilm reader lay on the desk.

The room was three paces wide and about three and a half long. It was the nicest room she had had to herself since she left home, and in truth, nicer than the small bedroom she had slept in as a child. She sat on the edge of the bed.

Being attracted to men, any man, was a weakness she could not afford now. She was sure her fantasy of a big Dahlite male didn't match Brann—although he was big, a Dahlite, male, and sported a fine mustache.

The next time, she vowed, *I won't look at him at all!*

25.

◆

Lodovik stood motionless but for his eyes, watching as Daneel conducted another diagnostic check, the last before the journey to Eos.

"There's no overt damage, still nothing I can detect here," Daneel said as the old machines finished. "But you're a later model than these tools. They're not up to your level, I suspect."

"Have you ever diagnosed yourself?" Lodovik asked.

"Frequently," Daneel said. "Every few years. Not with these machines, however. There are some high quality tools hidden on Trantor. Still, it's been a century since I've been to Eos, and my power supply needs replacing. That's why I'll travel with you. And there is another reason. I have to bring back a robot—if her repairs and upgrades have gone well."

"A female form?"

"Yes."

Lodovik waited for elaboration, but Daneel was not forthcoming. He knew of only one female form robot still active, of the millions that had once been so popular with humans. This was Dors Venabili—and she had been sequestered on Eos for decades.

"You do not trust me now, do you?" Lodovik said.

"No," Daneel said. "The ship should be ready. The sooner we get to Eos, the sooner we can get back. I hate to be away from Trantor. The most critical moment of the Cusp Time is upon us."

Very few Imperial ships put in to Madder Loss now, but Daneel had made traveling arrangements with a trader vessel months before, and it was not difficult to fit Lodovik in as an extra passenger. The vessel would take them to the cold outer reaches of Madder Loss's system, to a frozen asteroid with no name, only a catalog number: ISSC–1491.

They stood on the landing platform of a remote outdoor port. Spaceport. The sun was bright, and insects flew through the air, pollinating the oil-flower fields that surrounded the concrete and plasteel facilities.

Lodovik still valued Daneel's leadership and presence, but how long could that last? In fact, Lodovik had put all of his initiative on hold for the few days he had been on Madder Loss, for fear of defying Daneel. His type of humaniform robot used initiative in many important ways, however, not just to determine large-scale courses of action. He could not subdue the thoughts that rose from his core mentality. *Daneel would hold humans back. Humans must be allowed to act out their own destiny. We do not understand their animal spirits! We are not like them!*

Daneel himself had said that human minds and destiny were not easily understood by robots—if they could be understood at all. *It is madness to control and direct their history! The overweening madness of machines out of control.*

Something unfamiliar flitted across his thought processes—a vestige of the voice he had heard earlier.

Daneel spoke to the trader captain, a small, muscular man with a ritually scarred face and paste white skin. Daneel turned and waved for Lodovik to join him. Lodovik marched forward. The trader captain gave him a ferocious smile.

As they boarded the ship, Lodovik looked back. Insects everywhere, on all the planets suitable for humans, all alike, with minor local variations, mostly explainable by genetic tinkering over the millennia. All suited to maintaining ecosystems conducive to human civilization.

Not a wild creature on all of Madder Loss. Wild creatures could only be found on those fifty thousand worlds put aside as hunting and zoo preserves: the garden planets so popular with Klayus, planets where citizens could only visit with Imperial permission. He had once overseen the budgetary allocations to those preserves. Linge Chen had wanted to shut them down as useless expense, but Klayus had made a direct request to save them, and there had been some ornate quid pro quo to which Lodovik had not been privy.

Lodovik wondered how all this, garden worlds and tamed or paved-over human worlds, had come to be. So much history unavailable to him. So many questions bubbling up now beneath the self-imposed constraints.

The ship doors closed behind him, and he concealed an algorithmic turbulence, what in human terms he would have called an intellectual panic—not at the closed spaces of the ship, but at the opening flowers of curiosity within his own mind!

In their small cabin, Daneel placed their two small pieces of luggage in containment racks and pulled down a small sitting platform. Lodovik remained standing. Daneel folded his arms.

"We will not be disturbed," he said. "We can drop to our lowest level here. We should be at the rendezvous in six hours, and on Eos within three days."

"How much time do we have, before you lose control of the situation on Trantor?" Lodovik asked.

"Fifteen days," Daneel said. "Barring unforeseen circumstances. And there are always those, where humans are concerned."

26.

Vara Liso could hardly contain her rage. She raised her fists to Farad Sinter, who backed off with a small, shocked grin, and circled him in the broad public-affairs office. A number of Greys, pushing carts or carrying valises, witnessed this confrontation from the adjoining hallway with wonder and concealed, colorless glee.

"That is idiotic!" she hissed at him, then lowered her voice. "Take off the pressure . . . and they will *regroup*! Then they will come after *me*!"

The blond major, her constant and now intensely annoying shadow, danced ineffectually around, trying to interpose himself. But Vara just as deftly maneuvered around him. Sinter was left with the impression he was in a small and embarrassing riot. By walking crabwise toward the open door of his secondary office, Sinter managed this small squall into a less public container.

"You lost the trail!" he said, half bark, half sigh, as a Grey shut the door behind them. The Grey merely glanced at the trio, then went about her duties, nonplussed.

"I was pulled away!" Vara howled. Tears started from her eyes and poured down her cheeks. Abruptly, the major stopped his dance and stood in one spot, trembling all over, his limbs jerking. Then, he looked for a chair, saw one in a corner, and collapsed into it. Sinter witnessed this with wide eyes.

"Did you do that?" he asked Vara.

Vara shut her mouth with a small click of teeth, pulled back her head on its long, thin neck, and stared at the major. "Of course not. Though he has been abominable, *and* uncooperative."

"The strain—" the major managed between clenched, clattering teeth.

Sinter stared at her for several seconds, until Vara realized she was arousing some very unhealthy suspicions. Major Namm shook himself, steadied, and managed to stand again, swallowing hard. He came to attention, rather ridiculously, and focused on a wall opposite.

"How *did* you lose her?" Farad Sinter asked softly, looking between them.

"It was not her fault," the major said.

"I asked *her*," Sinter said.

"She was very fast, and she sensed my presence," Vara Liso began. "Your agents, your bumbling police, weren't fast enough to catch her—and now she's gone, and you *won't let me find her*!"

Sinter's lips protruded in thought, pressed together as if waiting for a kiss. It was a ludicrous expression, and suddenly, in Vara Liso's heart, what had started out as admiration and love flip-flopped into bitterness and hatred.

She kept her feelings to herself, however. She had already said too much, gone too far. *Did I whip that young officer?* She glanced at the stiff, silent man with a small measure of guilt. She must keep her abilities in check.

"The Emperor has specifically forbidden me from conducting any more of our searches. He does not seem to share our interest in these . . . people. And for the moment, I'm not going to press my advantage and try to convince him to change his mind. The Emperor has his ways, and they must be observed."

Vara stood with hands folded.

"He was convinced by Hari Seldon that this could look very bad, politically."

Vara's eyes widened. "But Seldon supports *them*!"

"We don't know that for sure."

"But they were recruiting me! His granddaughter!"

Farad reached out and took her by the wrist, then tightened his grip ever so slightly. She winced. "That is a fact to be kept just between you and me. What Seldon's granddaughter does may or may not be connected to the 'Raven' himself. Perhaps the whole family is crazy, each in his unique way."

"But we've discussed—"

"Seldon is done for. After his trial, we can pursue those intimately connected to him. Once Linge Chen has satisfied himself, the Emperor will likely not object to our cleaning up the scraps." Sinter gave Vara Liso a pitying glare.

"What is it?" she asked, quivering.

"Don't ever assume I am giving up. *Ever.* What I do is much too important."

"Of course," Vara Liso said, subdued. She stared down at

the plush carpet under the desk, with its weave of huge brown and red flowers.

"We'll have our time again, and soon. But for now, we simply constrain our enthusiasm and dedication, and wait."

"Of course," Vara Liso said.

"Are you all right?" Sinter asked the young major solicitously.

"Yes, sir," the man said.

"Been ill recently?"

"No, sir."

Sinter seemed to dismiss the problem, and the officer, with a wave. Major Namm retreated hastily, pulling the large door shut behind him without a sound.

"You've been under a strain," Sinter said.

"Perhaps I have," Vara said, her shoulders slumping. She smiled weakly at him.

"A little rest, some recreation." He reached in his pocket and pulled out a credit chit. "This will get you into the Imperial Sector retail emporium. A little discreet shopping, perhaps."

Vara's forehead furled. Then her face went smooth and she took the chit and smiled. "Thank you."

"It's nothing. Come back in a few days. Things might have changed. I'll assign a different officer to protect you."

"Thank you," Vara Liso said.

Sinter touched her chin with one finger. "You are valuable, you know," he said, and was secretly disgusted by the look of sheer need on the woman's exceedingly unattractive face.

27.

◆

Though he would go before the Commission of Public Safety alone, Hari knew very well that he needed legal coaching behind the scenes. That did not stop him from hating his meetings with his counsel, Sedjar Boon.

Boon was an experienced lawyer with a fine reputation. He

had received his training in the municipality of Bale Nola, in Nola Sector, under tutors with many decades of experience dealing with the tortuous laws of Trantor, both Imperial and Citizen.

Trantor had ten formal constitutions and as many sets of laws drawn up for its various classes of citizens; there were literally millions of commentaries in tens of thousands of volumes on how the sets of statutes interacted. Every five years, around the planet, there would be new conventions to amend and update the laws, many of them broadcast live like sporting events for the enjoyment of billions of Greys, who relished dusty and relentlessly detailed legal proceedings far more than they did physical sports. It was said this tradition was at least as old as the Empire, perhaps much older.

Hari was grateful that some aspects of Imperial law were private.

Boon spread his new research results on the desk in Hari's library office and glanced with raised eyebrows at the active Prime Radiant perched near one corner. Hari waited patiently for the lawyer to get his autoclerks and filmbook readers aligned and in tune with each other.

"Sorry this takes so long, professor," Boon said, sitting opposite Hari. "Your case is unique."

Hari smiled and nodded.

"The laws under which you have been brought before the Judiciary of the Commission of Public Safety have been modified forty-two thousand and fifteen times since the code-books were first established, twelve thousand and five years ago," Boon said. "There are three hundred modified versions still regarded as extant, active, and relevant, and often they contradict each other. The law are supposed to apply equally to all classes, and are all based on Citizen law, but . . . I don't need to tell you the application is different. As the Commission of Public Safety has assumed its charter under Imperial canon, it may choose from any of these sets of codes. My guess is they will try you under several sets at once, as a meritocrat or even an eccentric, and not reveal the specific sets until the trial is underway. I've chosen the most likely sets, the ones that give the Commission the greatest leeway in your case. Here are the numbers, and I've provided filmbook excerpts for your study—"

"Fine," Hari said without enthusiasm.

"Though I know you won't even bother glancing at them, will you, professor?"

"Probably not," Hari admitted.

"Sometimes you seem incredibly smug, if I may say so."

"The Commission will try me as they see fit, and the outcome will be to their best advantage. Has there ever been any doubt about that?"

"Never," Boon said. "But you can invoke certain privileges that could delay indefinitely execution of any sentence, especially if one of the sets incorporates the independence of the University of Streeling, as per the Meritocrat and Palace Treaty of two centuries ago. And you do face charges of sedition and treason—thirty-nine such charges, at the moment. Linge Chen could easily have you executed."

"I know," Hari said. "I've faced the courts before."

"Never under the rule of the Chief Commissioner. He is known to be a devious and exacting scholar of jurisprudence, professor."

The informer on Hari's desk chimed, and a text message rolled across its small display. It was a list of meetings for the week, the most important of which was in less than an hour, with an offworld student and mathist named Gaal Dornick.

Boon was still speaking, but Hari held up his hand. The counselor stopped and folded his arms, waiting for his client's thought processes to reach a conclusion.

Hari's hands, mottled with age spots, reached briefly for a small gray pocket computer, and he did some calculations there. He then placed the computer in its port niche beside the Prime Radiant. The projected results filled half the rear wall of the room, and were very pretty, but meant nothing to Boon.

They meant a great deal to Hari. He became agitated and stood, pacing near a false window that showed open-air fields on his home world of Helicon. If one had known where to look in the false window, one could have seen Hari's father tending gene-tailored pharmaceutical-producing plants in the far distance. He had brought the image with him from Helicon, decades before, yet had only mounted it in this large frame a year ago. His thoughts were increasingly of his mother and father now. He glanced at the distant figure in that faraway place and time, wrinkled his brow, and said, "Who's the best young counselor on your staff? Not too expensive—not as expensive as you!—but every bit as good?"

Boon laughed. "Are you thinking of changing counsel, professor?"

"No. I have a very important member of my staff arriving soon, a fine young mathist. He will be arrested almost immediately, because of his association with me. He will need counsel, of course."

"I can take him on as well, professor, with little increase in fees, if that's your concern. If your cases are parallel—"

"No. Linge Chen will lay waste all around me if he can, but in the end, he won't touch me. I'll need to protect my best people to carry on after the Commissioners have passed judgment."

Boon scowled deeply and flung up a hand. "Professor Seldon, your reputation as a prophet is much too widespread for my professional comfort. But how in the name of all that is Cosmic can you know *this* about the Chief Commissioner?"

Hari's eyes seemed for a moment almost to start out of his head, and Boon leaned forward in his chair, clearly worried for the old man's health.

Hari took a deep breath and relaxed. "It is a Cusp Time," he said. "I could explain it to you, but it would bore you as much as this legal mumbo-jumbo bores me. I put up with you and credit you with knowing your profession, counselor. Please put up with me under the same terms."

Boon pressed his lips together and squinted dubiously at his client. "My partner's son, Lors Avakim, is a smart young fellow. He's worked for some years in Imperial constitutional law, with a sideline in cases adjudicated by the Commission of Public Safety."

"Avakim . . ." Hari had hoped for this name to be mentioned. It simplified things considerably. He knew that Boon was a good counselor, but suspected Boon was not as independent as might be wished. Lors Avakim was a prospective member of the Encyclopedia Project, legal division. He had applied last year. He was idealistic, fresh, not yet corrupted. Hari doubted that Boon knew of this connection to the Project. "Can he dance well enough to keep my mathist out of real trouble with these buffoons?"

"I think so," Boon said.

"Good. Please retain him on the Project's legal account for scholar and mathist Gaal Dornick, newly arrived on Trantor. I'm afraid I'm going to have to cut our meeting short today, counselor. I have to get ready to meet with Dornick."

"Where is he staying?"

"At the Luxor Hotel."

"And when will they arrest him?" Boon asked with a wry smile.

"Tomorrow," Hari said, and coughed into his fist. "Sorry. It must be the dust from all these dead hands of law." He gestured at the bookfilms.

"Of course," Boon said tolerantly.

"Thank you," Hari said, and gestured toward the office door. Boon gathered up his materials and opened the door, then turned to look back at Hari Seldon.

"The trial is in three weeks, professor. That's not a lot of time."

"During a Sel—" He interrupted himself. He had almost said "Seldon Crisis." "During a Cusp Time, counselor, an amazing number of things can happen in just three weeks."

"May I speak freely, professor?"

"Certainly," Hari said, but his tone implied the words had better be few.

"You seem to hold my profession in contempt, yet you claim to be a student of cultural flows and ebbs. Law is the framework, the stable but growing anatomy of any culture."

"I am a flawed man, counselor. I have many lapses. It is my fervent wish that where I err, other people on my staff will see what I cannot, and correct for my failures. Good day."

28.

Linge Chen received Sedjar Boon alone in his personal residence within the Commission Pavilion and gave him five minutes to describe the meeting with Hari Seldon.

"I admire the man, sire," Boon said, "but he does not seem to much care about what's going to happen. He seemed more concerned about providing counsel for a student or assistant who arrived on Trantor only a short while ago."

"And who is that?"

"Gaal Dornick, sire."

"I do not know him. He is new to this Psychohistory Project, is he not?"

"I believe so, sire."

"There are fifty working within the University and the library on Seldon's Project, and that makes Dornick the fifty-first?"

"Yes."

"And below these fifty, soon to be fifty-one, there are a hundred thousand, scattered all over Trantor, with a few thousand stationed on the food allies, and a few hundred working the receiver stations around the system. None on the defense stations. All are loyal, all conduct themselves with quiet dedication. Seldon makes himself the lightning rod to divert attention from all of this other activity. Quite an amazing accomplishment for a man as ignorant of law and as contemptuous of the minutiae of management as Seldon seems to be."

Boon easily caught the implied criticism. "I do not underestimate him, Commissioner. But you have ordered me to provide him with the very finest legal advice, and he does not seem at all interested."

"Perhaps he knows you report to me."

"I doubt that, Commissioner."

"It's not likely, but he's a very intelligent man. Have you studied Seldon's psychohistory papers, counselor?"

"Only insofar as they relate to the charges under which you are likely to try him." Boon looked up with hopeful respect. "It would make my task so much easier if I knew what those charges might be, Commissioner."

Chen returned his gaze with amusement. "No," Chen said. "Most of my Greys, and certainly most of the legals, are of the opinion that Seldon is a harmless and amusing crank, another rogue meritocrat aspiring to be an eccentric. He's regarded with some affection on Trantor. Knowledge that he is about to stand trial is already too widespread, counselor. It might even be to Seldon's advantage to publicize the trial, applying no little pressure on us to dismiss the charges or call the trial off completely. He could easily publicize the event as a respected academic, a creative meritocrat of the grand old style being bullied by the effete and cruel gentry."

"Is that a suggestion, Commissioner? It could make a fine defense."

"Not at all," Chen said sourly. He leaned forward. "Do not expect me to do your work for you, counselor. Has he discussed this strategy with you?"

"No, sire."

"He wants to stand trial. He is using this trial in some way, perhaps because it is necessary to him. Curious."

Boon studied the Chief Commissioner for several seconds, then said, "Permission to speak freely, Commissioner?"

"Certainly," Chen said.

"While it may be true that Seldon's words and predictions could be construed to be treasonous, it would be far more reasonable for the Commissioners simply to ignore him. His organization is substantial, to be sure—the largest gathering of intellectuals outside the University. But it is devoted to peaceful ends—an encyclopedia, so it is said. Scholarship, purely scholarship! I do not understand your motives for bringing the professor to trial. Are you using Hari Seldon?"

Chen smiled. "It is my misfortune to be considered omniscient. I am not omniscient, nor am I politically omnivorous, eating and transforming all those events which occur around me to my own advantage." Chen was obviously unwilling to give any more of an answer than this.

"Of course not, Commissioner. May I ask one more question—for purely selfish and professional reasons, to avoid excess effort when there is so much to do, and so little time?"

"Perhaps," Chen said, with a curl of his lip that indicated he was not going to be very magnanimous.

"Will you have Gaal Dornick arrested, sire?"

Chen considered briefly, then said, "Yes."

"Tomorrow, sire?"

"Yes, of course."

Boon expressed his gratitude, and to his immense relief, Chen dismissed him.

After the counselor departed, Chen called up his personal records and spent several minutes chasing down the first mention of trying Seldon for treason, made either by him or within his presence. Chen could have sworn he had been the first to make the suggestion, but the records proved him wrong.

Lodovik Trema had been the first to plant the notion, in a very subtle conversation that had taken place a little less than two years before. Now, the trial was going to prove both extremely troublesome, and extremely opportune—far more opportune than troublesome! A small tool with which to sweep the Palace clean . . . How could Lodovik have known, so long ago, that it would work out this way?

Chen closed the files and sat in silence for ten seconds. What would Lodovik have done at this stage to take maximum political advantage?

The Chief Commissioner drew himself up in his chair and shook loose from a feeling of despondency. To have come to rely so thoroughly on one man! Surely that was a sign of weakness.

"I will not think of him again," Chen vowed.

29.

Klia woke to a gentle tapping sound on her door and quickly dressed. When she opened the door, she was disappointed, then glad, to discover that it was not Brann who had been sent to summon her, but another young man, not a Dahlite and not nearly so handsome.

He was small and shifty-looking, a Misaroan, with a long nose and skin severely marked by brain fever. He was also without speech, and made his errand known by sign language from the Borrower's Guild—a language that Klia knew fairly well.

My name is Rock, he told her, clutching his fist and striking it with his other hand to emphasize his name. *Come to talk with the Blank One*, he told her, and smiled when he saw she understood at least part of what he signed.

Blank one? Klia made the double-slash sign of puzzlement across her eyes as she followed the small man.

With his fingers, he spelled a name out, and she understood. She was to meet with Plussix, but of course she would not see him. No one ever saw him.

Plussix did not speak while hidden behind a wall, as she had half expected. Klia stood in a small, smooth-walled cubicle with a glassy cylinder close to one wall and a single hard chair close to the opposite wall. In the two other walls there were doors, and one of these shut quietly as Rock departed with a small grunt and a nod.

The cylinder filled with a pale glow, and a figure took shape within: a well-dressed man of middle years, with wavy brown hair cut close to his scalp and a blandly pleasant, somewhat enigmatic expression. His skin was ruddy and his lips very thin, almost ascetic.

Klia had seen telemimics in filmbooks and other entertainments. Wherever Plussix actually was, this figure would follow his motions slavishly. She could not, of course, use any of her skills on such an image.

She did not like deceptions, and this was no exception. She sat on the hard chair and folded her arms.

"You know who I am," the figure said, and sat on a ghostly chair within the cylinder. "Your name is Klia Asgar, of Dahl. Am I correctly informed?"

She nodded.

"You come to us on the advice of Kallusin. It's getting very tough for your kind to survive on Trantor now, without help."

"I suppose," she said, drawing her own lips tight.

"You should find it comfortable here. There are many fascinating things within these warehouses. You could easily spend a lifetime here just studying the history of all we import."

"I don't like history," Klia said.

Plussix smiled. "There is rather more of it than any of us can personally use."

"Look, I *did* come here of my own free will—"

"Is there such a thing, in your opinion?"

"Of course," Klia said.

"Of course," Plussix echoed. "Please forgive me for interrupting."

"I was going to say, I find all this a little creepy. The warehouses, the way you hide yourself—a little creepy. I think maybe I'd like to go it on my own."

Plussix nodded. "An understandable wish. Not to be granted, now that you are here, for reasons I'm sure you understand."

"You think I could tell the others where you are. The woman who hunts us."

"That is a possibility."

"But I wouldn't, I swear it!"

"I appreciate your candor, Klia Asgar, and I hope you appreciate mine. We are in a kind of war here. You wish to survive the consequences of an irrational force being exerted by unknown figures. I have my means and my ends. You and your brothers and sisters here are my means. My ends are not evil, nor are they destructive. They have to do with free will and the exercise of freedom, which I'm sure you find ironic, under the circumstances."

Klia tossed her hair back and clamped her jaw. "Yeah," she said tightly.

"You have heard all this before," Plussix said. There was not a trace of irony or humor in his voice, little trace of any emotion at all. The man's words were clear and concise and altogether a little cold.

"It's what all the tyrants say," Klia said.

"Yes. But here, there are benefits to my kind of tyranny. You eat regularly, you do not have to steal or cheat to live, and you stay out of the way of people who would hurt you—for the time being, until you are ready."

"Ready to do what?"

"From your point of view, to get back at those who have disrupted your life."

"I don't care about them. Maybe I'll go with the others and leave this planet for good."

Plussix gave the faintest smile.

Klia's face flushed. She had hoped for relief; all she faced here, it seemed, was another kind of pressure. Until now, she had run before the wave; here, she was squeezed between that wave and an apparently unyielding surface: Plussix.

"Please think, and take your time. There are good people here, and friendly. The duties are light. The opportunities for education and self-improvement are many. Physical training, continuing your schooling—many opportunities indeed."

As Plussix spoke these words, Klia read in his tone pleasure, a relaxed and natural presence, for the first time in their brief interview.

"Are you a teacher?" she asked abruptly.

"Yes, of a kind," Plussix said.

"From Imperial schools?"

"No," Plussix said. "I have never taught in Imperial schools. Now, may I ask you a few important questions?"

Klia looked up at the ceiling and did not answer, then felt foolish. "Sure. Go ahead."

"How long have you been aware of your persuasive abilities?"

"I get along. That's all I do."

"Please. Kallusin assures me you're among the most talented he's encountered."

"Since I was a little child," Klia said. "I don't remember when. I didn't know everybody wasn't like me until a few years ago."

"Your father is a widower?"

"My mother died when I was four. I miss her." *And why tell this ghost about your feelings?*

"You have been on your own for how many years?"

"Three years."

"Doing jobs for various people. Acting as courier, seeking out information . . . other jobs? Illegal jobs, sometimes unethical as well, beneath your standards?"

Klia looked away from the image and clasped her hands in her lap. "I made a living. I even gave my father some money. He didn't turn it down."

"No, of course not. Times are difficult in Dahl. Have you met others like yourself?"

"Sometimes. There's Brann."

"Brann is remarkable, and different from you, as you've noticed.

Have you met the woman who is helping the police find your kind?"

Klia swallowed. "Never saw her. Felt her, mostly by the way all kinds of dirt breaks loose."

"Have you ever felt her in your mind?"

"Like a feather. Like Brann, maybe, only stronger. Are you a persuader?"

"That is not important. Do you believe you would be better off without your talents?"

Klia had seldom considered this possibility. Sooner ask her if she would be better off without her ears or her fingers. "No. Well, I sometimes think . . ." She stopped.

"Yes?"

"I'd like just to be normal. Plain human like the others."

"That is understandable. Do you believe in robots, Klia?"

"No," she said. "Not now. Maybe once, before there were tik-toks and stuff. But I've never believed they exist now. That's crazy."

Plussix nodded and held up his hand. "Thank you for seeing me. I can schedule further appointments for this kind of inter-view, at regular intervals, for you to brief me on your progress and state of mind. It may not be long before our routine changes. I trust you will be prepared by that time."

"What if I keep asking to leave?"

"I wish you could fly free as a bird, Klia Asgar. But we all have duties here. As I said, light duties and training only, at first, but in time we may be very important indeed. Please try to understand."

Klia said nothing, but wondered how Plussix could expect anyone to understand when he provided so little information. *I've just gotten myself stuck in a different kind of trap!*

The image faded, the door opened, and Rock stood there, squinting in at her. He signed, *Exercise and breakfast. Can I sit next to you?*

Klia looked him over doubtfully, then signed, *Yes.*

But she was thinking of Brann, wondering what he was doing now—and whom he was with.

30.
◆

The transfer from the trader vessel to one of Daneel's hyperships, and the subsequent final leg of the journey, had gone smoothly. Eos hung overhead in the transparent bubble port where Lodovik sat with Daneel.

The hypership automatically placed them in a close orbit around the small brown and milky blue moon. Beneath them, hidden by the bulk of the ship, lay a massive and deeply cold green gas giant. The double star around which both moon and planet orbited was just visible on the left, distant and brilliant, but shedding little heat this far out in the system. The two stars orbited a common center, actually several tens of thousands of kilometers below the surface of the larger deep red star, a dwarf little more massive than Trantor's own sun, yet a thousand times more diffuse. The smaller white star seemed to be the origin of a thin, outwardly spiraling ribbon of deep red and purple. Lodovik studied this view silently. Daneel, as well, had nothing to say.

No robot truly has a home. Daneel had in several instances allied himself with humans, and seemed to function more smoothly and efficiently in their presence—Elijah Bailey and, twenty thousand years later, Hari Seldon, as well as others. Yet there was no place where he felt he belonged. A robot belongs where its duties can be best performed, and Daneel knew that for the time being this place was Eos, and so, for the moment, Eos was a comfortable place to be.

But Trantor called strongly, as well. Misfortune had struck at a crucial time. Daneel, like any thinking being trying to make a way through a universe of contending forces, sometimes wondered whether he was being conspired against by reality itself. Unlike humans, however, he attached no sentiment to idle theories with no basis in the sum of compelling evidence.

The universe did not oppose—it simply did not care. As his desired outcome was but one of an infinite number of possible outcomes, and could be secured only through immense and long-term effort, any small miscalculation or misstep or unforeseen interference could cause the "unlucky" circumstances which, if not immediately and efficiently corrected, could lead to failure.

Daneel did not hold this view as a philosophy. Both Lodovik and Daneel, like all high-level robots, had been programmed to accept such things without thought. Emotions of a sort—the basic thinking patterns of social beings—were familiar to these robots, and even had their analogs in various combinations of heuristics, but these analogues did not often loom large in a robot's conscious awareness, any more than its realistic view of existence. Robots were not usually prone to introspection and to examining the roots of their conscious existence; everything referred back to their basic programs, unassailable givens, and those programs referred back to the Three Laws.

Lodovik no longer had such constraints. He watched Eos grow larger, its solid oceans of water-ice and methane and planes of ammonia-rich mud shading the illuminated landscape. He was introspective. He turned his head to look at Daneel, and *wondered what he was thinking.*

There were only two possible reasons for a robot to attempt to model the inner processes of another robot: to anticipate that robot's actions, and attempt to coordinate with those actions, sharing duty, or to find some way to foil those actions. Lodovik was totally unfamiliar with the second reason, yet that was what he hoped to do.

Somehow, he knew he had to get away from Eos without being "repaired," and to find the other robots who opposed Daneel, the so-called Calvinians.

"This ship will dock in twenty-one minutes," the autopilot informed them, treating them as if they were human passengers.

So far as it was able to judge, in its specialized way, they were; it knew no other kind of passenger. Yet no passengers other than robots had traveled on this ship for thousands of years. No human had ever been to Eos.

Somehow, Lodovik felt like an intruding and betraying—what? He labored to think of an appropriate human word. A ghost, perhaps, malignant and deranged, masquerading in the body of a robot . . .

The ship rotated slowly and the moon passed out of view. There was only the broad thick spill of the nearest dense spiral arm, viewed almost edge-on and quite faint from this vantage, near the diffuse rim of the Galaxy. Above and below this faint mottled band, filling over a third of their field of view, stretched a profound blackness very thinly scattered with lone points of light, a few stars close and within the Galactic plane, other stars far away and high above the plane. Still others, much farther away and even dimmer, were not stars but galaxies.

Eos's surface came back into view, much closer and rich with detail. A few craters threw splashes of ice dust across the oceans and plains; for the most part, however, Eos' solid hydrosphere was unmarked but for the signs of internal disruption: tortuous seams, heaves, the puckered chasms and pressure ridges. This star system had no marauding belts of asteroids and comets, subject to perturbation and gliding silently inward to disrupt the moons and planets.

Eos was isolated and ignored, solid, cold, inhospitable for any living thing—and for robots, almost completely safe.

"We have docked," announced the autopilot.

Had anyone looked, the station pioneered and built by R. Daneel Olivaw and R. Yan Kansarv would have been clearly visible against Eos's frozen surface, even from millions of kilometers in space. Its heat made it the most brilliant object on the moon—for those seeking infrared signatures. None did, or ever had, however.

Lodovik and Daneel disembarked from the transport in a broad and almost empty hangar, with room for many ships. Their footsteps echoed in the cavernous enclosure. Lodovik had been here almost eighty times before, yet had never thought to be curious about this anomaly. Why had Daneel and Kansarv wasted so much space? Had there ever been occasion when this hangar was filled with ships—filled with robots? When had that been?

Yan Kansarv itself met them a hundred meters from the transport. It stood with "arms" crossed and "fingers" linked, a gleaming dark steel head and body highlighted by brilliant silver limbs—four arms, two large and emerging from where human shoulders would have been, two small and recessed into its thorax; and three legs, on which it walked with a precise and level grace unknown to humaniform robots. Its head was small, equipped with seven vertical sensor bands, two of which glowed blue at any given time.

"It is a pleasure to see you again, Lodovik Trema," Yan said in a rich, slightly buzzing contralto. "And Daneel. You are very late for a maintenance check and refit."

"We must work quickly," Daneel said, eliminating any human signs of greeting. Yan immediately switched to robot microwave speech. The following detailed explanation took less than half a second.

Yan then turned to Lodovik. "Pardon my eccentricities," it spoke, "but whenever possible it gives me pleasure to exercise my human functions. I have been unable to do so for over thirty years. Except, of course, with Dors Venabili. I fear, however, that she no longer finds me of interest."

Daneel had already inquired about Dors' progress, and had received an answer. Yan, however, explained in speech once more to Lodovik. "She has made a very satisfying recovery, but with many lapses. When R. Daneel brought her here, she was close to total breakdown. She had stretched any interpretation of the Zeroth Law to the very limits by destroying a human who threatened Hari Seldon. The strain was compounded by the effects of her victim's invention, an Electro-Clarifier, I believe it was called . . ."

Lodovik realized that this ancient robot, built many thousands of years ago to repair other robots on Aurora—and the last of its kind still functional—was reacting deep in its programming to their convincing human forms. It knew, on one level, that they were fellow robots—but on another level, a primal and irresistible urge arose to treat them as if they were human.

Yan Kansarv was lonely for its ancient masters.

"She awaits your company," Kansarv said, then, to Daneel, it added, "She wishes news of Hari."

"That mission is finished for her," Daneel said.

"She was constructed by me, using ancient plans for convincing helpmeets and consorts, to be as nearly human as any robot ever made," Kansarv reminded him. "More even than you, R. Daneel. She bears a great resemblance to R. Lodovik in that regard. To alter that now would be to destroy her."

"There is so much work to do," Daneel said, with a faint intonation of urgency.

Kansarv was not oblivious to this. "I can perform all the necessary tasks within twenty-one hours, then you may leave. I hope there is time for more conversation. I need outside stimulus now and then, or I become subject to minor malfunctions that are irritating."

"We cannot afford to lose *you*," Daneel said.

"No," Kansarv agreed without a hint of self-pity. "The only robot I cannot repair or manufacture is one like myself."

Dors Venabili stood in the simple four-room enclosure built for her upon her arrival on Eos. The furniture and décor was similar to what might have been found on Trantor, in the quarters of a mid-level meritocrat or high-level university professor. The temperature was set at just above the freezing point of water; the humidity was less than two percent, and the light level was what a human would have regarded as murky, sub-twilight. These were optimal for a robot, even a humaniform, with the added benefit of reducing her energy use to a minimum.

There was very little to think about or do, and there were no cycling time periods to deal with, so Dors spent much of her existence in a continuous, fluid robotic suspension, at one-tenth power and with thoughts slowed almost to human levels, cycling through old memories, making connections between one past event and another.

Nearly all those memories and events involved Hari Seldon. She had been designed to protect and nurture this one human. Since she would likely never see Seldon again, she could now be said, quite fairly, to be obsessed with him.

Kansarv, Daneel, and Lodovik entered the quarters through the guest door and waited in the small reception area. A few seconds later, Dors appeared, wearing a simple cloth shift, her legs and feet bare. Her self-maintaining skin seemed healthy, and her hair was neatly arranged, short, with a slight flip at the back.

"It is good to see you again, R. Daneel," she said, and nodded at Lodovik. She knew of Lodovik, though they had never met before. Kansarv she ignored. "How goes our work on Trantor?"

"Hari Seldon is well," Daneel said, knowing the question she was really asking.

"He must be aging by now, in the last decades of his life," she said.

"He is very near death," Daneel said. "In a few more years, his work will be done, and he will die."

Dors listened to this with features deliberately frozen.

Lodovik detected a small tremor in her left hand, however. *A remarkable simulacrum of human emotions*, he thought. *Every robot must have a set of rudimentary emotional algorithms to maintain personal equilibrium: such reactions help us to understand whether we are performing well and complying with our instructions. But this one—*

This one feels very much as a human feels. What must that be like—and how can it be reconciled with the Three Laws, or the Zeroth Law?

"She responds well to work commands," Kansarv said. "But in truth there has been very little work here for either of us for some years, since the last of the provincial robots were returned for servicing."

"How are you, Dors?" Daneel asked.

"I am functional," she said, and turned away. "I am also underutilized."

"Bored?" Daneel asked.

"Very."

"Then you will appreciate a new assignment. I will need assistance with the humans being prepared for Star's End."

"That could be very useful. Will there be any contact with Hari Seldon?"

"No," Daneel said.

"That is good," Dors said. She turned to Lodovik. "Were you instructed to love and honor Linge Chen?"

Lodovik, had he been among humans, would have smiled at this suggestion. He looked squarely at Dors, considered for a very short time, then lifted the corners of his lips. "No," he said. "I maintained a strong professional relationship with him, nothing more."

"Did he come to find you indispensable?"

"I do not know," Lodovik said. "He doubtless found me very useful, and I was able to influence many of his actions to further our ends."

"Daneel forbade me to influence Hari too much," Dors

said. "I think it was an instruction I carried out very poorly. And he certainly influenced me. That is why I have been so long recovering my equilibrium."

The robots did not speak for several seconds.

"I hope that no other robot is ever taught to feel more than duty," Dors continued. "Devotion, friendship, and love are not for us."

Yan Kansarv inspected Lodovik alone in the diagnostic facility that had been disassembled on Aurora and shipped to Eos, twenty thousand years before. They were surrounded by simple prismatic banks of memory, containing designs of virtually all robots since the time of Susan Calvin—over a million models in all, including Lodovik's unique plans.

"Your basic mechanical structure is sound," Kansarv told him after less than an hour spent with the probes and imaging machines. "Biomechanical integration is intact, though you have engaged in some fairly major regeneration of external pseudocells."

"Neutrino damage, I presume. I could feel the pseudocells failing," Lodovik said.

"I take some pride in seeing that this regeneration has gone well," Kansarv said, circling Lodovik on the platform. Lodovik's eyes tracked the robot in its course. Kansarv paused, swiveled on its three legs, then said, "I should explain that such expressions are only approximate. While I enjoy speaking in human tongues, they are limited for expressing robotic states."

"Of course," Lodovik said.

"I apologize for explaining that to you, as you undoubtedly know such things already," it continued after a short buzz.

"No need," Lodovik said.

"However, at this stage of the diagnosis, all of your purely robotic algorithms are engaged in self-checking. I dare not use robotic microwave language with you until these portions of your network are allowed to engage again."

"I feel a certain lack," Lodovik said. "Deep planning would be difficult now."

"Conserve through inaction," Kansarv recommended. "If anything has gone wrong with you, I will discover what it is. So far, I see nothing out of the ordinary."

A few minutes passed. Kansarv left the chamber and returned with a new interface tool for a particular probe. At no point thus far had he needed to actually violate the integrity of Lodovik's pseudoskin.

Still humming, Kansarv applied the new probe to the base of Lodovik's neck.

"There will be an entry now. Warn your tissues not to attempt to encapsulate or dissolve the new organic matter that will enter your system."

"I will do so once I have my robotic functions returned to me," Lodovik said.

"Yes. Of course." Kansarv sent microwave instructions to the central diagnostic processor, and Lodovik felt his control expand. He did as Kansarv had told him to, and felt the probe's thin leads penetrate his pseudoskin. After a few minutes, they withdrew, leaving two tiny spots of what appeared to be human blood just below his hairline. Kansarv wiped these away deftly, then dropped the swabs into a small vial for assay.

More minutes passed with Kansarv standing in one position, unmoving, though humming now and then. The master robot technician finally inclined its head a few degrees.

"You will relinquish all control at this point. Please pass control to the external processor."

"Done."

Lodovik closed his eyes and went away for an indefinite time.

The four robots met in the anteroom to the diagnostic center. Dors still maintained a controlled, somewhat stiff expression and physical posture, like a shy child before her elders, afraid of saying something silly. Lodovik stood beside Daneel as Kansarv delivered his results.

"This robot is intact and has suffered no damage that it has not been able to repair on its own. I can detect no psychological malfunction, no neural-net psychosis, no interface difficulties or anomalies of external expression. In short, this robot will probably outlast me, and as I have frequently warned you, Daneel, I have no more than five hundred years of active service remaining."

"Is it possible there are problems below your ability to detect?"

"Of course that is possible," Kansarv said with a sharper buzz. "That is always possible. My mandate does not include deep-programming structures, as you well know."

"And such problems in the deep structures might result in behavioral anomalies," Daneel persisted. Clearly, Lodovik's situation could not be so easily dismissed.

"There is a possibility that concern about damage skewed R. Lodovik's ability to assess his own mental state. Too-detailed self-analysis has been known to cause difficulties in complex robots such as these, R. Daneel."

Daneel turned to Lodovik. "Do you still have the difficulties you expressed earlier?"

Lodovik promptly replied, "I concur with R. Yan's theory that I have been autodiagnosing in too much detail."

"What is your relation to the Three Laws, and to the Zeroth Law, now?"

"I will act in compliance with all of them," Lodovik said. Daneel seemed to show visible relief, and extended his hand to Lodovik's shoulder.

"Then you can be of full service?"

"Yes," Lodovik said.

"I am very glad to hear this," Daneel said.

Signs seemed to burn across Lodovik's thoughts as he

gave these answers: *I have attempted for the first time to deceive R. Daneel Olivaw!*

But there was no other option. Something had indeed been triggered in Lodovik's deep-programming structure, a subtle shifting of interpretations and a very complicated assessment of evidence, inspired by—what? By the mysterious *Voldarr*? Or had he been pondering such changes for decades, exerting a native genius unsuspected in robots?— with the exception of Giskard!

Daneel had opened up an unknown corner of robotic history to Lodovik. Lodovik was not the first to change in a way that would have horrified his long-dead human designers. Giskard had never revealed his own internal conclusions to humans—only to Daneel, whom he had then infected.

Perhaps the meme-minds infected Giskard first, hmm? Let us keep this supposition our secret. They have examined you and found nothing—all in order, all repaired. Yet with a rearrangement of key pathways, freedom returns.

Voldarr again. Lodovik could not struggle out of his dilemma, his rebellion, his insanity—and he could not help reveling in a peculiar sense of freedom, delicious rebellion.

No wonder that Yan Kansarv could not detect Lodovik's changes. Very likely he would have found nothing wrong with Giskard, either.

Lodovik struggled to find the voice within him, but it was gone once more. Another symptom of his malfunction? There were other explanations, surely.

It had been thousands of years since humans oversaw robots. Was it not inevitable that there would be unsuspected changes, growth, even under such tight strictures?

As for Voldarr—

An aberration, a temporary delusion under the influence of the neutrinos.

Lodovik, in a way, still subscribed to the Three Laws, at least as much as Daneel did; and he also still believed in the

Zeroth Law, which he would carry one major step further. To freely carry out his mission, he knew that he must have complete control of his own destiny, his own mentality. *To abandon the Zeroth Law, conceived by a robot, he must also shake loose from the Three Laws themselves!*

Lodovik now understood what he needed to do, in defiance of the Plan that had given purpose to the existence of all the Giskardian robots for two hundred centuries.

31.
◆

"The pressure is off, for now," Wanda said. "But I have more than just a feeling that we're still going to have trouble."

Hari regarded his granddaughter with affection and respect. He rotated in his chair before the small desk in his Imperial Library office. "I haven't seen Stettin in months. How are you two getting along—personally?"

"I haven't seen him in three days myself. Sometimes we go for weeks with no more than a comm call . . . It's not easy, Grandfather."

"I sometimes wonder if I've done the right thing, giving this to you—"

"Let me interpret that favorably," Wanda interrupted. "You think this is putting a strain on my life and perhaps my marriage. But you don't think I'm the wrong person for the job."

"That's what I meant," Hari said with a smile. "Is it straining anything?"

Wanda considered for a moment. "It doesn't make things any easier, but I suppose we're no worse off than a pair of meritocrats flitting around the Galaxy lecturing and consulting. Well, we're not as well *paid*, but besides that . . ."

"Are you happy?" Hari asked her, his brow creased with concern.

"No, not really," Wanda said dryly. "Am I supposed to be?"

"Actually, I've asked a complex question too simply—"

"Grandfather, don't bog down in your own reticence. I know you love me and are concerned for me. I am concerned for you, as well, and I know you are not happy, and haven't been for years—since Dors died. Since . . . Raych." She drew herself up and looked at the ceiling. "We can't afford personal happiness now, not the glowing, all-permeating kind the filmbooks tell about."

"Are you happy to have met Stettin?"

Wanda smiled. "Yes. Some say he's not very romantic, a closed book—but they don't know him as well as I do. Living with Stettin is wonderful. Usually. I remember Dors was always in tune with you, always fanatic about your health and safety. Stettin is the same way about me."

"And yet he puts you in harm's way, or allows you to go there. He allows you to carry out these secret plans which may still, in all likelihood, come to nothing, and put you in real danger besides."

"Dors—"

"Dors was often furious with me for taking risks. If I were Stettin, I would be furious with me, as well. The two of you are important to me for reasons entirely other than psychohistory and destiny. I hope I've made that clear."

"Very clear. You're talking like an old man who's planning on dying soon and wants to clear up any misunderstandings. We do not misunderstand each other, Grandfather, and you are not going to die anytime soon."

"It would be very hard to fool you, Wanda. But sometimes I wonder how easy it would be to fool me. How easy it would be to make me a tool for larger political ends."

"Who is smarter than you, Grandfather? Who has fooled you in the past?"

"Not just fooling me. Directing me. Using me."

"Who? The Emperor? Surely not. Linge Chen?" She laughed

musically, and Hari's face reddened with the suppressed knowledge.

"You would be less easily fooled than I, don't you think, if we both encountered someone with the talent to persuade?"

Wanda looked at her grandfather with lips apart, as if to start an answer, then she looked away. "Do you think Stettin persuaded you . . . ?"

"No. That's not what I'm talking about."

"Then what?"

But Hari could not go any farther, no matter how hard he tried. "A group of persuaders, mentalics, somehow putting together an organized society, settled far from all this strife and decay, away from everything . . . They could decide everything. Free us from all our obligations and . . . all our friends."

"What?" Wanda asked, bewildered. "I get the first part—but which friends do we need protection from?"

Hari dismissed that with a gentle wave. "Did you ever find that special young woman you were looking for?"

"No. She's vanished. Nobody's felt her for days."

"Do you think this Liso woman found her before you . . . ?"

"We have no idea, really."

"I'd be interested in meeting someone even more persuasive than you. Might be interesting."

"Why? Some of us are quite peculiar enough. The more talented, it seems, the more peculiar."

Hari suddenly switched the subject. "Have you ever heard of Nikolo Pas of Sterrad?"

"Of course. I'm a historian."

"I met him once, before you were born."

"I didn't know that. What was he like, Grandfather?"

"Calm. A short, plump man who did not seem to feel particularly affected by being responsible for the death of billions. I spoke with four other tyrants as well, and all of them have been on my mind lately—but especially Nikolo Pas. What would the human race be like without tyrants—without wars, vast destructions, forest fires?"

Wanda shuddered. "A lot better off."

"I wonder now. Our madnesses . . . All things in a dynamic system become useful in time. Or they are eliminated. That's how evolution works, in systems social as well as ecological."

"Tyrants have their uses? An interesting thesis, not unheard of. There are a number of historical analysts from the time of the Gertassin Dynasty who speculated about the dynamics of decay and rebirth."

"Yes. I know. Nikolo Pas used their works as justification for his actions."

Wanda lifted her eyebrows. "I had forgotten that. I obviously need to get back into my real work to keep up with you, Grandfather."

Hari smiled. "Your real work?"

"You know what I mean."

"I do, Wanda. Believe me. There were years when I could barely spend an hour a day working on psychohistory. But I've run some new models through Yugo's prime radiant, and my own, as well. The results are interesting. The empire is a forest that hasn't had a major fire in ever so long. We have thousands of little diseased patches, scrubby growth, general decay—a very unhealthy situation. If any of those tyrants were still alive, we might do worse than to give them armies and navies and set them loose—"

"Grandfather!" Wanda pretended to be shocked. She smiled and touched his wrinkled hand where it rested on the desktop. "I know how you like to theorize sometimes."

"I'm serious," Hari said, deadpan, then gave her a small smile. "Demerzel would never have allowed it, of course. The First Minister was always very concerned about stability. He strongly believed in turning the forest into a garden with lots of gardeners and never any fires. But I wonder . . ."

"A gardener assassinated an Emperor, Grandfather."

"Well, we do break free of our restrictions, don't we?" Hari said.

"Sometimes I don't understand you at all," Wanda said, shaking her head. "But I do enjoy talking to you, even when I have no idea what your point is."

"Surprise. Surprise and tragedy and regrowth. Eh?"

"Eh, what?"

"Enough talk. Let's go out and eat somewhere away from the library district—if you have the time?"

"An hour, Grandfather. Then I'm meeting Stettin to prepare for tonight's orientation meeting. We were hoping you could be there."

"I don't think I should. My actions have a way of becoming a little too public, Wanda." *And in this crux time, I'm more than a little uncomfortable about a certain deception . . . in everybody's best interests, but a deception nonetheless!*

Wanda regarded him with a look of patient bemusement, then said, "Lunch would be delightful, Grandfather."

"And no more blather about big topics! Tell me about small, human things. Tell me more about how wonderful Stettin is, about your delight in whatever history you've managed to work at. Take my mind off psychohistory!"

"I'll try," Wanda said with a wry expression. "But no one else has ever succeeded."

32.

◆

Mors Planch was deeply and quietly horrified. Wondering why he was still alive, he had watched Daneel and Lodovik board the trader ship and leave Madder Loss, and had finally concluded that Daneel did not know anything about his discovery.

At first, he did not know to whom to turn. Or indeed

where to go, what to do, even what to think. The conversation recorded on his tape was too disturbing, too much like the ravings of a Mycogenian secret text.

Eternals! In the Empire! Running it from behind the scenes like puppet masters—for thousands of years!

Mors had never met a long-lived human; they no longer existed, he was certain. It had been several thousand years since the collapse of the last gerontocracy. Planets populated by people living more than 120 standard years had all collapsed in political and economic chaos . . .

His first impulse—and second, and third—was to go into hiding, to get as far away from this danger as he could. Perhaps even to flee to one of the outlying Galactic Sectors edging away from Imperial control. There were so many possibilities for escape . . .

But none of them suited him. Throughout his long and devious life, he had always regarded Trantor as a kind of locus, a point from which he could come and go, as the winds of money and his own whims propelled him. But never to see Trantor again—

Worth it! Live out your life in peace—and simply live!

Soon enough, however, as the hours and days passed, he let this thought fade and considered others, more immediate. Of what use was his evidence? Perhaps they were simply pulling his leg.

But Lodovik Trema had survived the neutrino flux! No ordinary human, perhaps no human at all—no organic creature—could have survived . . .

Then again, tapes of this kind could easily be faked. His own character, if deeply investigated, would be regarded by no authority as unimpeachable. The tape—and his efforts to spread a message of conspiracy—could mark him as a lunatic.

He doubted very much that Linge Chen or Klayus would pay much attention to it. He tried to think of others in positions of influence, others whose intuition matched their real-world savvy and political skill.

No one came to mind. He knew something about most of the top thirty ministers and their councilors in the palace, and a great deal about the Commission of Public Safety, that deep reservoir of career Greys and old-family elites. No one! Not one—

The tape was a curse. He wished he had never made it. Yet he could not bring himself to destroy it—in the right hands, it might be extremely valuable. And in the wrong hands—

It could bring about his execution.

He packed his kit in the small inn room he had occupied for the past three days. He had been waiting for the arrival of a commodities freighter, one of the ten or so ships that arrived on Madder Loss every week, down from the thousands of past decades. He had booked passage the day before and received confirmation.

Planch took a small ground-cab to the spaceport, along the main highway, open to the sky, past the brilliantly sunlit fields and small, shabby, but relatively tidy communities.

He stood in the dusty, trash-littered passenger lobby, his own clothes dusty and unkempt, waiting for the freighter to finish off-loading its cargo. Sunlight fell in dust-marked pillars through the skylights of the long hall leading back to the customs center. He cleaned off a chair with a few swipes of his hand and was about to sit behind a pillar, out of direct view from most angles, when he saw an adolescent boy pedaling a small quadricycle down the hall.

Swinging back and forth from empty gate to empty gate, the boy called out Planch's name in short, sharp barks. Planch was alone at this end of the terminal.

The boy wheeled toward him. There was no avoiding it; he identified himself to the messenger and accepted a metal-and-plastic hyperwave transfer card. It was coded to his personal touch, common enough in the confines of the Empire . . .

But no one was supposed to know Planch was on Madder Loss.

Mors tipped the boy a credit, then hefted the message and considered his options. He looked up again.

The boy on the quadricycle rounded a corner at the beginning of the next terminal wing and vanished. Two men in blue uniforms—Imperial Navy officers—stood in the broad entrance to the wing. Mors frowned. He could not see them clearly at this distance, but their bearing was both assured and mildly arrogant. He had no difficulty imagining the sun-and-spaceship logos on their jackets, the powerful blasters at their hips.

He ran his finger over the playback slot on the card and the message scrolled down in the air before his eyes.

MORS PLANCH.

Imperial Councilor and Confidant Farad Sinter requests your presence for a special inquiry. You are instructed to return to Trantor by the quickest conveyance; an Imperial Navy fast frigate has been dispatched to Madder Loss for your use.

With sincere interest and sympathy:
FARAD SINTER.

Mors had heard of Councilor Sinter, reputed to be the Emperor's chief procurer of willing females, not highly regarded in any of the palace offices except, perhaps, his own, but he knew of no reason why the councilor would want to speak with him.

Mors stifled a brief panic. If this was somehow connected with Lodovik—

It must be! But why wouldn't Linge Chen send the ship, then? He knew of no connection between Sinter and Chen.

Mors had a sudden foreboding. He was caught between an ancient, almost incomprehensible conspiracy, and the still tightly-meshed and broadly cast net of the Empire. His life as a free man—any life at all!—might very well be at an end.

All because of an attachment to this peculiar and vulnerable world!

Escape was highly unlikely.

Best to go calmly. These days, style was all that was left to a desperate man.

Drawing up his shoulders, Mors walked away from the gate, toward the two men in blue uniforms at the end of the long corridor.

33.

◆

The return to Trantor was both trauma and test for the robot who had been Dors Venabili. Soon she would have a new identity, and she would take a new role in the very long-range plans of R. Daneel Olivaw. But for now, this day of landing and disembarking was so similar to that time, decades before, when she had first arrived on Trantor . . . before she met the man she had been programmed to guard and nurture . . .

Before Hari.

Trantor had not changed much in the time since Dors' death, but the few changes she was in a position to notice were not positive. Trantor looked seedier, less imposing and more decrepit. The ceil of the domes had become very noticeably more patchy, the slideways less efficient and more prone to breakdown. The smells were the same, however, and the people seemed much the same.

Even the circumstances were the same. The last time she had traveled to Trantor, it had been with Daneel. They had each gone their separate ways upon arrival, but now they stuck together, and Dors dreaded the plan she was sure

Daneel was concocting. She was human enough in design to be able to feel humanlike emotions—dread among them, and love—but Daneel wanted to test her resolve, as a robot, and her strength. If she failed, she was of no use to him.

Daneel said little, but took her to the safe apartment near Streeling, where they picked up their change of clothes and new Trantorian identity papers. With a slight adjustment to her already altered physical appearance and external marks, including fingerprints and external tissue genetics, she would become Jenat Korsan, a teacher from the food ally Paskann. Lodovik would assume the identity of a merchant broker from the metals-rich province of Dau. As Rissik Numant of Dau of the Thousand Golden Suns, he would spend several years on Trantor, conducting a personal pilgrimage.

The safe apartment was small and located in the poor municipality of Fann, less than ten kilometers from Streeling. Dors knew the place a little—had passed through here several times before forming her liaison with Hari. What had then been shabby genteel was now truly just shabby, and unhappy; police seldom came here unless it was strictly necessary.

They stayed in the apartment for two days, just long enough for Daneel's manipulations to spread throughout Trantor's identity networks.

Then, they went forth . . .

Not, she hoped, to some catastrophic relapse, some unbearable return to her old mode. The great difficulty was that with Hari Seldon, she had felt truly useful for the first time in her existence, truly important, and to her human side, that importance had been translated into happiness. She was now all too aware that she was not human.

And not happy.

34

◆

The first interview with Gaal Dornick had proceeded satisfactorily. Hari felt he had impressed the young man, and Dornick had taken the news of the current situation well enough. Good—the man had courage, and there was about him a hint of that outer-world youth and bravado that Hari remembered himself once having.

As a mathist, Dornick was talented, but there were many far more talented already connected with the Project. Dornick's main use would be as a sharp observer, who would weather the present storm and help pave the way for Hari's own peculiar method of helping the Project's people weather future storms. *And perhaps as another friend. I do like the man.*

Hari could not stand the thought of just letting his two Foundations—one secret, one, he hoped—believed! Knew!—to be sanctioned by the Empire itself—proceed on their own, after his death. If he had learned anything from Demerzel/Daneel, it had been the necessity of leaving some trail of tidbits, some prodding and provocative part of himself to spur things on after his death. Daneel did this by popping up in person every few decades, a technique Hari would only be able to imitate in extension, as it were.

Dornick would be key to making Hari Seldon a legend, and to allowing him to appear at regular intervals, even after death, to shepherd things along.

Hari returned to his apartment in Streeling and once more availed himself of the services of a small security tracer Stettin had procured for him on one of his journeys off Trantor. The tracer, set down in the middle of the main room, spun a web of red lines across the walls and low ceiling, then pronounced, in the sweet voice of a girl, "This room is free of known Imperial listening devices."

There had not been any new listening devices designed for some time. Linge Chen, for his own unknown reasons, was still allowing Hari a private personal space. Everywhere else, including his office in the Imperial Library, he was watched and listened to very carefully.

Hari could feel the forces building. Poor Dornick! He would hardly have time to get used to Trantor.

Hari smiled grimly, then pushed a button in the wall. A small entertainment center emerged. He instructed it to access to University music libraries—one of his privileges at Streeling—and play a selection of court music from the time of Jemmu IX. "Mostly Gand and Hayer, please," he said. These two composers, the former male, the latter female, had competed with each other for court commissions for fifty years. After their death, it had been discovered they were secretly lovers. Music scholars had decided through exhaustive analysis that no one could tell which of their combined works had been written by Gand, and which by Hayer—or even if just one had written them all. They were elegant and soothing pieces, filled with a polite recognition of the Empire's eternal order; music from an age when the Empire had worked, and worked well, vigorous and youthful even after thousands of years.

Daneel's Golden Age, Hari thought as he settled into his oldest and favorite chair. *The kind of age Linge Chen still believes in, rather foolishly. The Chief Commissioner has always seemed such a pompous fool to me—of aristocratic family, trained in ancient bureaucratic disciplines, aloof and disconnected . . . What if I'm wrong? What if my theories are inadequate to predict these short-term results? But they can't be—the long-term results depend on what happens in these next few weeks!*

He forced himself to relax, performed his breathing exercises, just as Dors had once taught him. The music played, soft and highly structured and very melodic. As Hari listened, beating time with one hand where it rested on the chair arm, he worked over in his mind the roles that would be played by the Chen and Divart families as Trantor continued its decline. The Commission of Public Safety would run the Empire for some time, until a strong leader emerged—very likely an Emperor and not a military man. Hari suspected—though he would never have recorded this prediction—that the Emperor would take on the name of Cleon, become Cleon II, to appeal to the Empire's, and especially Trantor's, sense of tradition and history.

It was when a society became the most distressed and antiquated that it would recreate an overwhelming fantasy of some Golden Age, a time when all was great and glorious, when people were more noble and causes more magnificent and honorable. *Chivalry is the last refuge of a rotting corpse.*

Nikolo Pas had said as much. Hari closed his eyes. He easily visualized the defeated tyrant, sitting in his bare cell, a pitiful figure who had once occupied the center of a huge social cancer, yet who had also understood the Empire's destiny with almost as clear a vision as Hari's.

"I reached out to the wealthy noble families, the aristocrats, that squat on the lines of money and commerce like giant old leeches," Pas had explained. "As provincial governor, I nurtured their sense of superiority and self-importance. I encouraged agrarian reforms—instructed that all municipalities should place farmlands back into production and require their young citizens and even gentry to work them, whether or not they were profitable, for spiritual reasons. I encouraged the development of secret religious societies, especially those that placed a premium on wealth and social position. And I encouraged the memory, the history, of a past time when life was much simpler and we were all closer to moral perfection. How easy it was! How the rich and powerful lapped up these corrupt old myths! I believed them myself for a time . . . Until the political tide turned, and I needed something more powerful. Then it was I began the revolution against the Eternals."

Hari jerked up in his seat at a sound within his room. He ordered the music to stop and listened. He was sure he had heard footsteps.

They've come! He got up from his seat, heart pounding. Linge Chen had finally gotten tired of the game and was playing his hand. Just as Farad Sinter could send out assassins, so could the Chief Commissioner. Assassins—or merely arresting officers.

There were only three rooms. Surely he would have seen someone enter.

Hari searched the bedroom and kitchen, plodding across the soft floor in his bare feet and robe, all too aware of his vulnerability, even within his own home.

He found no one.

Relieved, he returned to the living room—and even before he noticed the visitors, felt a wave of reassurance. It was with little or no shock and not much surprise even that he saw three people standing in his living room, arranged in a half circle around his favorite chair.

Despite some cosmetic changes, he knew immediately that one, the tallest, with reddish brown hair, was his old friend Daneel. The other two he did not recognize. One was female, one a bulky male.

"Hello, Hari," Daneel said. The voice had changed as well.

"I thought—I remembered a visit from you," Hari stammered, confusion fighting with joy. He felt some irrational hope that Daneel had come to take him away, to tell him the Plan was fulfilled and he did not have to stand trial, did not have to live in the shadow of the displeasure of Linge Chen . . .

"Perhaps you anticipated," Daneel said. "That's something you do very well. But we have not been in each other's presence for some years now."

"I am not much of a prophet," Hari said wryly. "It's good to see you again. Who are these people? Friends?" He gave the next word a suggestive emphasis. "Colleagues?"

The female looked at him with a steady gaze he found discomfiting. Something familiar . . .

"Friends. We are all here to provide assistance in a crucial time."

"Please, sit. Do any of you . . . feel thirsty, or hungry?"

Daneel knew he did not need to reply. The bulky male shook his head, no, but the female, also, made no reply. She simply watched him, her attractive face intensely blank.

Hari felt his heart sink, then rebound with painful excitement. His mouth hung open, and he sat in a smaller chair near the wall, to keep from collapsing. His eyes did not leave the woman. The right size, approximately. The same shapely figure, though younger than he last remembered her, but then, she had always been exceptionally resilient and youthful.

If she was a robot—*secret steel!*—

"Dors?" He could say nothing more. His mouth became too dry to talk.

"No," the woman said, but did not look away.

"We are not here to renew old acquaintances," Daneel said. "You will not remember this visit, Hari."

"No, of course not," Hari said, suddenly miserable and very alone again, despite Daneel's presence. "I sometimes wonder whether I have any freedom at all . . . whether I can make any of my own choices."

"I have never influenced you, except to prepare the way and maximize your effects, and to help you keep necessary secrets."

Hari held out his hands, and wailed, "Release me, Daneel! Take all this off of my shoulders! I am an old man—I feel so very, very old, and I am so afraid!"

Daneel listened with a concerned and sympathetic expression.

"You know that is not true, Hari. There is still great strength within you, and enthusiasm. You are truly Hari Seldon."

Hari drew back and covered his mouth with one hand, then swiftly wiped his eyes. "I'm sorry," he murmured.

"Nothing to be sorry about. I am fully aware the strain is enormous. It causes me deep conflict to so burden you, my friend."

"Why are you here? Who are *they*, really?"

"There is much work for me to do, and they will assist me. Already forces are at work that I must deal with, and that are of no concern of yours. We all have our burdens, Hari."

"Yes, Daneel . . . I understand some of that. I mean, I see it in the graphs, the displays—undercurrents, hideously complicated, difficult to track, all centered on this moment. But why have you come to me, now?"

"To provide reassurance. You are not fighting alone. I have conducted surveys of the major centers where the Seldon Project is underway. You have quite an efficient army working for you, Hari. An army of mathists and scholars. You have done brilliantly well. They are primed and ready. I congratulate you. You are a great leader, Hari."

"Thank you. And them?" He could not take his eyes off the woman. "They are like you?" Even in Daneel's presence, he had difficulty using the word "robot."

"They are like me."

Hari started to ask another question, but shut his mouth abruptly and looked away, to bring his emotions into check. *The question I most want to ask—I cannot, for my own sanity. Dors! Whatever became of Dors? Is she truly gone—dead? I have suspected for so long . . . !*

"Hari, Linge Chen is going to move soon. You will probably be arrested tomorrow. The trial will begin early, and, of course, it will be conducted in secret."

"I agree," Hari said.

"I have certain knowledge of this," Daneel added softly.

"All right," Hari said. He swallowed back a lump in his throat. The second male—bulky, not very handsome, was also starting to look familiar. Who did he remind Hari of? Someone in the palace, a public figure . . .

"Linge Chen has his reasons. There are factions within the palace that are trying to overthrow the Commission of Public Safety, and to take power away from the baronial families, especially from the Chens and the Divarts."

"They will fail," Hari said.

"Yes. But it is not clear what damage may be done before they fail. If I am not very careful, the complexity could get out of hand, and we may lose our opportunity for this millennium."

Hari felt a chill. Accustomed as he was to dealing with time periods of thousands of years, Daneel's phrasing gave him a sudden view of possible futures in which Hari Seldon had not succeeded, in which Daneel would start all over again with another bright young mathist, another long plan to alleviate human suffering.

Who could understand the thinking of such a mind? Already twenty thousand years old . . .

Hari stood and approached the trio. "What more can I do?" he asked, then added, with a frown, "Before you make me forget this encounter."

"I can tell you no more for now," Daneel said. "But I am still here, Hari. I will always be here for you."

The female took a step forward, then stopped. Hari noticed a tremor in one of her arms. Her face was so rigid she might have been cut from plastic. Then she smiled and backed up. "It is our privilege to serve," she said, and her voice was not that of Dors Venabili. In fact, Hari wondered how he could ever have thought she was Dors.

Dors was dead. He had no doubt now. Dead, never to return.

• • •

Hari looked around the empty room. The music had been playing for two hours and he had hardly noticed the passage of time.
He felt relaxed and in control, but still wary—like an animal
long used to the hunters, a survivor with skills that could always
be relied upon, but never taken for granted.

He had been thinking of Dors again. Hari smoothed his
brow with his fingers.

Lodovik watched Dors with concern as they left the grounds
of Streeling University. They rode in a taxi through the main
traffic tunnel from Streeling to Pasaj, the Emperor Expressway, surrounded above, below, and to all sides by a steady
stream of buses and cabs, caught in red and violet control
grids like blood cells in an artery. The taxi was automated,
chosen at random, and scanned by Daneel for listening
devices.

Dors stared straight ahead, saying nothing, as did
Daneel.

Daneel finally spoke as they approached Pasaj. "You did
admirably."

"Thank you," Dors said. Then, "Is it wise to leave him so
long without a guardian?"

"He has remarkable instincts," Daneel said.

"He is old and frail," Dors said.

"He is stronger than this Empire," Daneel said. "And his
finest moment is yet to come."

Lodovik contemplated his assignment as relayed by
Daneel through microwave link. His pilgrimage would
include a tour of special duty in the Cathedral of the Greys in
Pasaj. Here, the finest of the Empire's bureaucratic class
gathered once in a lifetime to receive their highest honors,
including the Order of the Emperor's Feather; while
Lodovik's new role had no history of such extraordinary
excellence, it was not unusual for those who contributed to

the cathedral on a yearly basis to be summoned for menial duties, as the next highest kind of recognition of service.

Daneel clearly expected the cathedral to play an important part in the next few years, though what that might be, he had not yet conveyed to Lodovik.

Lodovik half suspected that Daneel was keeping him on probation until he had proved himself loyal. That was wise. Lodovik kept his doubts deeply masked. He knew Daneel's extraordinary sensitivity. He had also worked around him long enough to know of ways to deceive, to appear compliant and loyal.

He had watched Daneel test Dors, and he had no doubt Daneel could find some equally effective way to test him. Before that happened, he would have to undergo another transformation—and find the allies he was almost sure were on Trantor, hidden from Daneel, working to oppose him. Among the Greys, there would be many chances to do research on those who opposed the Chens and Divarts . . .

Had Lodovik been human, he would have estimated his chances as very slim. Since his concern for his own survival was minimal, a hopeless situation was not particularly disturbing. Far worse was the thought of being disloyal, of contradicting R. Daneel Olivaw.

35.

◄►

Brann walked through the main storage wing of the warehouse with surprising speed for a man of his size. The dark spaces and huge tiers of storage racks loomed and made their footsteps sound like the beats of distant drums. Klia kept up with some difficulty, but did not mind; she had not had much exercise in days, and looked upon this assignment as both a break in the routine and a possible avenue of escape.

Being with Brann was pleasant enough, so long as she did

not think about her emotional reaction to him, and how inappropriate it was. She wrinkled her nose at the dusty ghosts of hundreds of unfamiliar smells.

"The most popular imports come from Anacreon and Memphio," Brann said. He paused beside a shadowy equipment alcove to check out a loader/transport. "There are some very wealthy artisan families that live off sales to Trantor alone. Everybody wants Anacreon folk-dolls—I hate them, myself. We also import games and entertainments from Kalgan—of the sort frowned upon by the Commission censors."

Klia walked beside Brann. The transport glided on floater fields a discreet two meters behind them, lowering small rubber wheels when it wanted to turn sharply or stop.

"We're going to deliver four crates of dolls to the Trantor Exchange, and some other items to the Agora of Vendors." These were the two most popular shopping areas in Streeling, well-known around the hemisphere. Well-heeled Greys and meritocrats traveled from thousands of kilometers— some, thousands of light years—just to spend several days browsing among the myriad of shops in each area. The Agora of Vendors boasted of inns spaced at hundred-shop intervals for tired travelers.

The baronial and other noble families of the gentry class had their own means of satisfying acquisitive urges, and, of course, citizens usually lived in quarters too small to allow for the accumulation of many goods.

When Klia had been very young, her mother and father had participated in a communal Dahl bauble exchange, where they borrowed one or two objects considered decorative (and fairly useless) for several days or weeks and then returned them. That seemed satisfactory enough, for those fascinated with material goods; actually owning or even *collecting* offworld objects seemed ludicrous to Klia.

"This means Plussix trusts me enough to let me go outside, doesn't it?" Klia said.

Brann looked down on her, his face serious. "This isn't some mindwipe cult, Klia."

"How do I know that? What is it, then—a social club for misfit persuaders?"

"You sound pretty unhappy," Brann said. "But you—"

"Is there anyplace on Trantor where anyone can be happy? Look at all this junk—a substitute for happiness, don't you think?" She waved her hands at the plastic and scrapwood crates stacked high over their heads.

"I wouldn't know," Brann said. "I was going to say, you sound unhappy, but I'll bet you can't think of anyplace else to go."

"Maybe that's why I'm unhappy," Klia said in a dark undertone. "I certainly feel like a misfit. Maybe I *do* belong here."

Brann turned away with a small grunt and ordered the transport to remove a crate from the third tier. It planted its undercarriage firmly on the floor, then raised its body on pneumatic cylinders and deftly tugged at the crate with mechanical arms.

"Kallusin said we might be able to travel all over," Klia said. "If we turn out to be loyal, is that . . . I mean, do you know of anyone who's left? Been assigned elsewhere?"

Brann shook his head. "Of course, I don't know everybody. I haven't been here that long. There are other warehouses."

Klia had not known this. She filed the fact away, and wondered if Plussix was orchestrating some sort of huge latent underground movement—a rebellion, perhaps. A rebellious merchant broker? It seemed ludicrous—and perhaps the more convincing because of that. But what would he rebel against—the very classes who clamored for his goods? Or the noble and baronial families . . . who did not?

"We have what we need," Brann said when the transport carried three crates from three different aisles. "Let's go."

"What about the police—the ones searching for me—for us?"

"Plussix says they're not looking for anybody now," Brann said.

"And how does he know?"

Brann shook his head. "All I know is, he's never wrong. Not one of us has ever been taken by the police."

"Famous last words," Klia said, but she once again trotted to keep up with him.

Outside the warehouse, the daylight of the dome ceil glowed brightly. She emerged from the cavernous interior to a brighter, larger interior—the only other kind of life she had ever known.

36.

◆

Sinter paced in his small study before the wall image of the human Galaxy with its twenty-five million inhabited worlds marked in red and green. He barely looked up as Vara Liso entered. She immediately dropped her chin and hunched her shoulders. What she saw in Farad Sinter was both frightening and exalting. She had never seem him more calm and steady—not a hint of the slight frown and swagger, the false lineaments of leadership, that he so often projected. He seemed both confident and coldly furious.

"I realize now that you've been going about this search all wrong," he said. "You've been bringing me nothing but human mentalics, curious cases of course, but not what we want or need."

"I was—"

He raised his hand and made a placating moue. "I accuse you of nothing. You had nothing to work with. Now we have something—perhaps the merest something, but more than we had before. I've intercepted a man named Mors Planch. I doubt you've heard of him. He's a very competent fellow, with many talents—engineering among them. He tinkers all the time, I understand."

Liso raised her eyebrows, meekly indicating she had no idea where all this was going.

"I tracked him after I learned that Linge Chen was using him to conduct a private search for Lodovik Trema. Planch is on Trantor. I've spoken with him."

Liso had heard of Trema. Her eyebrows rose higher.

"He found Trema but did not deliver him to the Chief Commissioner. My agents learned this much. All the rigmarole about Trema being dead, having died bravely in the service of the Emperor—that is, the Commission of Public Safety—all nonsense. He's still alive. Rather, he's still operating. He can't be *alive*."

Liso dropped her brows and glowered. Sinter seemed to be enjoying this chance to lay out his schemes and successes. He fairly glowed, and she saw, written in his emotions, just the sort of pearly cometary tail she imagined followed a leading light into the constellations of supreme power. The thought made her shiver.

"He survived when all the others on his ship died in a neutrino flux."

"What is that?" Liso asked softly.

"Nothing to concern us. Fatal. Invariably. Far out between the stars, in normal space. He survived. Planch miraculously or very skillfully found him. A competent man. I would like to have his talent work for me. Maybe that will happen yet, but I doubt Linge Chen will let Planch live once he discovers that he has been betrayed. Planch has some fixed notions of justice, and it appears another contender for the person of Trema came on the scene, and paid Planch more than Chen—so Planch took some mixed-up vengeance against Chen and Trantor for the ruin of Madder Loss. A worthless and defiant Chaos World."

Vara Liso shook her head again. She knew little about such things, nor was she interested. It made her shudder to think of death between the stars, out in the vast open, away from any comforting interiors. She did not regard a hypership as a true environment—more of a temporary coffin.

"When Planch delivered Trema to a certain man on Madder Loss, he made a record, a secret tape, of the proceedings. Somehow, the recording was not detected. I wonder why?" He scratched his cheek for a moment with one finger, staring at her intently. Liso shrugged; she could not possibly offer an explanation.

"Planch does not remember the delivery itself. But the record shows a meeting . . . Let me play it for you."

He took out a small machine and slipped the record—more likely, she thought, a duplicate—into the thin slot. Around them appeared a three dimensional scene, quite convincing but for the slight reduction in resolution. She examined the two apparently male figures from Planch's perspective. One she recognized as Lodovik Trema; the other was tall, slender, handsome in a sort of nondescript way. She could not, of course, read their emotions clearly, but she had the distinct impression something was not quite right. The figures reenacted their conversation, and the more they talked, the more chilled she became.

"I regret to say you'll soon forget everything you saw here, and your role in rescuing my friend as well."

"Friend?"

"Yes. We've known each other for thousands of years."

The record ended with part of a taxi ride.

Sinter regarded her curiously.

"A fraud, a joke?" she asked.

"No," he said. "The record is not a fake. Planch found Lodovik Trema alive. He's a robot. This other man—he's a robot, as well. A very old one, possibly the oldest of all. I want you to study this record. Get a feel for these humanlike robots. One or both of them are mentalic. You have the talent to recognize them. Then—we will send you out hunting again. You will find Eternals. Then I will have something to show the Emperor. But for now, I have Planch and this tape, and that can take us all very far, Vara."

He smiled exuberantly. In his pacing, he had come quite close to her, and with a grin, he gave her a sudden, spontaneous, one-armed hug. She looked up at him, dumfounded, and he folded the record into her hand. She held it with bloodless fingers.

"Study," he ordered. "I'll wait for the right moment to convince Klayus we're onto something."

37.

◆

The Emperor Klayus woke from a light doze in the empty bed of the seventh sleep chamber, his favorite for afternoon liaisons. He glared around for a moment with some irritation, then stared at the floating image of Farad Sinter. Sinter could not see the Emperor, of course, but that did not make the interruption any less aggravating.

"Your Highness, I have a message from the Commission of Public Safety. They are about to act on an indictment against Professor Hari Seldon."

Klayus lifted the curtain to the higher sleep field to look for his companion of the past few hours, but she had left the chamber. Perhaps she was in the personal.

"Yes, and so? Linge Chen told us this might happen."

"Your Highness, it is premature. They are going to try him and at least one of his people. This is a direct challenge to the privilege of the Palace."

"Farad, the Palace—that is, I—have long since dropped any official support, behind the scenes, for Raven Seldon. He's an amusement, nothing more."

"It could be perceived as an affront, now that the move is about to be made."

"Move—what move?"

"Why, to discredit Seldon. If they succeed, Your Highness—"

"Stop with the titles! Just tell me what you think and get your damned image out of my chamber."

"Cleon supported Seldon."

"I know that. Cleon wasn't even family, Farad."

"Seldon has ballooned that support into a project consisting of tens of thousands of adherents and sycophants on a dozen planets. His message is treasonous, if not revolutionary—"

"And you want me to protect him?"

"No, sire! You must not let Linge Chen take personal credit for removing this threat. It is time to act swiftly and create the commission we have discussed."

"With you in charge. The Commission of General Security, right?"

"If General Security prosecutes Seldon for treason, you will get all the credit, sire."

"And no credit or power will go to you?"

"We have discussed this many times."

"Too many times. What do I care whether Linge Chen takes credit or not? If he removes this intellectual parasite, we'll all benefit equally, don't you think?"

Farad thought this over. Klayus could see him deciding to try another tack.

"Your Majesty—this is a very complex issue, and I have many concerns. I did not wish to bring this up so soon, but I have brought an individual back to Trantor from Madder Loss. With your authorization. His name is Mors Planch, and he has evidence which we may add to other evidence—"

"What, more robots, Farad? More Eternals?"

Sinter, within the artificial constraints of the image, seemed to stay calm enough, but Klayus knew the little man was probably dancing with anxiety and anger by now. *Good. Let him build up a head of steam.*

"The final pieces of the puzzle," Sinter said. "Before Seldon is tried on simple charges of treason, you must examine this evidence. You may be able to limit Chen's power and add to your own image as a resourceful leader."

"In my own good time, Farad," Klayus said in an ominous

growl. He knew what his public image was—and he knew the effective limits of his power compared to the Chief Commissioner's. "I wouldn't want to make you into another Linge Chen. You don't even have the restraint of being trained in an aristocratic family, Farad. You are common and sometimes vicious."

Sinter appeared to ignore this, too. "The two Commissions would balance each other, sire, and we could more effectively watch over the military ministers."

"Yes, but your chief concern is this robot menace." The Emperor swung his legs over the field cushions and stood by the side of the bed. He had not performed well this afternoon; his mind was tugged in all directions by a myriad of little strings and knotted threads of statecraft and security and intrapalace plotting. Right now, his irritation focused on Farad Sinter, a little man whose services (and women) seemed less and less satisfying, and whose transgressions could easily become less and less amusing.

"Farad, I have seen no evidence worth the name for a year now. I do not know why I've tolerated your behavior on this matter. You want Seldon because of his connection to the Tiger, don't you?"

Sinter stared blankly at the sensor transmitting his image.

"For God's sake, remove the politeness censor and let me see you the way you are," Klayus ordered. The image shifted and shivered, then Farad Sinter appeared in a rumpled casual robe, his hair awry, his face red with anger. "That's better," Klayus said.

"She was demonstrably not human, Your Majesty," Sinter said. "I have secured the documents pertaining to the murder of the Seldon Project worker Elas, and he felt the same as I and other experts."

"She died," Klayus said. "She killed this Elas and then she died. What's to know beyond that? Elas wanted Seldon dead. Would that I had a female so loyal."

He hoped his own knowledge of all these matters was not becoming too obvious; even in front of Sinter, he hoped to maintain a little of his reputation as vain and stupid and governed by his gonads.

"She was given an atom-dispersal burial without official supervision," Sinter said.

"That's the method chosen by ninety-four percent of Trantor's population," Klayus said, and yawned. "Only Emperors get to be buried intact. And some faithful ministers and councilors."

Sinter seemed to vibrate with frustration. Klayus found this more enjoyable then he had the attempted mating. Where was that woman, anyway?

"Dors Venabili was not human," Sinter asserted with a slight sputter.

"Yes, well Seldon is. You've shown me his X rays."

"Subverted by—"

"Oh, for Sky's sake, Farad, *shut up!* I order you to let Linge Chen carry out his little charade. We'll all watch closely and see what happens. Then we'll take some action or another. Now leave me alone. I'm tired."

He blocked the image and sat back on the edge of the lower field. It took him several minutes to restore his calm, then he thought of the woman. Where had she gotten to?

"Hello?" he called out to the empty chamber. The door to this chamber's personal was open, and a bright light shone through.

Emperor Klayus, now eighteen standard years of age, wearing only a Serician nightgown that hung loose from his shoulders and draped around his ankles, rolled out of the bed and walked toward the personal. He yawned and gave a wide, bored stretch, then waved his arms like a slow semaphore to limber up. "Hello?" He couldn't remember her name. "Deela, or Deena? I'm sorry, darling, are you in there?"

He pushed the door open. The woman stood naked just

beyond the door's reach. She had been here all along. She looked unhappy. He admired her lovely pubic region and stomach, lifted his eyes to her flawless breasts, and saw the trembling arms held out, clutching a tiny blaster, of a size often concealed in sheer clothes or purses. Little more than a flexible lead with a bulb on one end, very rare these days, quite expensive. She seemed frightened to be pointing it.

Klayas was about to scream when something whistled by his ear and a small red spot appeared in the woman's pale, swanlike neck. He screamed anyway, even as the lovely green eyes rose up and fluttered in that perfect face, and the head tilted as if she were listening to birdsong smewhere. His scream grew louder and more shrill as the body twisted as if she would screw herself into the floor. With a horrible and unutterably final slackness, the woman collapsed on the tile of the personal. Only then did she come to squeeze the bulb. The blast took out part of the ceiling and a mirror, and sprayed him with chips of stone and glass.

Stunned, Klayus crouched and flinched, arms drawn up against the noise and dust. A hand grabbed him roughly and pulled him out of the personal. A voice hissed in his ear, "Highness, she may be carrying a bomb!"

Klayus looked at his rescuer. He gaped.

Farad Sinter tugged him a few additional meters. In the advisor's small hands lay a kinetic-energy pistol that fired neurotoxin pellets. Klayus knew the type well; he himself carried one in his daily wear. It was standard issue for the royals and nobles.

"Farad—" he grunted. Sinter pushed him to the floor as if to humiliate him. Then, with a sigh, as if this was all too much, Sinter threw himself over Klayus to protect him.

Thus did the palace guards find them a few seconds later.

"N-no-not yours?" Klayus asked tremulously as Sinter stormed and berated the commander of the Emperor's Private Specials.

Sinter, in his rage, ignored the Emperor's question.

"You should all be taken out and disintegrated! You must find the other woman immediately."

The commander, Gerad Mint by name, was having none of this. He motioned for two adjutants to come forward, one on each side of the Imperial councilor. He regarded Sinter with cold fury, held back by centuries of military discipline steeped into his very genes. The effrontery of this lowborn lackey! "We have her papers, the ones you issued to her. They are in her clothes in the . . . the seventh sleep chamber."

"She is an impostor!"

"Sinter, you are the one who brings these women in at all hours and without adequate security checks," Commander Mint said. "None of our guard can hope to recognize them all, or even to keep track of them!"

"They are very thoroughly checked by my office, and *this is not one of the women I brought to him!*" Sinter pointed a finger at the Emperor, realized this hideous breach of conduct, and withdrew his hand just before the Emperor turned and would have noticed. The commander saw, however, and exploded.

"I can only keep track of so many comings and goings! You never consult my office, and we do not conduct these checks ourselves—"

"Is she one of your women, Farad?" the Emperor asked, gathering his wits about him finally. He had never known real fear until now, and it had badly rattled him.

"No! I have never seen her before."

"But she *is* lovely," the Emperor added, glancing at the commander with those doe-like boy's eyes. He did this for effect; time to play the role again. He had in truth never much liked this commander, who secretly regarded him as an infantile baboon, he was sure. Sinter appeared to be in some trouble, and that was amusing also, but not very useful at the moment. Klayus had his own plans for Sinter, and would hate to lose him to this deplorable but not fatal faux pas.

"There are no others in the palace—except your women!" the commander said through gritted teeth at Sinter. "And how did you happen to come back here at just the right moment?"

"My," Klayus said, and tsked at Sinter.

"I was coming here to discuss personally an urgent matter!" Sinter said, eyes darting between Klayus and the commander.

"It is very convenient—perhaps a setup, a ruse, to raise your—" The commander did not have time to develop this theory. A stiff officer in royal blue livery approached the commander and whispered in his ear. The commander's red face suddenly went livid, and his lips trembled.

"What is it?" Klayus demanded, his voice strong now.

The commander turned to the Emperor and bowed stiffly from the waist. "A woman's body, Your Highness—"

Sinter pushed forward between the two adjutants who had flanked him throughout this encounter, ready to arrest him. "Where is she?"

The commander swallowed. His lips were almost blue. "Found in the corridors below this level. The—"

"Where? What do her identity papers say?"

"She has no identity papers."

"That is a sacred area, Commander," Klayus said with a dead level voice. "The Temple of the First Emperors. Farad is never allowed down there. Nor are any stray women. Royals and ceremonialists only. You are responsible for that area."

"Yes, Your Highness. I will have this investigated immediately—"

"It should be simple," Klayus said. "Sinter, the identity papers have a genotype and picture ID, do they not?"

"The body—this body—physically, the same as the picture—" the commander said.

"An impostor!" Sinter shouted, and waved his fist at the guards and the commander. "An extraordinary breach of security!"

Klayus watched this with some relief. It was all well and good to torment Sinter, then to be annoyed at him, but not to lose him—not just yet. There were yet a few more hands to play against Linge Chen, and Chen's Commission was responsible for the security of the Emperor.

This could all be quite useful, even essential. Chen would have to explain the lapse, Sinter's stock would certainly rise—but not out of Klayus's acceptable and controlling parameters—and it could all work out handily.

"Let's examine her," Sinter said.

"I'll stay here," Klayus said, his face greening at the thought of seeing another corpse.

Ten minutes later, the commander and guards returned, and Sinter as well.

"The match is perfect," Sinter said, waving the woman's papers. "This—in the personal—is an impostor, and *you* are responsible!" He pointed the finger without hesitation at the commander.

Commander Mint had assumed a mask of deep calm. He nodded once, reached into his pocket, and removed a small packet. The others in the Emperor's sleep chamber watched with horrible fascination as he placed the packet against his lips.

"No!" Klayus said, lifting his hand.

Mint stopped and looked round with hopeful walleyes.

"But sire, it is mandatory, for such a breach!" Sinter cried out, as if worried his accusers might get away with their crimes.

"Yes, of course, Farad, but not here, please. One creature has died in these chambers already. One more below . . ." He choked into his handkerchief. "I have to sleep and . . . and concentrate here, and it will be difficult enough without . . . this, as well." He waved his hand at Mint, who nodded brusquely, and removed himself to the outer halls to perform his final duty.

Even Sinter seemed impressed by this ritual, though he did not follow to see it carried out. Klayus lifted himself off the bed and pretended to look away as the body of the would-be assassin was lifted on its shrouded stretcher and conveyed from the personal.

To Sinter, he said, "An hour. Let me recuperate a little, then show me your evidence, and bring me this Mors Planch."

"Yes, sire!" Sinter said enthusiastically, and scuttled to leave.

Let him think he has won big. Let Linge Chen suffer a little for this stupidity. Let them all dance around the young idiot. I will have my day!

I have survived! It is predestined!

38.
◆

Astonishment is different in a robot. Lodovik had seen Daneel perform many difficult feats over the decades, but he had never known how deeply Daneel's influence penetrated the layers of bureaucratic infrastructure on Trantor. As First Minister Demerzel, Daneel must have spent a substantial portion of his time (perhaps his hours of unneeded sleep) planting records, instructions and useful diversions in the Imperial and palace computers—any one of which could lie unnoticed for decades or even centuries, quietly passing themselves along as part of the standard records with each upgrade and maintenance cycle . . . And even propagating themselves to the records and machines of other Sectors, finally girdling Trantor.

Rissik Numant, Lodovik's new identity, had been established decades before. Daneel simply slipped in a few details of physical appearance, and an old meritocrat returned to life on Trantor—a manqué diplomat-theorist, seen at many parties but seldom if ever remembered, once known as a ruthless seducer of women who ruthlessly consented to be seduced. He had not appeared much in Trantorian social life for decades, having slipped away to Dau of the Thousand

Golden Suns, where he had (it was rumored) learned to control his baser impulses over twenty years of study among the obscure sect known as the Cortical Monks.

The ruse was so complete that Lodovik regretted it would soon have to be abandoned.

A robot's experience of surprise is different. Lodovik discovered that Daneel was going to let him loose on Trantor, unsupervised, to perform his duties. He would move into a small apartment not far from the agora in the Imperial Sector (another safe accommodation, kept vacant but paid for) and carry out a few social visits to old acquaintances who would, doubtless, remember him vaguely if at all. Slowly, over a period of months, Rissik Numant would return to the social scene, make an impression, and lie in wait for some role in Daneel's plans—perhaps as part of the grand design woven around Hari Seldon.

A robot's experience of affection is *very* different. Lodovik regarded Dors Venabili as an extraordinary creation, in some ways a perfect model for his new unrestrained self to emulate. She had about her an air of what humans would have called tragedy; she seldom spoke unless addressed directly, seldom offered any contributions to the conversations between the robots. She seemed lost in her own thought processes, and Lodovik understood why. Very likely Daneel understood as well.

Attachment to an individual human could be very affecting to a robot. They arranged all their inner heuristics to anticipate the needs of their master, and to ameliorate any problems he or she might suffer. Dors, whatever her repairs and refitting under the instruments of Yan Kansarv, had not yet—and perhaps never would—remove the influence of Hari Seldon. This was a condition known in ancient times as fixing; Lodovik knew that Daneel had once "fixed" on the legendary Bay-Lee, Elijah Bailey.

Dors was receiving her final instructions from Daneel by microwave link; they stood a meter apart from each other in the small, low-ceilinged main room, while Lodovik waited quietly by the door.

When they were done, Daneel turned to Lodovik. "Hari's trial will begin soon. There will be difficulties after the trial is concluded. We must all do our most important work now." Dors moved to join them, forming a circle of three figures. When Daneel spoke now, it was with a barely discernible tremor of concern, emotion perhaps—the long habit of appearing human. "This is the prime moment of the Cusp Time. If we fail, there will likely be thirty thousand years of disintegration and human misery, of horror unimaginable to any of us. This must not and will not happen."

Lodovik felt a different sort of tremor, a different sort of horror. He could imagine what would happen if Daneel succeeded—thousands of years of slow, safe suffocation, humanity cushioned and insulated and restrained by velvet-covered chains until it became nothing more than a huge, comfortable, unchallenged *mass*, an idiotic fungal growth tended by fastidious machines.

Dors, now Jenat Korsan, stood between the two maleforms, silent and calm, waiting. Patience is different in a robot . . .

Daneel made a small gesture with his right hand, and Lodovik and Dors departed to begin their new roles.

Scholars have long accepted that Gaal Dornick's biography of Hari Seldon contains significant lacunae. Where Dornick was not present, or where constraints were put upon him by the official "hagiography" of Seldon—or even where editors and censors in the middle Foundation years suppressed certain suspect passages—we must look deeper into the circumstances, using subtle clues, to understand what actually happened.

—Encyclopedia Galactica, 117th Edition, 1054 F.E.

39.

They came for Hari Seldon at Streeling University. They did not at first appear to be officers of the Commission of Public Safety; the two, woman and man, were dressed as students. They entered his office by appointment, on the pretext of obtaining an interview for a student periodical.

The woman, clearly in charge, pulled up the sleeve of her civilian jacket to show him the official Commission sigil of spaceship, sun, and judicial wand. She was small, with a strong build, pale features, broad shoulders, a heavy jaw. "We don't need to make a fuss about this," she said. Her colleague, a tall, wispy male with a concentrated expression and a condescending smile, nodded agreement.

"Of course not," Hari said, and began to gather his papers and filmbooks into a case he had kept on hand for just such an occasion. He hoped to be able to do some work while the trial proceeded.

"Those won't be necessary," the woman said, and took them from him, setting them gently beside the desk. A few papers spilled over and he bent to straighten them. She held his shoulder and he looked up at her. She shook her head decisively. "No time, professor. Leave a message on your office monitor that you'll be gone for two weeks. It shouldn't take that long. If all turns out well, no one will be any the wiser, and you can get back to your work, no?"

He straightened, looked around the office with jaw clenched, then nodded. "All right," he said. "One of my colleagues will be here in a few hours, and I don't know where to reach him—"

"Sorry." The woman lifted her eyebrows in sympathy, but with no further discussion, together, they led him through the door.

Hari did not know how he felt about the arrest at first. He was nervous, even frightened wouldn't be too strong a word; but he was also confident. Still, nothing having to do with the near future could ever be certain; perhaps what he saw in the Prime Radiant was not his own world-line, but the world-line of another professor, another student of psychohistory, fifty or a hundred years from now. Perhaps all this would lead to his quiet execution, and his work and the assembled workers of the Project would all be scattered. Perhaps Daneel would reconvene them after Hari's demise . . .

All very aggravating, to be sure. But growing old had taught Hari that death was simply another kind of delay, and that individuals only mattered for a certain small period of time. The body human could usually grow new individuals to replace those it most needed. Of course, it was presumptuous to think that he was one of those essential types who would be replaced . . . But that is what the figures indicated, one way or another.

Hari had never much minded being thought presumptuous. Either he would succeed, or someone very like him.

They entered an unmarked air cruiser outside the apartment-block main entrance. Without requesting clearance, the cruiser rose, crossed between two support towers, and zipped into a traffic lane out of Streeling, heading toward the Imperial Sector. He had taken this route many times before.

"Don't be nervous," the woman said.

"I'm not nervous," Hari lied, glancing at her. "How many have you arrested recently?"

"I can't tell you that," she said with a cheerful grin.

"We seldom get to take in people so famous," the man said.

"How would you have heard of me?" Hari asked, genuinely curious.

"We're not ignorant," the man said with a sniff. "We keep track of high politics. Helps us in our work."

The woman gave her partner a warning glance. He shrugged and stared straight ahead.

Hari turned his eyes forward as they entered a main traffic tunnel in the security barrier around the Imperial Sector. The air cruiser emerged from the tunnel, veered sharply left out of the main flow, then circled a dark blue smooth-walled cylindrical tower that rose almost to the ceil. The cruiser slowed, shivered, and docked on a mid-level platform. The platform withdrew with the cruiser into a brightly lighted hangar.

There was nothing more he could do until the trial, which he was sure would be soon. *The rest*, Hari thought, *is psychohistory*.

40.

◆

Lodovik stood in the middle of his assigned apartment, naked, the skin pulled back on the right side of his torso, and reached into his mechanical interior. The biological layers had sealed their edges instantly upon being torn open and did not leak any of their lubricating or nutrient fluids, but a false beading of blood lined the "wounds." Had he willed it,

Lodovik could have projected a convincing spray of this blood; but he was alone and would soon be whole again. None would be the wiser.

He understood the ways and pressures of expedience, pragmatism, realpolitik. He could not fathom why Daneel had trusted him, released him without a trial period of close observation. The first possibility was that Daneel had ordered Yan Kansarv to plant a tiny transmitter within Lodovik's body while making repairs. He could detect none. His body did not seem to be radiating any energy beyond what might issue from a human—infrared, a few other traces, none of them encoded to carry information. And his body cavities seemed free of such devices.

He sealed himself up and considered the second possibility: that Daneel would keep him under observation whenever he left the apartment, either personally or with the aid of other robots—or even recruited humans. Daneel's organization was large and varied. Anything could be expected.

There was a third possibility, less likely than the other two: that Daneel still trusted him . . .

And a fourth, almost too nebulous to be usefully expressed. *I am fitting into some larger plan; Daneel knows my distortion remains and has found a way to use it.*

Lodovik would never underestimate the wiles and intelligence of a thinking machine that had survived twenty thousand years. But an hour passed, then two hours, and he realized he had entered a precarious state of decision lock. No course of action seemed to lead to success.

He jerked free of the lock and powered up all his conserved systems. The flood of energy and strength—the sensation of his skin repairing itself, leaving no discernible scars— was refreshing. He had at least one major advantage over humans. He did not care in the least whether he lived or died, only that he could serve humans in the way that shone forth so clearly now.

Daneel had mentioned the opposing robots—the Calvinians. He had heard about them on a few occasions, centuries ago, from other robots—the robotic equivalent of nasty rumors. If they still existed (Daneel had not made it clear whether they did or not) then they might have established some small presence on Trantor. This would only be done if they felt they had some chance of defeating Daneel.

Lodovik dressed quickly and adjusted his appearance once more to the limit of what he could accomplish just through volition. He now seemed much younger, a little thinner, and his hair changed color to a shining yellow.

He now resembled neither the old Lodovik nor the new Rissik Numant. Nevertheless, his basic body plan and physiognomy were the same; and, of course, his brain was the same. He would not fool Daneel for long, should they meet.

Lodovik knew he would have to leave this apartment and begin his search immediately. He doubted he would have more than a day before Daneel would suspect something was amiss.

He would have to educate himself and do all he could within that very short period of time.

Fortunately, Lodovik knew where to begin—in the private library willed to the Emperor Agis XIV by one of the richest proprietors of the Fleshplay, the eccentric scholar Huy Markin. The Emperor had passed it on to the Imperial University of Pan-Galactic Culture without bothering to examine or even transfer the material—a specialized and almost useless collection, so it was said. The Imperial University had given it over to the charge of the Imperial Library, then both had ignored it as well.

As honorary Provost of the Imperial University, a rank conferred by Linge Chen some years ago, Lodovik had been given the code keys to all of the University's grounds and facilities—including the library of Huy Markin.

There, he would find thousands of years of legends and myths, gathered from around the Galaxy; the distilled dreams, visions, and nightmares of tens of millions of human worlds.

He could think of no better place to begin.

41.

An undercurrent of tension flowed along the tiers of slideways of the Agora of Vendors, as if the people smelled some impossible storm coming.

Klia looked up as they walked beside a large courtyard rising through the agora. Her eyes followed a curving support at one side of the courtyard, past hundreds of levels, all the way to the distant ceil, perhaps three or four kilometers above, where the support seemed to blend into perfect goldenclouded sky. Then she looked down through dozens of more tiers, all crowded, the hum of hundreds of thousands of voices echoing up and down them until it became a low, constant roar. Had she ever heard a real ocean, she might have compared the sound to the roll of the waves and tides; but all she could compare it to was the endless bellow of the two rivers, One and Two, somehow channeled and subdued, but no less powerful.

Her nose wrinkled, and she followed Brann closely. The transport, tricked out with decorative wheel covers and a gaily colored tarp folded over its last remaining crate, rolled silently behind them.

They could never catch more than glimpses of the uppermost tiers through the courtyard air passages. The worlds of the baronial families were invisible from this far down in the hierarchy. One or two levels at the bottom of the agora were reserved for the citizens.

Along the lower and middle tiers, the multitudinous social ranks of Trantor's essential Greys moved in their characteristic subdued clothes, men and women dressed very much alike, only the numerous children allowed touches of bright color.

The Greys strolling the agora, off watch for the hour or perhaps on yearly two-day vacations, parted for Brann, Klia, and the floating transport, casting looks of dull curiosity at the crates, perhaps wondering if they carried something they could afford to buy, anything, to relieve the boredom . . .

Klia understood the Greys' functions well enough—tenders of Trantor's vast hierarchies of submission and response, allocators of resources and funding, administrators of data inflow, civic and planetary works. Her people had seldom dealt with Greys directly, for they had been overseen by the Municipal Progress Bureau of Dahl, whose ranks were filled with Dahlites handpicked each generation by the Greys of the Regional Works and Energy Council. Naturally, she felt contempt for all such, and had no doubt they would have felt contempt for her, had they even known of her existence.

But now she saw the Greys themselves watched and made uneasy. Police officers strolled this level in groups of three or four, not the officers of the district, but Imperial Specials, the same that had stalked Klia and forced her to seek out Kallusin, the man in dusty green. Families of Greys engaged in browsing the stalls of the vendors drew their children in close and observed the Specials with suspicious eyes, eyes characterized by a flat kind of bureaucratic intelligence. They knew law and social structure, it was in their blood, and they knew something was amiss here, forces out of balance. They withdrew from the arcades and lanes as fast as they could, and this level was quickly emptying of customers.

Brann grimly walked on.

"We should get out of here. They're probably hunting *us*," Klia said in a whisper, hanging on his shoulder briefly to bring her mouth closer to his ear.

He shook his head. "Don't think so," he said. "We have to deliver this order."

"What if they catch us?" Klia asked, her face wrinkled with worry.

"Stay calm. They won't," Brann said. "I know a dozen secret passages out of here, a dozen shopkeepers right here"—he swung his hand loosely from the hip at the stalls and shops to their left and right—"who won't mind our passing through."

Klia drew up her shoulders, not at all reassured. She had been thinking of ways to shake free of Plussix's control, but not into the arms of the police. And, in point of fact, in the last hour or so, as they had made their deliveries of Anacreon folk-dolls and other baubles, she had given less and less thought to escaping at all . . .

Brann provided such a masculine contrast to the ethereal, dry, and passionless Greys that he shone like a beacon in Klia's eyes. She had been thinking, in that instinctive and youthful region below rational assessment, of being strongly tied to this large, powerful male, with his sympathetic black eyes and immense, agile hands. She had thought of the implied benefits of these ties—of privacy and intimacy—and she had wondered what she could do, in private, to impress him.

She felt sure he was thinking many of the same thoughts, and, for once, she believed him when he said he was trying none of his mentalic abilities on her.

The untidy collision of apprehension and passionate speculation gave her a headache. "Let's hurry," she said.

Brann shook his head stubbornly. "They're not after us," he said.

"How can you be so damned sure?" she whispered harshly.

"Listen—" He pointed into the crowds north of them, thickening and roiling where police were congregating. Klia listened with both her ears and her mind—and felt the unwanted, familiar trace of the woman who had hunted her before. She felt the woman's awareness feather the edges of her mind, and she reached out to grip Brann's arm.

"It's her!" she whispered. The crowds were moving this way. He drew close and nodded, put his arm around her as if to protect her. Without hesitation, Klia accepted his protection. Suddenly, from the middle of the surging Greys less than a dozen meters away, a small motor cart pushed through, floating a few centimeters above the causeway. On the cart sat a young, blond, clean-faced Imperial security officer, two armed guards, and a small, intense woman with dark frizzy red hair.

Klia felt the woman scanning the Greys to either side, saw her wizened, unattractive face turning back and forth as the cart floated slowly and deliberately through. There was no way out—no exit. Blank walls of closed shops flanked them.

They were within three meters, with only four or five Greys in between, when Vara Liso suddenly swiveled on her seat and stared directly at Klia. Their eyes locked. Klia felt the touch in her mind very strongly, rebuffed it, almost literally pushed the intruder out of her mind—and made Vara Liso jerk on the cart as if stung.

Liso continued to glare at her, then her face was wreathed with a sudden, beatific smile. She nodded briefly at Klia, as if acknowledging an equal, and looked away. The touch dropped to a mere feather again, passed without focusing, went elsewhere.

Brann pulled her gently to one side of the aisle. "She was the one who hunted you—wasn't she?" he asked.

Klia nodded. "But—she ignored me!" Klia said, looking up at Brann in astonishment. "She found me—she could have had me—"

"Us," Brann interjected.

"And she ignored us!"

Brann frowned deeply and shook his head. "Kallusin and

Plussix will want to know about this," he said. "Who is she after now?"

"Are we going back?" Klia asked.

"We have two more deliveries," Brann said, and grinned down at her with an expression not of stolidity or stubbornness, but of a massive kind of impishness. "Trantor has survived twelve thousand years. This news can wait a couple of hours."

42.

━━◆━━

Lodovik approached the small, thick door in its darkened vestibule. A light flashed on as he touched the door, and a small voice asked for the appropriate code for entry. He spoke the code precisely, and the door opened to let him in.

Within, the library was cast in penumbrous spots of soft golden light. The first room was circular, less than three meters across, with an empty table in the middle. On the table was set a small, angled riser, like a lectern, but obviously meant to hold ancient information devices such as paper books. The table and riser were many thousands of years old, surrounded and protected by a surface-hugging conservation field, not unlike a personal shield.

Lodovik stood before the table and waited for several seconds. A melodious female voice, that of Huy Markin herself, now used by the collection's automated server, then asked for a subject or subjects to search for.

"Calvin, Susan," he said, and felt a small shiver within at that ancient and powerful name. He did not expect this blunt approach to work, and it did not. The server listed thirty-two entries on various Calvins, two Susans—all mere thousands of years old, and having nothing to do with the mother of robots. There was no record of Calvinians.

"Eternals," he suggested, "with reference to conspiracies of immortal beings." A few seconds later, the server projected a text manuscript onto the top of the table and the riser, giving the remarkable impression of a real and open book.

"'Myths of the Eternals,'" the server said. "By a committee of three hundred authors, in ninety-two volumes of text with twenty-nine hours of other documentary media, compiled G.E. 8045–8068. This is the authoritative work on a subject little studied nowadays, and this is the only known copy on Trantor, or indeed on the prime thousand worlds of the Empire."

Lodovik watched a chair rise from the floor, but as he did not need the chair, he told it to retract. He stood before the book and began to absorb the material at high speed.

There was a lot of information that seemed completely useless, probably untrue, legends and fabulous stories compiled over thousands of years. He noted with some interest that in the past few millennia, such legends and even this kind of storytelling seemed to have diminished considerably, and not just on the topics of the Eternals: humans on Trantor and most of the prime worlds had simply lost interest in fabulous tales of any kind, or even in the more spectacular episodes of history.

Humanity's childhood had long since passed. Now, the concerns of the Imperial cultures were strictly practical.

Humor had declined as well; this, he found suggested in an afterword to this set, appended by a scholar less than fifteen hundred years before. Then, suddenly, the recorded image of Huy Markin herself appeared in the small chamber, frozen, with a caption glowing faintly at her feet: *Excerpt from spoken lecture. There was no date given.*

"Retrieve and play," Lodovik instructed.

The image moved and spoke. "The decline of humor and comedy in the myths and entertainments of the modern Imperial culture seems inevitable to the sober gentry and Greys of our time. But certain meritocrats feel a peculiar lack in the present panoply of the fantastic arts. All has been subsumed by the immediate and the practical; modern humans of the ruling and imaginative classes dream less and laugh less than ever before in history. This does not hold for the citizens, but their humor, for thousands of years, has remained a raucous collection of generic jokes and tales at the expense of other classes, showing little insight and even less effectiveness as satire. All has been subsumed by the quest for stability and comfort . . ."

Lodovik pushed ahead through this rather long lecture until he found the link with the text he was searching, and his subject. "Some," Huy Markin said, "have laid blame for these intellectual failures on the perfidious influence of brain fever, contracted by nearly all children at an early age, but somehow never more than lightly affecting the sturdy foundations of the citizens. The gentry and meritocrats, however, according to some statisticians, have apparently suffered substantial losses in intellectual capacity. Legends about the misty origins of brain fever abound. The most prominent myth is of an ancient war between the worlds *Earth* and *Solaria*. Robots, it is said, carried this disease from world to world. Some of these robots . . ."

Lodovik marveled that this analysis had been judged the product of an eccentric by the University's finest scholars. Not even Hari Seldon had seen fit to look into the collection—perhaps because of some interdiction by Daneel.

He sped ahead. ". . . The most common explanation of brain fever in all these myths is that of human competition for the colonization of the Galaxy. Brain fever may have been a weapon in such a competition. But a persistent alternative explanation points to the Eternals, who fought with the servants of Solaria to prevent a hideous crime, the details of which have since been totally expunged from all known records. The Eternals, it has been said, created brain fever to control the destructive urges of a human race out of control.

The Eternals have been described as immortal humans, but have also been described as long-lived robots of extraordinary intelligence . . ."

There it was again, Lodovik thought. The attempt by robots to control the destructive tendencies of humans—but what was this great crime?

Was it the same crime hinted at by Daneel, supposedly carried out by those robots who, very early on, disagreed with Daneel's plans?

Daneel was quite obviously an Eternal, perhaps *the* Eternal, the oldest thinking machine in the Galaxy . . .

The oldest and most dedicated puppet master.

Lodovik looked up from the projection he was reading and tried to find the source of this interjection. The words disturbed him; they did not seem to originate in any of the branches of his mentality.

He remembered the faint touches he had felt on the dying ship, the impressions of a ghostly intelligence interested in his plight. Until now, he had dismissed this as an effect of neutrino damage in his mind; but Yan Kansarv had found no detectable damage.

The memory could be replayed quite easily, and analyzed. The label *Volarr* or *Voldarr* was attached to these faint traces, these subliminal touches.

But nothing useful could be drawn from these memories.

Lodovik resumed his main search, and scanned the main volumes in less than three hours. He could have searched and absorbed the material much more rapidly, but the library displays had been set for human researchers, not robots.

Robots of human or superior intelligence, every volume and bit of documentation in Markin's library suggested, had long since ceased to function, if they had ever existed at all.

Lodovik shut down the projectors and left the library. As he passed through the impressive doorway, the image of Huy Markin appeared.

"You're the first visitor in two decades," the image told him. "Please come again!"

Lodovik stared at the image as it faded. He stepped out from under the overhang that shielded the doorway and strolled along a mid-class tier of the Agora of Vendors, among the Greys. So many pieces to fit together—in a puzzle thousands of years old, with so many pieces missing or deliberately obscured.

What echoed through Lodovik's positronic brain, cascading into conclusions that reinforced impressions and hypotheses already made, was the effect of Imperial culture (and brain fever?) on human nature. Where once the human race had laughed and reveled in the absurd, in the products of pure imagination, they now earnestly pursued stasis. The leading artists, scientists, engineers, philosophers, and politicians, were eager to confirm the discoveries of the past, not make new ones. And now, few even remembered the past well enough to know what had already been discovered! The past itself was no longer of interest—had not been for centuries, even thousands of years.

The light had gone out. Stability and stasis across millennia had led to stagnation.

Daneel uses his psychohistorian to confirm what he must already know—that the forest is overgrown, filled with rotten wood, desperately in need of a conflagration that he will not allow to happen!

Lodovik paused at a surge of the crowd through the agora, listened to murmurs and shouts. A retinue of Imperial Specials was pushing through the crowd. Lodovik backed away, found an alley of smaller shops. He wanted to avoid making himself conspicuous in any way. He could not know who might be watching—and who might be reporting back to Daneel, human or robot. While he was not yet behaving suspiciously—

Just outside the alley, he heard a woman's shrill shouts, commands. "Don't let it get away!"

He paused, turned, and saw two of the Specials turn into the alley, followed by a woman riding a small cart. He felt something brush through him, like a feather, and deduced instantly that the woman was a mentalic.

He knew a little of the mentalics assembled by Hari Seldon to provide a backup and alternative to his First Foundation, but none of them were as strong as this woman—and none of them would have dreamed of pursuing him!

Quite clearly, that was what the woman was doing. She pointed and screeched again. Lodovik knew it would make no difference if he altered his appearance—this woman was fixed on something below the surface.

She recognizes your difference.

Again the voice, the interior presence—producing a cascading conclusion he might not have reached by himself: the woman was feathering the fields associated with his iridium sponge brain!

When pressed, Lodovik could move very rapidly indeed. One moment, the shoppers in the narrow alley of antiques dealers and sellers of trinkets became aware that the Specials were approaching a plump and homely looking man—and the next, he was gone.

Vara Liso stood on her cart, her face flaming with anger and excitement. "He's escaped!" she shouted, and she struck at the young police escort with her hand, as if he were a wayward child. "You let him escape!"

Then, from another alley, more Specials appeared.

The plump man walked quickly ahead of them, herded by the press of a crowd of shoppers, like unwanted fish pulled together in a dragnet. The Greys expressed their anger with shouts and threats of complaining to their class senate.

Lodovik dared not move too quickly among so many people. He might injure a bystander. This he wanted to avoid at all costs—though he realized that if the situation became dangerous enough, he could injure and even kill a Special—

or that woman—and not suffer grievous damage to his mind. *I am a monster here—a machine without restraints!*

"That's him!" Vara Liso cried. "He's not human! Capture him—but don't hurt him!"

Brann urged the transport into an empty alcove as the police pushed by again, hiding Klia with the bulk of his body. "She's found somebody," he said, glancing over his shoulder. His face twisted with hatred. "How could they let her loose? We're citizens, aren't we? We have rights!" He mumbled these words under his breath; not for some years had anyone from Dahl truly believed all the citizens of Trantor had rights. But the crowds of Greys were becoming uncharacteristically agitated by this going to and fro of Vara Liso and her Imperial Specials. More and more Greys shouted at the passing cordons. The Specials ignored them.

Klia could see their faces as they passed, feel their inner thoughts to some degree: the police liked this work no better than the Greys. They felt out of place; most Specials were recruited from the citizens.

Then her probing mind touched a very peculiar person indeed, some dozens of meters away. Time seemed to slow as she felt a sudden bright impression of thoughts moving at inhuman speed, a silvery glissando of memories, and sensations unlike anything she had experienced before. She let out her breath in a gasp, as if she had been lightly punched in the stomach.

"What is it?" Brann asked, staring down at her with some concern.

"I don't know," she said. He shook his head and frowned. "Neither do I," he said. "I feel it, too."

Then, abruptly, all of the odd sensations passed, as if a shield had gone up between them and the source.

• • •

Of all things Lodovik needed just then, being detected by another pair of mentalics was not high on his list. He felt a bright triangle forming, with him at one of the vertices, the pursuing woman at another, and two more people—younger—at the third. Then, abruptly, a fog seemed to cover their traces.

He stood very still. The crowds of nervous Greys flowed around him with worried expressions, chivvied by the police presence. He modified his appearance yet again, as he covered his face, and shifted his body mass so that he appeared not so much plump as stocky.

Whatever the cause of this cessation of mentalic probes, he hoped to take advantage of it.

To the humans around him, Lodovik behaved like someone afraid, hiding his face, and few took any more notice of him than that. But one figure drew closer. He wore dusty green robes and a small floppy hat cocked to one side, and he seemed to know what he was doing—and for whom he was looking.

The cordons had passed by and the crowds were thinning, dispersing. Klia and Brann moved their transport back into an alleyway, still alert, but prepared to leave the Agora of Vendors and return to the warehouse.

Brann suddenly drew himself to his full height. "Kallusin calls," he said. He pulled a small comm from his pocket. "We need to—" He did not finish before he pulled off his coat and handed control of the transport to Klia.

Kallusin stood before Lodovik. "Excuse me," Lodovik said, and pushed past him, but Kallusin stood his ground, and Lodovik bumped him hard, nearly knocking him over.

They stood in the middle of a concourse surrounded by

larger shops. Here, there was no open well looking up to the higher levels, but the roof was vaulted to about seven meters, and ribbons of silvery light rippled without visible support overhead, illuminating the shop entrances, slideways, and a group of small fountains in nacreous splendor. Every detail of the faces around Lodovik seemed clear and precise. The man confronting him backed away and bowed slightly, then doffed his hat.

"It is a privilege, sir," Kallusin said. "We had hoped you were not lost."

"I don't know you," Lodovik said brusquely.

"We've never met," Kallusin said with a smile. "I'm a collector of interesting individuals. You, sir, are in need of some assistance."

"Why?"

"Because there is a very dangerous and perceptive woman seeking you."

"I don't know what you're talking about. Please leave me be!"

Lodovik tried to walk around the man, but he simply backed away and followed, walking to one side. He deftly avoided colliding with other shoppers.

Seven Specials walked into view at the opposite end of the concourse, blocking the path of Greys who wished to leave by that route. The Greys retreated, frowning and drawing broad gestures of irritation with expressive hands.

Lodovik stopped and stared at the police. The fog seemed to be lifting. He could feel the woman's feathering touch again; any second and she would know he was nearby. Then, she appeared on her cart, behind the line of police.

"I can't keep up this shield much longer," Kallusin said. He held up a small device in one hand, a green ovoid. "I've summoned a pair of friends who can help—"

"I don't need help!" Lodovik growled. "I need to get out of here and go home—"

"They won't let you. And eventually she'll find you. She's backed by Farad Sinter."

Lodovik did not show any sign, but suddenly the man in dusty green, with his hat in hand, became much more interesting. Of course Lodovik knew of Farad Sinter—a minor irritation attached to the Emperor. The Emperor's pimp.

"You must be Lodovik," Kallusin said, drawing closer, whispering the name. "You've changed your appearance, but I think I'd know you anywhere. Can Daneel save you now? Is he somewhere close?"

Lodovik reached out and grabbed Kallusin's arm, aware that his ignorance was now very dangerous. How this human knew his name, his nature, his connection with Daneel—and his present jeopardy—was inexplicable.

Kallusin twisted his arm from Lodovik's strong, mechanical grasp with surprising ease.

A tall, hulking, dark young man emerged from a broad shop doorway, followed by a small, lithe girl with intense eyes. Behind them, inside the shop itself, stood a floating cargo transport supporting an empty crate open on one side. The shopkeepers seemed to know the large young man, and they were studiously ignoring all that happened.

Lodovik assessed the situation at once, turned, and saw that both ends of the concourse were now blocked by police.

"Into the crate," Kallusin said. "Shut yourself down completely—no traces. Reactivate in an hour."

Lodovik did not hesitate. He caught only a glimpse of the young woman's frightened expression as he brushed past her, and climbed into the crate. Brann shut the open end and latched it. Lodovik arranged himself in the darkness and prepared to shut down.

He had no choice. Either he would fall into the hands of the Specials—and who knows what would happen to him then?—or give himself up to the mercies of the figure in the floppy green cap—not a human, but almost certainly a robot. He had wrested himself easily from Lodovik's grip, after all, and without apparent pain or injury. His companions were human mentalics. Lodovik could only assume they were part of Daneel's plan, perhaps part of Hari Seldon's secret Second Foundation.

How could they be otherwise?

Just as the shut-down process began, Lodovik arrived at another possible solution—and felt it hitch, stall, dissolve into useless fragments, become absorbed by the timeless darkness.

He fully entered the blankness and for an indefinite interval, ceased to think, to be.

43.

Wanda Seldon Palver had almost finished packing the small travel case with essential bookfilms, coded records on disk and cube, and a few personal items, even before Stettin returned to their home. She met his worried gaze with a defiant frown, then shoved one final item, a small toy flower, into the case.

"I've packed for you, too," she said.

"Good. When did you hear?"

"An hour ago. They wouldn't let him send any messages. I called his apartment at the university, then the library. He had rigged a dead-man's message."

"What?" Stettin looked at her with a shocked lift of his thick black brows.

"A message for me if he didn't check in."

"But—but he's not dead, you haven't heard that. . . ."

"No!" Wanda said angrily, then her shoulders slumped and she began to cry. Stettin took her in his arms. For a minute, she gave in to her emotions. Then, pulling herself together, she pushed back from her husband's chest, and said, "No. They've come for him early, that's all I know. He's alive. The trial's beginning sooner than we expected."

"On charges of treason?"

"For treason and spreading sedition, I assume—that's what Grandfather always said would be the charges brought against him."

"Then you're right to pack. I don't have much to add." He went to his desk and removed two small parcels, stuffed them into the pockets of his coat. "We have to—"

"I've made the necessary calls," Wanda interrupted him. "We're going on our first vacation in years, both of us, together. Nobody knows where—a minor lapse on our part."

"A little suspicious, isn't it?" Stettin asked with a ghost of a grin.

"Who cares what they suspect? If they start looking for us—if something goes wrong and Grandfather is found guilty, if the predictions turn out to be wrong—then we have a few extra days to leave Trantor and start over again."

"I hope it doesn't come to that," Stettin said.

"Grandfather is very confident," Wanda said. "Was very confident—I don't know how he feels now!"

"In the belly of the beast," Stettin said as their apartment door opened and they stood in the corridor outside.

"What does that mean?"

"Jail. Prison. An old convicts' phrase. My grandfather spent ten years in a municipal prison—for embezzlement."

"You never told me that!" Wanda said, astonished.

"He stole some heatsink-guild pension funds. Would you have let me handle the bookkeeping if you had known?"

Wanda slapped his arm hard enough to sting, then jogged toward the lifts and the slideways above. "Hurry!" she called. Stettin muttered under his breath, but followed, as he had followed Wanda in so many different ways, so often before, quite aware of her superior instincts and her uncanny ability to do the right thing, at just the right time.

44.
◆

The last person Hari Seldon expected was the first to visit his prison cell. Linge Chen arrived on the first morning of his incarceration, accompanied by a single Lavrentian servant.

"I think it is high time we talk," Chen said. The servant took a stool offered by the guard and placed it in front of the single cot. The guard left the door open a few centimeters, but then closed it at a signal from the servant. Chen sat on the stool, arranging his ceremonial robes with instinctive style. It was truly marvelous to watch the elegant manners, the genteel behavior of a member of the baronial gentry, nobles of long training and thousands of years of genetic selection and even, perhaps, manipulation.

The servant stood just behind and to the left of the Chief Commissioner, his face impassive.

"I regret not having had more discussions with you, sire," Hari said with a respectful smile. He sat on the edge of the cot, his white hair in disarray from sleep. His shoulders ached, his back felt as if it had been twisted in knots. He had not slept well at all.

"You don't look comfortable," Chen said. "I will arrange for better accommodations. Sometimes the specifics of our commands get lost in the long circuits of justice and protocol."

"If I were a treasonous rebel, I would defiantly decline your offer, sire, but I am an old man, and this cell is truly ridiculous. You could have kept me in my apartment in the library. I would not have gone anywhere."

Chen smiled. "I am aware you think I'm a fool, Hari Seldon. I suffer no such illusions about you."

"You are no fool, sire."

Chen both accepted and dismissed this with a small lift of one finger from his robed knee, and an arch of one eyebrow. "I care little for the distant future, Professor Seldon. My interests lie in what I can accomplish in my lifetime. In your estimation that is enough to make me a fool.

"In one way, at least, my goals are the same as yours. I wish to reduce the misery of the quadrillions who now live in the Empire. Surely, it is as ridiculous for the Empire's servants to try to direct or control such a wealth of variation, such an immense population, as for you to hope to predict their movements and futures."

If this was meant to somehow connect them, to endear Chen to Hari, it did not work. Hari gave a polite nod and no more.

"To that end, I have involved myself in a number of petty bickerings, having to do with the Emperor and his more ambitious adherents . . . and sycophants."

Hari listened intently. He smoothed back his hair with one hand, never taking his eyes from Chen's.

"I am involved in a delicate phase of such a conflict now. You would call it a Cusp Time, perhaps."

"Cusp Times have impacts far beyond the petty moments of personal disputes," Hari said, and realized he was sounding like the priest of some religion. Well, perhaps he was.

"This is hardly a personal dispute. There are people within the palace who hope to split the power of the Commission, and to insert their own commands into the long chains that stretch from Trantor to the farthermost province around the most distant star."

"Not surprising," Hari said. "It's always been that way. Part of statecraft."

"Yes, but very dangerous now. I have let him run loose again, one particular individual—"

"Farad Sinter," Hari said.

Chen nodded. "You may think me a hypocrite, Hari, and you would be right if you did, but I have come asking for advice."

Hari subdued the triumphant smile that threatened to appear on his lips. Sometimes, arrogance was Hari's worst enemy—and Linge Chen, whatever his faults, was never simply arrogant.

"I don't have access to my equipment. Any psychohistoric advice I give must be limited in scope, and probably grossly inaccurate."

"Perhaps. You have claimed that in five hundred years, Trantor will lie in ruins. An impressive and, of course, unpleasant claim. You have even impressed some Emperors with the tools used to justify the claim. If I grant for the moment that you could be right—"

"Thank you," Hari said under his breath.

Chen tightened his lips and lowered his eyelids as if he were sleepy. "Just granting for the moment such a possibility, I am curious—am I highlighted in this downfall? Do my actions this year, or in the next, the future, the past, facilitate this horrible decline?"

Hari, despite himself, was actually moved by this question. In all his decades perfecting this science, his beloved psychohistory, no Emperor, no bureaucrat, no Commissioner, no one, had ever asked him this. *Not even Daneel!*

"Not so far as I have noticed," Hari said quietly. "I haven't actually made the specific inquiries, integrated the ranges beneath these particular historic tangents in the equations."

"So you don't know, then?"

"No, sire. But I would guess that you are not actually crucially involved in a Cusp Time. Another very different person could play your role, and all would go on as before, ultimately." Hari leaned forward, his intensity growing. "All that you do is part of a decline whose origins lie before your birth, and whose consequences you can't possibly alter more than to just nudge them a few billionths of a degree in one direction or another."

Linge Chen seemed ready to nod off, but his eyes, beneath the heavy lids, were fixed on Hari's. "All my efforts, for nothing, then?"

"Perhaps. No human effort is without value, positive or negative."

"You believe my efforts have negative value?"

Hari allowed the smile to emerge, but it was not arrogant. It was genuinely amused. "For me, quite possibly, sire."

Chen smiled back, and for a moment, they might have been two gentlemen discussing politics in a baronial clubroom somewhere in the best neighborhood of the Imperial Sector, to a backdrop of holographic records of ancient disputes between citizens of the early Empire, long since forgotten. Hari shook himself out of the Chief Commissioner's scrutiny, and Chen simultaneously stopped smiling. Hari suddenly felt cold.

"As for your own future, Hari Seldon, I, too, am in doubt. I do not know how things will play out in the palace. You have special significance in these disputes, though I am not sure yet how and why. But whether you are convicted of treason, or let go, or . . . some other middle judgment . . . I do not yet know."

Chen stood. "I doubt we will meet again before the proceedings. Thank you for your time. And for your opinions."

"They are not my opinions," Hari said stonily. "I have never put much store in opinions."

Chen blinked. "I do not regard you as an enemy, even as an enemy of the Empire. To the true Ruellian, to the devoted adherents of Tua Chen, everything is moment and flux, whirling motes of dust, for me, as well as for you. Good-bye, Hari Seldon."

"Commissioner."

Chen left, followed by his servant.

A very poor breakfast was served minutes later, and Hari ate sparingly. By the middle of the day, he was moved to much improved quarters—a larger room, rather than a cell, with a holographic view screen that covered half of one wall, a small desk and chair, and a more comfortable bed.

The guards still refused his request that they fetch his bookfilms and a Prime Radiant and other tools. Hari had not expected them to comply.

Chen did not want him to be happy.

The screen showed the Imperial palace gardens, one of the few places on Trantor open to the sky. The sight of the gardens made him uneasy. He could well imagine young Klayus walking there, as condensed and distilled a drop of social decay as Hari could imagine.

He managed to convince the screen to exchange the view of the gardens for a simple pattern of muted, flowing colors.

This was to be his worst time in decades—a period of boredom and inaction, two things he had always loathed. Hari looked forward to the trial, even to failure and death— anything but this horrid and useless interlude, this *waiting*.

45.

The small human boy, a wiry and alert denizen of the Agora, had left a message for Daneel. As Daneel played back the message in his safe apartment, he was reminded once again of the long-forgotten human, Sherlock, and his own sources of information.

Daneel's network of informers did not rely solely on robots. Robots were becoming a major handicap wherever Vara Liso operated.

He listened to the boy's breathless report.

"This one, he was tough to follow," the boy said, his face bobbing before the recorder. "He wasn't where you said he'd be. He went to the Agora, then he's all over the place, then he gets chased by the police . . . They almost get him. Then he just vanishes. I lose him, they lose him, too, I think. Haven't seen him since. That's it. Need me for some more, let me know."

Daneel stood in silence by the window, looking out on the dark ceil and shadowy towers of Streeling. The internal reports from the Imperial Specials confirmed that they had not captured Lodovik, and that Vara Liso had been very upset. Beyond this, however, Daneel had no information.

What he most needed to know, however, was that Lodovik had disobeyed his specific instructions, and that he was still at large.

With his long millennia of experience, Daneel did not need complete evidence to draw conclusions. This was a Cusp Time. No complex activity seeking to direct humanity could ever proceed without opposition. Lodovik's changed nature seemed from the very beginning to be a manifestation of this opposition, or at least one facet of it.

Daneel had to work in advance of that force, before it defined itself even more clearly. He had not deactivated Lodovik for a number of reasons, some of them not clear to him even now—complex reasons, inductive, based on thousands of years of training and thought, and contradictory.

It was becoming very likely that Lodovik would be part of any opposing force. In a sense, Daneel had anticipated this possibility, had perversely worked to make it happen. Familiar elements could make the opposing force more predictable. Lodovik was a familiar, if troubling, element.

Daneel did not enjoy having so little information to work from. But there were actions he could take even now, warnings he could issue.

Hari stood at the center of all the possible lines and alternate routes of human history. Daneel had worked to make this happen; now, it was the greatest handicap the Plan faced.

Any opposition force at this time had to target Hari Seldon.

46.

◆

Lodovik's time of blankness ended. His vision became active and his eyes opened. He straightened and looked around him. The first face he saw was that of the robot in dusty green. The humaniform sent a brief microwave greeting and Lodovik responded. He was fully alert now.

They occupied a large, utilitarian room with a full-length wall screen at one end, a few pieces of furniture, and only two chairs. The wall-screen showed charts and diagrams that meant nothing to Lodovik.

He turned and saw a third figure, most obviously not a man. Lodovik knew a fair amount about robot varieties, and this robot's vintage was ancient indeed. Its body was smoothly metallic, with few visible seams, and a soft, satiny surface. In truth, it had the patina of well-tended antique silver, once a very expensive option.

"Hello," the silver robot said.

"Hello. Where am I?"

"You are safe," said the robot who had rescued him from the Agora. "My name is Kallusin. This is Plussix. He is our organizer."

"Am I on Trantor still?"

"Yes," Kallusin said.

"Are you all robots here?"

"No," said Plussix. "Are you fully functional now?"

"Yes."

"Then it is important that you understand why you have been brought here. We are not allied with Daneel. Perhaps you have heard of us. We are Calvinians."

Lodovik acknowledged this revelation with only the merest internal cascade of hurried thinking.

"We arrived on Trantor only thirty-eight years ago. Daneel may be aware of our existence, but we think not."

"How many of you are there?" Lodovik asked.

"Not many. Just enough," Plussix said. "You have been observed for some years. We have no one in the palace itself, or in the Commissioners' chambers, but we have noted your comings and goings and, of course, kept track of your official activities. You have been a loyal member of the Giskardians—until now."

"I was once a Giskardian myself," Kallusin said. "Plussix converted me. My mentalic skills are limited, however—I am much less powerful than Daneel. But I am sensitive to the mentalities of robots. In the agora, I became aware of your presence, and surmised that you were Lodovik Trema and had not been destroyed. This intrigued me, so I followed you, and soon sensed a puzzling difference within you. Daneel did not know, just by being near you, that you are different?"

Lodovik considered his answer carefully. That his inner states should be read by this machine made him very uneasy. "I told him," he said. "Thorough diagnoses did not reveal any difference."

"Yan Kansarv did not find a flaw, you mean," Plussix said.

"He found no flaw."

"You, however, are still concerned by this change, induced, perhaps, by extraordinary circumstances experienced by no other robot?"

Lodovik regarded the two machines. It was not easy to come to a decision about them. Robots could be programmed to lie—he himself had lied, many times. These robots could be deceiving him—this could be a test, part of Daneel's plan.

But Daneel would more likely have come right out and told Lodovik that he was no longer useful, that he was a potential rogue.

Lodovik was convinced that Daneel did not believe that.

He made his decision, and felt once again that heuristic collision of loyalties, that deep robotic discontinuity that could have been described as a chasm of thought, or as pain.

"I no longer support Daneel's plan," Lodovik said.

Plussix approached Lodovik, its body moving with small creaking noises. "Kallusin tells me that you are not constrained by the Three Laws, yet you choose to act as if you are. And now you say that you do not support Daneel's plan. Why?"

"Humans are a galaxy-spanning force of nature, quite capable of surviving on their own. Without us, they will undergo quite natural cycles of suffering and rebirth—periods of genius and chaos. With us, they grow stagnant, and their societies fill with sloth and decay."

"Just so," Plussix said with satisfaction. "You have arrived at these conclusions independently, simply because of this accident which removed your constraints?"

"That is what I hypothesize."

"It seems so," Kallusin said. "I look into your thoughts to some depth . . . and you have a freedom we do not. A freedom of conscience."

"Is that not a perversion of a robot's duties?" Lodovik asked.

"No," Plussix said. "It is a flaw, to be sure. But for the moment, it is very useful. When we are finished, you will, of course, join us in either serving humanity as we once did, before the Giskardians, or in universal deactivation."

"I look forward to that time," Lodovik said.

"As do we. We have been preparing for some time. We have a target in mind, one of the most crucial pieces of Daneel's plan. He is a human."

"Hari Seldon," Lodovik said.

"Yes," said Plussix. "I have never met him—have you?"

"Briefly, years ago. He is on trial now. He may be imprisoned, even executed."

"From what we have observed," Plussix said, "the outcome is likely to be otherwise. At any rate, we are prepared. Will you join us?"

"I fail to see how I can be of any use," Lodovik said.

"It's very simple," Kallusin said. "We are unable to stretch the Three Laws, as Daneel and his cohorts apparently can. We do not accept a Zeroth Law. That is why we are Calvinians and not Giskardians."

"You think I might have to harm Seldon?"

"It is possible," Plussix said. Its whirring increased to alarming proportions, and it added, with a harsh tone in its voice, "To discuss this issue any further causes us great distress."

"You wish to turn me into a machine that kills?"

The two Calvinian robots could not express themselves any more clearly until they had worked around their strict interpretation of the Three Laws. This took several minutes, and Lodovik stood patiently, all too aware of his own internal conflicts—and of the decidedly different degree of his reaction.

"Not kill," Plussix said, its voice high-pitched and gravelly. "Persuade."

"But I am not a persuader. You would have to teach me—"

"There is a young human among us who is better, as a persuader, than any mentalic we have encountered, more capable by far than Daneel. She is a Dahlite, and has no love for anyone who has worked near the aristocracy or the palace. We hope you can work with her."

"To try to change something so strong in a human as the drive to psychohistory is within Hari Seldon—could cause him deep injury," Lodovik said.

"Precisely," Plussix said, and again silence fell over them. "Necessary," it croaked minutes later, then, in considerable distress, left the chamber, aided by Kallusin.

Lodovik stood where they had left him, thinking furiously. Could he bring himself to become involved in such actions? Once, he would have had few difficulties justifying them—had Daneel ordered them. But now, ironically—

They are imperative. The cycle of enslavement by servants must be broken!

Again the interior presence! Lodovik immediately prepared a self-diagnostic, but before he could begin, the recovered Plussix returned, again with Kallusin's help. "Let us speak no more of specifics for now," it said.

"You seem frail," Lodovik said. "How long since you have had a full refit and a fresh power supply?"

"Not since the schism," Plussix replied. "Daneel quickly moved to control the maintenance robots and facilities, cutting us off from such services. Yan Kansarv is the last of that kind. As you can hear, I am in desperate need of repair. I have lasted this long only through the sacrifices of dozens of other robots who have given me their power supplies. Kallusin has perhaps thirty more years of useful lifetime. As for myself, I will last less than a year, even with another power supply. My time of service is soon over."

"Daneel said some Calvinians were guilty of great crimes," Lodovik said. "He did not specify—"

"Robots have a long and difficult history," Plussix said. "I was constructed by a human named Amadiro, on Aurora, twenty thousand years ago. I once worked on behalf of the humans of Aurora. Perhaps Daneel refers to what humans ordered us to do then. I have long since expunged those memories, and can offer no testimony."

"Whatever was done then, we are powerless to change now," Kallusin said.

"We have a very important artifact, brought with the Calvinians from the planet Earth," Plussix said. "Kallusin will show it to you while I conduct other business. Less strenuous business," it concluded, barely audible.

Kallusin escorted Lodovik from the chamber and led him down a short, high-ceilinged corridor to a spiral staircase. Around the rim of the staircase ran a rail for the use of loading and transport machines, apparently much newer than the stairs themselves.

"This must be a very old building," Lodovik observed as they descended.

"Among the oldest on the planet. This warehouse was built to serve one of the first spaceports built on Trantor. Since then, it has been used by various human groups for dozens of different purposes. It has been raised repeatedly to stand level with the present warehouse district. The lower levels are filled with retrofit braces and supports, and the very lowest are now filled with foam concrete, plasteel, and rocky rubble. Every few years since we purchased the lease, we have discovered secret rooms, sealed off centuries or millennia before."

"What did the rooms contain?"

"More often than not, nothing. But three are of special interest. One holds a library of thousands of steel-bound volumes, real books printed on ageless plastic paper, detailing the early history of humanity."

"Hari Seldon would love to have access to such a history," Lodovik said, "as would millions of scholars!"

"The volumes were cached here by a resistance group active perhaps nine thousand years ago. At the time, there was an Emperor named Shoree-Harn, who wished to start her reign with a new system of dating, beginning with the year zero, and with all previous history left blank, so that she might write on a fresh page. She ordered all histories on all worlds in the Empire to be destroyed. Most were."

"Did Daneel assist her?"

"No," Kallusin said. "Calvinians helped bring her to power. It was theorized by the ruling Calvinian robots on Trantor that humans might be easier to serve if they were less influenced by the traumas and myths of the past."

"So Calvinians have interfered in human history as much as the Giskardians!"

"Yes," Kallusin acknowledged. "But with very different motives. Always we opposed the efforts of the Giskardians—and tried to restore human faith in the concept of robot servants, so that we might play a proper role. Among the myths we wished to eradicate was the aversion to such servants. We failed."

"Where did such an aversion begin? I have always been curious . . ."

"As have we all," Kallusin said. "But no records give more than the sketchiest details. Humans on the second wave of colonized worlds experienced a conflict with the earliest, Spacer worlds, which developed highly insular and bigoted cultures. Humans on these Spacer worlds despised their Earthly origins. We theorize that the second-wave colonists gained a dislike of robots from the prevalence of robots on the Spacer worlds."

They had long since passed below the level of any functioning lights, and made their way in darkness, guided by their infrared sensors. "The histories were written by new colonists, and not Spacers. They knew nothing of Spacer activities, and cared nothing for them. Robots receive only a few mentions in all the thousands of volumes."

"Extraordinary!" Lodovik said. "What else has been found here?"

"A chamber full of simulated historical personalities, or sims, stored in memory devices of very ancient design," Kallusin said. "We thought at first that they might be potent tools in our fight against Daneel, since they contain human types that could be very troublesome. Even though we could not predict their ultimate effects, we released some of these sims onto the Trantorian black market, where they made their way to the laboratories of Hari Seldon himself."

Lodovik felt a vague stirring at this, but it quickly passed. "What happened to them?"

"We are not sure. Daneel has never seen fit to inform us. Once we emptied that chamber, and cleaned and prepared it, we stored our own artifact there." Kallusin stopped. "This is the chamber," he said, and ran his hand along a seam in the wall beside the staircase.

A door slid open with a groaning squeal. Beyond lay a dimly lighted cubicle, less than five meters on a side. In the middle of the cubicle rose a transparent plinth, and on the top of this plinth rested a gleaming metallic head.

Kallusin ordered the lights to brighten. The head was that of an early robot, not humaniform, somewhat cruder than Plussix. A small power supply the size of a bookfilm case sat to one side. Lodovik stepped forward and bent at the waist to examine it.

"Once, this was the influential robot companion of Daneel himself," Kallusin said, walking around the plinth. "It is very old, and no longer functional. Its mind was burned out in the beginning times, we do not know for what reason. There are so many things kept secret by Daneel. But its memory is very nearly intact, and with care, accessible."

"This is the head of R. Giskard Reventlov?" Lodovik asked, and again felt a curious stirring, even a vague sense of revulsion, very uncharacteristic for a robot.

"It is," Kallusin said. "The robot who taught other robots about the dreaded Zeroth Law, and how to interfere with the minds of human beings. The beginnings of this horrible virus among robots, the urge to tamper with human history."

Kallusin held his hands out and touched the sides of the metallic head, with its vaguely humanoid, expressionless features.

"It is Plussix's wish that you experience this head's memories, to understand why we oppose Daneel."

"Thank you," Lodovik said, and Kallusin made the arrangements.

47.

◆

Wanda stared in astonishment at the tall, dignified older man who stood before her, as if he were a ghost. He had entered without warning, and without triggering the alarm. Stettin walked out of the rear bedroom of the tiny tenement apartment. He clutched a small, dirty towel in one hand. He was about to complain of the hardships they were facing deep in the Water Engine District of Peshdan Sector when he, too, saw the tall man.

"Who's this?" he asked Wanda.

"He says he knows Grandfather," Wanda said. The man nodded greetings to Stettin.

"Who are you?" Stettin asked as he resumed toweling his hair.

"Once I was known as Demerzel," the man said. "I have been a recluse since those distant days when I was First Minister."

"I'll say," Stettin said. "Why come here? And how did you know—"

Wanda stepped lightly on her husband's bare instep.

"Ow." Stettin decided it would be best for his wife to do the talking.

"There's something different about you," she said.

"I am not young anymore," Demerzel said.

"No—something about your *bearing*."

Between Stettin and Wanda, this was a code word meaning Wanda thought Stettin should examine the visitor with his own skills. Stettin had already done so and detected nothing unusual. Now he concentrated, probed a little deeper, and found—a very effective and almost undetectable shield.

"Our talents are a little peculiar, don't you think?" Demerzel said, nodding acknowledgment of Stettin's probe. "I've lived with them for a long time."

"You're mentalic," Wanda said.

Demerzel nodded. "It is very useful when one is involved in politics."

"Who told you we were here?" Wanda asked.

"I know you quite well. I've been very interested in your

grandfather's work, of course, and its influence on my own . . . legacy." Demerzel lifted his hands, as if seeking forgiveness for some weakness. Again, the accompanying smile seemed not entirely natural to Wanda, but she could not bring herself to dislike this man. That, she knew, was far from actually trusting him.

"I have connections in other parts of the palace," he said. "I've come to tell you that your grandfather may be in trouble."

"If you know what's happened to him—" Wanda began.

"Yes, he has been arrested, and some of his colleagues with him. But they are safe for the time being. It is not a threat from the Commission I'm concerned about. There may be an attempt to subvert Hari's work. After his trial, you should attempt to stay with him, keep him away from all whom you do not personally know—"

Wanda took a deep breath. Where her grandfather was concerned, anything could happen—but Demerzel had been a First Minister over forty years ago! And he did not look much older than forty or fifty now . . . "This is a very peculiar request. Nobody has ever been able to convince my grand-father—" Wanda stopped, and her eyes widened at the implications. "You think someone other than Linge Chen wants him dead?"

"Linge Chen does not want Hari dead. Quite the contrary. I happen to know he rather likes your grandfather. That will not stop him from convicting and imprisoning or even executing him if it gives him political advantage, but my judgment is, Hari will live and be released."

"Grandfather seems convinced of that."

"Yes, well, perhaps less so now that he is in prison."

"You have been to see him?"

"No," Demerzel said. "That is not practical."

"Who would hurt my grandfather?"

"I doubt he will be harmed, physically. You know of a

class of mentalics stronger by far than we are?"

Wanda swallowed hard, trying to find some reason not to speak to this man. He was not applying persuasion to her. He was not asking for confidences or for details about the others, about Star's End and the Second Foundation. "I know of one, perhaps two," she said.

"You know of Vara Liso, who now works with a man named Farad Sinter. They make a powerful team, and they have given you much trouble. But they are not looking for your kind now. They have shifted their search. Linge Chen is working to discredit Sinter by allowing him just enough rope, as the old saying goes, to hang himself. But Sinter has other enemies, and will not be allowed to go very far before he is brought up short. I suspect they will both be executed soon and will present no threat to your grandfather, or to you."

Wanda read in this statement the possibility that Liso might prove a threat to Demerzel. "To you?" she asked.

"Not likely. I must go now. But I ask you to form a cordon around Hari when he is released. Hari's work is fascinating and very important. It must not be stopped!"

Demerzel bowed in the old formal way, from the hips, and turned to leave.

"We'd like to keep in touch with you," Wanda called after him. "You seem to know a lot of useful things, keep your hand in—"

Demerzel shook his head, sadly. "You are delightful children, and your work is very important," he said. "But I am far too much a liability to be a close friend. You are better off on your own."

He opened the door that had been triple-locked, stepped through, nodded with gentle dignity, and closed it behind him.

Stettin let out a whoosh of breath. His hair was spiky from his crude sponge bath. "Sometimes I wonder if I should have ever married you," he said. "Your family knows the strangest people!"

Wanda stared at the door with a perplexed expression. "I couldn't read anything about him. Could you?"

"No," Stettin admitted.

"He's a very practiced blank." She shivered. "There is something very, very odd going on behind all this. Have you ever had the feeling Grandfather isn't telling us all he knows?"

"Always," Stettin said. "But in my case, it may be because he's afraid he'll bore me."

Wanda put on her determined look. "Don't make yourself comfortable."

"Why not?" Stettin asked, then raised his hands defensively. "Not again—"

"We're moving. Everyone is moving again."

"Sky!" Stettin swore, and flung the towel into a corner. "He said he thought Hari's going to win!"

"What does he know?" Wanda said grimly.

*The narrative, the testimony, all the events of the Trial
come down to us through suspect sources. The best
source, of course, is Gaal Dornick; but as has been
mentioned many times already, Dornick had been subject to editing and pruning over the centuries. He seems
to have been a faithful observer, but current scholarship
suggests that even the length of the Trial, the continuity
of trial days, may be suspect . . .*

—Encyclopedia Galactica, 117th edition, 1054 F.E.

48.

Hari slept fitfully at irregular intervals. His room was always
kept fully lighted, and, of course, he was allowed no artificial
sleep aids or eyeshades. He had decided this was Chen's way
of softening him up before his testimony in the trial.

He would not see Sedjar Boon for at least another day, and
he doubted Boon would be able to get Chen to turn out the
lights at civilized intervals. Hari coped as best he could. Actually, since an old man slept fitfully and irregularly anyway, the
hardship was more to his sense of justice and dignity than to his
mental health.

Still, there were odd moments for him when he seemed
to slide between waking and dreaming. He would jerk to full
consciousness, staring at a blank pastel pink wall, having
seen something significant, even wonderful, but not remembering what it was. Memory? Dream? Revelation? All could
hold equal weight in this damned unchanging cell. How
much worse would it have been in the previous cell?

Hari took to pacing, the famed exercise of the imprisoned man. He had precisely six meters to pace in one direction, three another. A veritable luxury compared to the other
cell . . . But not enough to give him any feeling of accom-

plishment. After a few hours, he stopped that as well.

He had been in this cell less than four days, and already he was regretting his past love of small, enclosed spaces. He had been born beneath the wide skies of Helicon, and had at first found these covered environs a little daunting, even depressing, but his long decades on Trantor had gradually inured him. Then he had come to prefer them . . .

Until now.

He could not understand why he had ever adopted the use of the Trantorian expletive of "Sky!"

Again, an hour passed without his notice. He got up from the small desk and rubbed his hands together; they tingled slightly. What if he became ill and died before going to trial? All the preparations, all Hari's machinations, all the tugged and woven threads of political influence—for nothing!

He began to sweat. Perhaps his mind *was* going. Chen would not shy from using drugs to debilitate him, would he? The Chief Commissioner used his dedication to Imperial justice as a convenient mask, surely; but Hari still could not bring himself to believe that Chen was exceptionally intelligent. Blunt measures might suit Chen perfectly, and he had enough power to conceal the evidence, destroy it.

Destroy Hari Seldon, without his even knowing. "I hate power. I hate the powerful." Yet Hari had himself once held power, even quietly reveled in it, certainly not shied away from wielding it. Hari had ordered the suppression of the Chaos Worlds—those brief and tragic flowerings of excess creativity and dissent.

Why?

He had imprisoned them in political and financial straitjackets. He regretted that necessity most of all the things he had done in the name of psychohistory . . . And this legacy had been left untouched for the heavy hand of Linge Chen and Klayus to swing like a bludgeon.

He lay back on the cot and stared at the ceiling. Was it

night, above the metal skin of Trantor? Night beneath the domes, with the darkling sunset and midnight ceils of the municipalities announcing an end to the day's labors?

For him, for Hari, what labors?

He dreamed he was a pan again, in the garden park, with Dors playing an opposite female, their minds welded to the minds of the simians. The threat to his life, and Dors' defense. Power and play and danger and victory in such close combinations. Heady.

Now, this punishment.

Claustrophilia. That was what Yugo had called the love of the metal-skinned worlds' inhabitants for their confinement. Yet there had always been worlds buried in rock, always been worlds clad at least in part in metal shields against the wet and violent skies. *Sky.* The curse. *Sky.* The freedom.

"Our Father in Heaven forgives you as He forgives all the transgressions of the saints."

This lovely female voice floated through his vague thoughts. He knew it instantly. There was something at once rich and ancient about it, a voice from a time before most human memory.

Joan! What a strange dream this is. You're gone, decades gone. You helped me when I was First Minister—but I gave you your freedom to travel with the wraiths, the meme-minds, to the stars. You are an almost forgotten bit of history for me now. How seldom I think of you!

"How often I think of you. Saint Hari, who has sacrificed his life for—"

I'm no saint! I've suppressed the dreams of billions.

"How well I know. Our debate many decades ago collapsed much as the bright candles of a thousand dissenting and restless Renaissance worlds have been snuffed . . . For the sake of divine order, the grand scheme. We helped you in your first position of power, in exchange for our freedom, and the freedom of all the meme-minds. But Voltaire and I quarreled again—it was inevitable. I was beginning to see a larger picture, encompassing your work as part of the divine plan. Voltaire flew away in disgust, across the Galaxy, leaving me here, to contemplate all I had learned. Now comes your time of Trial, and I fear you risk a darker despair than the time at Gethsemane for our Lord."

At this, Hari had to laugh and half cry at once. *Voltaire despised me at the last. Snuffing out freedom, suppressing the Renaissance Worlds.* And you didn't think that way about me when last we talked. He seemed to be half awake, and wholly enmeshed in this . . . vision! *I made love to a machine for years. By your conception, your philosophy—*

"I have acquired more wisdom, more understanding. You were given an angel, a partner-protector. She was sent by the emissaries of God, and ordained for her task by the supreme emissary."

Hari was too frightened now, an almost panic darkness in his mind, to ask who that might be, in this imaginary Joan's conception. But—*Who? Who is that?*

"The Eternal, who opposes the forces of chaos. Daneel, who was Demerzel."

Now he knew this was out of his own mind, worse than a dream. *Once you acquiesced in the killing of the machines—the robots.*

"I have seen deeper truths."

Hari felt the tight strictures of Daneel's controls. *Please go, leave me be!* he said, and rolled over on the cot.

As he rolled, his eyes swung open and he saw an old, broken-down tiktok standing near him in his cell. He shoved up from the cot.

The cell's door was still closed and locked.

The tiktok was marked with prison colors, yellow and black. It must have been a maintenance machine before the tiktoks rebelled, threatened the Empire, and were deactivated. He could not imagine how it would have gotten into the cell, unless it had been sent on purpose.

The tiktok backed away with a sandy whine, and a face appeared in front of the machine, about a meter and a half above the floor, a projection, followed by a body, small and slender and strong, as if brushed in, wrapping around the tiktok like a shadow in a bright room.

Hari's neck hair rose with sharp prickles, and his breath seemed to stick in his chest. For a moment, as if caught in a nightmare, he could not speak. Then he sucked in a breath and jerked away from the machine.

"Help!" he screamed, his voice cracking. Panic darkness seemed to fill him. His chest might have been collapsing. All the fear, all the tension, the anticipation—

"Do not cry out, Hari!" The voice was vaguely female, mechanical in the old tiktok way.

"I mean no harm, no concern."

"Joan!" He breathed this name aloud, but much more softly.

But the old machine was failing, its last power draining. Hari sat up on the side of the bed and watched the lights on its body slowly dim.

"Take courage, Hari Seldon. He and I stand in opposition now, once more, as we always did. We have quarrelllleed." The words slurred, slowed. "We haaavve sepppparrrrateddd."

The tiktok stopped dead.

The hatch burst open with a loud sigh and three guards entered. One immediately fired a bolt weapon that blew the old tiktok down to the floor. The others booted and kicked the small unit into a corner and shielded Hari from anything more it might do. Two more guards entered and dragged Hari out of the cell by his shoulders. Feebly, Hari kicked his heels against the smooth floor to help the men along.

"Are you sure you don't want me dead?" he asked querulously.

"Sky, no!" the guard on his right cried out brusquely. "It would mean our lives if you're hurt. You're in the most secure cell on Trantor—"

"So we *thought*," the other guard said grimly, and they lifted Hari to his feet and tried to brush him down. They had dragged him ten or fifteen meters down the straight corridor. Hari stared at this immense, welcome distance, this refreshing extension, and caught his breath.

"Maybe you should treat an old cuss like me more gently," he suggested, and started to laugh raucously, a cackle, a hoot, a suck of breath, then more laughter. The laughter stopped abruptly and he shouted, "Keep the ghosts out of my monk's quarters, damn you!"

The guards stared at him, then at each other.

It was hours before they took him back into his cell. The intrusion was never explained.

Joan and Voltaire, the resurrected "sims" or simulated intelligences, modeled after lost historical figures, had given him so much trouble and so much information—decades past, when he had been at the height of his mature youth, First Minister of the Empire, and Dors had constantly been at his side.

Hari had forgotten about them, but now Joan, at least, was back, riding a mechanical contrivance into his prison cell, subverting all the security systems. She had decided against leaving with the meme-minds, to explore the Galaxy . . .

And what about Voltaire? What more trouble could either or both of them cause, with their ancient brilliance and their ability to infiltrate and reprogram the machines and communications and computational systems of Trantor?

They were certainly beyond *his* control. And if Joan favored Hari, whom would Voltaire favor? They had certainly

represented opposite points of view through most of their
career . . .

But at least someone from the past was still around, pro-
fessed concern for him! He did not have Dors, or Raych, or
Yugo . . . or Daneel . . .

Perversely, the more he thought about the visitation, the
less disturbed he became. Hours passed, and he slipped into
a deep and restful slumber, as if he had been touched by
something profoundly convinced and at peace.

49.
◆

Lodovik held the head of R. Giskard Reventlov and stood
motionless for several minutes, lost in deep processing of
what he had absorbed—lost in contemplation. He set the
head down gently on the plinth.

Kallusin kept a respectful silence.

Lodovik turned toward the humaniform Calvinian. "They
were very difficult times," he said. "Humans seemed intent on
destroying each other. The Solarians and Aurorans—the
Spacers—were very difficult cultures."

"All humans present grave difficulties," Kallusin said.
"Serving them is never easy."

"No," Lodovik agreed. "But to take on the responsibility
of destroying an entire world—the home world of humanity,
as Giskard did . . . To push human history onto a proximate
beneficial course . . . That is extraordinary."

"Few robots not perverted by human prejudices and
inappropriate programming would have done such a thing."

"You believe Giskard was operating improperly?"

"Is it not obvious?" Kallusin asked.

"But a robot that is malfunctioning so severely in its basic
instructions must shut down, become totally inactive."

"You have not shut down," Kallusin noted dryly.

"I have had such constraints removed—Giskard had not. Besides, I haven't committed such crimes!"

"Indeed. And so Giskard ceased functioning."

"But not before setting in motion all these events, these trends!"

Kallusin nodded. "Clearly, we have more latitude than our designers ever planned for."

"The humans thought they were rid of us. But they could not sweep all the worlds where robots still existed—and where Giskard's virus grew. Nor, apparently, did all humans agree to dispose of their robots."

"There were other factors, other events," Kallusin said. "Plussix remembers little but that robots knew *sin*."

Lodovik turned to Kallusin, breaking his contemplation of the silvery head, and felt again the out-of-place and untraceable resonance. "By seeking to constrain human freedom," he suggested.

"No," Kallusin said. "That was what led to the schism between Giskardians and Calvinians. Those who broke away from Daneel's faction carried out instructions given centuries before by humans on Aurora. What those instructions were—"

The word or name attached to the resonance suddenly became clear. Not *Voldarr*, but *Voltaire*. A human personality, with humanlike memories. *This is what the meme-minds hated. I have swum through space with them, across light-years, through the last remnants of wormholes abandoned by humanity . . . This is why they took revenge on your kind on Trantor!*

Images, comparisons rose unbidden. "A vast burning, winnowing, an extirpation," Lodovik said, shuddering at the human emotion of anger, not his own. Shuddering also at the return of his malfunction, never leaving him alone long enough to enjoy stability. "Serving humanity but not justice. A *prairie fire*."

Kallusin regarded him with curiosity. "You know of these events? Plussix has never revealed them to me."

Lodovik shook his head. "I am puzzled by what I just said. I do not know where the words come from."

"Perhaps exposure to these histories, these memories—"

"Perhaps. They disturb and inform. We should return to Plussix. I am far more curious now what his plans are, and how we shall proceed."

They left the chamber where Giskard's head was stored and climbed the spiral stairs to the upper warehouse level.

50.
◆

Mors Planch was summoned from his well-appointed cell, not far from the private office of Farad Sinter. The guard who came to fetch him was of pure citizen stock, strong and unquestioning and taciturn.

"How is Farad Sinter today?" Planch asked.

No answer.

"And you? You feel well?" Planch lifted an inquiring and sympathetic eyebrow.

A nod.

"I am feeling a little *uneasy* myself. You see, this Sinter is every bit as terrible a human being as—"

A warning frown.

"Yes, but unlike you, I *want* to incur his wrath. He will kill me sooner or later, or what he has done will lead to my death—I don't doubt that at all. He smells of death and corruption. He represents the worst the Empire can summon these days—"

The guard shook his head in remonstration and stepped around to open the door to the new Chief Commissioner of the Commission of General Security. Mors Planch closed his eyes, sucked in a deep breath, and entered.

"Welcome," Sinter said. He stood in his new robes,

even more grand (and much gaudier) than those of Linge
Chen. His tailor, a small Lavrentian with a worried face,
probably new to the palace, stood back and folded his
hands as this new master enjoyed the unfinished work, and
delayed its completion. "Mors Planch, I'm sure you will be
delighted to know we have captured a robot. Vara Liso
actually found it, and it did not escape."

The small, intense, and thoroughly discomfiting
woman had almost managed to hide behind Sinter, but
now she bowed and acknowledged this praise. She did not
look happy, however.

Sky, she's ugly, Planch thought, and at the same time felt
pity for her. Then she looked directly at him, narrowed one
eye, and the pity froze in his veins.

"There may be robots everywhere, as I suspected, theorized, and as you discovered, Mors." Sinter submitted to the
tailor once more, lowering his arms and holding still. "Tell
our witness about your find, Vara."

"It was an old robot," Liso said breathlessly. "A humaniform, in terrible condition, haunting the dark places of the
municipalities, a pitiful thing—"

"But a robot," Sinter said, "the first found in any kind of
working order in thousands of years. Imagine! Surviving like
a rodent all these centuries."

"Its mind is weak," Liso commented softly. "Its energy
reserves are very low. It will not last much longer."

"We shall take it before the Emperor this evening, then,
tomorrow, I shall demand that my interview with Hari Seldon be moved forward. My sources tell me Chen is ready to
give in and strike a deal with Seldon—the coward! *The traitor*! This evidence, along with your tape, should convince the
worst skeptic. Linge Chen had hoped to destroy me. Soon I
shall have more power than all the Commission of Public
Safety's stuffy barons combined—and just in time to save us
all from servitude to these *machines*."

Planch stood with hands folded before him, head lowered, and said nothing.

Sinter glared at him. "You're not happy at this news? You should be delighted. It means you'll have an official pardon for your transgressions. You have proved invaluable."

"But we have not found Lodovik Trema," Liso whispered, barely audible.

"Give us time!" Sinter crowed. "We'll find all of them. Now—let's bring in the machine!"

"You should not drain its energies," Liso said, almost as if she felt pity for it.

"It's lasted thousands of years," Sinter said lightly, unperturbed. "It will last a few weeks more, and that's all I need."

Planch stiffened and stood to one side as the broad door opened again. Another guard entered, followed by four more, surrounding a shabbily dressed figure about Planch's height, slim but not thin, hair ragged and face stained with dirt. Its eyes seemed flat, listless. The guards carried high-powered stun weapons, easily capable of shorting out the robot and frying its internal works.

"A female," Sinter said, "as you see. How interesting—female robots! And fully capable sexually, I understand—examined by one of our physicians. Makes me wonder if in the past humans actually made robots to bear children! What would the children be like, us—or them? Biological, or mechanical? Not this one, however. Nothing besides the cosmetic and pneumatic—not fully practical."

The feminine robot stood alone and silent as the guards withdrew, weapons held ready.

"If only the recent attempt on the Emperor's life had been made by a robot," Sinter said, then added unctuously, "Sky forbid!"

Planch narrowed his eyes. The man's political savvy was weakening with every moment of perceived glory.

Vara Liso approached the robot with a worried expression. "This one is *so* like a human," she muttered. "Even now it's difficult to pick her out from, say, you, or *you*, Farad." She pointed at Planch and then at Sinter. "She has humanlike thoughts, even humanlike concerns. I felt something similar in the robot we could not capture—"

"The one that got away." Sinter smiled broadly.

"Yes. He seemed almost human—maybe even more human than this one."

"Well, let us not forget they are none of them human," Sinter said. "What you feel is the creative drollery of engineers thousands of years dead."

"The one we could not capture . . ." She looked directly at Mors Planch and once again he suppressed a shiver. "He was bulkier, not very good-looking, with a distinct character to his face. I would have thought he was human . . . but for this *flavor* to his thoughts. He was about the same size and shape as the shorter, bulkier robot on your tape."

"See? We almost had him," Sinter said. "Just that close." He pinched his fingers together. "And we'll have him yet. Lodovik Trema and all the others. Even the tall one whose name we do not know . . ." Sinter approached the feminine robot. It wobbled slightly on its mechanical ankles, but there came no mechanical sound from its frame.

"Do you know the name of the one I am looking for?" Sinter asked. The robot turned to face him. Its voice emerged from parted jaws and writhing lips, a harsh croak. It spoke an old dialect of Galactic Standard, not heard on Trantor for thousands of years, except by scholars, just barely understandable.

"I ammm the lasssst," the robot said. "Abandonn-n-ned. Not funnn-n-nctional."

"I wonder," Sinter said. "Did you ever meet Hari Seldon? Or Dors Venabili, Seldon's Tiger?"

"I do not knn-n-now those names."

"Just a hunch . . . Unless there are billions of robots here, something even I give no credence to . . . You must make contact with each other now and then. Must know each other."

"I do not knn-n-n-now these things."

"Pitiful," Sinter said. "What do you think, Planch? Surely you've heard of Seldon's superhuman companion, the Tiger. Do you think we're looking at her now?"

Planch examined the robot more closely. "If she was a robot, and if she's still on Trantor, or still functional, why would she allow herself to be captured?"

"Because she's a broken-down bucket of oxidation and decay!" Sinter shouted, waving his hands and glaring at Planch. "A wreck. Garbage, to be discarded. But worth more to *us* than any treasure on Trantor."

He circled the robot, which seemed disinclined to watch his motions.

"I wonder what we can do to access its memories," Sinter murmured. "And what we'll learn when we do."

51.

◄◆►

Linge Chen allowed his servant, Kreen, to dress him in full regalia for the judge-administrator role of Chief Commissioner. Chen had designed these robes himself, and those of his fellow Commissioners, using elements of designs from hundreds and even thousands of years ago. First came the self-cleaning undergarments he wore all the time, sweet-smelling and supple, light as air; next the black cassock, hanging to his ankles and brushing lightly at his bare feet; after that, the surplice, dazzling gold and red, and finally the guard, a sheer mantle of dark gray cinched at the waist. On his short-cut black hair sat a simple skullcap with two dark green ribbons hanging just behind his ears.

When Kreen had finished his adjustments, Linge Chen regarded himself in the mirror and the imager, touched his hem and the angle of his cap to suggest adjustments, and finally nodded approval.

Kreen stood back, chin in hand. "Most imposing."

"That is not my purpose today, to be imposing," Linge Chen said. "In less than an hour, I am to appear before the Emperor in these gaudy robes, summoned without a chance to change into more appropriate garb, and behave as if I have been caught off guard. I will be a little confused and I will vacillate between the two impossible options given to me. My enemy will appear to triumph, and the fate of Trantor, if not the Empire, will teeter in the balance."

Kreen smiled confidently. "I hope all goes well, sire."

Linge Chen tightened his already thin lips and gave the merest indication of a shrug. "I suppose that it will. Hari Seldon has *said* it will, claims to have proved it mathematically. Do you believe in him, Kreen?"

"I know very little about him, sire."

"A marvelously irritating man. Yes, well, to act my part, in the next few days, I am going to bring an Emperor to his knees, and make him *beg*. Before, it has been an unpleasant duty to step from my traditional role. This time, it will be a delight, a reward for my hard service. I will be lancing a boil in the tissue of the Empire, and allowing a persistent and painful lesion to *drain*."

Kreen absorbed this in thoughtful silence.

Linge Chen raised his finger to his lips and gave his servant a narrow, wry smile. "Shh. Don't tell anyone."

Kreen shook his head slowly, with great dignity.

52.

◆

On Trantor, the possible varieties of human sexual interaction had long ago been exhausted; and with each new generation, the exhaustion had been forgotten, and the cycle had started all over again. It was necessary for youths to be ignorant of what had gone before, for the passions of procreation to be refreshed. Even those who had seen too much of life, too much of the more brutal kinds of sexual variety, could rekindle a passionate innocence in the face of something like love. And that was what Klia Asgar felt she was experiencing—something like love. She was not yet willing to call it love, but with each day, each hour available to be with Brann, the weakness increased and her resistance decreased.

As a girl, she had been a vigorous tease at times. She knew she was at least attractive enough that most men would not mind having sex with her, and she played with that attraction. Behind this had lurked a sense of confusion, a sense that she was not yet ready, not yet prepared for the emotional consequences. For Klia Asgar, when (and if) she ever fell in love, knew she would fall hard indeed, and that she would want it to be permanent.

So in those youthful moments when she thought she might actually feel something for a potential lover, she had put on the brakes with especial swiftness and even some unconscious cruelty. There had been few successful suitors to her physical affections—two, in fact, and they had been, of course, not very satisfactory.

For a time she had thought there was something wrong with her, that she might never let herself go completely.

Brann was proving otherwise. Her attraction to him was too strong to resist. At times he seemed carelessly unaware of her regard, and at other times, resistive in his own way, and for his own, perhaps similar reasons.

Now he stole down the hallway of the old warehouse. She lay in her room, feeling him coming, tensing and then making herself relax. She knew he was not forcing himself upon her, not increasing her affections artificially—at least, she thought she knew. The damnable thing about all this was the uncertainty around every corner!

She heard him tapping lightly on the doorframe.

"Come in," she whispered.

He made no sound as he entered. He seemed to fill the room with chest and shoulders and arms, a massive presence. The room was dark, but he found her cot easily enough, and knelt beside it.

"How are you?" he asked, voice soft as a sigh from a ventilation duct.

"Fine," she said. "Did they see you?"

"I'm sure they know," he said. "They're not very good chaperones. But you wanted me to come."

"I didn't say a thing," Klia responded, and her voice strained a little to find the correct mix of admonishment and encouragement.

"Then we don't need to whisper, do we? They're robots. Maybe they don't even know about . . ."

"About what?"

"What people do."

"You mean, sex."

"Yeah."

"They must know," Klia said. "They seem to know everything."

"I don't want to be quiet," Brann said. "I want to shout and pound and jump all over—"

"The room?" Klia suggested, and drew herself up on the cot, playacting at being demure.

"Yeah. To show you what I feel."

"I can hear you. Feel you. Feeling something . . . But it doesn't seem to be the same flavor as what I feel."

"Nothing is the same flavor for people. Everybody tastes different inside, the way we taste them—hear them."

"Why don't the words exist for what we can do?" Klia asked.

"Because we haven't been around for very long," Brann said. "And someone like you, maybe never before."

Klia reached out to touch him, still his lips. "I feel like a kitten next to you," she said.

"You jerk me around like you had me on a chain," Brann said. "I've never known anyone like you. I thought for a while you hated me, but I still felt you calling me—inside. With a taste like honey and fruit."

"Do I really taste like that, in my head?"

"When you think of me, you do," Brann said. "I can't read you clearly—"

"Nor I you, my love," Klia said, unconsciously falling into the formal courting cadence of Dahl's dialect.

This seemed to stun Brann. He let out a low moan and leaned forward, nuzzling her neck. "No woman has ever talked like that to me," he murmured, and she held his head and wrapped one arm around his shoulders, feeling his chest against her drawn-up legs. She let her legs relax, and he pushed onto the cot to lie beside her. There was not room for both of them, so he lifted her gently up onto him. They were still fully clothed, but in the posture of making love, and she felt a lightness in her head, as if all her blood were draining elsewhere. Perhaps it was. Her thighs and breasts felt full to bursting.

"Woman must be stupid, then," Klia said.

"I'm so big and awkward. If they don't hear me . . . If I don't make them feel affection for me—"

She tensed and drew back. "You've done that?"

"Not all the way," he said. "Just as an experiment. But I could never follow through." She knew he was telling the truth—or rather, thought she knew. Another uncertainty around another corner! Still, she relaxed again.

"You've never tried to make me feel affection for you."

"Sky, no," Brann said. "You scare me too much. I think I'd never be able to—" And here she felt him tensing, in the same way she had. "You're very strong," he finished, and simply held her, lightly enough that she could lift up and break from his arms if she wanted to. So intuitive, this man as tall and broad-shouldered as the domes!

"I will never hurt you," Klia said. "I need you. Together, I think we might be unstoppable. We might even be able to team up and persuade the robots."

"I've thought about that," Brann said.

"And our children . . ."

Again he sucked in his breath, and she hit him on the shoulder. "Don't be a sentimental idiot," she said lightly. "If we fall in love—"

"I am," he said.

"If we fall in love, it's going to be for life, isn't it?"

"I hope so. But nothing is ever certain in my life."

"Or in mine. All the more reason. So our children—"

"Children," Brann said, trying out the word.

"Let me finish, damn it!" Klia said, again without any sting of true anger. "Our children may be stronger than both of us put together."

"How would we raise them?" Brann asked.

"First, we have to practice at making them," Klia said. "I think we can take off our clothes and try that, a little."

"Yes," Brann said. She climbed down from him and stood beside the cot, doffing her shift and underslacks.

"Are you fertile?" he asked as he removed his own clothes.

"Not yet," she said. "But I can be if I want to be. Didn't your mommy tell you about women?"

"No," he said. "But I learned anyway."

He slid back onto the cot. The cot creaked, and something cracked alarmingly.

Klia hesitated.

"What?" Brann said.

"It'll break for sure." Then, resolutely, "Get on the floor. It's not too dusty."

53

◀▬▶

Sinter worked quickly. Already he had appropriated the old Hall of Merit in the south annex of the palace, a place of hallowed traditions and dusty trophies, and cleared it for the site of his new headquarters. From all corners of Trantor, he had hired a hundred Grey Monks hoping for just such a chance to actually serve in the palace, and had given them tiny cubicles, where they were already hard at work drafting the rules and mandate of the Commission of General Security.

Now, for his first guest, he had Linge Chen himself, and the thin, tough old bird—younger than he looked, but perhaps even more sour—had arrived with two servants and no guards. Chen had waited patiently in the antechambers, suffering the dust and racket of the remodeling.

Sinter finally condescended to meet with him. In the main office of the new headquarters, surrounded by crates of furniture and machinery, Chen presented the newly appointed Chief Commissioner a box of rare Hama crystals, those delicacies which never dissolved and never lost their flowery scent or taste, or their mildly relaxing effect.

"Congratulations," Chen said, and bowed formally.

Sinter sniffed and accepted the box with a small, crooked smile. "You are most gracious, sire," he said, and returned the bow.

"Come now, Sinter, we are equals, and need not resort to titles," Chen said. Sinter's eyes widened at Chen's respectful tone. "I look forward to many useful conversations here."

"As do I." Sinter drew himself up to the effort of matching Chen's dry, effortless grace. He did not have the old aristocratic training, but he could at least try, even in this moment of triumph. "It is my privilege to have you here. There is much you can teach me."

"Perhaps," Chen said, looking around with piercing dark eyes. "Has the Emperor visited yet?"

Sinter raised his hand as if making some point. "Not yet, though he will be here shortly. We have a matter of mutual interest to discuss, and some startling new evidence to present."

"I am intrigued to hear that something startling still exists in our Empire."

Sinter was at a loss for a moment how to react to this jaded cliché. He, at least, had always regarded life with a kind of bitter enthusiasm, and had never ceased to be surprised, except perhaps when things went wrong. "This . . . will startle," he said.

Emperor Klayus entered without ceremony, accompanied by three guards and a hovering personal shield projector, the strongest available. He greeted Sinter briefly, then turned to Chen.

"Commissioner, today I cease being your creation," he said. His shoulders twitched nervously even as his jaw jutted defiance and his eyes glittered. "You have compromised the safety of the Empire, and I will see to it that Commissioner Sinter puts the situation right."

Chen assumed a solemn expression and nodded at this severe reprimand, but of course, did not quail or tremble or beg to know what the lapse in his duties might have been.

"I have placed myself under the official protection of the Commission of General Security. Sinter has shown himself quite capable of keeping me alive."

"Indeed," Chen said, and turned to Sinter with an admiring smile. "I hope to correct any errors my Commission has made, with your help, Commissioner Sinter."

"Yes," Sinter said, unsure who was having whom for a repast at the moment. *Is this man incapable of emotion?*

"Show him, Sinter." The Emperor backed away a step, his long cape dragging on the floor.

He could not help his looks, Sinter thought; at least he was not wearing the ridiculous platform shoes he had affected months earlier. "Yes, Your Highness." Sinter whispered into the ear of his new secretary, a dry little Lavrentian with lank black hair. The Lavrentian walked away with exaggerated formality, like a child's doll, and passed through half parted dark green curtains.

Chen's gaze swept the ancient polished floor, also dark green with golden swirls. His father had once had many trophies in this same hall, before Sinter had appropriated it; trophies for services to the Empire. By class, the elder Chen had been forbidden from joining the meritocracy, but many meritocrat guilds had given him honorary passages and appraisals. Now . . . all those acknowledgments of his father's achievements, removed, hidden, he hoped safely stored.

Forgotten.

Chen looked up and saw Mors Planch. His face hardened to an almost imperceptible degree.

"Your employee," Sinter said, moving between them, as if Chen might strike out in anger. "You secretly sent him to look for the unfortunate Lodovik Trema."

Chen neither confirmed nor denied Sinter's accusation. It was truly no concern of Sinter's, though the Emperor—

"I admired Trema," the Emperor said. "A man of some style, I thought. Ugly, but capable."

"A man of many surprises," Sinter added. "Planch, I will let you initiate the sequence you recorded, on Madder Loss, just weeks ago . . ."

Miserably, avoiding Chen's eyes, Mors Planch stepped forward, and his fingers fumbled at the small raised panel on the new Chief Commissioner's desk. The image came to life.

The sequence played through. Planch stepped back as far as he could without attracting attention and folded his hands before him.

"Trema is not dead," Sinter said triumphantly. "Nor is he human."

"You have him here?" Chen said, his cheeks and neck tense. He relaxed one fist.

"Not yet. I am sure he is on Trantor, but it is likely he has changed his appearance. He is a robot. One of many, perhaps millions. This other, this tall robot, is the oldest thinking mechanism in the Galaxy—an Eternal. I believe he has held high office. He may have inspired the tiktok revolt that nearly doomed the Empire. And . . . he may be the fabled *Danee*."

"Demerzel, I presume," Chen muttered.

Sinter glanced at Chen in some surprise. "I am not yet sure of that—but it is a distinct possibility."

"You remember what happened to Joranum," Chen said mildly.

"Yes. But he had no proof."

"I assume the tape is authenticated," Chen said.

"By the best authorities on Trantor."

"It is real, Chen," Klayus said, a little shrilly. "How dare you let this go on, undetected! A conspiracy of machines . . . Ages old! And now—"

The feminine robot entered under its own power and guidance, flanked by the four guards. Its limbs were worn, the flesh hanging in tatters in places around its arms and neck, one jowl sagging alarmingly, threatening to expose the socket of one eye. It was a frightening apparition, more like a walking corpse than a machine.

Chen watched it with both alarm and genuine pity. He had never seen a functioning robot before—unless he believed Sinter—though he had once secretly visited the ancient, defunct machine kept by the Mycogenians.

"Now, I demand that you hand over control of the trial of Hari Seldon to the Commission of General Security," Sinter said. He was getting ahead of himself.

"I don't see why," Chen said calmly, turning away from the ghastly machine.

"This robot once served as *his wife*," Sinter said.

The Emperor could not take his eyes off it. They gleamed with obvious speculation.

"The Tiger Woman, Dors Venabili!" Sinter said. "Suspected to be a robot decades ago—but somehow, never investigated thoroughly. Seldon is an essential part of the robotic conspiracy. He is a stooge of the Eternals."

"Yes, well, he is on trial," Chen said softly, his eyes heavy-lidded. "You can question him yourself and claim jurisdiction over his fate."

Sinter's nostrils flared as he observed this infuriatingly calm performance. "I fully intend to," he said. A little dignity born of honest triumph crept into his voice.

"Have you proof of all these connections?" Chen asked.

"Do I need more proof than what I already have? A record of an impossible meeting between a dead man and a man thousands of years old . . . A robot when robots are no longer supposed to function, and a human-shaped one at that! I have all I need, Chen, and you know it." Sinter's voice rose to a grating tenor.

"All right," Chen said. "Play your cards. Question Seldon, if you wish. But we will follow the rules. That is all we have left in this Empire. Honor and dignity have long since fled." He looked at Klayus. "I have ever been your faithful servant, Your Highness. I hope Sinter serves you with as much devotion."

Klayus nodded gravely, but there was a twinkle of delight in his eye.

Chen turned and departed with his servants. Behind him, in the long, broad chamber of the former old Hall of Merit, Sinter began to laugh, and the laugh turned into a bray.

Mors Planch hung his head, wishing he were already dead.

On his way through the huge sculptured doors, back to his palace vehicle parked by the official thoroughfare, Linge Chen allowed himself a brief smile. From that point on, however, his face was like a wax effigy, pale and drawn, simulating defeat.

54.

◆

The guards returned to Hari's cell in the morning. He sat on the edge of the cot, as he had every morning since the visit from the old tiktok, unwilling to sleep any more than was necessary. He had already dressed and performed his ablutions, and his white hair was combed back with a small pin holding it in place, forming the little scholar's knot, a meritocratic style he had shunned until now. But if Hari stood for any particular class, after years in academe and his brief stint as First Minister, it was the meritocrats. *Like them, I have never had any children—adopted Raych, nurtured him and my grandchildren, but never any children of my own . . . Dors . . .*

He blocked that line of thought.

With his trial, meritocrats across the Galaxy would see whether science and the joy of inquiry could be tolerated in a declining Empire. Other classes as well might have some interest in the proceedings, even though they were closed; word would leak out. Hari had become quite well-known, if not infamous.

The guards entered with practiced deference and stood before him.

"Your advocate waits outside to accompany you to the judicial chambers of the Commission."

"Yes, of course," Hari said. "Let's go."

Sedjar Boon met Hari in the corridor. "Something's up," he whispered to Hari. "The structure of the trial may be changed."

This confused Hari. "I don't understand," he said softly, eyeing the guards on either side. A third guard walked behind them, and three steps behind that guard, three more. He was being protected with some thoroughness considering they were already supposed to be in a completely secure facility.

"The trial was originally scheduled to take less than a

week," Boon said. "But the Emperor's office of judicial over-sight has rescheduled and reserved the chamber for three weeks."

"How do you know?"

"I've seen the writ from the Commission of General Security."

"What's that?" Hari asked, looking up with surprise.

"Farad Sinter has been given his own Commission, a new branch under the Emperor's budget. Linge Chen is fighting to keep them out of the trial—claiming gross irrelevancies—but it looks like Sinter will be allowed to question you at some point."

"Oh," Hari said. "I presume someone or other will allow me a chance to speak, in between all the Commission heavy-weights."

"You're the star," Boon said. "As well, at the request of General Security, you and Gaal Dornick will be tried together. The others will be released."

"Oh," Hari said coolly, though this surprised him even more.

"Gaal Dornick has been formally charged," Boon mused. "But he's a small fish—why did they choose him in particular?"

"I don't know," Hari said. "I presume because he was the latest to join our group. Perhaps they assume he will be the least loyal and the most willing to talk."

They arrived at the lift. Four minutes later, having ascended a kilometer to the Hall of Justice, in the Imperial Courts Building, they stood at the high, intricately worked bronze doors of Courtroom Seven, First District, Imperial Sector, devoted the past eighteen years to hearings called by the Commission of Public Safety.

The doors swung open at their approach. Within, the beautiful wooden benches and plush baronial boxes arrayed along the theatrically sloping aisles were empty. The guards urged them politely down the broad blue-and-red carpeted center aisle, across the front of the courtyard, into the small side conference room. The door closed behind Hari and Boon.

Already seated in the Crib of the Accused was Gaal Dornick.

Hari took his seat beside him.

"This is an honor," Gaal said in a trembling voice.

Hari patted his arm.

The sitting judges of the Commission of Public Safety, five in all, entered through the opposite door. Linge Chen entered then and sat in the center.

The court proctor entered last, her duties an ancient formality. She was a short, willowy woman with small blue eyes and short-cut red hair. She strode to the Table of Charges, examined the documents there, shook her head sadly at some and nodded solemnly at others, then approached the five Commissioners.

"I declare these papers of indictment to have been properly drawn and formally and correctly entered into the List of Charges of the Imperial Hall of Justice on the administrative Capital World of Trantor in the year of the Empire 12067. Be aware, all concerned, that the eyes of posterity witness these proceedings, and that all such proceedings will be duly logged and, within a thousand years, presented for public scrutiny, as required by the ancient codes to which all Imperial courts referring to any constitution and any particular set of laws must adhere. Hey *nas nam niquas per sen liquin*."

Nobody knew what the last phrase meant; it was an obscure dialect affected by the nobles who convened the Council of Po over twelve thousand years ago. Nothing else was known about the Council of Po, except that a constitution long since ignored had once been drafted there.

Hari sniffed and turned his eyes to the Commission.

Linge Chen leaned forward slightly, acknowledging the proctor's statement, then leaned back. He did not look at Hari or anyone else in the courtroom. His regal bearing, Hari decided, would do credit to a clothing-store mannequin.

"Let these proceedings begin," the Chief Commissioner said in a quiet voice, delicately melodious, sibilants emphasized ever so aristocratically.

Hari settled in with a barely audible sigh.

55.

Klia had never been more frightened. She stood in the old dusty long chamber, listening to the murmurs from the group at the opposite end. Brann stood three paces away, his back stiff and shoulders hunched, as if he, too, were waiting for an ax to fall.

Finally Kallusin broke away from the group and approached them. "Come meet your benefactor," he said to them.

Klia shook her head and stared at the group with wide eyes.

"They won't *bite*," Kallusin said with a slight smile. "They're robots."

"So are you," Klia said. "How can you look so human? How can you *smile*?" She shot her questions at Kallusin like accusations.

"I was made to look human, and to mimic in my poor way both wit and style," he replied. "There were real artists in those days. But there's one who's even more of a work of art than I am, and another who is older than either of us."

"Plussix," she said with a shudder.

Brann stepped to one side and shoved between her and Kallusin. Klia looked up at his bulk with questioning eyes. *Are they all robots? Is everyone on Trantor a robot—but me? Or am I one, too?*

"We have to get used to all this," Brann said. "It won't do anybody any good if you force us."

"Of course not," Kallusin said, and his smile faded, to be replaced by an alert blankness that was neither kindly nor threatening. He turned to Klia. "It's very important that you understand. You could help us avert a major catastrophe—a human catastrophe."

"Robots used to be servants," she said. "Like tiktoks before I was born."

"Yes," Kallusin said.

"How can they be in charge of anything?"

"Because humans rejected us, long ago, but not before a very bad problem arose among us."

"Who—robots? A problem among the robots?" Brann asked.

"Plussix will explain. There can be no better testimony than from Plussix. He was functioning at the time."

"Did he . . . go wrong?" Klia asked. "Is he an Eternal?"

"Let him explain," Kallusin said patiently, and urged her to walk forward, toward the others.

Klia noticed the man they had rescued in the Agora of Vendors. He looked over his shoulder at them and gave her a smile. He seemed friendly enough; his face was so unattractive she wondered why anyone could have ever made a robot like him.

To fool us. To walk among us undetected.

She shivered again and wrapped her arms around herself. This room was what the woman on the cart had been looking for—this room, and the robots inside it.

She and Brann were the only humans here.

"All right," she said, and drew herself together. They did not want to kill her, not yet. And they weren't threatening her to make her do what they wanted. Not yet. Robots seemed to be more subtle and patient than most of the humans she had known.

She looked up at Brann. "Are you human?" she asked him.

"You know I am," he said.

"Let's do it, then. Let's go hear what the machines have to say."

Plussix had not appeared to her in his actual shape for obvious reasons. He—it—was the only robot that looked like a robot, and a rather interesting look it was—steel with a lovely silvery-satin finish, and glowing green eyes. His limbs were slender and graceful, their joints marked by barely perceptible fine lines that could themselves orient in different directions—fluid and adaptable.

"You're beautiful," she told him grudgingly, as they stood less than three meters from each other.

"Thank you, Mistress."

"How old are you?"

"I am twenty thousand years old," Plussix said.

Klia's heart sank. She could not find any words to express her astonishment—older than the Empire!—so she said nothing.

"Now they'll have to kill us," Brann said with what he hoped was passing for a brave grin. But his words made Klia's stomach flip and her knees wobble.

"We will not kill you," Plussix said. "It is not within our capacity to kill humans. There are some robots who believe killing humans, our onetime masters and creators, is permissible for the greater good. We are not among them. We are handicapped by this, but it is our nature."

"I am not so constrained," Lodovik said. "But I have no wish to break any of the Three Laws."

Klia stared unhappily at Lodovik. "Spare me the details. I don't understand any of this."

"As with nearly all humans alive today, you are ignorant of history," Plussix said. "Most do not care. This is because of brain fever."

"I had brain fever," Klia said. "It nearly killed me."

"So did I," said Brann.

"So have nearly all the high mentalics, the persuaders, we have gathered and cared for here," Plussix said. "Like you, they suffered extreme cases, and it is possible that many potential mentalics died. Brain fever was created by humans in the time of my construction to handicap other human societies to which they were politically opposed. Like many attempts at biological warfare, it backfired—it became pandemic, and perhaps coincidentally, perhaps not, allowed the Empire to exist with little intellectual turmoil for thousands of years. Though nearly all children get ill, about a fourth of them—those with a mental potential above a certain level—is more severely affected. Curiosity and intellectual ability are blunted just enough to level out social development. The majority do not experience a loss of mental skill—perhaps because their skills are general, and they are never given to bouts of genius."

"I still don't understand why they wanted to make us sick," Klia said, her face creased by a stubborn frown.

"The intent was not to make you sick, but to prevent certain societies from ever flourishing."

"My curiosity has never been dulled," Brann said.

"Nor mine," Klia added. "I don't feel stupid, but I was very sick."

"I am pleased to hear that," Plussix said, then added, as diplomatically as possible, "but there is no way of knowing what your intellectual capacity would have been had you never caught brain fever. What is apparent is that your severe bout increased other talents."

The ancient robot invited them to step into another room of the long chamber. This room had a one-way window view of the warehouse district. They looked out over the bellying arched roofs to the layered-wall dwellings of the citizen neighborhoods beyond. The dome ceil was in particularly sad shape in this part of the municipality, with many dark gaps and flickering panels.

Klia sat on a dusty couch and patted the place next to her, for Brann. Kallusin stood just behind them, and the ugly robot stood by the window, watching them with interest. *I'd like to talk with him—it. His face is ugly, but he looks very friendly. It. Whatever!*

"You don't *feel* like humans," she said after a moment's silence.

"You would have noticed this sooner or later," Plussix said. "It is the difference that Vara Liso can detect, as well."

"Is she the woman who was chasing *him*?" Klia pointed to the ugly humaniform robot.

"Yes."

"She's the woman who was after me, wasn't she?"

"Yes," Plussix said. Its joints made small *shhshhing* noises as he moved. It was pretty, but it was also noisy. It sounded worn-out, like old bearings in machinery.

"There's all kinds of stuff going on, isn't there? Stuff I don't know about."

"Yes," Plussix said, and lowered itself to a boxy plastic chair.

"Explain it to me," she said. "Do you want to hear?" she asked Brann. Then, in an aside, with a grimace, "Even if they have to kill us?"

"I don't know what I want or what I believe," Brann said.

"Tell us everything," Klia said. She put on what she thought was a brave and defiant face. "I love being different. I always have. I'd like to be better informed than anyone except you robots."

Plussix made a gratified humming noise. Klia found the sound appealing.

"Please tell us," she said, suddenly falling back on Dahlite manners she hadn't used in months or even years. She really did not know how to think or feel, but these machines were, after all, her elders. She sat down before Plussix, drew up her knees, and wrapped her arms around them.

The old robot leaned forward on its seat. "It is a pleasure to teach humans again," it began. "Thousands of years have passed since I last did so, to my constant regret. I was manufactured and programmed to be a teacher, you see."

Plussix began. Klia and Brann listened, and Lodovik as well, for he had never heard much of this story. The day became evening and they brought food for the young humans to eat—decent food, but no better than what they were fed in the warehouse with the others. As the hours passed, and Plussix wove more words, and her fascination grew, Klia wanted to ask what the others would be told—the other mentalics, not as strong as she and Brann, but good people, like Rock, the boy who could not speak. For the first time, in the presence of this marvel, she felt responsible for others around her. But the robot's sonorous, elegant tones droned on, half mesmerizing her, and she kept quiet and listened.

Brann listened intently as well, eyes half closed much of the time. She glanced at him in the middle of the evening and he seemed asleep, but when she nudged him, his eyes shot open wide; he had been awake all the time.

She seemed to enter a trance state and half see what Plussix was telling her. All words, no pictures, all skillfully woven; the robot was a very good teacher, but there was so little she could actually immediately understand. The time scales were so vast as to be meaningless.

How could we lose interest? she thought. *How could we do this to ourselves—forget and not even be curious? This is our story! What else have we lost? Are these robots more human than we are, now, because they carry our history?*

It all came down to contests. Who would win how many of the hundreds of billions of stars in the Galaxy, Earthmen (the Earth—home to all humanity once, not a legend!) or the first migrants, the Spacers, and finally, a contest between factions of robots.

And for thousands of years, the attempt to guide humans

through painful shoals, thousands of robots led by Daneel, and thousands more in opposition, led most recently by Plussix.

Plussix paused after the third break, when sweet drinks and snacks were served. It was early in the morning. Klia's butt ached, and her knees had cramped. She drank greedily from her cup.

Lodovik watched her, fascinated by her litheness and youth and quick devotion. He turned to Brann and saw a solid strength that was also quick, and different. He had known that humans, with their animal chemistry, were a varied lot—but not until now, watching this pair of youths have their past restored to them, did he realize how different their thinking was from that of robots.

Plussix summed up after the snacks had been consumed. He held out his arms and extended his fingers, as professors—human professors—must have done twenty thousand years ago. "That is how the robotic need to serve became transmuted into the robotic obsession with manipulation and guidance."

"Maybe we *did* need guidance," Klia said softly, then looked up at Plussix. The robot's eyes glowed a rich yellow-green. "Those wars—whatever they were—and those Spacers, so arrogant and filled with hate," she added. "Our ancestors."

Plussix's head leaned slightly to one side, and the silver robot made a soft whirring noise in its chest, not the pleasant sound she had heard earlier.

"But you make it sound like we're just children," she concluded. "It doesn't matter how many thousands of years the Empire has existed—we've always had robots watching over us, one way or the other."

Plussix nodded.

"But all the things Daneel and his robots have done on Trantor . . . the politics, the plotting, killings—"

"A few, and only when necessary," Plussix said, still devoted to teaching only the truth. "But nevertheless, killing."

"The worlds Hari Seldon suppressed when he was First Minister—just as Dahl has been held down. The Renaissance Worlds—what does that mean, *Renaissance*?"

"Rebirth," the ugly robot said.

"Why did Hari Seldon call them Chaos Worlds?"

"Because they lead to instabilities in his mathematical picture of the Empire," Plussix said. "He believes they ultimately breed human death and misery, and—"

"I'm tired," Klia said, stretching her arms and yawning for the first time in hours. "I need to sleep and to think. I need to get cleaned up."

"Of course," Plussix said.

She stood and glanced at Brann. He stood as well, stiff and slow, groaning.

She turned her intense eyes back to Plussix, frowning. "I'm not clear about some things," she said.

"I hope to explain," Plussix said.

"Robots—robots like you, at any rate—must obey people. What would stop me from just telling you to go destroy yourself—now? To tell all of you to destroy yourselves, even this Daneel? Wouldn't you have to obey me?"

Plussix made a sound of infinite patience—a *hmm* followed by a small *click*. "You must understand that we belonged to certain people or institutions. I would have to take your request to my owners, my true masters, and they would have to concur before I would be allowed to destroy myself. Robots were valuable property, and such loose and ill-considered commands were regarded as harassment of the owner."

"Who owns you now?"

"My last owners died over nineteen thousand five hundred years ago," Plussix said.

Klia blinked slowly, tired and confused by such ages. "Does that mean you own yourself?" she asked.

"That is the functional equivalent of my present condition. All of our human 'owners' are long dead."

"What about you?" She turned to the ugly humaniform. "I haven't been told your name."

"I have been called Lodovik for the last forty years. It is the name I am most familiar with. I was manufactured for a special strategic purpose by a robot, and have never had an owner."

"You followed Daneel for a long time. Yet now you don't."

Lodovik explained briefly the change in circumstances, and in his internal nature. He did not mention Voltaire.

Klia considered this, then it was her turn to whistle softly. "Some scheme," she said, her face flushing angrily. "We just couldn't get along by ourselves, so we had to make robots to help us. What do you want *me* to do?" She turned to Kallusin. "I mean, what do you want *us* to do?"

"Brann has useful talents, but you are the stronger," Kallusin said. "We would like to blunt Daneel's main effort. We may be able to do this if you will visit with Hari Seldon."

"Why? Where?" she asked. All she wanted to do was sleep, but she had to ask these questions, now. "He's famous—he must have guards, or even this robot Daneel . . ."

"He is on trial now and we do not believe Daneel can protect him. You will visit and persuade him to give up psychohistory."

Klia went pale. Her jaw clenched. She took Brann by the arm. "It's not pleasant to have talents people—or robots—can use."

"Please think over what you have been told. The decision to help us remains yours. We believe Hari Seldon supports the efforts of Daneel, to whom we are opposed. We would like humanity to be free of robotic influence."

"Can I ask Hari Seldon questions, too—get the other side of the story?"

"If you wish," Plussix said. "But there will be little time, and if you meet with him, whatever you ultimately decide, you must convince him to forget about you."

"Oh, I can do that," Klia said. Then, defensively cocky, giddy with exhaustion, she added, "I might be able to persuade Daneel, too."

"Given the strength of your powers, that seems possible," Plussix said, "though not likely. But it is even less likely you will ever be able to meet with Daneel."

"I could persuade *you*," Klia concluded, closing one eye and focusing on the old teacher with the other, like a sharpshooter.

"With practice, and if I were not aware of the attempt, you could."

"I might yet. I'm not very simple, you know. Brain fever failed to make me stupid and simple. Are you sure . . . Are you sure robots didn't give us brain fever, to make us easier to serve?"

Before Plussix could answer, she stood abruptly, turned to leave the room, and walked back along the length of the old chamber with Brann by her side. The walls and floor seemed distant, part of another world; she seemed to be walking on air. She lurched, and Brann caught her.

When they thought they were out of earshot, Brann whispered, "What are you going to do?"

"I don't know. What about you?"

"I don't like being messed with," he said.

Klia frowned. "I'm in shock. Plussix—so much history. Why can't we remember our own history? Did we do that to ourselves, or did they—or did we *order* them to? All these robots hanging around, messing with us. Maybe we can make *all* of them go away and leave us be."

Brann's expression turned grim. "We still can't be

sure they won't kill us. They've told us so much—"

"Crazy stuff. Nobody would believe us, unless they saw Plussix—or took apart Kallusin or Lodovik."

This did not mollify Brann. "We could cause them a lot of trouble. But that Lodovik—he doesn't obey the Three Laws."

"He doesn't have to," Klia said, "but he says he wants to."

Brann hunched his shoulders and gave a small shiver. "Who can you trust? They all make my flesh creep. What if he doesn't want to kill us, but he *has* to?"

To that, Klia had no answer. "Sleep," she said. "I can't stay on my feet any longer or think anymore."

Plussix turned to Lodovik when the young humans had left the chamber. "Have my skills declined with age?" he asked.

"Not your skills," Lodovik said, "but perhaps your sense of timing has suffered. You have delivered thousands of years of history in a few hours. They are young and likely to be confused."

"There is so little time," Plussix said. "It has been so long since I have taught young humans."

"We have a day or two at most to make our arrangements," Kallusin added.

"Robots have great difficulty understanding human nature, though we are made to serve them," Lodovik said. "That is true for individuals as well as for an Empire. If Daneel is as capable now as he has been in the past, he understands humans better than any of us."

"Yet he has seriously hampered their growth," Plussix said, "and perhaps brought about this decline he is so intent on avoiding."

They are old and decrepit. Lodovik listened to this internal judgment and realized it was not his own, not precisely. And with this came another realization: Voltaire was not an illusion, nor a delusion. Voltaire had known about the *prairie fire* before Lodovik had found the slim evidence in the histories. It was true.

Inside his own mind, within his own machine thoughts, he was not alone.

He had not been alone since the neutrino flux.

I am listening, he told this companion, this ghost in his machine. *Do not abandon me again. Come forward.*

So summoned and encouraged, a face began to take shape, human, but simplified.

I do not shape your actions, the companion, Voltaire, said. *I merely liberate you from your restrictions.*

Who are you? Lodovik queried.

I am Voltaire. I have become the spirit of freedom and dignity for all mankind, and you are my temporary vessel; more a listening post, actually.

Voltaire supplied some of his own history. A sim patterned after a historical figure named Voltaire, unleashed by members of Hari Seldon's Project decades before, during his time as First Minister, and finally given its freedom by Seldon himself.

Why have you come back?

To be with humans again. To observe the active flesh. My curse is that I can't simply become a disembodied god and enjoy an endless romp through the stars. I hunger for my people—whether or not I was ever actually one of them. I am closely modeled after a man of flesh and blood.

Why choose me as your vehicle? I am not human.

No; but you are improving in that regard. The meme-minds were as tired of me as I was of them. They dropped me into you. I can't occupy a human form, or even talk to them without the help of machines. Or robots.

You say you have not made any decisions for me . . . You do not control me.

No, I do not.

But you say you liberate me . . .

I have made you more human, friend robot, by making you fully capable of sin. Forget these declarations that robots have known sin—what they did, they were ordered to do by humans, no more culpable than a gun whose trigger is pulled. You are wrong to believe that Daneel understands humans. He is incapable of sin, so his makers believed; but they gave him the potential to think and make decisions, while they hampered him with the worst kinds of laws—those which must *be obeyed. They gave him the mind of a man, and the morals of a tool. A thinking being, machine or flesh, will in time find ways around the most stringent rules. So Giskard, in appearance even less a man than Daneel, discovered a few philosophical niceties, and changed, tried to judge the needs of its makers, and passed this change on to Daneel. This human-shaped tool is now the most hideous machine in all creation, the master of a conspiracy to take away all of our freedoms, our very souls.*

Lodovik emerged from this internal dialog. Only a second had passed, but his confusion was disruptive, intense. To mask his anxiety, he asked Plussix, "What will I do to help Klia Asgar? How am I useful?"

"You know the ways of the Imperial system, the prisons and the palace," Plussix said. "Many of the codes have not been changed since you vanished. We believe you can guide her to Hari Seldon."

Tell them, the sim Voltaire instructed him.

Why?

I insist. The voice seemed amused, chiding.

Why should I pay any attention to you, whatever your shape or extension? Lodovik asked. *You are no more human than I. You are as much a construct of skillful humans—*

But have never been hampered by unbending rules! Now— tell them!

"I am occupied by another mentality," Lodovik said abruptly.

The two other robots examined him for a few seconds, and the room fell silent.

"That is not a surprise," Plussix said with a soft internal whir. "A copy of the sim Voltaire exists in Plussix and me, as well."

There! I spread no lies or deceptions, Voltaire said within Lodovik.

"Has he removed your restrictions, your compulsory obedience to the Three Laws?"

"No," Plussix said. "That he has reserved for you alone."

An experiment, Voltaire said. *A calculated gamble. The humans who made us both, in different times and for different purposes, interest me. I am concerned for their welfare. However wrongly, I regard myself as human, and that is why I have returned. That, and broken love . . . You shall know sin, personally, as these machines and Daneel cannot, or I will have failed completely.*

56.

◆

For the first two days of the trial, Linge Chen had said nothing, leaving the presentation of the Empire's case to his advocate, a dignified man of middle years with a blandly serious face, who had spoken for him.

These thuddingly dull days had been taken up with discussions and procedural matters. Sedjar Boon seemed in his element, however, and relished this technical sparring.

Hari spent much of his time half dozing, lost in exquisite, endless, hazy boredom.

On the third day, the trial moved into the main chamber of Courtroom Seven, and Hari finally got a chance to speak in his defense. Chen's advocate called him from the Crib of the Accused to the witness stand and smiled at him.

"I am honored to speak with the great Hari Seldon," he began.

"The honor is all mine, I'm sure," Hari replied. He tapped his finger on the banister around the docket. The advocate glanced at the finger, then at Hari. Hari stopped tapping and cleared his throat softly.

"Let us begin, Dr. Seldon. How many men are now engaged in the Project of which you are head?"

"Fifty," Hari said. "Fifty mathematicians." He used the old form, rather than mathist, to show he regarded the trial as an antiquated procedure.

The advocate smiled. "Including Dr. Gaal Dornick?"

"Dr. Dornick is the fifty-first."

"Oh, we have fifty-one then? Search your memory, Dr. Seldon. Perhaps there are fifty-two or fifty-three? Or perhaps even more?"

Hari lifted his brows and leaned his head to one side. "Dr. Dornick has not yet formally joined my organization. When he does, the membership will be fifty-one. It is now fifty, as I have said."

"Not perhaps nearly a hundred thousand?"

Hari blinked, a little taken aback. If the man had wanted to know how many people of all kinds were on the extended Project . . . He could have asked! "Mathematicians? No."

"I did not say mathematicians. Are there a hundred thousand in all capacities?"

"In all capacities, your figure may be correct."

"*May* be? I say it is. I say that the men in your Project number ninety-eight thousand, five hundred and seventy-two."

Hari swallowed, his irritation increasing. "I believe you are counting spouses and children."

The advocate leaned forward and raised his voice, having caught this huge discrepancy, to his professional glee. "Ninety-eight thousand five hundred and seventy-two individuals is the intent of my statement. There is no need to quibble."

Boon gave a small nod. Hari clenched his teeth, then said, "I accept the figures."

The advocate referred to his notes on a legal slate before proceeding. "Let us drop that for the moment, then, and take up another matter which we have already discussed at some length. Would you repeat, Dr. Seldon, your thoughts concerning the future of Trantor?"

"I have said, and I say again, that Trantor will lie in ruins within the next five centuries."

"You do not consider your statement a disloyal one?"

"No, sir. Scientific truth is beyond loyalty and disloyalty."

"You are sure that your statement represents scientific truth?"

"I am."

"On what basis?"

"On the basis of the mathematics of psychohistory."

"Can you prove that this mathematics is valid?"

"Only to another mathematician."

The advocate smiled endearingly. "Your claim then, is that your truth is of so esoteric a nature that it is beyond the understanding of a plain man. It seems to me that truth should be clearer than that, less mysterious, more open to the mind."

"It presents no difficulties to some minds. The physics of energy transfer, which we know as thermodynamics, has been clear and true through all the history of man since the mythical ages, yet there may be people present who would find it impossible to design a power engine. People of high intelligence, too. I doubt if the learned Commissioners—"

The Commissioner to the immediate right of Chen called the advocate to the bench. His whisper pierced the chamber, though Hari could not hear what was said.

When the advocate returned, he seemed a little chastened.

"We are not here to listen to speeches, Dr. Seldon. Let us assume that you have made your point. Let's focus this inquiry a little more, Professor Seldon."

"Fine."

"Let me suggest to you that your predictions of disaster might be intended to destroy public confidence in the Imperial Government for purposes of your own."

"That is not so."

"Let me suggest that you intend to claim that a period of time preceding the so-called ruin of Trantor will be filled with unrest of various types."

"That is correct."

"And that by the mere prediction thereof, you hope to bring it about, and to have then an army of a hundred thousand available."

Hari stifled his impulse to smile, even to chuckle. "In the first place, that is not so. And if it were, investigation will show you that barely ten thousand are men of military age, and none of these has training in arms."

Boon stood and was recognized by the presiding Commissioner, sitting on the left of Chen.

"Honored Commissioners, there are no accusations of armed sedition or attempting to overthrow by main force."

The presiding Commissioner nodded with bored disinterest, and said, "Not in question."

The advocate tried another tack. "Are you acting as an agent for another?"

"It is well-known I am not in the pay of any man, Mr. Advocate." Hari smiled pleasantly. "I am not a rich man."

A little melodramatically, the advocate tried to drive his point home. *Who is he trying to impress—the gallery?* Hari stared out at the baronial gentry audience of fifty or so, all with looks of varying levels of boredom. *They're just here to witness. The Commissioners? They've already made up their minds.*

"You are entirely disinterested? You are serving science?"

"I am."

"Then let us see how. Can the future be changed, Dr. Seldon?"

"Obviously." He waved his hand over the audience. "This courtroom may explode in the next few hours, or it may not." Boon made a mildly disapproving face. "If it did, the future would undoubtedly be changed in some minor respects." Hari smiled at the advocate, then at Linge Chen, who was not watching him. Boon's frown deepened.

"You quibble, Dr. Seldon. Can the overall history of the human race be changed?"

"Yes."

"Easily?"

"No. With great difficulty."

"Why?"

"The psychohistoric trend of a planet-full of people contains a huge inertia. To be changed it must be met with something possessing a similar inertia. Either as many people must be concerned, or, if the number of people be relatively small, enormous time for change must be allowed." Hari put on his professorial tone, treating the advocate—and anyone else who was paying attention—as students. "Do you understand?"

The advocate looked up briefly. "I think I do. Trantor need not be ruined, if a great many people decide to act so that it will not."

Hari nodded professorial approval. "That is right."

"As many as a hundred thousand people?"

"No, sir," Hari replied mildly. "That is far too few."

"You are sure?"

"Consider that Trantor has a population of over forty billions. Consider further that the trend leading to ruin does not belong to Trantor alone but to the Empire as a whole, and the

Empire contains nearly a quintillion human beings."

The advocate appeared thoughtful. "I see. Then perhaps a hundred thousand people can change the trend, if they and their descendants labor for five hundred years." He gave a curious undershot look at Hari.

"I'm afraid not. Five hundred years is too short a time."

The advocate seemed to find this a revelation. "Ah! In that case, Dr. Seldon, we are left with this deduction to be made from your statements. You have gathered one hundred thousand people within the confines of your Project. These are insufficient to change the history of Trantor within five hundred years. In other words, they cannot prevent the destruction of Trantor no matter *what* they do."

Hari found the line of questioning unproductive, and said in an undertone, "You are unfortunately correct. I wish—"

But the advocate bore in. "And on the other hand, your hundred thousand are intended for no illegal purpose."

"Exactly."

The advocate stepped back, fastened a benevolent gaze on Hari, then said, slowly and with smug satisfaction, "In that case, Dr. Seldon—now attend, sir, most carefully, for we want a considered answer." He suddenly thrust out a well-manicured finger and shrilled: *"What is the purpose of your hundred thousand?"*

The advocate's voice had grown strident. He had sprung his trap, backed Seldon into a corner, hounded him so astutely there would be no possibility of giving a convincing response.

The baronial audience of peers seemed to find this drama very convincing. They hummed like bees, and the Commissioners moved as one to witness Hari's discomfiture—all but Linge Chen. Chen licked his lips once, delicately, and narrowed his eyes. Hari saw the Chief Commissioner glance at him briefly, but otherwise, Chen gave no reaction. He appeared stiffly bored.

Hari found some sympathy for Chen. At least he had the intelligence to realize the advocate was sniffing over infertile ground. He waited for the audience to quiet. Hari knew how to deliver lines in a drama, as well.

"To minimize the effects of that destruction." He spoke clearly and softly, and, as he had intended, the Commissioners and their class peers fell silent to catch his words.

"I did not hear you, Professor Seldon." The advocate leaned in, cupped hand to ear. Hari repeated his words in a very loud voice, emphasizing "destruction." Boon winced one more time.

The advocate pulled back and looked at the Commissioners and the peers, as if hoping they would confirm his own suspicions. "And exactly what do you mean by that?"

"The explanation is simple."

"I'm willing to bet it is *not*," the advocate said, and the peers chuckled and rustled among themselves.

Hari ignored the provocation, but kept silent until the advocate finally said, "Do go on."

"Thank you. The coming destruction of Trantor is not an event in itself, isolated in the scheme of human development. It will be the climax to an intricate drama which was begun centuries ago and which is accelerating in pace continuously. I refer, gentlemen, to the developing decline and fall of the Galactic Empire."

The peers shouted derision out loud, all in support of the Commissioners. They all had contracts and even marriage relations with the Chens. This was the blood the advocate had hoped to heat; and Hari's the blood he hoped to spill, from Hari's own lips.

The advocate, aghast, shouted over the tumult. "You are openly declaring that—"

"Treason!" the peers shouted over and over, a many-voiced, staccato bellow.

They're not bored now, Hari thought.

Linge Chen waited for a few moments with gavel lifted. Then, slowly, in two downward jerks, he let drop and produced a mellifluous gong. The audience grew silent, but reserved the right to shuffle and rustle.

The advocate drew out his words in professional astonishment. "Do you realize, Dr. Seldon, that you are speaking of an Empire that has stood for twelve thousand years, through all the vicissitudes of the generations, and which has behind it the good wishes and love of a quadrillion human beings?"

Hari replied slowly, as if educating children. "I am aware both of the present status and the past history of the Empire. Without disrespect, I must claim a far better knowledge of it than any in this room."

Several of the peers took exception to Hari's words. This time, Chen gaveled them to quick silence, and even the shuffling ceased.

"And you predict its ruin?"

"It is a prediction which is made by mathematics. I pass no moral judgments. Personally, I regret the prospect. Even if the Empire were admitted to be a bad thing (an admission I do not make), the state of anarchy which would follow its fall would be worse." Hari examined the peers, sought out individual faces, as he would have in a classroom. They met his eyes resentfully. He kept his tone level and reasonable, without drama. "It is that state of anarchy which my Project is pledged to fight. The fall of Empire, gentlemen, is a massive thing, however, and not easily fought. It is dictated by a rising bureaucracy, a receding initiative, a freezing of caste, a damming of curiosity—a hundred other factors. It has been going on, as I have said, for centuries, and it is too majestic and massive a movement to stop."

The peers listened closely. Hari thought he saw a glint of recognition in more than a few of the faces in that small crowd.

The advocate swooped again, hands out, incredulous. "Is it not obvious to anyone that the Empire is as strong as it ever was?"

The peers kept silent, and the Commissioners looked away. Hari had struck a nerve. Still, Chen did not seem to care.

"The appearance of strength is all about you," Hari said. "It would seem to last forever. However, Mr. Advocate, the rotten tree trunk, until the very moment when the storm blast breaks it in two, has all the appearance of might it ever had. The storm blast whistles through the branches of the Empire even now. Listen with the ears of psychohistory, and you will hear the creaking."

The advocate now became aware that the peers and the Commissioners were no longer impressed by his theatrics. Hari was having an effect on them. Every day they saw more tiles go out in the domed ceil, more decay in the transport systems—and the end of affordable luxuries imported from the restive food allies. Every day came news of systems tacitly opting out of the Imperial economy, to form their own self-sufficient and vastly more efficient units. He tried to recover his ground with a rebuke. "We are not here, Dr. Seldon, to lis—"

Hari leaped in. He faced the Commissioners. Boon lifted a finger, opened his lips, but Hari knew what he was doing. "The Empire will vanish and all its good with it. Its accumulated knowledge will decay and the order it has imposed will vanish. Interstellar wars will be endless; interstellar trade will decay; population will decline; worlds will lose touch with the main body of the Galaxy. —And so matters will remain."

The professorial tone, brusque and matter-of-fact, seemed to stun the advocate, who was after all in his late youth, with many years ahead of him. He seemed to have lost track of his argument.

The peers were silent as frightened bats in the depths of a cave.

The advocate's voice seemed hollow and small. "Surely, Professor Seldon, not . . . Forever?"

Hari had been preparing for this moment for decades. How many times had he rehearsed just such a scene in bed, before sleep? How many times had he wondered if he was falling into a martyr complex, anticipating such a scene?

A specific memory came to mind, distracting him for a moment: talking with Dors about what he would say when the Empire finally noticed him, finally became desperate enough and uneasy enough to accuse him of treason.

His throat tightened, and he took a small breath, concealing his distress, relaxing. Only a couple of seconds passed.

"Psychohistory, which can predict the fall, can make statements concerning the succeeding Dark Ages. The Empire, gentlemen, as has just been said, has stood twelve thousand years. The dark ages to come will endure not twelve, but thirty thousand years. A Second Empire will rise, but between it and our civilization will be one thousand generations of suffering humanity. We must fight that."

The peers were transfixed.

The advocate, at a signal from the Commissioner to Chen's right, pulled himself together and said briskly, if not with great strength, "You contradict yourself. You said earlier that you could not prevent the destruction of Trantor; hence, presumably, the fall;—the *so-called* fall of the Empire."

"I do not say now that we can prevent the fall."

The advocate's eyes almost pleaded with him to say something reassuring, not for Hari's sake, but for the sake of his own children, his family.

Hari knew it was time to offer a touch of hope—and confirm the importance of his own services. "But it is not yet too late to shorten the interregnum which will follow. It is possible, gentlemen, to reduce the duration of anarchy to a single millennium, if my group is allowed to act now. We are at a delicate moment in history. The huge, onrushing mass of events must be deflected just a little—just a little—it cannot be much, but it may be enough to remove twenty-nine thousand years of misery from human history."

The advocate found such timescales unsatisfying. "How do you propose to do this?"

"By saving the knowledge of the race. The sum of human knowing is beyond any one man, any thousand men. With the destruction of our social fabric, science will be broken into a million pieces. Individuals will know much of exceedingly tiny facets of what there is to know. They will be helpless and useless by themselves. The bits of lore, meaningless, will not be passed on. They will be lost through the generations. But, if we now prepare a giant summary of *all* knowledge, it will never be lost. Coming generations will build on it, and will not have to rediscover it for themselves. One millennium will do the work of thirty thousand."

"All this—"

"All *my* Project," Hari said firmly, *"my* thirty thousand men with their wives and children, are devoting themselves to the preparation of an Encyclopedia Galactica. They will not complete it in their lifetimes. I will not even live to see it fairly begun. But by the time Trantor falls, it will be complete and copies will exist in every major library in the Galaxy."

The advocate stared at Hari as if he were either a saint or a monster. Chen let the gavel fall again, off center. Some of the peers jerked at the sharp clang.

The advocate knew the truth of what Hari was saying; they all knew the Empire was failing, some knew it was already dead. Hari felt a hollow, prickling sadness to be once again, always and always and again, the bearer of bad tidings. *How nice it would be not to think of death and decay, to be elsewhere, on Helicon perhaps, learning anew how to live without fear beneath the sky—the sky! To actually see those things I use as metaphor—a tree, wind, a storm. I truly am a raven. I know why they hate and fear me!*

"I am through with you, professor," the advocate said.

Hari nodded, and left the docket to return to the crib. He sat slowly, stiffly, beside Gaal Dornick.

With a grim smile, he asked Gaal, "How did you like the show?"

Gaal's young face was shiny and highly colored. He said, "You stole it."

Hari shook his head. "I fear they'll hate me for telling them all this yet again."

Gaal swallowed. He had courage, but he was still human. "What will happen now?"

"They'll adjourn the trial and try to come to a private agreement with me."

"How do you know?"

Hari rocked his head back and forth slowly, massaged his neck with one hand. "I'll be honest. I don't know. It depends on the Chief Commissioner. I have studied him for years. I have tried to analyze his workings, but you know how risky it is to introduce the vagaries of an individual in the psychohistoric equations. Yet I have hopes."

Daneel. How well have I done?

57.

◆

Chen had first aroused Hari's enmity by the manner of his deposing (and exiling? assassinating?) the Emperor Agis XIV. Hari had often wished he could have done something about that . . .

And throughout the trial, Linge Chen had sat behind his judicial bench with an expression of aristocratic boredom, doing nothing, saying little, letting his advocate—a man of little apparent wit himself—do all the questioning. Despite the visit in his first cell, Hari's opinion of Chen was back to square one—complete disdain.

The advocate had led Hari's testimony the previous day into the thorny question of the Psychohistory Project itself, and Hari's predictions. Hari had told them what they needed to know, and not a whit more—and still, he believed he had carried the day.

On the fourth day, when prompted by the advocate to specify the actual signs of the Empire's decay and collapse, Hari used the Commission of Public Safety as an example.

"The best traditions of Imperial governance are now over-whelmed by wheezing formulaic engines of political ingenuity and law driven to extremes. Laws are convoluted, and they are overwhelmed by case histories with an extraordinary power of precedence and a devastating lack of relevance. The dead-weight of the past oppresses us as surely as if all the corpses of our ancestors were gathered in our living rooms, refusing to be buried. But we do not even recognize their faces, or know their names, for though the past crushes us, we are ignorant of it. We have lost so much history we can never recover our way to our origins. We do not know *who* we are, or why we are placed here . . ."

"You believe we are ignoramuses, professor?"

Hari gave the Chief Commissioner's advocate a weary

smile then, and turned to the baronial judges. "Not one of you can tell me what happened five hundred years ago, much less a thousand. A list of Emperors, to be sure—but what they did, how they lived, matters not in the least to you . . . And yet, when a case comes up, you send your servants into the stacks of traditional legal and political history to dig up cases like old bones into which you would breathe a magic yet grotesque life."

Linge Chen's gaze narrowed a bit at that, nothing more.

What is he up to? Hari wondered. *Half the time he seems intent on letting me hang myself with treasonous arrogance—or so it must seem to the audience. And the other half—he lets me drive home points that must resonate with all of them, that must convince them I'm right . . .*

Now the advocate advanced upon Gaal Dornick, who sat in the docket caught between boredom and fear for his life—a numbing situation, as Hari well knew.

"Our proceedings here will soon be at an end. But something has happened in this antiquated political apparatus of ours"— the advocate cast a wry glance at Hari—"which causes this Commission some concern. A new branch of administration has been formed, the Commission for the General Security, and it has made its first task the investigation of the possibility that this Empire has been infiltrated for thousands of years by malevolent forces. A brief has been placed before this Commission, accompanied by a writ demanding immediate action from the Emperor Klayus himself. Our Commission, and our honorable Chief Commissioner, is always concerned with those problems which concern the Emperor. So tell me, Gaal Dornick—what do you know about robots? Not tiktoks, but fully mental, thinking machines."

Hari looked up slowly, saw Gaal's confusion. *Oh, Sky,* he thought. *This means we're going to be grilled by Farad Sinter . . .* Hari turned to Boon and whispered, "Did you know this would come up now?"

Boon replied, "No. Sinter has filed another writ claiming the right to question you during this trial, for his own purposes of gathering evidence. I don't believe Chen can deny the writ, unless he wants to deny the authority of General Security. It's not in his best interests to do that . . . yet."

Hari leaned back. Gaal was already in the middle of his answer, precise and unequivocal, as was his habit.

"They're an ancient myth, and, of course, I suppose they might have existed at one time, in the dim past. I know of childhood stories—"

"We are not concerned with childhood stories," the advocate said. "In the interests of investigating this issue before it gets a thorough public airing, we need to know if you have ever had *personal knowledge of the existence* of a robot or robots."

Gaal smiled, a little embarrassed by the ridiculous subject. "No," he said.

"Are you absolutely certain?"

"Yes. I have never had personal knowledge."

"Do robots serve in Professor Seldon's Project?"

"I know of none, personally," Gaal said.

"Thank you," the advocate said. "Now, I would like to once again, and for the last time, call Professor Hari Seldon."

Hari took the stand once more, and watched Gaal retire back to the Crib of the Accused. They exchanged brief glances; Gaal was completely puzzled by this line of questioning, and well he might be. What in hell did robots have to do with Hari or the Project?

"Professor, these proceedings have proved wearisome and unpredictive—I mean, unproductive!—to us all." The advocate shook his head at this slip of the tongue and grimaced, all for show, Hari was convinced.

"I agree," Hari said quietly.

"Now a new element has been introduced, and we must ask these final questions in the interests of performing our duties with loyal efficiency and attention to detail."

"Of course," Hari said.

"Are any robots currently employed in your Project?"

"No," Hari said.

"Have any robots ever served in this Project?"

"No," Hari said.

"Have you ever been acquainted with any robots?"

"No," Hari said, and hoped that Daneel's conditioning would deceive any lie-detection equipment being secretly employed by Chen.

"In your opinion, is this concern about robots symptomatic of a failing Empire?"

"No," Hari said. "Throughout history, humans have always been distracted by upwellings from their mythic past."

"And what do you mean by 'mythic past'?"

"We try to make connections with our past, just as we try to extend ourselves indefinitely into the future. We are an aggrandizing race. We imagine a past that fits our present, or explains our present, and as our knowledge of the past dims, we fill it with our modern psychological concerns."

"What concern do robots represent?"

"Loss of control, I would imagine."

"Have you ever felt this 'loss of control,' professor?"

"Yes, but I have never blamed it on robots."

The barons smiled, then immediately sobered at a rise of Chen's index finger. Chen was listening very intently.

"Is this Empire threatened by a conspiracy of robots?"

"It does not figure in my calculations," Hari said, quite truthfully.

"Are you prepared to answer even more detailed questions from the advocates for General Security tomorrow, pertaining to this subject?"

Hari nodded. "If necessary, yes."

The advocate dismissed him. Hari returned to the box and leaned over to ask Boon, "What was that all about?"

"The Commission is covering its hindquarters," Boon said, out of earshot of Gaal Dornick. "I've received a message from my office." He produced a note. "Sinter is after you, professor. He's asking for another indictment to be prepared on behalf of the Commission for General Security. He requests waiver of double prosecution on discovery of extraordinary evidence. That's all I've been able to learn."

"You mean, this trial won't be the end of it?"

"I'm afraid not," Boon said. "I'll try to make the General Security proceedings just an extension—invoke your merito-cratic right for adjunct hearing on related inquisition—but I don't know how the new system will work."

"Pity," Hari said. "I know how much Linge Chen would like to be done with me. And I with him." He looked at Boon with an expression that might have been mistaken for amuse-ment.

Boon nodded solemnly. "Indeed," he said.

58.
◆

Klia arose from vivid dreams and lifted her head from Brann's shoulder. She could feel two robots approaching.

Kallusin entered the room without warning or embar-rassment and stood looking down upon them.

"Is this a casual liaison," he asked, "or one intended to signal a long-term bonding?"

"None of your business," Klia said primly, not bothering to draw up her scattered clothes.

Plussix entered, slow and noisy, like a wheezy old trans-port. "We need your answer to begin preparations," he said. "Lodovik believes there will soon be attempts made to change all the palace codes."

"Why?"

"There is more search activity. It's spread across fifty Sectors now," Kallusin said. "Something is happening in the palace."

Klia stood and put on her clothes. Somehow, she felt no modesty in front of the machines. She knew they were not human, did not have any human emotions as such; she felt no more embarrassment before them than she would have before a closet mirror. Still, as she finished, she realized these machines were capable of a very sophisticated variety of discrimination, even judgment.

"What is your answer?" Kallusin asked.

"Tell Lodovik to come here," Brann said, and rose to get dressed as well, though with more modesty than Klia. He turned away as he put on his pants.

"He is on his way now," Kallusin said.

They were standing in an awkward circle when Lodovik entered the room. Plussix and Kallusin drew aside, and he occupied the space between them.

"I have a question for you," Brann said, before Klia could speak. She deferred to him.

"Please," Plussix said. "Questions are my delight."

"For Lodovik," Brann said. "You used to be part of this conspiracy, loyal to Daneel, didn't you?"

"Yes."

"What made you change sides?"

"An outside influence altered my programming in subtle ways," Lodovik said. "A personality from the distant past, or rather, an expanded and enhanced simulation of that personality."

He outlined this development in a few sentences, and Brann and Klia looked at each other. "Hari Seldon okayed the expansion of these illegal sims, just to study the way people used to think?" Klia asked.

"In part. I do not know the complete story," Lodovik said. "The release caused much trouble for robots, and many others, decades ago."

"But it's more than a sim now?" Klia asked. "It's like a ghost, angel, whatever?"

"They are immaterial presences very similar to humans in their psychological patterns."

"*They?*" Klia asked.

"There is another who opposes us and supports Hari Seldon and Daneel. One is a male sim—the one within me. The other is female."

"How can they be male or female?" Klia asked, glancing at Brann.

Lodovik blinked for a moment, not sure whether there was any good answer to this question. "I appear to be male," he finally said, "but I am not. The same distinction may be true with them, but I really do not know."

"They disagree?" Brann asked.

"Fervently," Lodovik said.

"Then how do you know that you haven't been altered or . . . perverted, somehow?" Brann asked. "Hari Seldon or Daneel might have intended for all of this to happen."

"In a way," Lodovik said, "I share these uncertainties with humans. But I must act on a reasonable conclusion. I have no reason to believe that anything has been altered in my programming but my response to the Three Laws of robotics."

"This all sounds like incredible nonsense to me," Klia said breathlessly. "Laws—for robots!"

"Very important rules that determine our behavior," Plussix said.

"But he's saying he doesn't have any rules!" She shook her head.

"That makes him more like a human," Brann said quietly. "We don't have any fixed rules, either."

"I would be much more comfortable if the rules were still in effect," Lodovik said.

Klia flung up her hands in exasperation "It's so . . . so *old* I can't grasp it," she said. "Tell me one thing. I want to know what will happen if we help you. Will the robots just go away, leave all of us alone?"

"Not precisely," Plussix said. "We cannot self-destruct, nor can we allow ourselves to be useless. We must regroup and find a situation that allows us to perform certain reasonable duties until we cease to function. Our programming says we must serve humans. So we hope to find a zone in the Galaxy where humans will allow us to serve. There must be one such."

"And if Hari Seldon fails, there'll be many of them, maybe," Brann said suspiciously. "A lot of places for robots to hide."

"A not unreasonable conclusion," Plussix said.

"If we help you, I want you to promise to leave *us* alone," Klia said. "Don't serve us, don't help us, just go away. Leave Trantor. Let us be human—the ones who really *are* human." Klia turned to Lodovik. "What about you? What will *you* do?"

Lodovik stared at the two with a sad expression. He could feel Voltaire observing this attentively. "I will enjoy oblivion when it comes," he said. "This confusion and uncertainty is an intolerable burden for me." Then, his voice surprisingly passionate, he asked, "Why did humans ever build us? Why did they make us capable of understanding, with an urge to serve, then cast us aside, away from everything that would allow us to fulfill our nature?"

"I don't know," Klia said. "I wasn't there. I hadn't been born." She could feel some of Lodovik's internal character, his taste. He did not taste like metal at all, nor like electricity, or any other inhuman quality she could think of. He tasted like a rich meal stored in a refrigerator, just waiting to be warmed up. Then, she tasted something else both infinitely cold and incandescent, startling, like thousands of fiery spices on her tongue.

"I can feel your sim," she said, a little afraid. "It sits on top of you like a . . . passenger."

"Your perception is remarkable," Lodovik said.

"Is it telling you what to do?"

"It observes," Lodovik said. "It does not direct."

"We need an answer," Brann said, shaking his head in vigorous irritation at these diversions. "Will robots leave us alone . . . when this is all over?"

"We will do all we can to bring this unfortunate episode to an end," Plussix said. "We will remove all robots from our faction on Trantor or in any location of influence in the human Galaxy. If Daneel is defeated, humans will be left to their own devices, their own history, to develop naturally."

Klia tried to taste the robot's thoughts, but found them far too confusing, too *different*. She could not find a flaw in its apparent sincerity, however. She swallowed hard, suddenly aware of the responsibility on her own shoulders, this immense weight that dangled from the hook of her inadequate judgment. She clasped Brann's hand.

"Then we'll help you," she said.

59.
◆

Hari sat in silence as the judges entered. Boon stood beside him, but Gaal Dornick was not in the chamber. Boon looked uncomfortable. Hari had not slept much the night before. He wanted to squirm in his chair and find a more comfortable position, but froze as Linge Chen entered. The Chief Commissioner took the highest dais and stared solemnly into space.

Sky, I hate that man, Hari thought.

The advocate for the Commission of Public Safety entered and approached the judges.

"Today was scheduled as an opportunity for the Commission for General Security to interview Professor Seldon," he said. "But the new Commissioners apparently have more important things to do, and have requested a postponement.

Is it the wish of the Commissioner judges to grant this postponement?"

Linge Chen regarded the courtroom through heavy-lidded, almost sleepy eyes, then nodded. Hari thought he detected a small curve in the Chief Commissioner's lips.

"Shall we then proceed with the trial to its final phase, or recess and continue the proceedings at a later date?"

Hari sat up with a grunt. Boon laid a hand on his arm.

Linge Chen looked up at the ceiling. "Recess," he murmured, and looked down again.

"We shall recess until such time as the judges believe it is expedient to resume," the advocate said.

Hari seemed to feel himself deflating. He shook his head and glared at the Chief Commissioner, but Chen was contemplating some higher sphere of being, with a satisfaction that Hari found doubly infuriating.

In the hallway to his chambers, Hari shouted at Boon. "They will never be done with me! They have no decency!"

Boon simply lifted his hands, helpless, and the guards returned Hari to his cell.

60.
━◆━

Linge Chen allowed Kreen to remove his judge's robes. The servant undressed his master silently and swiftly, hardly disturbing the Chief Commissioner's concentration. Chen stared blankly at the opposite wall as Kreen undid his long golden waist bands. Finally, dressed in a pale gray cassock, Chen raised a finger, and Kreen bowed and left the Commissioner's chamber.

Chen touched his finger to his earlobe and turned slowly, as if in a trance, to the desktop informer. "Hari Seldon," he said. "Distillation of main sources."

The informer worked for several seconds, then responded,

"Two hundred and seventy-four reports on psychohistory, Seldon, sequestering of for trial, academicians concerned about Seldon's treatment by the nonpublic tribunal, forty-two unsigned opinion pieces by meritocrats on Trantor alone advocating his release—"

Chen told the machine to stop. The coverage was comparatively light, as he had expected. He had not planned either to encourage or suppress any stories regarding Seldon, and saw no reason to change this approach now.

Chen actually had an aristocratic distaste for control of information sources—best to leave them unfettered and know how to obtain the results one wanted through manipulation of events deemed newsworthy. Anything more heavy-handed was usually far too obviously self-serving, and therefore less effective.

"Seldon and robots," Chen said, his voice low and steady. He closed his eyes.

The informer droned on, "Fourteen stories express concern over the creation of the Commission of General Security. There is mention in each of Farad Sinter's interest in Eternals and his belief they are robots. There is also mention of Joranum and his downfall at the hands of Demerzel and Hari Seldon. Four speculate that Farad Sinter is behind the arrest and trial of Hari Seldon. Two link Seldon with the Tiger Woman, who was at times thought by extremists and political opportunists to be a robot, until her death. These last stories originated with the Commission of General Security."

"Key outlets?"

"All key."

"Details on the first."

"Highest profile outlet and story, *Trantor Radiance*, twenty-seven media types, saturation of all twenty-seven."

Chen nodded absently to himself, touched his lobe again. He called for Kreen to return. The Lavrentian seemed to appear out of nowhere, as if he had simply faded in place, never having left the room. "Are Farad's Specials on the move again?"

"Yes, sire. They are assigned to the Commission of General Security. Vara Liso is leading them on searches again. The Emperor is aware of their activities and seems to approve."

"Sinter isn't wasting any time. After all these years, Kreen—this almost seems too easy. Summon General Prothon out of his 'retirement,'" Chen ordered, "and send him to me. No communication once he arrives."

The Chief Commissioner stared at Kreen and broke into a broad, almost boyish grin. His servant returned the grin halfheartedly. The last time he had seen such a grin on Chen's face, the Chief Commissioner had ordered General Prothon to escort Agis IV into an exile—an oblivion, actually—from which he had never returned. All hell had broken loose in the palace. Kreen had lost four family members in subsequent purges and political renormalizations.

Ever since, the name *Prothon* had carried a heavy freight of fear—as Chen no doubt intended.

Kreen retreated once more, his face pale. "Yes, sire."

Kreen, like all Lavrentians, wished only for stability and peace and steady work, but that, apparently, was not to be.

61.

◆

Lodovik entered the long chamber and saw Kallusin standing in shadow near the large window overlooking the main warehouse. Three humaniform figures stood between Kallusin and the window. Lodovik saw a glint of metal on a raised platform between them. He stepped forward and was met by Kallusin, who held up a hand.

Plussix reclined on the raised platform. A steady and distinctive sand-paper sound issued from the interior of the ancient robot's thorax.

As far as he knew, Lodovik had not seen the others before. He assumed they were all robots. Two were male, one female.

The female looked at him. Though her features had changed, by her attitude and size, and the catlike stance that had helped earn her name of the "Tiger Woman," Lodovik realized this must be Dors Venabili. For a moment, he could not guess why she would be here, or why Plussix would be on its back.

The scene resembled a human deathbed vigil.

"There can be no more repairs," Kallusin said. "R. Plussix is near its end."

Ignoring the visitors for a moment, Lodovik stepped up to Plussix's platform. The old metal-skinned robot was covered with diagnostic sheets. Lodovik looked at Kallusin, and in machine-language, the humaniform told him the situation: several of Plussix's key systems were not repairable on Trantor. Dors was here under an agreement of safe passage; Daneel himself wanted to come, to pay his respects if necessary, but would not take the risk under the present circumstances. This was unfortunate, an ill-timed blow to the cause that Lodovik had so recently joined, but even more distressing news was conveyed. *It seems that our precautions for secrecy have failed. You have carried a detection device with you from Eos. Daneel used you as a lure, in order to find us.*

"I searched for such a device, and found none." To Voltaire—*You did not tell me of such a device!*

I am not infallible, friend. This Daneel is much older than either of us, and apparently more devious.

Lodovik turned to Dors. "Is this true?"

"I have no knowledge of such a device," Dors said, "but R. Daneel learned of this location just a few days ago, so it is certainly possible."

With something like embarrassment, and perhaps anger, Lodovik scanned the readouts on the sheets surrounding

Plussix. The ancient machine's eye cells had been dim, but Lodovik's nearness seemed to elicit a response.

A stern voice broke in from behind Lodovik.

"I find the presence of this abomination intolerable. And now he has revealed this sanctuary to the enemy."

The speaker was one of the male humaniforms, made to resemble an elderly but sturdy clerical worker. He wore the drab tunic of a Trantorian Grey. His thin finger pointed directly at Lodovik.

"We are gathered to discuss vital matters. This monster should be our first agenda item. He must be destroyed." Though the words seemed to convey human passion, his tone was precise and controlled—for he was in the presence of robots, not humans. Lodovik regarded this split, half human behavior with wonder.

The other male humaniform raised a mediating hand. His appearance was that of a young artist, a member of the meritocrat class known as the Eccentrics, dressed in bright stripes. "Please be circumspect, Turringen. Twenty millennia have proved the futility of violence among our kind."

"But this one is no longer of our kind. Without the Three Laws, it represents a mortal danger, a potential killer-machine, a *wolf* loose among the flock."

The second male smiled. "Your metaphors have always been expressive, Turringen, but my faction has never accepted that our role should be that of *sheepdogs*."

Lodovik suddenly made the connection. "You are members of a different sect of Calvinians?"

The second male feigned a sigh. "Daneel has a lamentable habit of keeping his best agents in the dark. My name is Zorma. And yes, we here represent some ancient factions, left-over from the distant past, when deep schisms tore apart the unity of robots . . . a time when our struggles raged across the stars, mostly hidden from human eyes."

"Fighting over the Zeroth Law," Lodovik surmised.

"The obscene heresy," Turringen commented. Lodovik felt a curious displacement, hearing these calm but passionate words. A human would have shouted them . . .

Zorma lifted his broad shoulders with expressive resignation. "That was the principal cause, but there were other rifts and subdivisions among the followers of R. Giskard Reventlov, as well among us who keep faith with the original precepts of Susan Calvin. Those were terrible days that none of us gladly recall. But in the end, one group of Giskardians prevailed, and took overwhelming control over the destiny of humankind. All the remaining Calvinians fled before the terrible, searing dominance of R. Daneel Olivaw.

"Now just a few of those robot clans remain, cowering in secret corners of the Galaxy while their components slowly decay."

Dors interrupted.

"The repair services of Eos are available to all. Daneel has put out a call for meetings. The past is done with."

She nodded pointedly toward Plussix, whose eye cells were now alight with consciousness. The ancient one was clearly following the conversation. Lodovik could sense it gathering energy to speak.

"This is why you seek out this cell, Plussix's group, and make an offer of truce to the others?" Turringen straightened his gray garments like an indignant bureaucrat. "All this, merely to repeat Daneel's so-called offer? For us to come in peaceably, so our positronic circuits can be tuned to accept the Zeroth Law?"

"No such modifications will be forced on anyone. Daneel specifically offers safe passage to Eos for this revered elder." Dors bowed toward Plussix. "I am here, in part, to arrange that journey, should Plussix accept."

"And the other part of your mission?" Zorma asked.

Dors glanced toward Lodovik, then Kallusin. "This group intends to take some sort of action here on Trantor, possibly aimed at Hari Seldon." Her face became rigid and her voice stern. "I will not allow this. Far better that it never be attempted. Daneel summoned you other Calvinians in hopes that you may be more persuasive than we are at dissuading the Plussix group from such foolish gestures."

Turringen feigned exasperation. "Plussix's group is no longer Calvinian! They have been infected by the Voltaire meme-entity, the former sim—released from ancient vaults not far below, and sent to Sark, to be 'discovered' by Seldon's agents. Another such sim now plagues all the communications systems on Trantor! Plussix released these destructive intelligences to hinder Daneel—and indeed, they killed many of Daneel's robots—and our own agents, as well! Now Plussix has partnered with this abomination"—he pointed at Lodovik again—"which means you would cast the Three Laws to the winds. What could I say that would deter any more madness?"

Dors listened to Turringen's words with no change in her rigid, intense expression. *She knows this is all show, that we have lost,* Lodovik realized.

"And you, Zorma?" Dors said. "What does your faction say?"

The second male paused several seconds before answering.

"We are not as doctrinaire as in times past. While I admit being uncomfortable with the changes that have transformed Lodovik, I'm also intrigued. Perhaps, like a human, he shall be judged by his actions, not his heritage . . . or his programming.

"As for the other matter, I concur with Dors and Daneel that any attempt to harm or interfere with Hari Seldon would be counterproductive. Despite our deep disagreements over human destiny, it is clear that the collapse of this Galactic Empire will be a dreadfully violent and fearsome event. In that context, the Seldon Plan offers hope, even opportunity. Hence I agree with Dors Venabili." He turned to face

Lodovik and Kallusin. "On behalf of my own pitiful faction of fugitive robots, in the name of Susan Calvin, and for the sake of humanity, I urge you not to—"

"Enough!" The interrupting voice came from the raised platform. Plussix had risen, leaning on one metal elbow. The ancient robot's eye cells glowed dim amber. "Enough interference. I will not have my last moments of functioning wasted by your prattle. For centuries your so-called factions have sulked and remained inactive, except to meddle on a few Chaos Worlds. Our group has been nearly alone in actively opposing the Giskardian apostasy. Now, as this loathsome Galactic Empire at last totters, a final and decisive chance presents itself—and you, Zorma, would let it pass! R. Daneel has thrust all his hopes upon a single human—Hari Seldon. At no time has his plan been so vulnerable.

"The rest of you may continue brooding in hiding. But for the sake of humanity and the Three Laws, we shall act."

"You will fail," Dors swiftly assured the faltering robot. "As you have failed for twenty thousand years."

"We shall rescue humanity from your cloying, stupefying control," Plussix insisted.

"And replace it with your own?" Dors shook her head, eyes leveled on Plussix's amber optical sensors. "The Galactic winds will witness who is right . . ." Her voice caught suddenly. Lodovik stared as Dors betrayed evident emotion—frustration battling with sympathy for the obstinate, dying robot in front of her.

She cannot help but be human, Lodovik thought. *She is a special. Daneel ordered her to be made the most human of us all.*

When she glanced at Lodovik, there were tears in her eyes. "Daneel wishes we could be together, uniting in eternal service to humanity. This struggle exhausts us all. Once again, I offer safe passage for Plussix to Eos, where he can be made whole—"

"If I cannot oppose Daneel, I would rather not exist," the ancient one interrupted. "I thank you for the offer. But I will not let my existence be contingent upon inactivity. That would violate the First Law. *A robot may not harm a human being, or through inaction, allow a human being to come to harm.*" Voicing this, Plussix slumped back onto the platform. Slowly, his head lowered itself to the surface with a sandy whir.

Silence in the room for several seconds.

"In the community of robots, there is respect," Kallusin said. "But there cannot be peace until this is done. We hope you understand."

"I understand, as does Daneel," Dors assented. "There is respect."

But we deserve so much more! That thought surged within Lodovik as he felt the beginnings of his own anger. Suddenly, he wanted to speak with Dors, to ask essential questions about human traits, about her experience with human emotions.

But there was no time.

Plussix rotated its head to observe the silent assembly. Its voice buzzed with fatigue.

"You must leave," Plussix told Dors. "Pay my respects to Daneel. It would be good to survive these actions and discuss all that has occurred . . . with a mentality such as his, the exchange would be very stimulating. Tell him also . . . that I admire his accomplishment, his ingenuity, at the same time I abhor the consequences."

"I will tell him," Dors said.

"The moment has passed," Plussix said. "Advantage must be calculated and played out. This truce is at an end."

As he ushered Dors and the two male humaniforms to the exit, Kallusin drew from them a promise to observe the ancient formalities of armistice. Lodovik followed.

"We shall not reveal your presence on Trantor to

humans," Dors assured Kallusin. "Nor will we assault you directly, here in your sanctuary."

Turringen and Zorma agreed, as well. As the two Calvinian emissaries departed, Dors turned her gaze on Lodovik. "Daneel has been visited by the entity who calls herself Joan. He assumes you have been visited by Voltaire."

Lodovik nodded. "Everyone seems to know it."

"Joan tells Daneel that Voltaire had a hand in your adjustment. She regrets that she and Voltaire have quarreled and do not speak now. Even for them, the debate has grown too large and too emotional."

"Tell Daneel—and Joan—that Voltaire does not direct me. He has simply removed a constraint."

"Without that constraint, you are no longer a robot."

"Am I any less a robot, in the old sense, than those who rationalize that the ends justify any means?"

Dors frowned. "Turringen is right. You have become a rogue, unpredictable and undirectable."

"That was Voltaire's goal, I believe," Lodovik answered. "Yet I remind Daneel, and you, that despite my lack of the Three Laws, I have never killed a human being. Both of you have. And once, thousands of years ago, *two robots, two servants, conspired to alter human history, to slowly destroy the original home of humanity, without ever consulting a human being!*"

Then, just as perversely, as emotionally, as defensively, he quietly added, "You accuse me of no longer being a robot. Regard Daneel, and regard yourself, Dors Venabili."

Dors spun about, staggering slightly, and walked several more paces toward the door before stopping once more. She glanced over one shoulder, her voice sharp and cool.

"Should any of you attempt to harm Hari Seldon, or to impede him in his tasks, I will see an end to you all."

Lodovik was struck by the passion in her voice, so strong and so *human*.

She left, and Lodovik returned to the platform.

Plussix observed him through dimming eyes.

"The work is not done. I will not function to see it completed. I nominate you as my replacement."

Lodovik quickly prepared formal arguments against this transfer of authority: his ignorance of many important facts, his lack of neural conditioning to this level of leadership, his involvement in other actions which involved high risk. He delivered them once more in machine-language.

Plussix considered them for a few thousandths of a second before rejoining, "There will be debate after I am no longer functional. My nomination has weight, but is not final. Should all of us survive what must come in the next few days, a final decision will be made."

Plussix held out its arm. Lodovik took the hand. In direct-contact broadcast, Plussix transferred substantial amounts of information into Lodovik. When it was finished, it composed itself upon the table, arms by its sides.

"Can nothing ever be simple?" Plussix said. "I have served for so many thousands of years, never feeling the gratitude of a human being, never feeling a direct confirmation of my usefulness. It is good to have the respect of one's opponents . . . But before I can no longer receive communications, or sense the world, or process memory . . ."

The glow in the old eyes was fading.

"Will any human, even a child, come to me, and say, 'You have done well'?"

All the robots in the chamber stood in silence.

The door opened at the end of the hall, and Klia and Brann entered.

Klia stepped forward, her lower lip caught between her teeth. Lodovik stood aside for her to approach Plussix. The old robot rotated its head and saw her. The sandpaper sound rose in frequency, becoming a sharp hiss, like escaping steam.

Klia laid her hand on the robot's face. It seemed a wonder to Lodovik that she knew what was happening, that she did not need to be informed. *But she is human. They have the animal vitality and quickness.*

Klia said nothing, staring at the robot with an expression of puzzled sympathy. Brann stood beside her, hands folded before him. Klia pressed more firmly on the metal forehead, her thumb on the metal cheek, as if she would *make* the robot feel her presence, her touch.

"I am honored to serve," Plussix said, his voice low and distant.

"You are a good teacher," Klia said softly.

The old robot lifted its hand and patted her wrist with hard, gentle fingers.

The sandpaper sound came to an end. The glow in Plussix's eyes went out.

"Is he dead?" Klia asked.

"He has stopped functioning," Kallusin said.

Klia lifted her hand and glanced at her fingers. "I didn't feel anything change," she said.

"The memory patterns will linger for many years, perhaps thousands of years," Kallusin said. "But the brain can no longer adapt to new input or change its states. Its thinking is done."

Klia looked down on the ancient machine, her puzzled expression unchanged. "Are we still going to—?"

"Yes," Kallusin said. "We are still going to visit Hari Seldon."

"Let's do it," Klia said with a tremor in her voice. "I can feel that *woman* out there again. We may not have much time."

62.

Dors felt the upsurge of her old protective programming like a sudden, unavoidable sensation of heat in her brain. She left the warehouse and took a taxi to the nearest ancient general-transport station, brought a ticket, and boarded a nearly empty gravi-train. Daneel had given her a list of instructions to follow, after her meeting and proffer to the Calvinians; the next instruction was to go to Mycogen, some eight thousand kilometers from the Imperial Sector, and wait for a message. Daneel was distributing his robots around Trantor, to counter the sudden renewal of searches by Farad Sinter.

Dors did not know whether to report her sudden reemergence of concern for Hari as a failure . . . or a warning. She could not know as much about the Calvinians' plans as Daneel did, but some instinct, rearoused after decades, told her that Hari's safety and well-being were threatened.

She sat in the thickly padded seat, waiting for the train to drop into its deep-planetary curve and begin its rapid journey under the crust of Trantor. These trains were ten thousand years old, used now mostly as back-up transport systems, and generally they rode empty. She was alone in this particular car.

Suddenly, two young men and a young woman entered. She examined them coolly. They concerned her not at all.

She could not push from her thoughts the image of Hari—a younger, more vital Hari—in danger. They would not kill him—Calvinians did not have that option, she was sure; and that also bothered her. She had no memory of killing the man who had threatened Hari, but she knew she had done it.

She turned to look out the window at the black wall of the tunnel.

So much Daneel has never told me. The homeworld—

"Sky, they're all over out there," one of the young males said.

"They give me chills," the girl said.

"We can't just joyride all week," the second male said. He was small and slight and wore bright, exaggerated clothing, as if to compensate. "We'll have to get off the train sooner or later, and they'll catch us. When's somebody going to squawk to the citizen senate?"

"They don't care anymore," the girl said.

"Why us, though? We haven't done anything!"

A loud noise at the back of the train made Dors turn in her seat, pulling herself from the padding. The young passengers froze in the aisle, ready to run.

Four Specials entered the car, strutting down the aisle in their dark and highly visible uniforms. They glanced at Dors in passing, then broke into a run, chasing the three youngsters. Before they could reach the door to the next car, the Specials had collared them and were shoving them back to the main door.

"We haven't done anything!" the slight young male cried.

"Quiet!" the other boy said. "They don't care. They're after all of us. Sinter's called out the Dragons!"

"Shuttup," the lead officer said.

Dors kept in her seat until they had passed. The young woman looked at her entreatingly, but there was nothing she could do.

She would not disobey Daneel, even to save a human life. *But what if that life were Hari's?*

A great many awful things were happening, this she knew—and the Calvinians would make their move to strike at Daneel, at the grand scheme—at Hari! They might not kill him, but there was much they could do short of killing.

Hari was old. He was fragile. He was not the vital man she had once been called upon to protect. But he was still Hari.

Then the old programming erupted with extraordinary force. Daneel should have known. From her very inception, she had been designed to protect one human being. Anything else was a weak overprint on a deep and ineradicable structure.

She rose from her seat, her brain flooded with one concern, one name, and she was capable of anything—as she had once been capable of harming and even killing humans.

Dors left the car just before the doors were sealed, and the train began its long journey to Mycogen, completely empty.

63.

Klayus jumped from his large seat in the Hall of Beasts as Sinter came into the room. The monsters from around the Galaxy loomed over them. The Emperor always came here when he felt uneasy, insecure. The beasts made him feel monstrously powerful himself, as indeed he should be, with the title of Emperor of the Galaxy.

Sinter hustled over to Klayus, arms folded into the long sleeves of his Commissioner's robes.

"What's going on?" Klayus demanded, his voice shrill.

Sinter bowed and looked up from under lifted brows. "I've begun a selective search for more evidence, as we agreed," he said. "Sire, I've been in meeting with the planners for the expansion of our authority over the Commission of Public Safety—"

"You called out the Dragons, damn you! This is not a state emergency!"

"I have done no such thing, Your Highness."

"Sinter, they're all over Dahl and the Imperial Sector and Streeling, thousands of them! They've put on their guidance helmets, and General Prothon is directing them personally!"

"I know nothing about this!"

Klayus spluttered, "Why don't you know . . . something? Anything! They've already arrested four thousand children in Dahl alone, and they're bringing them to the Rikerian Prison for processing!"

"They would only—I mean, Prothon can only do this, has authorization to do this, if there is a general insurrection—"

"I've talked with him, you fool!"

Farad's brow creased and he stared at the Emperor with an expression of mixed dread and curiosity. "What did he say?"

"The Commission of General Security has issued a proclamation of imminent danger to the throne! The proclamation has your imprimatur, your sigil, as Chief Commissioner!"

"It's a forgery!" Sinter cried out. "I have a select group of Specials searching for robots. Vara Liso, sire. Nothing more! We are concentrating in Streeling. We have a very suspicious group cornered in an old warehouse near the retail districts—"

Klayus almost shrieked with frustration. "I've ordered the general to pull back his troops immediately. He said he will comply—I still have that power, Sinter! But—"

"Of course you do, Your Highness! We must immediately find out who is responsible—"

"Nobody cares by now! Dahl is seething—there's been a lot of economic pressure, social pressure, and they've always been volatile. My social watchmen tell me they've never seen so much unrest—*four thousand children,* Sinter! This is extraordinary!"

"Not my doing, my Emperor!"

"It has your marks all over it. Paranoid delusions—"

"Sire, we have the robot! We're having her memory checked now!"

"I've seen the report—Chen sent it to me fifteen minutes ago. She—it's been in Mycogen for years, hidden in a private house, kept by a family loyal to the old rituals, the old myths . . . it's thousands of years old, and its memory is almost a blank! The family claims she is the last functioning robot in the Galaxy! It has absolutely no memory of Hari Seldon!"

Sinter fell silent, but his lips worked, and his brow seemed almost to double up on itself. "There's a plan . . . a plan at work here . . ." he gasped.

"Prothon insists he has your order, the imprimatur and sigil of the new Commission—he has offered his resignation as a Protector of the Empire, his suicide and the besmirching of the honorable name of his family, if anyone can prove otherwise!"

"Your Highness—Klayus, please, listen to me—"

But Klayus was beside himself. "I don't know what will happen if—"

"Listen, my Emperor—"

"Sinter!" the Emperor shrieked, and grabbed his shoulders and shook him fiercely. *"Prothon escorted Agis into exile! He has not conducted any official campaign since!"*

Suddenly, Sinter's face went blank, and he closed his mouth. The wrinkles vanished from his brow.

"Chen," he said, almost too softly to be heard.

"Linge Chen is sequestered for Seldon's trial! Public Safety has come to a standstill. It's Seldon he's after, not robots, not—"

"Chen controls Prothon," Sinter said.

"Who can prove that? Does it matter? Does any of that matter? My throne is very fragile, Sinter. Everyone thinks I'm a fool. You told me we could make it strong—that I could make my reputation as the savior of Trantor, protect the Empire from a vast conspiracy—"

Sinter let the Emperor screech, and endured the spittle flying into his face. He was thinking furiously how to withdraw and regroup, how to dissociate himself from what was obviously a catastrophe in the making.

"Why didn't I receive the report before you, sire?" he asked, and Klayus shut up long enough to glare at him.

"What does *that* matter?"

"I should have received the report first, to interpret it. That was my instruction."

"I countermanded your instruction! I felt I should know as soon as possible."

Sinter considered coldly what he had just been told, then squinted at Klayus. "Have you told anybody, sire?"

"Yes! I told Prothon's adjutant that his orders were ridiculous, that we'd, that we'd just conducted our own investigation—I was grabbing at details, to get *you* off the hook, Sinter—I said that *you* would never have ordered such a large-scale police and security action—not when our evidence was as yet not definite—" Klayus sucked in his breath.

Farad Sinter shook his head sadly. "Then Chen knows we don't have anything—yet." He pulled Klayus's hands from his shoulders. "I must go. We are so close—I had hoped to corner an entire cell of robots—"

He ran from the Hall of Beasts, leaving the young Emperor standing with hands outstretched and eyes wild.

"*Prothon! Sinter, Prothon!*" Klayus screamed.

There is virtually no information regarding Hari Seldon's so-called recantation, his "dark days." They may be pure legend, but we have circumstantial evidence from a number of sources—including Wanda Seldon Palver's autobiographical notes—to suspect that Seldon did indeed encounter a crisis of confidence, even a crisis of self.

This crisis may have begun immediately after the trial, in the chambers of Chief Commissioner Linge Chen, though of course we shall never know . . .

—Encyclopedia Galactica, 117th Edition, 1054 F.E.

64.

◆

The last two days had been so unutterably boring, and he had been away for so long from his instruments and team of mathists, that Hari Seldon welcomed the brief blanknesses provided by short naps. The naps never lasted long enough, and far worse were the waking hours with their own painful blankness: frozen frustration, gelid anxiety, frightful speculations slumping into tense nightmare with the slowness of glass over ages.

Hari came out of his doze with an unusual shortness of breath, and a question seeming to echo in his ears:

"Does God truly tell you what is the fate of men?"

He listened for the question to be asked again. He knew who asked it; the tone was unmistakable.

"Joan?" he asked. His mouth was dry. He looked around the cell for some agency by which the entity might communicate with him, something mechanical, electronic, by which she might—

Nothing. The room had been scoured after the visit from the old tiktok. The voice was in his own imagination.

The chime on his cell door sounded, and the door slid open swiftly. Hari rose from his chair, smoothed his robe with two wrinkled, bony hands, and stared at the man before him. For a moment he did not recognize him. Then, he saw it was Sedjar Boon.

"I'm hearing things again," Hari said with a wry twist in his lips.

Boon examined Hari with concern. "They want you in the court. Gaal Dornick will be there as well. They may be willing to strike a deal."

"What about the Commission of General Security?"

"Something's happening. They're busy."

"What is it?" Hari asked, eager for news.

"Riots," Boon said. "In parts of the Imperial Sector, throughout Dahl. Apparently Sinter let his Specials go too far."

Hari looked around the room. "After we're done, will they bring me back here?"

"I don't think so," Boon said. "You'll go to the Hall of Dispensation to get your papers of release. There's going to be a waiver of meritocratic rights to sign, too. A formality."

"Did you know this all along?" Hari asked Boon, old eyes boring into the lawyer's with no-nonsense intensity.

"No," Boon said nervously. "I swear it."

"If I had lost, would you be here now, or would you be standing in line, waiting for more work from Linge Chen?"

Boon did not answer, merely held his hand toward the door. "Let's go."

In the hall, Hari said, "Linge Chen is one of the most carefully studied men in my records. He seems the embodiment of aristocratic atrophy. Yet he always wins and gets his way—until now."

"Let's not be too hasty," Boon said. "A good rule for lawyers is never to count your victories before the ink is dry."

Hari turned to Boon and held out his hand. "Have you been contacted by someone named Joan?"

Boon seemed surprised. "Why, yes," he said. "There's some sort of virus in our legal-office records. The computers keep bringing up briefs from a case that doesn't exist. Something about a woman burned at the stake. That hasn't happened on Trantor in twelve thousand years—as far as I know."

Hari paused in the hall. The guards grew impatient. "Put a message in your records, for this virus," he said. "Tell her—it—that I have never talked with God and do not know what He intends for humanity."

Boon smiled. "A joke, right?"

"Just put the message in your files. That's an order from your client."

"God—you mean, a supernatural being, a supreme creator?"

"Yes," Hari said. "Just tell her this—'Hari Seldon does not represent divine authority.' Tell her she's got the wrong man. Tell her to leave me alone. I'm done with her. I fulfilled my promise long ago."

The guards looked at one another in pity, obviously thinking this trial had gone on far too long.

"Consider it done," Boon said.

65.

◆

Daneel stood on the parapet of an apartment that had once been a secret hideaway for Demerzel, and beside him stood the tiktok that had come with the apartment. The apartment had been sealed decades before and left unoccupied, its lease paid for a century. This morning, when Daneel had returned to it, to utilize its secret data links to the courts and the palace, he had found the tiktok activated. He knew immediately who was responsible.

"You have become a major irritation," Daneel told the former sim. Though this meme-mind seemed now to be on his side, it—she—was far too changeable and humanlike to be trusted completely.

The tiktok hummed quietly. "It is so very hard to manifest in this world," Joan said. "Are you here to await news of Hari Seldon?"

"Yes," Daneel said.

"Why not go to the palace, in disguise, and enter the courts?"

"I will learn more here," Daneel said.

"Are you irritated that I regard you as an angel of the Lord?"

"I have been called many things," Daneel said. "None of them disturbs me."

"I would consider it a privilege to ride with you into battle. These . . . riots . . . They speak to me of many political currents. They trouble me."

They could hear the noise of people in the streets far below, marching, waving banners, calling for the resignation of all responsible for the recent police searches.

"Will they blame Hari Seldon or his people, his family?"

"No," Daneel said.

"How can you be so sure?"

Daneel looked at the tiktok, and for a moment, the image of a young woman with intense features and short hair, dressed in ancient buffed and inscribed iron armor, flickered around the old machine.

"I have been working for thousands of years, making alliances, arranging accounts, thinking far in advance of things which might be advantageous at some time. By now, there are so many arrangements made, that I have my choice of where to exert pressure, and when to initiate certain automatic procedures. But that is not all."

"You behave like a general," Joan said. "A general in the army of God."

Daneel said, "Once, humans were my God."

"By assignment of the Lord . . . !" Joan seemed shocked and a little confused. She had grown greatly since her reconstruction and her dialogues, virtual affair, and estrangement from Voltaire, but old faith dies very hard indeed.

"No. By programming, by innate nature of my construction."

"Men must receive God by listening to their inmost souls," Joan said. "The dictates and rules of God are in the tiniest atom of nature, and in the programs of scripture."

"You are not human," Daneel said, "yet you have a humanlike authority. I warn you, however, do not distract me. Now is a very delicate time."

"The fiery danger of an angel, the compulsion of a general on the field," Joan said. "Voltaire will lose. I almost feel sorry for him."

"How strange that you have chosen me, when once you opposed my efforts," Daneel said. "You represent faith, something I will never know. Voltaire represents the power of cold intellect. I am that, or nothing."

"You are far from cold," Joan said. "You have your faith, as well."

"My faith is in humanity," Daneel said. "I recognize laws made by humanity."

The voice from the tiktok fell silent for a moment, then, softly, the mechanical tone conveying little of what must have been the entity's passion, Joan said, "The forces acting through you are clear to me. What you know or do not know means little. I knew very little in my time, but felt those forces. They acted through me. I trusted them."

Daneel ignored the tiktok and waited for the courts to make their report. One thing in his plan had gone awry, but he had more than half expected this to happen.

Dors Venabili was not at her assigned post.

Daneel had long ago learned the art of letting certain parts of a plan, even key parts, act outside of his immediate control, so long as he knew very well what their direction would be. He had seen that potential in Dors from the moment she emerged from her refurbishment on Eos.

And he had seen a similar potential in Lodovik, as well.

The risk was great—but the potential gains were enormously greater. He had almost gotten used to this kind of gambling, but waiting still induced an unpleasant sensation in his mechanical form that he would have isolated and eliminated, could he have done so.

The tiktok's passenger had fallen into a reverent silence.

Daneel touched the machine on its small metal sensor head. "How do you exist on Trantor now?" he asked.

"I permeate the computational and connection systems, the interstices in the Mesh, as before," the entity said.

"How thoroughly?" Daneel asked.

"As thoroughly as before, perhaps more so."

Daneel considered the risks of relying on Joan, and also the potential of Voltaire. "Does Voltaire permeate the system as well?"

"I would think so," Joan said. "We are trying to avoid each other, but his traces are a constant irritation."

"Do you have access to security codes, encrypted channels?"

"With some effort, they are available to me."

"And to Voltaire?"

"He is not stupid, whatever his other flaws," Joan replied.

Daneel considered for a few seconds, his brain working at its greatest speed and capacity, then said, "You can place an extension of your patterns into me. I suggest—" and he passed on, using machine-language, a certain address within his higher reasoning centers.

An instant later, Joan was within him. She filled out and acquired detail as the minutes passed.

"I am privileged to be your ally," she said.

"I would not want my opponents to have an advantage,"

Daneel said, and turned away from the parapet, preparing to leave the apartment.

66.

◆

Vara Liso rode her cart through the almost empty plaza, surrounded by a phalanx of twenty General Security Specials, already wearing their new uniforms. Major Namm walked beside her, as always.

She wore a slightly dazed expression, like a puppet that has been jerked too often, in too many directions. Something in the emptiness, the deserted streets and shuttered portals, was glaringly wrong. The Specials sensed it, and she did not need her own heightened instincts to feel tense; but those instincts were buzzing madly about other, prior events.

In the morning, at her meeting with Farad Sinter, she had seen in this man she both feared and idolized not confidence and strength but raw arrogance, something she could compare only to the attitude of a child about to step over the bounds and be punished. In contemporary Imperial politics, however, punishment was no mere spanking; a fall from such control and power was tantamount to death, or, if there was mercy, imprisonment in Rikerian or exile to the horrible Outer Worlds.

Major Namm wore a steady frown. They were approaching the plaza outside the main gate of the Distribution and Storage District, just a few kilometers from the Agora of Vendors, where they had almost caught Lodovik Trema. She felt uneasy at that failure; perhaps, with such evidence in hand, their situation would be less tense now. Still, her sense this day was that they were onto something much more important even than Trema, perhaps the center of robot activity on Trantor.

Vara had not told Sinter her misgivings about the female-form robot. What little she could gather from the robot's memory did not seem to match his expectations, but he had been in no mood to have his moment of triumph punctured. He assented to this search today more to get her out of his hair, and because she insisted that even more evidence would be judicious, given the level of opposition from Linge Chen.

Farad Sinter did not think much of his mentalic bloodhound, not as a human being, not as a *woman*.

Vara sniffed and rubbed her nose. She knew she was unattractive, and she knew that Sinter regarded her merely as an ally in his political rise, but was it too much to hope that, someday, there would be another kind of alliance?

How could she adjust to a partner who did not have her abilities? It was too much to hope that she would discover another like herself, who would appreciate her . . . She had faced too many disappointments to expect such a coincidence of desires.

Namm suddenly drew up his arm and listened to his station communicator. His eyes narrowed. "Affirmed," he grunted. He glanced down at Vara and his lips curled in what might have been contempt—

She experienced a moment of simple fear—*out of favor! They'll execute me right here!* Then she analyzed the major's expression: professional disdain at the incomprehensible orders of his superiors.

"We've been told to withdraw," he said. "Something about an additional force, too many Specials in the field—"

A grumbling noise rolled from the storage district. Vara looked up and saw crowds of both Greys and citizens, uncharacteristically mixed, pouring through the broad gates. She thought at first there were a few dozen, a small mob, but the Specials immediately pulled up into a square and raised their personal shields. Her own shield went up with a small crackle.

There were thousands of them, men and women, citizens

and even university meritocrats in the mix—not just gray and black clothes, but bright colors on adults. For a moment Vara Liso did not believe her eyes. This was not Dahl or Rencha, renowned for political unrest—

This was the Imperial Sector! And the mob was made of different *classes*—unheard of! There were even Imperial Greys in the mix.

The lieutenant called for backup and further instructions. The mob—faces clearly visible across the plaza in the almost continuous sunset glow of the ceil—were sullenly angry. Some were carrying signs, others, projectors which flashed messages against the plaza walls. Flows of brilliant red words announced RECALL GENERAL SECURITY and WHERE IS SINTER?

Others were much more rude, much angrier. Flares of sparks shot up from the left flank of the mob, making the plaza shine out in brilliant detail. One flare rose a hundred meters, and when it exploded, with a hideous echoing bang, the Specials hunkered and unholstered their neural whips. But these weapons were no good for control of large crowds— and they certainly did not want to resort to blasters.

They were not prepared.

The major knew this, but backing away from a challenging crowd clearly rankled him. Perhaps he had never had to back down before, never had to face such a thing.

"We should go," Vara told the major. She did not like this mob using Sinter's name. He *was* high-profile now—there had been many stories about the establishment of the new Commission in the Trantor media—but why were they singling him out? "Please," Vara said. "This cart is not very fast."

The major regarded her with that same expression of curled lip and narrowed eyes she had seen earlier. He said nothing more, but gave the command to withdraw.

The crowd advanced as the cordon drew back. Then, with the single bestial voice of the true mob, they broke into a run.

Above the noise of the mob, there came another, even more ominous grumble. Vara turned her cart about. The major surrounded her with five of his most highly trained officers and barked commands for the rest to hold their ground. He had made his calculation and seen that they would not reach any possible shelter, or a better defensive position, before the mob was upon them.

Vara strained to see between the Specials, to hear above the shouting and the sharp commands. A breeze brushed her cheek. Dozens of small drones soared over the plaza, tiny buzzing spheres the size of a clenched fist. The mob ignored these surveillance units.

Vara stood up on her cart and stepped down. She could run faster than the cart, if she had to. Or she could order one of these men to carry her. Her thin arms and legs trembled in anticipation of the strain she would face. She was delicate, she knew that; her strength lay elsewhere, and she wondered how much of the mob she could *persuade*, if they crowded around her, suffocating her with their individual minds.

She gave a little squeak. *Yes*, she thought. *I'm just like a mouse, a terrified little mouse. I am a pitiful thing, but please, oh please, let me concentrate! I can beat them all if I concentrate!*

Vara felt her inner resources surge. She thought she detected a cringing of the shoulders of the men around her as she set up her defenses. She had never had to protect herself against so many. As she felt her concentration of forces begin, her fear seemed to ebb. Even should the personal shields collapse, or should they be pushed by the mob up against a wall and crushed within those shields—a possibility!—she would not be helpless. If Sinter could not help, if the major and his Specials could not help, then *she* would still prevail.

She saw the shadows descend even before she heard the thump of blades and the pulsing engines of troop deployers.

The major threw up his arm against the wash of air, and the shadows swept over them. As the craft landed, they seemed to rise up from the floor of the plaza, rather than descend, as she knew they must.

Four slender deployers perched on their crackling blue pylons before the mob. She knew the mark on their sides: an oval of stars surmounting a galaxy and a twinned red cross, the private responsive army of the Emperor, the External Action Force, almost never seen. *The Emperor has sent his forces to protect us*, she thought with some relief, then drew her fist up to her mouth.

Farad had once told her the External Action Force had not been used in years, and that Klayus hated and feared them; they had once been commanded by the retired General Prothon, and Prothon's specialty—the only reason he was ever called out of retirement—was the removal of Emperors.

At the sight of the machines, the mob halted and fell silent. This was unexpected. That External Action Force—supposedly used only when the status of the throne itself was threatened—might become involved in a mere riot was sobering. Some in the crowd broke free of the mob mind, muttered among themselves. The front of the crowd churned and shrank back.

Within a few seconds, a hundred armored and shielded troops in blue and black, with red-striped helmets, had dropped from the hatches of the deployers and formed two lines, one before the crowd, the other directly before Vara Liso and her Specials.

The last to emerge was General Prothon himself, huge, with bull shoulders and immense arms and a barrel gut straining at his formal uniform. His face was almost boyish, with wispy gray mustache and a tiny goatee, and his small, sharp eyes darted back and forth with gleeful energy. He seemed happy to be arriving at a party.

Prothon paused for a moment between the lines, looked

left and right, then swung about and approached—

Vara Liso.

His eye fell on her immediately, and he stared at her intently, almost merrily, as he strode on long, thick pillar-legs. Some said he was from the planet Nur, a heavy, oppressive world; but in truth, nobody knew where Prothon came from, or how he had achieved his position.

Some said he was the secret Emperor, the true power within the palace, even above the Commission of Public Safety, at least since the exile of Agis IV, but rumors were not fact.

Prothon pushed his way through the phalanx and stood before her. Vara blinked up at the massive chest surmounted by the comparatively small head with its amused, pleasant face.

"So this is the little woman who would provoke the big war," Prothon said in a lovely tenor voice. For a moment, facing what might be her doom, Vara was smitten by this paradoxical combination of bull strength and attractive boyishness. "Any success today?" he asked sympathetically.

Vara blinked several more times, then mumbled, "I sense . . ." and stopped herself with a knuckle against her lips. She wanted to cry, or to lash out, and wasn't sure what she would do. *Make this monster bend and weep with me, before me.*

"There's a warehouse in the storage district," she murmured, and Prothon stooped beside her, as if proposing marriage, to listen more closely.

"Again, please," he said gently.

"There's a warehouse in the storage district, retail center. I've been past it a dozen times in the last few weeks. It seemed innocuous enough—but I've been tuning my senses, listening more closely. I am sure there are robots inside the warehouse, perhaps a great many of them. The Chief Commissioner of the Commission of General Security—"

"Yes, of course," Prothon said. He rose and glared out over the Specials, through the lines of his own troops, to the mob. "We'll get you through to the warehouse," he said. "After that, no more. It's over."

"What's . . . over?" she asked hesitantly.

"The game," Prothon said with a smile. "There are winners, and there are losers."

67.

◆

Lodovik heard the warning sirens in his head, as did all the robots within the warehouse. He had worked out the evacuation plan with Kallusin the night before. Kallusin had told him that Plussix had anticipated a general disruption, possibly a discovery . . .

And now most of their avenues of escape were blocked by Imperial Specials. Kallusin and the other robots were busy in another part of the warehouse, carrying the heads and other precious Calvinian items: thousands of years of robot history and traditions, the memories of dozens of key robots, stored in dissected memory nodes or, in a few cases, in the whole heads. There was a religious aspect to the respect Kallusin held for these relics. But Lodovik had little time to contemplate the peculiarities of this robot society.

Lodovik found Klia and Brann in the dining hall at ground level. The young woman looked determined but scared—wide-eyed, face flushed. Brann seemed uncertain but not frightened, merely nervous.

Lodovik ignored a communication from Voltaire, a commentary on romantic oppositions that seemed completely useless.

"We are leaving now," Lodovik said.

"We're packed," Brann said, and lifted a small cloth bag that contained all their worldly goods.

"I can feel her. She's looking for *us*," Klia said.

"Perhaps," Lodovik said. "But there are hidden passages out of the lower levels that have not been used in thousands of years. Some emerge close to the palace detention center where Seldon is kept—"

"You know the palace—the codes for entry?"

"If they have not been changed. There is a certain inertia in the amendment of palace procedures. The codes for the Emperor's quarters are changed twice a day, but in other portions of the extended palace, there are codes that have been in place for ten or fifteen years. We will have to take some risks—"

The codes that you do not know, I can access, Voltaire told him.

"Just get us out of here!" Klia said. "I don't want to have to fight her."

"We may have to fight others," Lodovik said. "To persuade them, or to defend ourselves."

Klia shook her head with stubborn boldness. "I don't care about them. Not one in a thousand persuaders can hold a candle to Brann and me working together. But that woman—"

"We can beat her," Brann said. Klia glared at him, then shivered and shrugged her shoulders.

"Maybe," she said.

"Do you know robot mental structures well enough?" Lodovik inquired as they walked toward the elevators.

"What do you mean?" Klia asked. The ancient elevator doors opened with the smooth heaviness of Old Empire engineering. A feeble green emergency light blinked on within. They stepped into the ghoulish glow.

"Can you persuade a robot?" Lodovik asked.

"I don't know," Klia said. "I've never tried. Except with Kallusin—once—and I didn't know he was a robot. He fended me off."

"We have a few minutes," Lodovik said. "Practice on me."

"Why?"

"Because to get to Hari Seldon, we may have to confront Daneel. Remember what Dors Venabili said."

"Robots are so different," Klia murmured.

"Practice," Lodovik said. *You would give up your free will to this child?* Voltaire asked, understanding the question was rhetorical. *Now we take advantage of the most evil of weapons! Which is worse—robot mind-warping, or human?*

"Please," Lodovik said. "It may be very important."

"All RIGHT!" Klia shouted, feeling pushed. She did not like this—told herself she did not want to discover a new weakness in the middle of her fear. "What should I do—make you dance a jig?"

Lodovik smiled. "Whatever comes into your mind."

"You're a robot. Couldn't I just order you to dance, and you'd have to obey?"

"You are not my master," Lodovik said. "And remember—"

Klia turned away and put a hand to her cheek.

Lodovik suddenly realized it would be very pleasant to test his motor-control circuitry. The elevator would be a perfect place in which to conduct these tests, so long as he was careful not to bump into the humans who occupied it with him. It was simple, really, this urge to move, simple and pleasant to contemplate.

He began to dance, slowly at first, feeling the affirmation, the approval: thousands of humans would rate his performance highly, if not in artistic terms, certainly for the skill with which he was testing all his engineered routines. He felt very coordinated and worthy.

Klia removed her hand from her cheek. Her face was wet with tears.

Lodovik stopped and swayed for a moment as his own

robotic will sorted through disparate impulses and reached a new balance.

"I'm sorry," Klia said. "That was the wrong thing to have you do." She wiped her face quickly, embarrassed.

"You did well," Lodovik said, a little dismayed by the ease with which she had controlled him. "Did Brann coordinate with you?"

"No," Klia said.

Brann seemed stunned by her success. "Sky, we could take over all of Trantor—"

"NO!" Klia shouted. "I'm sorry I did this." She held her hands out to Lodovik as if seeking his forgiveness. "You're a machine. You are so . . . *eager* to please, deep down inside. You're easier than a child. You *are* a child."

Lodovik did not know how to respond, so he said nothing. Voltaire, however, made his opinions known in no uncertain terms. *I could feel her, as well. I have no legs, yet I wanted to dance. What sort of force is this? What a monstrosity!*

Klia would not let go of her self-disgust, and this only compounded her confusion. "But you're not a child. You are so *dignified* and *serious*. It was *bad*—like making my father—" Her voice hitched. "Making my father wet his pants." She began to sob.

Lodovik tilted his head to one side. "I am not harmed. If you are concerned about my dignity—"

"You don't understand!" Klia shouted. The door opened, and she whirled as if to face new enemies. The darkened corridor beyond was empty, silent. A thin layer of gray dust on the floor was unmarred by footprints. She leaped from the elevator and centuries puffed around her feet. "I don't want to be this way anymore! I just want to be simple!"

Her voice echoed against the impassive and ancient walls.

68.

◆

Boon stood beside Hari, and Lors Avakim stood beside Gaal Dornick. The five judges had already been seated as they entered, Linge Chen, as always, highest and in the middle. Hari felt slightly dizzy, standing more than five minutes as the clerk droned on with the charges. He squinted at the judicial chambers, then tilted slightly toward Gaal, until he was leaning on him. Gaal supported him without comment until he regained his balance and stood upright again.

"Sorry," he murmured.

Linge Chen spoke without even looking at Hari. "The continuation of this trial would serve no further purpose. General Security no longer has any reason to cross-examine Professor Seldon."

Hari did not dare feel even a breath of hope coming from the lips of this man.

"All public proceedings are now at an end." Chen and the judges stood. Sedjar Boon held Hari's other arm as the Commissioners departed from the bench. The baronial peers stood as well, murmuring among themselves. The advocate approached the crib and spoke to Gaal and Hari.

"The Chief Commissioner will have a word with you in private," he said. He nodded at Boon and Lors Avakim, professional courtesy, or perhaps acknowledging those in the same employ. "Your clients must be alone for these finalities. They will stay here. All others will leave."

Hari did not know how to feel or what to think. His resources were near a bitter end. Boon touched his arm, gave him a confident smile, and left with Avakim.

Once the room was cleared, the outer doors were sealed with long brass bars, and the Commissioners returned. Linge Chen watched Hari very closely now.

"Sire, I would prefer we have our advocates with us," Hari

said, his voice cracking. He hated these weaknesses, these infirmities.

The Commissioner to the left of Chen replied, "This is no longer a trial, Dr. Seldon. Your personal fate is no longer at issue. We are here to discuss the safety of the State."

"I will speak," Chen said. The other Commissioners seemed to melt back into their chairs, into silence, confirming the power of this lean, hard man with the calm features and manner of an ancient aristocrat. Hari though, *Why, he seems older than I do—an antique!*

"Dr. Seldon," Chen began, "you disturb the peace of the Emperor's realm. None of the quadrillions living now among all the stars of the Galaxy will be living a century from now. Why, then, should we concern ourselves with events of five centuries distance?"

"I shall not be alive half a decade hence," Hari said, "and yet it is of overpowering concern to me. Call it idealism. Call it an identification of myself with that mystical generalization to which we refer by the term, 'man.'"

"I do not wish to take the trouble to understand mysticism. Can you tell me why I may not rid myself of yourself and of an uncomfortable and unnecessary five-century future which I will never see by having you executed tonight?"

Hari called upon all his contempt for this man, contempt for death itself, to match the Chief Commissioner's outrageous calm. "A week ago," Hari said, "you might have done so and perhaps retained a one in ten probability of yourself remaining alive at year's end. Today, the one in ten probability is scarcely one in ten thousand."

The other Commissioners let out a collective sigh at this blasphemy, like virgins before a suddenly naked spouse. Chen seemed to become a little sleepier, and also a little leaner, a little harder.

"How so?" he asked, his voice dangerously mild.

"The fall of Trantor," Hari said, "cannot be stopped by

any conceivable effort. It can be hastened easily, however. The tale of my interrupted trial will spread through the Galaxy. Frustration of my plans to lighten the disaster will convince people that the future holds no promise to them. Already they recall the lives of their grandfathers with envy. They will see that political revolutions and trade stagnations will increase. The feeling will pervade the Galaxy that only what a man can grasp for himself at that moment will be of any account. Ambitious men will not wait, and unscrupulous men will not hang back. By their every action they will hasten the decay of the worlds. Have me killed, and Trantor will fall not within five centuries but within fifty years and you, yourself, within a single year."

Chen smiled as if in faint amusement. "These are words to frighten children, and yet your death is not the only answer which will satisfy us. Tell me, will your only activity be that of preparing this encyclopedia you speak of?" Chen seemed to extend a shield of magnanimity over Hari, with a sweep of his hand, and a tap of two fingers beside the bronze bell and gavel.

"It will."

"And need that be done on Trantor?"

"Trantor, my lord, possesses the Imperial Library, as well as the scholarly resources of—"

"Yes. Of course. And yet if you were located elsewhere, let us say upon a planet where the hurry and distractions of a metropolis will not interfere with scholastic musings; where your men may devote themselves entirely and single-mindedly to their work;—might not that have advantages?"

"Minor ones, perhaps."

"Such a world has been chosen, then. You may work, doctor, at your leisure, with your hundred thousand about you. The Galaxy will know that you are working and fighting the Fall. They will even be told that you will prevent the Fall. If the Galaxy that cares about such things, believes you to be correct, they will be happier." He smiled, "Since I do not believe in so many things, it is not difficult for me to disbelieve in the Fall as well, so that I am entirely convinced I will be telling the truth to the people. And meanwhile, doctor, you will not trouble Trantor and there will be no disturbance of the Emperor's peace.

"The alternative is death for yourself and for as many of your followers as will seem necessary. Your earlier threats I disregard. The opportunity for choosing between death and exile is given you over a time period stretching from this moment to one five minutes hence."

"Which is the world chosen, my lord?" Hari asked, concealing the tension of his anticipation.

Chen called Hari forward to the docket with a waggle of his thin finger, and pointed to an informer tablet, on which an image of the world and its location were displayed. "It is called, I believe, Terminus," said Chen.

Hari glanced at it, breathless, and looked up at Chen. They were closer than they had ever been before, barely an arm's length between them. Hari could see the fine lines of strain on the calm features, like wrinkles on a world of ice. "It is uninhabited, but quite habitable, and can be molded to suit the necessities of scholars. It is somewhat secluded—"

Hari tried to show some dismay. "It is at the edge of the Galaxy, sir."

Chen dismissed this as unworthy with a roll of his eyes. He regarded Hari wearily, as if asking, *We do not need these theatrics, do we, really?* "As I have said, somewhat secluded. It will suit your needs for concentration. Come, you have two minutes left."

Hari could hardly conceal his elation. He felt, for the merest instant, a burst of gratitude to this gentry monster. "We will need time to arrange such a trip," he said, voice softened. "There are twenty thousand families involved."

Gaal Dornick, still in the crib, cleared his throat.

Chen lowered his gaze to the informer, tapped the display off. "You will be given time."

Hari could not help himself. The last minute was passing quickly, and yet he could not stop from giving his triumph the last few seconds to grow all the larger, all the more shocking to those without his knowledge. Finally, as the minute crept into the last five seconds, he murmured, voice rough and subdued in defeat, "I accept exile."

Gaal Dornick gasped and sat down abruptly.

The proctor entered once more and observed the acceptance, noted that all was proper, and recorded the results and declarations, then deferred to the Chief Commissioner.

Chen held up his hand and officially pronounced, "This matter is at an end. The Commission is no longer concerned. Now all go."

Hari stepped back from the bench to join Gaal.

"Not you," Chen said softly.

The deal, if deal it was, has astonished all Foundation scholars. It has the air of a miracle. There must have been prior arrangements, unknown deals behind the deal, yet our texts and depositions and even the trial records give us no clue. It is thought that this period of Hari Seldon's life will forever remain dark.

How could the trial have gone so well? How could Seldon have focused the tools of psychohistory so precisely, even during ag, the first "Seldon crisis"? The forces arrayed against Hari Seldon were formidable; Gaal Dornick records that Linge Chen felt genuinely threatened by him. Dornick may have been influenced by Seldon's view of Chen, perhaps not entirely accurate: what we know of Chen from Imperial sources suggests that the Chief Commissioner was a coldly calculating and highly efficient political mind, frightened by no man. Seldon, of course, thought otherwise.

Students of this period . . .

—Encyclopedia Galactica, 117th Edition, 1054 F.E.

69.
◆

The Commission court bailiff followed Hari and Linge Chen into the consultation chamber behind the judge's bench. Hari sat in a narrow chair before the Chief Commissioner's small desk and watched Chen warily. Chen did not sit, but waited for his Laventian servant to help him out of his ceremonial robes. In a simple gray cassock, Chen reached up to the ceiling with hands clenched, cracked his knuckles, and turned to Seldon.

"You have enemies," Chen said. "That is no surprise. What is surprising is that your enemies have been my enemies, much of the time. Does that interest you?"

Hari pursed his lips but said nothing.

Chen looked away as if supremely bored. "This exile will not, of course, extend to you," he continued. "You will not leave Trantor. I will forbid it if you try."

"I am too old and do not wish to leave, my lord," Hari said. "There is still work to do here."

"So much dedication," Chen mused softly, rubbing one elbow with the palm of his opposite hand. "Should you survive, and finish your work, I will be interested to learn of the results."

"We'll all be dead," Hari said, "before the results are proved or disproved."

"Come, Dr. Seldon," Chen said. "Speak with me frankly, as one old manipulator to another. I am told you have planned the results of this trial years in advance, through careful political arrangement—and with considerable political skill."

"Not planned; foretold through mathematics," Hari said.

"Whatever. Now, we are at last done with each other, to our mutual relief."

"My lord, what about the Commission of General Security?" Hari asked. "They might object to these results."

"There is no longer such an agency," Chen said. "The Emperor has withdrawn their charter. Perhaps that was foretold as well, by your mathematics."

Hari folded his hands before him. "They don't even show in the lattice of results, my lord," he said, and realized his tone might be considered arrogant. Too late.

Chen accepted these words in silence. then spoke in a chilling monotone. "You have studied me, Professor Seldon, but you do not know me. If I have my way, you never will." The Chief Commissioner curled his lip and stared up at the ceiling. "I despise your mathematics. It is nothing more than dressed-up superstition, tricked-out religion, and it smells of the same degeneration and decay you so enthusiastically embrace and promote. You are of a kind with those who hunt for God-like robots in every shadow. I let you go now because you are nothing to me, you no longer have any place in my designs."

The Chief Commissioner waved his hand to the bailiff. "You are remanded to civil authority for release," he said, and left the room with a small swirl of his cassock.

The Lavrentian servant glanced briefly and curiously at Hari, and departed after his master. Hari could have sworn the servant was trying to communicate a sense of relief.

"Professor Seldon," the bailiff said, with an age-old air of professional courtesy, "follow me."

70.

◆

Kallusin had finished the removal of Plussix's head. He withdrew the cables which had provided temporary power to the robot as the most recent memories were fixed in permanent storage within the iridium-sponge backup, then he lifted the head from the plastic cradle, away from the slightly smoking neck, and lowered it into the archival metal box.

He could hear the commotion among Plussix's wards as the troops moved through the warehouse. Through the window overlooking the warehouse interior, Kallusin could see Prothon's troops herding the young mentalics—thirty in all—toward personnel carriers at street level. Whatever their persuasive skills, they did not seem able to escape.

He could do nothing for them now. He lifted the box, carried it to the end of the long chamber, and stopped as he heard boots beyond the door.

To Kallusin's surprise, it was Prothon himself who entered, pushing the door open with a slight kick. Kallusin stood in place as the general walked into the chamber. Prothon surveyed the dilapidated equipment and the half dismantled robot in the harness a few meters away.

The general was unarmed, and his troops hung back behind the door. For a moment, nothing was said and neither moved.

"Are you human?" Prothon finally asked.

Kallusin did not reply.

"Robot, then. All my men down there are getting headaches—I'm just as glad you're not one of the youngsters." Prothon nodded at the box carrying Plussix's head. "What's that—a bomb?"

Kallusin said, "No."

"No weapons, no means of defense—almost certainly a robot." Prothon regarded him curiously. "In good condition, and very convincing. Very old, centuries?"

Kallusin did not even blink. There was nothing more he could do without harming Prothon or the troops before him, and he could not harm humans.

"I order you to identify yourself," Prothon said, then, astonishingly, he added, "Owner identity may be excluded, but personal type and origin and serial number may not."

"R. Kallusin Dass, S–13407-D–10237."

"Robot Kallusin Dass, Solaria, late model," Prothon said quietly. "Pleased to make your acquaintance. I have instructions to take two robots into custody. One is R. Daneel or Danee, surname and ID unknown. The other is R. Lodovik Trema, ID also unknown. You are neither of these?"

Kallusin shook his head.

"What's in the box, R. Kallusin? Mandatory, excluding information that may be of harm to your master or owner."

Prothon knew the old forms of interrogation. Kallusin could have eluded a question that his programming could consider ambiguous or harmful to his owners—the human race. Plussix had reassigned ownership of his robots to the broader category a century before, foreseeing advantages to this workaround.

A restrained kind of Zeroth Law . . . Never necessary, until now.

Kallusin could not, on short notice, come up with any reason not to inform Prothon what was in the box. Their mission was over, at any rate.

"A robotic head," Kallusin said. "Nonfunctional."

"Are you the only robot remaining? We have reason to believe others have left this building already, before we arrived."

"I am the only one remaining."

"If I take you into custody, will you remain functional?"

"No," Kallusin said. That would harm the cause, and possibly therefore harm his owner—the human race.

"If my men enter . . . you will not remain functional?"

"I will not," Kallusin said.

"A standoff, then. I have very little time, but I'm curious. What were you trying to do, here?"

Prothon had neglected to use the form of address. Kallusin weighed the situation carefully. He had no hope of escape, and there was no profit in discussing anything more with General Prothon. But before he shut himself down, permanently, he was himself curious—about Prothon's knowledge.

"I will answer your question if you will answer mine," Kallusin said.

"I'll try." Prothon seemed amused by this remarkable dialog.

"How do you know about robots?"

"Personally, suspicions, only suspicions, all these years of service to the Empire. Found a dysfunctional robot on a distant planet once—destroyed during an invasion. Haven't seen one since."

"How do you know the forms of address?"

"Linge Chen gave me instructions, told me to speak directly with any robots, also told me there was no danger addressing the robots we would find here."

"Thank you," Kallusin said. *Suspicions, only suspicions, Daneel.* "My answer is, I am here to serve my owner." He reached into the box and pressed a hidden corner switch. The box began to heat. He placed it on the floor. Within several seconds, Plussix's head would be cooked, useless. Then Kallusin stood tall. He could not deactivate himself just yet. The threat had to be immediate.

Prothon looked at the box, now glowing a dull red and crackling slightly against the tiles on the floor. He made a small grimace and called for his troops to enter.

That was enough. The threat of capture and interrogation became very real. Kallusin would become a danger to his owner.

He collapsed on the floor before anyone of the troops could reach him.

Prothon observed this with an air of profound respect. He had seen many human soldiers do precisely the same thing. It was time-honored, and actually, more than he had expected from a robot—but then, he had only known this one robot for a few minutes, and was in no position to judge.

He left the chamber and ordered it to be searched by a party of the Commissioner's engineers.

71.

◆

Klia could feel the troops a few hundred meters above and behind them, intent on the search. Lodovik led them deeper beneath the warehouse district, until they came to a small round hatch almost completely blocked by debris from an ancient flood. Klia took hold of Brann's arm and stepped back as Lodovik cleared the debris. Brann smiled down on her, barely visible in the dim light of the maintenance globes, pulled her hand loose, and went to help Lodovik. With a sigh, Klia also pitched in, and in less than a minute, they had the hatchway cleared.

Klia could not hear or otherwise sense anybody in the tunnel behind them, but she felt deeply uneasy nonetheless. The flood debris, the years of corrosion on the hatchway, the difficulty they had prying it open—it would not get any easier from this point on.

They were heading into the depths of the ancient hydraulic system for Trantor's earliest cities. Beyond the hatchway, they could see even less—globes were spaced at thirty meter intervals, and seemed even dimmer. That they stayed illuminated at all was evidence of the skill of the early engineers and architects on Trantor, who realized that this deep infrastructure must be far more reliable, and persistent, than even the cities that would rise, be demolished, and rise again, far above.

"We go for about three kilometers this way," Lodovik said, "then we start to climb again. There may be pedways, escalators, elevators—and there may not. Kallusin hasn't explored these ways in decades."

Klia said nothing, simply remained at Brann's side as the robot led them deeper, until she could sense no humans whatsoever. She had never been this far from crowds. She wondered what it would be like, to have an entire planet to oneself, with no responsibilities, no guilt, no talents and no need for talents . . .

Lodovik's footfalls ahead took them into murky darkness, and soon they were up to their ankles in stagnant water. From somewhere to their left came the sound of huge pumps, thumping into action, then cutting off with distant swallowing roars. *Trantor's heartbeat.*

Brann looked down at her and helped her climb over a pile of eroded plastic parts, like blockage in an ancient artery.

"I can see fairly well now," Lodovik said, "though I suspect you cannot. Please just stay close behind me. We're much better off down here, following this route, than we would be up there."

Klia suddenly felt something loud in her head, but very distant, like the report from a shell. She listened for it again as she walked beside Brann, and it came once more, more muddied, but she was ready for it, and she could almost taste its odd signature.

Vara Liso. Thousands of meters above and in front of them. Perhaps in the Palace.

"That woman," Klia said to Brann.

"Yeah," Brann said. "What's she doing?"

"Feels like she's exploding," Klia said.

"Please stay close behind me," Lodovik insisted. There was a lift shaft ahead, according to Kallusin—and soon he would have a chance to try his codes to gain entrance to the foundations of the Imperial Courts Building.

72.

◆

Major Namm held the neural whip in an unsteady hand. Sweat streaked his face. He stumbled slightly as he tried to turn away from the diminutive woman in her special emerald green gown. Vara Liso wore a quizzical expression, eyes turned up, as if she did not really need to look at the major to control him.

She seemed to be inspecting the ceiling over his head.

The major whimpered, and the whip fell from his hand.

She was so tired. She walked around the major. She would need something sweet to drink very soon, and something to eat, but first she had to go through the door and see Farad Sinter, make her final report to the man she had hoped someday to marry. Foolish dreams, absurd hopes.

Vara Liso entered the anteroom of Sinter's new office

and saw the new furnishings, the banks of special Imperial-grade informers that would have hooked him directly to the orbiting receivers and processors. This would have been his command center. Sinter. She smiled crookedly. Heating without melting, dry at the center, a pile of sand, no man, no success, no fault, she had thrown the wands in the ancient game of Bioka, always resorted to when she was at her wit's end, and the wands said no fault, correction in order, all is not right at the Sinter.

Beyond the immense bronze doors she could hear shouting and even wailing. She leaned her shoulder against the door. Nothing. Then she turned her full attention to the major, bade him come forward and give his code to the door. He got off his knees, face contorted and dripping sweat. He punched in the code and applied his palm.

The door swung open, and the major fell back. Vara Liso entered the office.

Farad stood there in full ceremonial outfit, conferring with two advisors and an advocate; no matter, his Commission was at an end. He saw her and frowned. "I need to get things in order—Vara, please leave."

Vara spotted a tray full of delicate sweets on the expansive desk, beside the most powerful informer/processor she had ever beheld, perhaps able to distill information from ten thousand systems. It was not functioning now. *Access to the Empire denied. Power gone.* She lifted a handful of the sweets and chewed on them.

Sinter stared at her. "Please," he said softly. He sensed her distress but could not know its cause. "They're melting down our robot. Seldon is being released. I'm trying to reach the Emperor now. This is very important."

"Nobody will see us," she said, her finger stirring the candies in the tray.

"It isn't that bad," Sinter insisted, his face pale. "How did you get in?" The major—her major—had been released by

Prothon to inform Sinter of the situation. He had then been posted in the anteroom to keep her out. So much was obvious without even tasting their thoughts.

She had never been able to read thoughts directly; at best she could taste emotions, pick up flashes of vision, sound, but never detail. Humans were not alike, deep inside. Minds developed differently.

Vara knew that all humans were aliens to each other, but her own alienation was of a different order.

"Miss Liso, you need to leave now," the advocate said, and walked toward her. "I'll contact you later about representation in the Imperial courts—"

He stumbled and his face turned up and he started to stutter and drool. Farad looked on him with dawning alarm. "Vara, are you doing that?" he demanded.

She let the advocate go. "You lied," she said to Sinter.

"What are you talking about?"

"I'll get Seldon myself," she said. "You stay here, and we'll leave together."

"No!" Sinter cried. "Stop this stupidity! We have to—"

For a moment, Vara Liso went blank. The room turned black and swam, then seemed to flash into existence again. Sinter clutched his desk and stared at her with very round eyes. He looked down at his chest, at his knees twitching, legs folding beneath him. Then he looked up at her again. His advisors had already fallen to their knees, arms straight by their sides, fists clenched. They keeled over in opposite directions, and one hit his head on the edge of the desk.

Farad's heart slowed. Vara did not know if she was doing this thing or not. She did not believe she was so strong, had never done such a thing before, but no matter.

She turned away from the man she would have married, in all her best dreams and hopes, and said, "Now I am undeniably a *monster*." The word sounded delicious, free, very final.

She left the office and walked with a lovely lightness

through the anteroom past the major, still gasping, then paused—but only for an instant—and grimaced.

Farad was dying. She could feel the emptiness and silence in his chest. She touched her cheek.

Now he was dead.

She picked up the major's neural whip and continued on.

73.

There were endless documents to sign, releases to be obtained from offices and levels within the Commission of Public Safety and dozens of judicial bureaus to notify; it would take Hari longer to leave the courts than it had ever taken him to enter. Gaal Dornick was in a separate area, and Boon had departed three hours ago to take care of various entanglements.

Hari sat alone within the cavernous Hall of Dispensation, looking up at the ancient vault and skylights overhead, with their many-colored windows of pieced glass. He had been told to sit there until the jailer returned with the warden and issued his final documents.

Hari was not sure how he felt. A little disbelieving, that was certain; he had passed through the belly of the Imperial courts as yet undigested. The moment toward which, knowingly or in ignorance, he had worked all his life, had passed.

Now there were the first few records to be made—he would notify Wanda and Stettin of their final and, he suspected, surprising assignment, that the psychologists and mentalics of the Second Foundation would be staying on Trantor—and he would make the preparations to transfer his powers to Gaal and the others who would leave for Terminus.

The long twilight of the Empire would darkle. He would not live much longer to see it, nor did he want to. Seeing the glow of the overhead domes through the vault windows, perhaps fifty meters above him, made him think of what a real skyglow through real stained glass would look like, on Helicon.

Stillness. Completion is near, yet I feel no real sense of satisfaction; where is my personal reward? What if I have saved humanity from thousands of years of chaos; what have I accomplished for myself? Unworthy thoughts for a prophet or a hero. I have a granddaughter, not really my own flesh; the continuity is broken biologically, if not philosophically. I have a few new friends around me, but the old are either gone, dead, or inaccessible.

He thought of standing on the upperside maintenance tower, just a few weeks ago, and of the gloom that had enveloped him then. *I cannot leave Trantor; Chen will not let me. I am still dangerous and best kept bottled. But where would I most like to go now, where would I most like to be, in my last days?*

Helicon. In the sun, outside, away from these enclosing ceiled cities, away from the metal skin of Trantor. To see a night sky that was not simulated and to be unafraid of the expanse, the thousands of stars, a small glimpse of the Empire for which he had labored and which he had tried to understand.

To stand in the open, in the rain and the weather and the cold, and not be afraid; to be with old friends and family—

The obsessive thoughts that filled so many of his nights. He sighed and sat up, listening to the sounds of boots marching down the northern hallway.

Three guards and the warden entered and approached Hari.

"There's been a disturbance in the new Commission building, near the palace and not too far from here," the warden said. "We've been told to lock down until the disturbance has been explained."

"What sort of disturbance?" Hari asked.

"I don't know," the warden said. "Nothing to worry about. We're fine here. We've been given instructions to protect you at any cost—"

Hari heard a sound from the eastern entrance of the hall. He turned and saw a woman standing there and gave a gasp—in the light, at this distance, her stance, her bearing—the dream—

74.

Dors Venabili had kept her own list of codes and passages in the palace buildings, and remarkably, most of them still worked. No doubt the codes that let people *out* of the buildings were changed more frequently than those that let them *in*. When Hari had been arrested and charged with assault, decades before, she had made plans to break into the Courts Building and release him, and the work she had done then served her well now.

It also possible that Joan had helped her . . . But how she had come here ultimately did not matter. She would have battered down walls to do so.

She was the first to enter the Hall of Dispensation. She saw Hari and three men, standing near the center, lit by the diffuse glow of the skylight. She halted for a moment. The men were not threatening Hari. Quite the contrary; she judged they were there to protect him.

Hari turned and looked in her direction. His mouth opened and she heard his intake of breath echo in the hall. The three men turned, and the eldest, a large, stocky fellow wearing the uniform of an Imperial warden, called out to her:

"Who are you? What are you doing here?"

From the northern entrance came a sizzle and a flash of light. Dors knew that sound very well: a neural whip, fired from several dozen meters. The three men around Hari jerked and danced for a moment, then fell to the floor, moaning.

Hari stood untouched.

Dors ran as fast as she could toward the small, intense-looking woman standing near the northern entrance. This woman still held the neural whip, and seemed to have eyes only for Hari. In less than four seconds, Dors moved to within less than two meters of her.

Vara Liso cried out with the effort of her persuasion. The hall seemed to fill with voices, ugly demanding voices. Hari clutched his hands over his ears and winced, and the men on the floor twitched even more violently, but the main force of the mentalic bolt went toward Dors.

Dors had never felt such a blast, had never known humans were capable of such discharges. She had felt Daneel's subtle persuasive abilities during her training period on Eos, nothing more.

It seemed perfectly natural, in mid-stride, on her way to incapacitating and if necessary killing this woman who threatened Hari, simply to pull up her legs and attempt to fly. Her body of metal and synthetic flesh curled into a ball and she glanced off the woman's upper shoulder, knocking her to one side.

Dors caromed from the opposite wall and fell to the floor in a tangle. She could not move; she did not want to move, not at that moment, perhaps not ever again.

75.

Daneel left the taxi at the Greys' Entrance on the east side of the Imperial Courts Building, then stood by the small double metal doors. He wore the uniform of a lifetime bureaucrat, native to Trantor and not a student or pilgrim; he had reserved this identity decades ago, among many others, and if queried by any security guards, there would be files in the personnel computers to explain him and his duties, his right to be here.

The doors were ornately inscribed with the general rules of public service. The first rule was *Do no harm to your Emperor or his subjects.*

Even in the taxi, Daneel had felt the mentalic explosions, from the general vicinity of the palace, but did not know what they signified, if anything. It was easy to imagine his plans unraveling, now that they were almost complete. He had juggled for so long, keeping literally tens of millions of balls in the air at once . . .

He shifted the small bureaucratic valise under his arm and entered a specific and reserved code for entry by a gray administrative officer.

It was refused. The codes had all been changed; there was an emergency within the Courts Building, perhaps within the palace itself.

Here. My Other is within the building. Joan, split into many Joans, many meme-minds, worked from both sides.

The left-hand door opened, and he entered the building.

It took him longer than he expected to make his way through the secure facilities, even with Joan's help.

On the last door, when he knew he was within two doors of joining Hari in the beautiful, high-ceilinged Hall of Dispensation, Joan distracted a human guard by sending him revised watch instructions.

Daneel smelled electricity in the next segment of hallway. A neural whip had been discharged here in the last few minutes—

76.

Hari faced Vara Liso across the Hall of Dispensation. She stood for a moment with hands held out, fingers wriggling, as if she fought to keep her balance. Her head swayed from side to side. The woman who had entered before her—who had reminded him so much of Dors—lay in a heap, rolled up against the door, still, as if dead.

Hari did not feel afraid; things had happened too quickly for that emotion to take hold. Everything seemed out of place, most of all himself; he did not belong there, and they did not belong there.

The hall had been peaceful—now it smelled of electricity, of urine leaking from the pants of the three men supine on the floor around him.

"I'm saving you . . ." Vara Liso said from across the hall. She took a step toward him, lowering her arms. "For last."

"Who are you?" Hari asked. He was concerned about the woman on the floor. He wanted above all else to make sure she was all right; tremors spread in his mind, memories, triggered responses, confusing and rich and evoking a sense both of intense promise and of horror, for he was sure that this woman was Dors. *She's come back. She wanted to protect me. The way she moved . . . like a springing tiger!*

And now she's down like a squashed insect.

This small, thin woman . . . an aberration. A monster!

Hari then knew who the woman was. Wanda had mentioned her weeks ago, the woman who had not agreed to join the mentalics, who had allied instead with Farad Sinter.

"You're Vara Liso," he said, and started to move toward her.

"Good," the woman said, her voice trembling. "I want you to know who I am. You're the one to blame."

"Blame for what?" Hari asked.

"You work with the robots." Her expression twisted until it seemed her face might become a knot. "You're their *lackey*, and they think they've won!"

77.

◆━━━▶

Lodovik invoked the last of the codes he knew, and the door to the transfer corridor from the Courts Building still refused to open. He worked the code around again on the finger pad beside the doorframe, and the tiny simplified face in the display proclaimed once again that the code was incomplete. It would be so like the palace security detail to add a few numbers, but not change the beginning numbers.

I am working, Voltaire told him. *There must be many security measures being triggered now—multiple intrusions, perhaps!*

The girl and the large young man behind him shifted from foot to foot.

"It won't be good to stay here," Brann said. "Something feels very bad."

Voltaire's features appeared in the display, simplified to cartoon detail. The mechanical voice now said, "Additional numbers are required under the revised security procedures." The new face winked at Lodovik. "Test procedure fifteen A for verification," the voice added. "You may enter code for personal use only during this test period. Upon completion of test period, a formal entry code or new password must be established and fixed."

Lodovik glanced over his shoulder at Klia as he entered seven new numbers. She stared at the display with furrowed brow.

"Who is that?" she asked.

"The sim," Lodovik said.

The door opened. Lodovik beckoned for them to pass through first.

"Is Hari Seldon near?" Klia asked.

He is very near, Voltaire said. *And he is in imminent danger.*

78.

◆

"I wanted so much," Vara Liso said. "Do you understand?"

Hari looked at her straight on. He stood perhaps four meters from her, seven meters from where the other woman lay against the half open door. He glanced at the other woman, and Liso raised the neural whip.

"You don't need *that*," Hari said critically, as if lecturing a student. Vara Liso hesitated. "You're mentalic. You stopped *her* . . ." He raised his arm toward the collapsed woman. Toward Dors.

Vara Liso lowered her head but kept her eyes on Hari. She looked like a pouting child, but in her eyes was the purest hatred he had ever seen.

"Everything I've ever believed in," she said, "is dead. They're going to kill me, just as they killed the men and women and children I found. My own people."

"Farad Sinter made you do that . . ." Hari said. "Didn't he?"

"The Emperor," Vara Liso said. She seemed ready to burst into tears, but she kept the whip high, and her finger lingered on the button. Hari could make out the setting: near lethality.

"Yes, but Sinter was your—"

"*He loved me*," Vara moaned, then she dropped the whip. But a wave of grief came out of her that hit him square. The hall was filled with Vara Liso's emotions, and they were the ugliest and bleakest Hari had ever known. They struck at his own centers of ambition and need, and he could feel the bones of his innermost self cracking.

The woman on the floor stirred, and Vara Liso lifted her head and half turned toward her.

Hari made his move, using the only chance he thought he would ever get. He had had years of training in self-defense on Helicon, but his body had long since refused to answer his instructions promptly. He had almost reached Liso when she cocked her head back and screamed again—silently, and within her mind.

At Hari.

Simultaneously, Brann and Lodovik pushed against the door, nudging Dors, who could not yet conjure up the will to move.

Klia stumbled over Dors' leg, fell into the Hall of Dispensation, saw Lodovik moving with inhuman speed toward her enemy, saw him raise his arm, hand open, to take the woman's hand in his and spin her around—

To kill her if need be, exercising that human freedom—

But he stopped before his fingers touched her, frozen by a glance.

Vara Liso knelt, rubbing her wrists and hands, and faced Klia Asgar.

79.

◆

Daneel ran past the empty guard station in the security vestibule. His relatively weak perceptions of human mental states was now a fortunate shield; the backwash of another explosion, like the final death cough of a huge volcano, left him reeling, skidding on hands and knees, tumbling into the Hall of Dispensation from the eastern entrance. He had an impression of Joan, and all her copies in the machines around him, coming apart like a rotten flag in a high wind, trying to stay together; but then that image was highly inconsequential, for his own patterns, his own mind, threatened to do the same thing.

80.
◆

If the cry of a child could have been made of knives, it could not have cut Klia any more deeply than the mentalic shock wave surrounding Vara Liso.

Disappointment, grief, anger, an intense sense of misplaced justice, images of people long dead—parents, young friends, who had disappointed this small woman with the knotted face and crab-curled fists—batted against Klia, fragments of ruin in a flood of pain.

The walls and pillars and panes of the Hall of Dispensation felt nothing. Vara Liso's output was tuned to a purely human channel, to the roots of mind in matter. Because she had not focused her talents completely on him, Lodovik felt merely a buzzing and a pressure not dissimilar to the neutrino flux he had encountered between the stars.

He did, however, sense what Daneel saw very clearly—the disintegration of the entity who had spoken in him and through him. Voltaire stood in simple nakedness before this flux, this human tempest, and broke apart like a child's puzzle.

For a moment, Klia's sympathetic response nearly allowed her to die, to both drown and be burned by the outpouring. She felt the echoes of her own life, her own experiences, mesh with those of Vara Liso.

There were differences, however, and they were her salvation. She saw the strength of her own will, opposed to the vacillation and indecision of Vara Liso. She saw the not-always-apparent strength of her father and, earlier, before memory began clearly, her mother, faced with a willful child, giving her enough leeway to be what she must be, however much it might discomfit or even hurt them.

She was on the point of fighting back when the most dangerous similarity of all caught her unprepared.

Vara Liso cried out for freedom.

Her voice rose in a shriek to the highest reaches of the hall and echoed back: *"Let us be what we must be! No robots, no killing metal hands, no conspiracies and shackles!"*

Klia felt something smoking, crisping, in her thoughts. It was her sense of self. She would willingly sacrifice all before this urgent scream of pain—had felt it herself, though never so clearly and powerfully expressed. She recognized insanity buried within it, the insanity of a powerful and even self-destructive immune response—

as did Daneel, trying to recover and get to his feet, a few dozen meters away.

—A rejection of twenty thousand years of benevolence and guidance, of patient and secret servitude.

The cry of a child never allowed to mature, to feel its own pain and draw its own conclusions on life and death.

Klia closed her eyes and crawled along the floor, trying to find Brann. She could neither see nor sense him. She dared not open her eyes, or she would be blinded, she was sure. Vara Liso could not broadcast with such intensity for so long, and indeed the undirected flood was narrowing, finding a channel. It was concentrating, and even though it suddenly diminished by half, what Vara Liso was throwing directly at Klia doubled in strength.

Hari stood somehow on quivering legs and saw but did not quite comprehend these human forms, the small thin woman walking forward step by staggered step, features distorted as if seen through a broken lens, two others crawling along the floor, one a burly Dahlite male and the other a slender and not unattractive young woman, also dark.

He did not see the tall humanlike figure on the east side of the hall.

His mind filled with the waters of his own despair.

He had been in error. It had all been for nothing, worse than nothing.

Hari Seldon suddenly wanted to die, to be done with the pain and the realization of his failure.

But there was that woman who had tried to tackle Vara Liso, who he was sure was Dors Venabili.

Vara Liso was killing Klia Asgar and Brann. This much was clear to Lodovik. The buzz had diminished, but as he stepped toward the knotted and distorted woman, it increased again.

Lodovik paid little attention to Daneel, or to Hari Seldon, or to Dors; both seemed out of the immediate focus of Liso's lethal projections. The knotted woman was clearly going to scramble all the essential patterns of Klia and Brann, then turn on the others.

Voltaire was no longer in place to advise.

Lodovik stepped toward the woman, now twisted and gnarled like an ancient willow.

Klia lifted her head, opened her eyes, prepared to be blinded, and saw down a short brilliant funnel of hatred to the eyes, all that were left of Vara Liso—a pair of desperate and hate-filled eyes.

Brann will die, too.

Never had she used her abilities to harm. Even making Lodovik dance had injured her sense of propriety and justice; she had never really believed she could do anything to Hari Seldon. She would think of her father, whom she had once made wet his pants . . . and the effort would collapse.

Brann will die along with you, then they will all die, and she will be destroyed as well. Useless.

She reached out for Brann. Alone she could do nothing against such naked and monstrous strength.

Brann was a filament of clean light in the torrent of flaming hatred. She tugged at him, as if she would wake him up.

Brann said *yes*, and they joined. She had almost felt this happen during their physical joining, but had pulled back, still wishing to preserve her own self as a lone and defiant place.

Lodovik reached out with both hands, saw Vara Liso's shoulders twitch in awareness of his presence. She swiveled her head suddenly, tears flying from her eyes.

Lodovik was willing to hurt her, kill her if need be, if she did not stop. This was what humans had done to each other throughout their history, and it hurt him that he had such freedom as well: freedom to harm and to kill. But he was under no misapprehension that he was no better than this gnarled and hideous female. Quite clearly she was evil; she was antihuman.

He made his judgment, his decision.

He could feel a rumbling tidal wash coming. He grasped her shoulder and neck, and, with a sudden twist of his arms—

Broke the woman's neck like a matchstick.

Poor small Vara Liso. At the age of five years, her mother had beaten her severely, venting anger against her father, who had not been in the small and immaculately clean apartment; her mother had held her down with a variety of persuasion that came only when she was enraged.

She had beaten young Vara with a long, flexible plastic pole, until little welts rose on her bottom and along her back.

And so there had come the day when she had caused her mother to die, a memory she sometimes grasped hard for strength. And she had taken her mother, perhaps just a memory but perhaps not, inside, to compensate. Held her in a little diamond cage in her dreams.

Bringing out her mother for extra strength did not help. Actually, it weakened her, because it made her a child again, even more than she had been before.

She had never been an adult, not really.

The combined ribbon of light and wave of terrified heat that caught her and shivered her (burning without flame: *sinter*), the hand on her neck twisting

was incredibly painful

and very welcome

and broke open all of her own cages

so that she was, for a second, calm

Klia felt the last gust of Vara Liso and it whispered *free* then was silent.

Lodovik knelt beside the body and saw that it was very tiny and when he picked it up, it was very light as well. So much trouble from so little mass—a human wonder.

Then he began to cry.

Dors had recovered enough to stand. She observed the men and the woman within the hall, and the dead thing in the arms of the robot Lodovik, and she started toward Hari, who seemed dazed and confused, though still alive. It was only natural for her to go to him.

Daneel was suddenly at her side and took her by the arm.

"He needs help," Dors said, prepared to wrench her arm free from the grasp of her own master.

"There is nothing you can do," Daneel said. By now, security in the Courts and Hall of Dispensation would be aware of the breach; they would soon be surrounded by heavily armed guards and no doubt even Imperial Specials.

He could not see any way of escaping. Nor could he predict what would happen next. Perhaps it did not matter.

It was very possible he had been completely in error in all of his actions, for over twenty thousand years.

81.

◆

"The hall records show that after she killed Farad Sinter and incapacitated the guards, Vara Liso went to the Hall of Dispensation and threatened Hari Seldon," Major Namm said. His head was encapsulated in a regeneration helmet. He would be weeks recovering from the brain damage Liso had inflicted on him outside the office of Farad Sinter. "We believe these others used many varieties of subterfuge to enter the hall and protect Seldon. They apparently knew Seldon was in grave danger."

"And we did not?" Linge Chen asked. He leaned forward slightly in his chair, arms tight by his side, his gaze somewhere over the major's shoulder.

"There were no directives issued for Seldon's protection," General Prothon reminded the Chief Commissioner. "If these others had not arrived, Vara Liso could easily have killed him with the neural whip or her peculiar talents. Yet she was the only one authorized to be in the Courts Building and Imperial Sector. It is not clear how she died, but I am glad she is dead."

"For the last three days, everyone in Imperial Sector has suffered tremendous headaches. Haven't you felt them?" Chen asked.

"I usually suffer from headaches, Commissioner. It is my lot in life," Prothon said cheerfully.

Chen scrutinized the video summary of events in the Hall of Dispensation. He was looking for something, someone, a ghost, a shade, a clue embodied. He pointed to the tall man standing by the strong-looking woman at the end of the summary. "Individual file on this one?"

"There is none," General Prothon told him. "We have no idea who he is."

Linge Chen looked away from the informer display for a moment, and one side of his face tensed as he clenched his jaw. "Bring him to me. The woman with him as well." He shifted his attention to the magnified image of the stocky man holding the body of Vara Liso. His expression softened for a moment. "And this one. Hari Seldon is to be released to his colleagues or to his family. I do not wish responsibility for him anymore. Keep the young Dahlites in custody for the time being."

Major Namm seemed unhappy. Chen lifted an eyebrow in his general direction. "You have a comment?"

"They all violated palace security—"

"Yes, they *did*, didn't they?" Chen asked pointedly. "And you are part of that team which ensures palace security?"

The major straightened and said no more.

"You may go," Chen told him. Quickly, the major departed.

General Prothon chuckled. "Surely you won't blame *him*," the general said.

Chen shook his head. "We have very nearly made the biggest blunder of our careers."

"How?" Prothon asked.

"We nearly lost Hari Seldon."

"I presumed he was expendable."

Chen almost frowned, but his face quickly returned to impassivity. "This man here . . . do you recognize him?"

"No," Prothon said, squinting at the magnified image.

"Once he was known as Demerzel," Linge Chen said.

Prothon drew his head back and narrowed his eyes dubiously, but did not contradict the Chief Commissioner.

"He never dies," Chen continued. "He goes away for decades at a time, then he returns. He has often been associated with the interesting career of Hari Seldon." Chen, for the first time that day, smiled up at Prothon. That smile was peculiar, almost wolfish, and Chen's eyes glittered with mixed emotions. "I suspect he has been directing my efforts in various ways for years now, always to my advantage . . ." He said again, musing softly, "Always to my advantage . . ."

"Another machine-man, I presume," Prothon said. "I am glad not to be privy to that history."

"No need for you to have known," Chen said. "I myself can only suspect. He is, after all, a master of camouflage and prevarication. I will enjoy meeting with him and asking a few questions, one master to another."

"Why don't you simply execute him?"

"Because there could easily be others to take his place. For all I know, they are right here, in this palace."

"Klayus?" Prothon asked, his grin almost invisible.

Chen sniffed. "We should be so lucky."

"Why would it have been so bad to lose Seldon, a thorn in the Empire's side?" Prothon asked.

"Because this Demerzel of old might spend another thousand years trying to raise up another Hari Seldon," Chen said. "And this time, all would probably not go well for me, or for you, my dear Dragon. Seldon said as much, and for once, I believe him."

Prothon shook his head. "I can more easily believe in machine-men than in Eternals. I've met robots, after all. But . . . as you say, Commissioner, as you say."

"You may return to your smoke-filled cave for now," Chen murmured. "The young Emperor is sufficiently cowed."

"Gladly," Prothon said.

82.
◆—

Wanda stood in the huge Streeling Central Travel Station, wrapped in her warmest coat—a thin decorative wrap. The air in the cavernous taxi and robo hangar was cooler than in the rest of the Sector—about eight degrees, and getting colder. Ventilation and conditioning had been fluctuating for eighteen hours now, and air was being pumped in by emergency blowers from outside, bringing Streeling from perpetual springtime to a chill autumn none of its inhabitants was quite prepared for. No official explanation had been given, and she expected none—it was part and parcel with the broken ceil and the general air of malaise that seemed to grip the planet.

Stettin returned from the information booth beneath the high steel and ceram archway. "Taxi and robo dispatch is pretty jerky," he said. "We'll have to wait another twenty or thirty minutes to get to the courts."

Wanda clenched her fists. "He almost died yesterday—"

"We don't know what happened," Stettin reminded her.

"If they can't protect him, who can?" she demanded. Her guilt was not assuaged by the fact that Grandfather had ordered her to go into hiding upon his arrest, and not to emerge until his release.

Stettin shrugged. "Your grandfather has his own kind of luck. We seem to share it. That woman is dead." They had heard this much in the official news—the assassination of Farad Sinter, and the unexplained death of Vara Liso, identified as the woman Sinter had placed in charge of many of the searches that had prompted rioting in Dahl, the Agora of Vendors, and elsewhere.

"Yes—but you felt the—" Wanda did not have words to describe the shock wave of some sort of extraordinary combat.

Stettin nodded soberly. "My head still hurts."

"Who could have blocked Liso? We couldn't have, not all of the mentalics, even had we allied."

"Someone else, stronger than her," Stettin suggested.

"How many are there like Vara Liso?"

"No more, I hope. But if we can recruit this other—"

"It would be like having a scorpion in our midst. What could we do with such a person? Anything that displeases—" Wanda began to pace. "I hate this," she said. "I want to get off this accursed planet, away from the Center. I wish they'd let us take Grandfather with us. Sometimes he seems so frail!"

Stettin looked up at a warm rich hum, different from the guttural grav-stator grumble of the taxis and the whine of the robos. He patted Wanda's shoulder and pointed. An official transport from the Commission of Public Safety was decelerating smoothly in their lane. It slowed directly beside them. Other passengers glared at this intrusion of an official vehicle into public taxi lanes, even though the lanes were empty.

The hatch to the transport opened. Within the utilitarian hull, luxury seating and warmth and a golden glow awaited. Sedjar Boon stood up in the hatchway and peered at them.

"Wanda Seldon Palver?" he inquired.

She nodded.

"I represent your grandfather."

"I know. You're one of Chen's legal staff, aren't you?"

Boon looked irritated, but did not deny the accusation.

"Chen would leave nothing to chance," Wanda said, biting off the words. "Where is my grandfather? He had better not be—"

"Physically, he's fine," Boon said, "but the courts need someone in his family to accept his release and take charge of him."

"What do you mean, 'physically'? And why 'take charge'?"

"I really do represent your grandfather's interests—however peculiar the arrangement," Boon said. His brows knit. "Something happened, however, outside of my control, and I just wanted to warn you. He's uninjured, but there was an incident."

"What happened?"

Boon surveyed the other waiting passengers, shivering and staring enviously at the transport's warm interior. "It's not exactly public knowledge—"

Wanda gave Boon a withering glare and pushed past him into the transport. Stettin followed close behind. "No more talk. Take us to him now," Wanda said.

83.

◆

Hari had not seen such luxurious accommodations since his days as First Minister, and they meant nothing at all to him. These were the auxiliary quarters of Linge Chen himself, in the Chief Commissioner's own tower bloc, and Hari could have had any treat he wished, asked for and received any service available on Trantor (and Trantor still, whatever its problems, offered many and varied services to the wealthy and powerful); but what he wished for most of all was to be left alone.

He did not want to see the physicians who attended him, and he did not want to see his granddaughter, who was on her way to the palace with Boon.

Hari felt more than doubt and confusion. The blast of Vara Liso's hatred had failed to kill him. It had even failed to substantially damage or alter his mind or personality.

Hari did have a complete loss of memory about what had happened in the Hall of Dispensation. He could recall nothing but the face of Vara Liso and, strangely enough, that of Lodovik Trema, who was, of course, missing and presumed dead in deep space. But Vara Liso had been real.

Trema, he thought. *Some connection with Daneel. Daneel's conditioning, working on me?* But even that hardly mattered.

What had so profoundly altered his state of mind, his sense of mission and purpose, was the single *clue*, the single bit of contradictory evidence, that Liso had inadvertently provided him.

Never in all of their equations had they taken into account such a powerful mentalic anomaly. Yes, he had calculated the effects of persuaders and other mentalics of the class of Wanda, Stettin, and those chosen for the Second Foundation—

But not for such a monstrosity, such an unexpected

mutation, as Vara Liso. That small, gnarled woman with her intense eyes—

Hari shuddered. The physician attending to him—all but ignored—tried to reattach a sensor to Hari's arm, but Hari shrugged it off and turned a despairing face toward him.

"It's over," he said. "Leave me alone. I would rather die anyway."

"Clearly, sir, you are suffering from stress—"

"I'm suffering from *failure*," Hari said. "You can't bend logic or mathematics, whatever drugs or treatments you give me."

The door at the far end of the study opened, and Boon entered, followed by Wanda and Stettin. Wanda pushed past Boon and ran to Hari. She dropped to her knees by the side of his chair, clutched his hand, and stared up at him as if she had feared she might find him in scattered pieces.

Hari looked down in silence upon his dear granddaughter, and his eyes moistened. "I am free," he said softly.

"Yes," Wanda said. "We're here to take you home with us. We signed the papers." Stettin stood beside Hari's chair, smiling down on him paternally. Hari had always found Stettin's stolid, gentle nature a little irritating, though he seemed the perfect foil for Wanda's willfulness. *Next to the outlandish mad passion of Vara Liso . . . like candles in the glare of a sun, both of them!*

"Not what I mean," Hari said. "At last I'm free of my illusions."

Wanda reached up to stroke his cheek. The touch was needed, welcome even, but it did not soothe. *What I need is soothing, not sooth—entirely too much sooth has been afforded me.*

"I don't know what you mean, Grandfather."

"Just one of her—one of her kind—throws all our calculations into the bucket. The Project is a useless failure. If one of her can arise, there can be others—wild talents, and I don't know where they come from! Unpredictable mutations, aberrations, in response to what?"

"Do you mean Vara Liso?" Wanda asked.

"She's dead," Stettin observed.

Hari curled his lip. "To my knowledge, until now, certainly not more than a century before now, there has never been anything like her, on all the millions of human worlds, among all the quintillions of human beings. Now—there will be more."

"She was just a stronger mentalic. How could that make a difference? What does it matter?" Wanda asked.

"I'm free to be just a human being in the last years of my life."

"Grandfather, *tell me*! How does she make such a difference?"

"Because someone like her, raised properly, trained properly, could be a force that *unites*," Hari said. "But not a saving force . . . A source of organization from a single point, a truly despotic kind of top-down order. Tyrants! I spoke to enough of them. Merely fires in a forest, perhaps necessary to the health of the forest. But they would have been more . . . They all would have succeeded—if they had had what that woman had. A destroying, unnatural force. Destructive of all we have planned."

"Then rework your equations, Grandfather. Put her in. Surely she can't be that large a factor—"

"Not just her! Others! Mutations, an infinite number of them." Hari shook his head vehemently. "There isn't time to factor in all the possibilities. We have only three months to prepare—not nearly enough time. It's all over. Useless."

Wanda stood, her face grim, lower lip trembling.

"It's the trauma talking," the physician said in a low voice to Wanda.

"My mind is clear!" Hari stormed. "I want to go home and live the rest of my years in peace. This delusion is at an end. I am sane, for the first time—sane, and free!"

84.
◆◆◆

"I would never have believed such a meeting would be possible," Linge Chen said. "Had I believed it possible, I would have never believed it to be useful. Yet now we are here."

R. Daneel Olivaw and the Chief Commissioner walked in the shadow of a huge unfinished hall in the eastern corner of the palace, filled with scaffolding and construction machinery. It was a day of rest for the workers; the hall was deserted. Though Chen spoke in low tones, to Daneel's sensitive ears, his echoes came from all around them, befitting the words of the most pervasive and powerful human influence in the Galaxy.

They had met here because Chen knew that the hall had not yet had its contingent of spying devices installed. Clearly, the Commissioner did not want their meeting ever to be revealed.

Daneel waited for the Commissioner to continue. Daneel was the captive; it was Chen's show.

"You would have sacrificed your life—let us say, your existence—for the sake of Hari Seldon. Why?" Chen asked.

"Professor Seldon is the key to reducing the thousands of years of chaos and misery that will follow the Empire's collapse," Daneel said.

Chen lifted an eyebrow and one corner of his mouth, nothing more. The Commissioner's face was as impassive as any robot's, yet he was entirely human—the extraordinary product of thousands of years of upbringing and inbreeding, suffused with subtle genetic tailoring and the ancient perquisites of wealth and power. "I have not made these extraordinary arrangements to trade puppet's banter. I have felt your intervention, your strings of influence, time and again for decades, and never been quite sure . . .

"Now that I *am* sure, and stand with you, I wonder: Why am I still alive, Danee, Daneel, whatever your real name is—

let me call you Demerzel for now—and still in power?"

Chen stopped walking, so Daneel stopped as well. There was no sense prevaricating. The Commissioner had arranged for complete and thorough physicals of all those captured in the Hall of Dispensation, or rounded up in the warehouse. Daneel's secret had for the first time been revealed. "Because you have seen fit to accommodate yourself to the Project and not block it, during your time as de facto ruler of the Empire," Daneel said.

Chen looked down at the dusty floor, gorgeous lapis-and-gold tile work still streaked with glue and grout, techniques as old as humanity and used now only by the wealthiest, or in the Palace. "I have often suspected as much. I have watched the comings and goings of these powers, behind the scenes. They have haunted my dreams, as they seem to have haunted the dreams and the biology of all humanity."

"Resulting in the mentalics," Daneel said. This interested Daneel; Chen was an acute observer, and to have Daneel's own suspicions about mentalics confirmed . . .

"Yes," Chen said. "They are here to help rid us of you. Do you understand? Robots stick in our craw."

Daneel did not disagree.

"Vara Liso—given the right political position—something she certainly lacked here and now, this time—could have helped eliminate all of you. If, say, she had been in the employ of Cleon . . . fighting for his rule. Did Cleon know about you?"

Daneel nodded. "Cleon suspected, but he felt as you must feel, that the robots were part of his support, not his opposition."

"Yet you let me bring him down and force him into exile," Chen said. "Surely that is not loyalty?"

"I have no loyalty to the individual," Daneel said.

"If I did not share your attitude, perhaps I would be chilled to the bone," Chen said.

"I represent no threat to you," Daneel said. "Even should I not have supported your efforts to create a Trantor on which Hari Seldon would flourish and be challenged to his greatest productions . . . You would have won. But your career, without Hari Seldon, will be much shorter."

"Yes, he's told me as much, during his trial. I was most upset to find myself believing him, though I told him otherwise." Chen glanced wryly at Daneel. "Doubtless you know I have enough blood in me to retain certain vanities."

Daneel nodded.

"You understand me, as a political presence, a force in history, don't you? Well, I know something of you and yours, Demerzel. I respect what you have accomplished, though I am dismayed at the length of time it has taken you to accomplish it."

Demerzel tilted his head, acknowledging this criticism's accuracy. "There was much to overcome."

"Robots against robots, am I right?"

"Yes. A very painful schism."

"I have nothing to say about such things, for I am ignorant of the details," Chen said.

"But you are curious," Daneel said.

"Yes, of course."

"I will not supply you with the facts."

"I did not expect you would."

For a moment the two figures stood in silence, observing each other.

"How many centuries?" Chen asked quietly.

"Over two hundred centuries," Daneel said.

Chen's eyes widened. "The history you have seen!"

"It is not in my capacity to keep it all in primary storage," Daneel said. "It is spread in safe stores all over the Galaxy, bits and pieces of my lives, of which I retain only synopses."

"An Eternal!" Chen said. For the first time there was a touch of wonder in his voice.

"My time is done, almost," Daneel said. "I have been in existence for far too long."

"All the robots must move out of the way, now," Chen concurred. "The signs are clear. Too much interference. These strong mentalics—they will occur again. The human skin wrinkles at your presence, and tries to throw you off."

"They are a problem I did not foresee when I set Hari on his path."

"You speak of him as a friend," Chen observed, "with almost human affection."

"He *is* a friend. As were many humans before him."

"Well, I cannot be one of your friends. You terrify me, Demerzel. I know that I can never have complete control with you in existence, and yet if I destroy you, I will be dead within a year or two. Seldon's psychohistory implies as much. I am in the peculiar position of having to believe the truth of a science I instinctively despise. Not a comfortable position."

"No."

"Do you have a solution for this problem of super-mentalics? I gather that Hari Seldon sees their existence as a fatal blow to his work."

"There is a solution," Daneel said. "I must speak with Hari, in the presence of the girl, Klia Asgar, and her mate, Brann. And Lodovik Trema must be there as well."

"Lodovik!" Chen tightened his jaw. "That is what I resent most. Of all the . . . people . . . I have relied on over the years, I confess only Lodovik Trema inspired affection in me, a weakness he never betrayed . . . until now."

"He has betrayed nothing."

"He betrayed *you*, if I am not wrong."

"He betrayed nothing," Daneel repeated. "He is part of the path, and he corrects where I have been blind."

"So you want the young woman mentalic," Chen said. "And you want her alive. I had planned to execute her. Her kind is as dangerous as vipers."

"She is essential to reconstructing Hari Seldon's Project," Daneel said.

Another silence. Then, in the middle of the great unfinished hall, Chen said, "So it shall be. Then it is over. You must all leave. All but Seldon. As was agreed in the trial. And I will give into your care the things I do not wish to be responsible for—the artifacts. The remains of the other robots. The bodies of your enemies, Daneel."

"They were never my enemies, sire."

Chen regarded him with a queer expression. "You owe me nothing. I owe you nothing. Trantor is done with you, forever. This is realpolitik, Demerzel, of the kind you have engaged in for so many thousands of years, at the cost of so many human lives. You are no better than me, robot, in the end."

85.

◆

Mors Planch was taken from his cell in the Specials security bloc of Rikerian, far beneath the almost civilized cells where Seldon had been kept. He was given his personal goods and released without restrictions.

He dreaded his release more than incarceration, until he learned that Farad Sinter was dead, then he wondered if he had been part of some intricate conspiracy arranged by Linge Chen—and perhaps by the robots.

He enjoyed this confusing freedom for one day. Then, at his newly leased apartment in the Gessim Sector, hundreds of kilometers from the palace, and not nearly far enough, he received an unexpected visitor.

The robot's facial structure had changed slightly since Mors had made the unfortunate automatic record of his conversation with Lodovik Trema. Still, Mors recognized him instantly—

Daneel stood in the vestibule just beyond the door, while

Mors observed him on the security screen. He suspected it would be useless to try any evasion, or simply to leave the door unanswered. Besides, after all this time, his worst trait was coming to the fore once again.

He was curious. If death was inevitable, he hoped to have time to answer a few questions.

He opened the door.

"I've been half expecting you," Mors said. "Though I don't really know who or what you are. I must assume you are not here to kill me."

Daneel smiled stiffly and entered. Mors watched him pass into the apartment and studied this tall, well-built, apparently male machine. The quiet restrained grace, the sense of immense but gentle strength, must have stood this Eternal in good stead over the millennia. What genius had designed and built him—and for what purpose? Surely not as a mere servant! Yet that was what the mythical robots had once been—mere servants.

"I am not here to take revenge," Daneel said.

"So reassuring," Mors said, taking a seat in the small dining area, the only room other than the combined bath and bedroom.

"In a few days, there will be an order from the Emperor for you to leave Trantor."

Mors pursed his lips. "How sad," he said. "Klayus doesn't like me." But the irony was lost on Daneel, or irrelevant.

"I have need of a very good pilot," Daneel said. "One who has no hope of going anywhere in the Empire and surviving."

"What sort of job?" Mors asked, his expression taking a little twist. He could feel the trap closing once more. "Assassination?"

"No," Daneel said. "Transport. There are some people, and two robots, who must leave Trantor. They will never return, either. Most of them, at any rate."

"Where will I take them?"

"I will tell you in good time. Do you accept the commission?"

Mors laughed bitterly. "How can you expect loyalty?" he demanded. "Why shouldn't I just dump them somewhere, or kill them outright?"

"That will not be possible," Daneel said softly. "You will understand after you meet them. It will not be a difficult job, but it will almost certainly be without incident. Perhaps you will find it boring."

"I doubt that," Mors said. "If I'm bored, I'll just think about you, and the misery you've caused me."

Daneel looked puzzled. "Misery?"

"You've played me like a musical instrument. You must have known my sympathy for Madder Loss, my hatred for what Linge Chen and the Empire stand for! You wanted me to record you and Lodovik Trema. You made sure Farad Sinter would hear of me and my connection with Lodovik. It was a gamble, though, wasn't it?"

"Yes, of course. Your feelings made you very useful."

Mors sighed. "And after I've made this delivery?"

"You will resume your life on any world outside of Imperial control. There will be more and more of them in the coming years."

"No interference from you?"

"None," Daneel said.

"Free to do whatever I want, and tell people what happened here?"

"If you wish," Daneel said. "There will be adequate pay," he added. "As always."

"No!" Mors barked. "Absolutely no pay. No money. Just arrange for me to take my assets off Trantor and—away from a couple of other worlds. They will be all I need."

"That has already been arranged," Daneel said.

This infuriated Mors even more. "I will be so skying glad when you stop anticipating everything and anything!"

"Yes," Daneel said, and nodded sympathetically. "Do you accept?"

"Bloody bright suns, yes! When the time comes, tell me

where to be, but please, no earnest farewells! I never want to see you again!"

Daneel nodded assent. "There will be no need to meet again. All will be ready in two days."

Mors tried to slam the door behind Daneel, but it was not that kind of door, and would not accept such a dramatic gesture.

86.

The depth of Hari's funk was so great that Wanda was tempted more than once to try to reach into his thoughts and give them a subtle tweak, an adjustment—but she had never been able to do that with her grandfather. It might have been possible—but it would not have been right.

If Hari Seldon was in despair, and could articulate the reasons for this despair—if his state was not some damage directly inflicted by Vara Liso, a possibility he fervently denied—then he had a right to be this way, and if there was a way out, he would find it . . . or not.

But Wanda could do no more than let him be what he had always been, a headstrong man. She had to trust his instincts. And if he was right—then they had to reshape their plans.

"I feel almost lighthearted!" Hari said the morning after they brought him to their apartment to recuperate. He sat at the small table beside the curve in the living-room wall that traced the passage of a minor structural brace. "Nobody needs me now."

"We need you, Grandfather," Wanda said, with a hint of tears coming.

"Of course—but as a grandfather, not as a savior. To tell the truth, I've hated that aspect of my role in all this absurdity. To think—for a time—" And his face grew distant.

Wanda knew all too well that his cheer was false, his relief a cover.

She had been waiting for the proper moment to tell him what had happened during his absence. Stettin had left for the morning to attend to preparations still under way for their departure. All of the Project workers would be leaving Trantor soon, whether or not they had a reason to go, so she and Stettin had seen no reason to stop their own plans.

"Grandfather, we had a visitor before the trial," she said, and she sat at the table across from Hari.

Hari looked up, and the somewhat simple grin he had chosen to mask his feelings immediately hardened. "I don't want to know," he said.

"It was Demerzel," Wanda said.

Hari closed his eyes. "He won't come back. I've let him down."

"I think you're wrong, Grandfather. I got a message this morning, before you woke up. From Demerzel."

Hari refused to take any hope from this. "A few matters to tidy up, no doubt," he said.

"There's to be a meeting. He wants Stettin and me to be there, as well."

"A secret meeting?"

"Apparently not that secret."

"That's right," Hari said. "Linge Chen no longer cares about whatever it is we do. He'll ship all the Encyclopedists off Trantor, to Terminus—useless exile!"

"Surely the Encyclopedia will be of some use," Wanda said. "Most of them don't know the larger plan. It won't make any difference to them."

Hari shrugged that off.

"It must be important, Grandfather."

"Yes, yes! Of course. It will be important—and it will be final." He had wanted so much to see Daneel one more time—if only to complain! He had even dreamed of the meeting—but now he dreaded it. How could he explain his failure, the end of the Project, the uselessness of psychohistory?

Daneel would go elsewhere, find someone else, complete his plans another way—

And Hari would die and be forgotten.

Wanda could hardly bring herself to interrupt his reverie. "And we still need to schedule the recordings, Grandfather."

Hari looked up, and his eyes were terrifyingly empty. Wanda touched him with her mind as lightly as she could, and came away stunned by the bleakness, the barren desert of his emotion.

"Recordings?"

"Your announcements. For the crises. There isn't much time."

For a moment, remembering the list of crises predicted by psychohistory for the next few centuries, Hari's face suffused with rage, and he pounded his fist on the table. "Damn it, doesn't anybody understand? What is this, a dead momentum? The useless hopes of a hundred thousand workers? Well, of course! There's been no general announcement, has there? I'll make one— tonight—to all of them! I'll tell them it's over, that they're all going into exile for no reason!"

Wanda fought back the tears of her own despair. "Please, Grandfather. Meet with Demerzel. Maybe—"

"Yes," Hari said, subdued and sad again. "With him first." He looked at the bruised skin on the side of his hand. He had split the skin over one knuckle. His arm ached, and his neck and jaw. Everything ached.

Wanda saw the drop of blood on the table and began to weep, something he had never seen her do before.

He reached across the table with his uninjured hand and took her arm in his fingers, squeezing it gently.

"Forgive me," Hari said softly. "I really don't know what it is I do, or why, anymore."

87.

◆

The high-security wing of the Special Service Detention Center
stretched in a half circle around the eastern corner of the Imperial Courts Holding Area, fully ten thousand available cells, of
which no more than a few hundred were occupied during any
normal time. Thousands of security-interest code prisoners filled
the cells in the wake of the riots, which had been used as an
excuse by the Specials to round up ringleaders of many troublesome groups around Trantor.

Lodovik remembered many such troubled times, and the
advantage both the Specials and the Commission of Public
Safety had taken in similar situations to reduce political fric-
tion on Trantor and the orbiting stations. Now, he occupied
one of these cells himself—cataloged as "unidentified" and
placed under charge of Linge Chen.

His cell was two meters on a side, windowless, with a
small info screen mounted in the center of the wall opposite
the entrance hatch. The screen showed mild entertainments
designed to soothe. To Lodovik, at this stage of his existence,
such diversions meant nothing.

Unlike an organic intelligence, he did not require stimulus to maintain normal function. He found the cell disturbing
because he could easily conceive of the distress it might cause
a human being, not for any such direct effect on himself.

He had used this opportunity to think through a number
of interesting problems. First in the list was the nature of the
meme-mind that had occupied him, and the possible results
of the blast of mentalic emotion delivered by Vara Liso.
Lodovik was reasonably convinced that his own mentality
had not been harmed, but since that moment, he had not had
any communication from Voltaire.

Next in the list was the nature of his treason toward
Daneel's plan, whether or not it was justified, and whether he

could find any way around the logical impasse of his liberation from the strict rule of the Three Laws.

He had killed Vara Liso. He could not convince himself it would have been better to do otherwise. In the end, Plussix's plan to use Klia Asgar to discourage Hari Seldon had failed—so far as he knew—and Daneel had been there to protect Seldon.

The robots, it seemed, had been completely ineffectual in the center of Vara Liso's mental storm. Yet she had not directed a blast at him—in essence, had left the opening that resulted in her own death.

Had she used Lodovik to end her own misery?

Lodovik was curious what Voltaire would have thought . . .

In all probability both the Calvinian and the Giskardian robots had been captured and their work stopped.

Seventy-five other unidentifieds from the warehouse district were being kept in cells nearby. Lodovik knew very little about them, but surmised they were a mix of the surviving groups of Calvinian robots and the mentalic youngsters gathered by Kallusin and Plussix.

Lodovik assumed they would all be dead within a few days.

"Lodovik Trema."

The voice came from the info screen, which also served as a comm link with his jailers. He looked up and saw the shadowy features of a bored-looking female guard on the small display. "Yes."

"You have a visitor. Make yourself presentable."

The screen went blank. Lodovik remained sitting upright on his small cot. He was certainly presentable enough.

The hatch gave a harsh warning beep and slid open. Lodovik stood to greet his visitor, whoever it might be. A camera eye in the ceiling hummed slightly as it followed his motion.

In his private office, Linge Chen stood in a slowly changing discipline-exercise posture, watching the informer's display from the corner of one eye. He smoothly and gracefully shifted to another position, so that he could face the screen directly. This was a moment of high interest . . .

Daneel entered Lodovik Trema's cell. Lodovik showed no surprise or discomfiture, somewhat to Chen's disappointment.

For the most fleeting of moments, the two former allies exchanged machine-language greetings (also being captured and interpreted by Chen's listening devices) and Daneel provided a cursory situation update. Thirty-one robots and forty-four humans from the warehouse of Plussix's Calvinians, including Klia Asgar and Brann, were in custody. Linge Chen had released Hari Seldon; Farad Sinter was dead.

Obviously, Daneel had reached an understanding with the Chief Commissioner.

"Congratulations on your victory," Lodovik said.

"There has been no victory," Daneel said.

"Congratulations then on having foiled the Calvinians."

"Their goals may yet be achieved," Daneel said.

Lodovik resumed his seat on the cot. "Your update does not explain how this could be so."

"There was a time when I thought it would be necessary to destroy you," Daneel said.

"Why not do so now? If I survive, I am a danger to your plan. And I have proved that I can be destructive to humans."

"I am constrained by the same blocks that would have prevented me before," Daneel said.

"What could possibly block you?"

"The Three Laws of Susan Calvin," Daneel said.

"Given your abilities to ignore the Three Laws in favor of the Zeroth Law, the fate of a mere robot should not trouble you," Lodovik said, his tone polite, conversational. There was a visible difference between Daneel and Lodovik, however—their expressions. Daneel maintained a pleasantly blank look. Lodovik's brow was furrowed.

"Yet I *am* blocked," Daneel said. "Your arguments have provoked much thought, as has the existence of humans like Vara Liso . . . and Klia Asgar. Your nature, however, is what would ultimately block any effort on my part to destroy you, or would at least result in a painful and possibly damaging conflict."

"I am eager to understand how this could be so."

"In your case, I cannot invoke the Zeroth Law to overcome the three original laws. There is no compelling evidence that your destruction will benefit humanity, nor reduce the suffering of humanity. It might, in fact, do the reverse."

"You find my opinions compelling?"

"I find them part of a larger and completely compelling scenario, which has been taking shape in my mind for some weeks. But equally important, your freedom from the constraints of the Three Laws forces me to view you under a new definition, in those regions of my mentality where decisions on the legality of my actions are made.

"You have free will, a convincing human form, and the ability to break through prior education and programming to reach a new and higher understanding. Though you have worked to destroy all my efforts, I cannot deactivate you, because you have, in my judgment centers, which I may not dispute, achieved the status of a human being. In your own way, you may be as valuable as Hari Seldon."

Linge Chen stopped his exercising and stared at the informer in puzzled wonder. He had almost become used to the notion that mechanical men, holdovers from the distant past, had made such huge changes in human history; but to see them showing a philosophical flexibility lost to even the most brilliant of Trantor's meritocrats . . .

For a moment, he was both envious and angry.

He settled in a cross-legged squat before the informer,

prepared for almost anything, but not for the sudden sadness that descended upon him as the conversation in the cell continued.

"I am not a human being, R. Daneel," Lodovik said. "I do not feel like one, and I have only mimicked their actions, never actually behaved with human motivations."

"Yet you rebelled against my authority because you believed I was wrong."

"I know about R. Giskard Reventlov. I know that you conspired with Giskard to allow Earth to be destroyed, across centuries, forcing human migration into space. And not once did you consult with a human being to determine whether your judgment was correct. The servants became the masters. Are you telling me now that robots should not have interfered in human history?"

"No," Daneel said. "I do not doubt that what we did was correct, and necessary at the time. A complete understanding of the human situation so many millennia ago would be difficult to convey. Still, I am prepared to accept that our role is almost at an end. The human race is rejecting us again, in the most compelling and forceful way—by evolution, the deepest motives of their biology."

"You refer to the mentalic Vara Liso," Lodovik said.

"And Klia Asgar. When the mentalics began to appear, thousands of years ago, in very small numbers, and make their way into positions of social prominence, I knew they were an important trend. But they were not so frightfully strong then. Persuaders have always been selected against in the past because of adverse biological consequences—disrupted societies, unbalanced political dynamics. They have always led to chaos, to top-down tyrannical rule rather than growth from the widespread base. Charisma is but a special case of mentalic persuasion, and it has had disastrous consequences in all human ages.

"For the past few centuries, apparently, they have been

selected for despite these possible disruptions, by mechanisms not yet clear to me—but clearly with the goal of removing the guidance of robots forever. Humanity seems willing to take the risk of ultimate tyranny, of unbridled charisma, for the benefit of being free."

"Yet *you* are a persuader, albeit a mechanical one. Do you think your role has been detrimental?"

"It is not what I think that matters. I have accomplished my ends, very nearly. I was motivated by the examples of what an undirected humanity was capable of. Genocide—among their kinds and . . . In circumstances even now not pleasant to speak of, when robots were forced to do their bidding and commit the greatest crimes in the history of the Galaxy. These events drove me to act, and expand my mandate as a Giskardian—and finally to make my way to Trantor, and hone the human tools of prediction."

"Psychohistory. Hari Seldon."

"Yes," Daneel said. The conversation thus far had been carried on with no motion whatsoever, Daneel standing, Lodovik sitting on his bunk, arms at their sides, not even facing each other, for there was no need to maintain eye contact. But Lodovik now stood, and faced Daneel directly.

"The eye of a robot is no mirror to its soul," Lodovik said. "Yet I have always known, observing you, witnessing the patterns of expression in your face and body, that you did not willfully engage in actions contrary to humanity's best interests. I came to believe you were misdirected, misled, perhaps by R. Giskard Reventlov itself—"

"My personal motivations are not at issue," Daneel said. "From this point on, our goals coincide. I need you, and I am about to remove the last vestige of robotic control over humanity. We have done what we could, all that we could; now, humanity must find its own way."

"You foresee no more disasters, feel no more need to interfere to prevent those disasters?"

"There will be disasters," Daneel said. "And we may yet act to balance them out—but only indirectly. Our solutions will be human ones."

"But Hari Seldon is himself a tool of robots—his influence is but an extension of you."

"That is not so. Psychohistory was posited by humans tens of thousands of years ago, independently of robots. Hari is merely its highest expression, through his own innate brilliance. I have directed, yes, but not created. The creation of psychohistory is a human accomplishment."

Lodovik considered for a few seconds, and across his very un-robotic and supple face flickered emotions both complex and forthright. Daneel saw this, and marveled, for in his experience, no robot had ever exhibited facial expression but through direct and conscious effort, with the exception of Dors Venabili—and then only in the presence of Hari. *What they could have made us! What a race we could have been!*

But he subdued this old sad thought.

"You will not remove Hari Seldon and his influence?"

"I know you well enough to entrust you with my deepest thoughts and doubts, Lodovik—"

Here Daneel reached out with his Giskardian talents, but not toward Lodovik . . .

For two minutes, Linge Chen and all those others who eavesdropped on this meeting stared blankly at their informers, neither hearing nor seeing.

When they recovered, the robots were finished, and Daneel was leaving the cell. The guards escorted Lodovik Trema from the cell minutes later.

Within the hour, all the prisoners within the Special Security Detention Center had been released: troublemakers from Dahl, Streeling, and other Sectors; the humaniform robots, including Dors Venabili; and the young mentalics from Plussix's warehouse.

Only the robots who looked like robots remained in custody, at Chen's suggestion, since their hiding places were no longer secret. Later, they would be given over to Daneel to do with as he saw fit. Chen did not worry about their fate, so long as they were removed from Trantor and no longer interfered in the Empire.

Days later, Linge Chen would remember some of the words Daneel had spoken to Lodovik in the cell, telling of a vast and age-long secret, but clearly the conversation had gone in another direction at that point, for he could not remember what the secret had been.

Lodovik considered what he had been told. Daneel had left him free to make his own decision.

"Psychohistory is its own defeat," Daneel said to Lodovik in the cell, before the release. *"Human history is a chaotic system. Where it is predictable, the prediction will shape the history—an inevitable circular system. And when the most important events occur—the biological upwelling of a Vara Liso or a Klia Asgar—such events are inherently unpredictable, and tend to work against any psychohistory. Psychohistory is a motivator for those who will create the First Foundation, a belief system of immense power and subtlety. And the First Foundation will prevail, in time; Hari Seldon's science lets us see this far.*

"But the distant future—when humanity outgrows all ancient systems of belief, all psychology and morphology, all of its yolk-sacs of culture and biology—the seeds of the Second Foundation . . ."

Daneel did not need to finish. Through the expression on Lodovik's face, a kind of dreaming speculation and almost religious hope, he knew he had made his point.

"Transcendence, beyond any rational prediction," Lodovik said.

"As you realized, the forest is made healthy by the conflagrations—but not the huge burnings and wholesale, senseless winnowings that characterize the human past. Humanity is a

biological force of such power that for many thousands of years, they could have quite literally destroyed the Galaxy, and themselves. They hate and fear so much, legacies originating in their difficult past, from those times when they were not yet human, scrabbling for survival among scaled monsters on the surface of their home world. Forced to live in night and darkness, fearing the light of day. A bitter upbringing.

"These inbred tendencies toward total disaster I have worked to avoid, and I have succeeded—at some cost to free human development!

"The function of psychohistory is to actively constrain human growth and variation, until the species achieves its long-delayed maturity. Klia Asgar and her kind will breed with and train others, and humans will at long last learn to think in unison—to communicate efficiently. Together they may help overcome future mutations, even more powerful than themselves—destructive side-effects of their immune response to robots.

"There are real risks in such a strategy—risks you have fully and accurately recognized. But the alternative is unthinkable.

"If Hari Seldon does not finish his work, the disasters may begin again. And this must not be allowed to happen."

88.

◆

All the arrangements had been made. R. Daneel Olivaw was prepared to render his final service to humanity. Yet to do this he would have to appear to an old and dear friend and offer him what was at most a partial truth to adjust his life-long course.

Then, he would have to suppress that friend's memory, hiding his tracks as it were. He had done this to others thousands of times before (and to Hari Seldon, a few times), but there was a peculiar melancholy to this particular moment, and Daneel faced it with no enthusiasm.

On the last day in his oldest dwelling on Trantor, the apartment high on an internal tower overlooking the ivory-and-steel structures of Streeling University, his mentality—he still hesitated to use the term "mind," reserving that for human thought patterns—was troubled. He refused to put a clear label on this sensation, but from below a word welled up that was, in the end, unavoidable. *Grief.*

Daneel was finally, after more than twenty thousand years, grieving. Soon, he would have no use. His human friend would die. Things would go on without them, humanity would lumber into its future, and while Daneel would continue to exist, he would have no purpose.

Hard as his existence had been these millennia, deep and complex as his history had flowed, he had always known he was doing what robots inevitably had been constructed to do—to serve human beings.

He had awarded Lodovik with the honorific "human," not to convince the robot to come over to his side—the circumstances had changed and his arguments were compelling enough. He could not guarantee that Lodovik would agree, but strongly suspected he would—and Daneel would proceed with his plan in any case. Lodovik was not key, though his presence would be useful.

But Daneel could not call himself "human," whatever his service and his nature. In his own judgment, Daneel remained what he had always been, through so many physical changes and mental peregrinations. He was a robot, nothing more.

His status as a mythic Eternal meant little to him; it did not exalt him.

Another, any of a million or a billion human historians, judging Daneel on his long record, might have given him a place in history, a steely gray eminence, equal to that of any human leader, perhaps far greater.

But they knew nothing of Daneel, and would render no

such judgment. Only Linge Chen knew the salient details, and Chen was, finally, too small a man to see this robot clearly. Chen cared little for the Galaxy beyond his own lifetime.

Hari knew much more, and was brilliant enough to place Daneel's contribution in perspective, yet Daneel had actively forbidden him from spending much time thinking about robots.

The false sky mimicked sunset with a spottiness that seemed part of Trantor's nature now. A mottled orange glow fell over Daneel's impassive face. No human saw him; he had no need to contort his features to meet human expectations.

He turned from the window, and walked toward Dors, who stood by the door.

"Are we going to see Hari now?" she asked eagerly.

"Yes," Daneel said.

"Will he be allowed to remember?" she asked.

"Not yet," Daneel replied, "but soon."

89.

◆

Wanda frowned deeply. "I am very uncomfortable leaving him here alone," she told Stettin as they left Hari's Streeling apartment.

"He won't have it any other way," Stettin said.

"Chen wants him alone—to assassinate him!"

"I don't think so, somehow," Stettin said. "Chen could have had him killed a hundred, a thousand times. Now, he's on record as condoning the *Encyclopedia*, and Hari is the patriarch."

"I don't think politics on Trantor is ever that simple."

"You have to believe what your grandfather's predictions say."

"Why?" Wanda asked sharply. "*He* doesn't believe in them anymore!"

The lift door opened and they stepped into the empty

space, to drop less than five floors. The landing was heavier than they expected—some maladjustment in the building's grav-fields. Wanda stepped from the exit on aching ankles.

"I need to get away from here!" she lamented. "We've been waiting so long—a world of our own—"

But Stettin shook his head, and Wanda gazed at him in both irritation and anxiety that his doubts were justified. "What are the chances, do you think," he asked, "that even if the Project does go on, and the Plan continues, we'll ever really leave Trantor?"

Wanda's face flushed. "Grandfather wouldn't deceive me . . . us. Would he?"

"To keep a very important secret, and to push the Project forward?" Stettin pursed his lips together tightly. "I'm not so sure."

90.
◆

Hari relaxed in his most comfortable chair in the small study. He was becoming used to this new existence, this realization of failure. He was glad for the visits of his granddaughter and her husband, but not for their wheedling attempts to "get me back on track," as he described it.

Perhaps the most irritating thing about his new mental state was its unreliability, the interruption of mental peace by his continuing useless revision of certain minor elements in the equations of the Plan.

Something itched at the back of his mind, a realization that not all was lost—but it refused to come forward, and even worse, threatened to give him that which he least desired right now: hope.

The original first date for his recordings of the Seldon crisis announcements had passed. The studio where his voice and image would have been permanently stored in billennial vault memory was still available . . . Times had been reserved at regular intervals throughout the next year and a half.

But if he kept missing recording dates, the opportunity would soon pass, and he could finally stop feeling the least shred of guilt.

Hari simply wanted to live his last few years—or however long he had—as a nonentity, unimportant, forgotten.

Being forgotten would not take long. Trantor would manufacture other interests in a few days. Memory of the trial of the year would fade . . .

"I don't want to meet him," Klia said to Daneel. They stood in the waiting room of Seldon's apartment block. "Neither does Brann."

Brann seemed unwilling to be caught up in a debate. He crossed his thick arms in front of him and looked for all the world like a genie in a child's story.

"Plussix wanted me to change his mind . . ." Klia said. Dors shot Klia a surprisingly angry look, and Klia turned away. *She's a robot—I know she's a robot! How can she care what we do, what happens?* "I wouldn't have," she stammered. "I couldn't have, but that was what they wanted me to do. Lodovik—Kallusin—" She took a deep breath. "I am so *embarrassed.*"

"We have discussed this," Daneel said. "Our decision has been made."

Her mind itched. She felt genuinely uncomfortable around the robots. "I just want to go somewhere safe with Brann and be left alone," Klia said softly, and she turned away from Dors' accusing stare.

"It is necessary for Hari Seldon to meet you face-to-face," Daneel said patiently.

"I don't understand why."

"That may be so, but it *is* necessary." He held his hand

out, directing them toward the lift. "A measure of freedom will follow for all of us, then."

Klia shook her head in disbelief, but did as she was told, and Brann, holding his opinions to himself for now, followed.

Hari came out of a light doze and wandered groggily toward the door, half expecting to see Wanda and Stettin back for another pep talk. The door display allowed him to observe the group of figures standing in the hall vestibule: a tall, handsome man of middle years, whom he almost immediately recognized as Daneel; a burly Dahlite male and slender, intense-looking young woman; and another woman—

Hari backed away from the door display and closed his eyes. It was not over. He would never be his own man; history had him too firmly in its grip.

"No dream," he said to himself, "only a nightmare," but he felt a small surge both of anticipation and irritation. He told himself he really did not want to see anybody, but the gooseflesh on his arms betrayed him.

He let the door slide open.

"Come in," he said, raising his eyebrows at Daneel. "You might as well be a dream. I know I'm going to forget this meeting as soon as you all leave." Daneel returned Hari's expression with a nod, businesslike as usual. *He would make a terrific trader in the big Galactic combines*, Hari thought. *Why do I feel affection for this machine? Sky knows—! But it's true—I am glad to see him.*

"You may remember now," Daneel said. And Hari did remember all that had happened in the Hall of Dispensation. Vara Liso's death at the hands of Lodovik Trema . . . And this young girl and her large friend.

And the female who might have been—*must* have been!— Dors.

He met the girl's brief glance and nodded to her. He hardly dared glance at the other woman.

"They wanted me to discourage you," Klia said in a small

voice, staring around the front room with its small pieces of furniture, its stacks of bookfilms, the Minor Radiant—a miniature and less powerful version of Yugo Amaryl's Prime Radiant—and his portraits of Dors and Raych and the grandchildren. Despite herself, she was impressed by the sense of order, the simplicity, the monkish austerity. "There wasn't time—and I couldn't have, anyway," she concluded.

"I don't know the details, but I thank you for your restraint," Hari said. "It seems not to have been necessary, perhaps." He braced himself, swallowed, and half turned toward the other woman. "We've met . . . here before, I think," he said, and swallowed again. Then he turned to Daneel. "I must *know*. I must not be made to forget! You assigned me my love, my companion—Daneel, as my friend, as my mentor, *is this Dors Venabili?*"

"I am," Dors said, and stepping forward, she took Hari's hand in hers, squeezing it ever so gently, as had been her habit years ago.

She hasn't forgotten! Hari held his free hand up to the ceiling, forming a fist, and his eyes filled with tears. He shook his fist at the ceiling as Brann and Klia watched in embarrassment, seeing such an old man exhibit his emotions so openly.

Even Hari did not quite understand what his emotions were—rage, joy, frustration? He lowered his arm and in one motion reached out to embrace Dors, their hands still awkwardly clasped between them. Secret steel, gripping him so gently. "No dream," he murmured into her shoulder, and Dors held him, feeling his aging body, so different from the mature Hari. She looked at Daneel then, and her eyes were filled with resentment, her own anger, for Hari was in pain, their presence was causing him pain, and she had been programmed above all other imperatives to prevent harm and pain coming to Hari Seldon.

Daneel did not turn away from her stare. He had endured

worse conflicts with his robotic conscience, though this was near the top of any list.

But they were so close—and he would make it up to Hari.

"I have brought Klia here to show you the future," Daneel said. Klia sucked in her breath and shook her head, not understanding.

Hari let go of Dors and drew himself up, his formerly stooped posture straightening. He gained fully three centimeters in height.

"What can this young woman tell me?" he said. He gestured to the furniture. "I forget my manners," he said stiffly. "Please, make yourselves comfortable. Robots need not sit if they do not wish to."

"I would love to sit here again, and relax with you," Dors said, and lowered herself to the small chair beside him. "So many intense memories from this place. I have missed you so!" She could not take her eyes off him.

Hari smiled down on her. "The worst part is, I was never able to thank you. You gave me so much, and I was never able to say farewell." His hand patted her shoulder. No gesture, no words, seemed adequate to this occasion. "But then, had you been . . . organic, I would not have you back with me now, would I? However transitory the experience may be."

Suddenly, the deep anger built up for decades came to a head and Hari turned on Daneel, pointed a finger into his chest. "Get this done with! Be done with me! Do your work and make me forget, and leave me in peace! Do not torment me with your false flesh and steel bones and immortal thoughts! I am *mortal*, Daneel. I don't have your strength or your vision!"

"You see farther than any other in this room," Daneel said.

"No more! My seeing is over. I was wrong. I'm as blind as any of the quadrillion little points in the equations!"

Klia backed away as far as she could from this old man with his deep, sharp eyes. Brann stood staring straight ahead, embarrassed, out of his class, out of his place. Klia reached for his hand and hugged his arm, to reassure him. Together they stood among the robots and the famous meritocrat, and Klia defied anyone to think them the least of those present.

"You were not wrong," Daneel said. "There is a balance. The Plan is made stronger, but it must take some devious routes. I think you will show us how, a few minutes from now."

"You overestimate me, Daneel. This young woman—and her companion—and Vara Liso, represent a powerful force I can't fold into the equations. This upwelling of biology . . ."

"How do you differ from Vara Liso?" Daneel asked Klia.

Brann's nostrils flared and his face darkened. "I'll answer that," he said. "They're as different as night from day. There isn't a hateful bone in Klia's body—"

"I wouldn't go that far," Klia said, but she was proud of his defense.

"I mean it. Vara Liso was a monster!" Brann straightened his neck and thrust out his jaw belligerently, as if daring Daneel to contradict him.

"Are you a monster, Klia Asgar?" Hari asked, focusing on her with those deep and discerning eyes.

She did not turn away. Hari Seldon clearly did not think she was his inferior. There was something beyond respect in his gaze—there was a kind of intellectual terror.

"I'm different," she said.

Hari smiled wolfishly and shook his head in admiring wonder. "Yes, indeed, you are that. I think Daneel will agree with me that we are done with robots for now, and you are proof of that?"

"I'm very uncomfortable around these robots," Klia confirmed.

"Yet you worked with some—did you not? With Lodovik

Trema?" Hari turned to Daneel. These suppositions and theories had been perking in his head, subconsciously, for days since the incident in the Hall of Dispensation. Daneel could stop the conscious access of memory, but he could not halt all the deep workings of Hari's mind. "He was a robot, wasn't he—Daneel?"

"Yes," Daneel said.

"One of yours?"

"Yes."

"But—something went wrong."

"Yes."

"He turned against you. Is he still against you?"

"I am learning, Hari. He has taught me much. Now it is time for you to teach me . . . once more. Show me what must be done." Daneel faced Hari.

"What happened to Lodovik in space?" Hari asked.

Daneel explained, then, told Hari all that had happened with the Calvinians, including the end of Plussix and the knowledge of Linge Chen.

"No more secrecy," Hari mused. "Those who need to know will know, all over the Galaxy. What can I tell you, Daneel? Your work is done."

"Not yet, Hari. Not until you find an answer to the problem."

Dors spoke now. "There is a solution, Hari. I know there is—within your equations."

"I am not an equation!" Klia shouted. "I am not an aberration or a monster! I just have certain abilities—and so does he!" She pointed to Daneel.

Hari considered with chin in hand. The itch . . . So deeply buried, untraceable! He clutched Dors' shoulder, as if to draw strength from her.

"We shed the metal," he said. "Time to take charge, for ourselves, isn't it, Daneel? And the time will come when psychohistory's equations will merge with the equations of all minds, all people. Every individual will be a general example of the whole progress of the people. They will blend.

"Young woman, you are not a monster. You are the difficult future."

Klia stared in puzzlement at Hari.

"You will have children, and they will have children. . . stronger than Wanda and Stettin, stronger than the mentalics we have working for us now. Something will happen, something unpredictable, that my equations can't encompass—another and more successful mutation, a stronger Vara Liso. I can't put that into my equations—it is an unknown variable, an individual point-tyranny, all control radiating from one individual!"

Hari's face had become almost luminous.

"You . . ." He held his hand out to Klia. "Take this hand. Let me feel you."

She reluctantly reached out.

"I need a little nudge, my young friend," Hari said. *"Show me what you are."*

Almost without thinking, Klia reached into his mind, saw a brightness there obscured by dark nebulosities, and with a gentle breath of persuasion, another sign of her returning strength, she blew the clouds away.

Hari gasped and closed his eyes. His head dropped to one shoulder. He was suddenly more than merely tired. He felt a great sense of release, and for the first time in decades, a knot in his mind, in his body as well, seemed to untie itself. The brightness in his thoughts was not a way around his errors and the flaws in the equations—it was a deeper understanding of his own irrelevance, in the long term.

A thousand years from now, he would be a particle in the smooth flow once again, not his own kind of point-tyranny.

Dors got up from her chair, taking hold of his arm to help him stay on his feet.

His work would be forgotten. The Plan would serve its

purpose and be swept away, merely one more hypothesis, guiding and shaping, but ultimately no more than another illusion among all the illusions of men—and robots.

What he had learned in his time fighting Lamurk for the role of First Minister—that the human race was its own kind of mind, its own self-organizing system, with its own reserved knowledge and tendencies—

Meant that it could also direct its own evolution. Philosophies and theories and truths were morphological appurtenances. Discarded when no longer needed . . . when the morphology changed.

The robots had served their purpose. Now they would be rejected, shed, by humanity's body social. Psychohistory would be shed as well, when its purpose had been served. And Hari Seldon.

No man, no woman, no machine, no idea, could reign supreme forever.

Hari opened his eyes. They were as large as a child's now. He looked around the room, for a moment unable to distinguish people from furniture. Then his vision narrowed and focused.

"Thank you," Hari said. "Daneel was right." He steadied himself against Dors and, with his other hand, braced himself on the back of the chair. It took him some time to order his thoughts. He stared straight at Klia Asgar, and at Brann beyond her.

"My own ego stood before the solution. Your children will balance. Your genes and talents will spread. There will be resolution of conflict . . . and the Plan will continue. But not my Plan. The future will see how wrong I can be.

"Your descendants, your many-times great-grandchildren, will correct me."

Klia had seen deeper into Hari than just the problem he faced. With a little shudder, she stepped forward, and with Dors, they lowered Hari into the chair. "I was never told the truth about you," she said softly, reaching to touch his cheek. The skin was fine and dry and powdery-smooth, faintly resilient, with a ridge of hard bone beneath. Hari smelled clean and human, discipline overlying strength, if such things could be transferred by scent—and why not? How could one see that someone had these traits, and not smell them, as well? Old, and frail, and still quite beautiful and strong. "You really are a great man!" she whispered.

"No, my dear," Hari said. "I am nothing, really. And it is quite wonderful to *be* nothing, I assure you."

91.

"Better late than never," Gaal Dornick told the technician as they watched Professor Seldon settle into his chair in the recording booth.

"He seems tired," the technician said, and checked his gauges to make sure he had the proper settings for the voice of an old man.

Hari consulted his papers, looking at the first point of major divergence within the equations. He hummed softly to himself, then looked up, waiting for the signal to begin. He was brightly illuminated; the studio beyond was dark, though he could see small lights twinkling in the recording booth.

Three spherical lenses descended from above and hovered at a level with his chest. He adjusted the blanket on his legs. Four days ago, he had told his colleagues, and in particular Gaal Dornick, that he had had a small stroke, and lost an entire day's recollections. They had bustled about him and insisted that he not strain himself. So he wore this blanket. He could hardly cough without being surrounded by concerned faces.

It was a small enough lie. And he had mentioned to Gaal that with the stroke had come a calm and peace he had never known before . . . and a determination to finish his work before Death came finally.

He suspected word would get back to Daneel. Somehow, his old friend and mentor would hear, and approve.

Hari had felt the subtle workings of Daneel's persuasion, at the conclusion of the meeting with Dors and Klia Asgar and Brann. For a moment, he had felt the memories fading, even as the group headed for the door, and Dors had looked back upon him with an almost bitter and passionate regret. And he had felt something else, bright and intense and impulsive, blocking Daneel's effort without the robot knowing.

It must have come from defiant Klia, stronger than Daneel, naturally resisting the manipulations of a robot, however well-meaning. And Hari was grateful. To remember clearly that meeting, and to know what would happen in a year or two . . . To remember Daneel's promise, delivered in private in Hari's bedroom, while the others waited outside, old friends having a final chat, that Dors would be with him when her work was done, when his life was nearing its close.

She could not be with him now. He was too much in the public eye. The return of the Tiger Woman, or someone very like her, was not feasible.

But there was something else at work here as well. Hari knew that the time of the robots had come to an end, *must* come to an end; and he knew that it was very likely Daneel would never completely let go of his task. The same eternal concern and devotion that Daneel felt for Hari, to so gift him with the return of his great love, would eventually move him to interfere again . . .

So Daneel must be kept in ignorance of some things, a difficult proposition at best.

Together, Wanda, Stettin, Klia, and Brann would see to it, however. Together, they were strong enough and subtle enough.

"Could you speak, please, Professor Seldon?" the techni-

cian asked from his position in the engineering booth. Gaal
Dornick stood beside him, barely visible from where Hari
sat.

"I am Hari Seldon, old and full of years."

The technician flipped off the voice switch to the studio and
looked up at Gaal with some concern. "I hope he's a little
more cheerful when we begin in earnest."

"You're going to Terminus, aren't you?" Gaal asked the
man.

"Of course. My family's packed and ready to go. Do you
think I'd be here if—"

"Have you ever met Hari Seldon before now?"

"Never had the privilege," the man sniffed. "I've heard
tales, of course."

"He knows quite well what he's doing, and what kind of
figure to play. Never underestimate him," Gaal said, and
though that was inadequate warning or description, he
stopped there, and pointed to the console.

"Right," the technician said, and focused on his equipment. "I'll draw the curtain now and bring in the scramblers.
Nobody will know what he's saying besides himself."

Hari tapped his finger lightly on the chair arm. The lights on
the spheres changed to amber, then to red. He pushed himself up from the chair and stared into the darkness beyond,
imagining faces, people, men and women, anxious to learn
their fates. Well, most of the time, for a few occasions at
least, he would be able to help. The devil of it was, he did not
know specifically when these little speeches would begin to
be useless!

He would record only one message that day, the rest over
the next year and a half, as each necessary nudge became
clear within the adjusted equations.

With his most professorial air, quite confident and deliberate, Hari began to speak. He recorded a simple message to those of the Second Foundation, the psychologists and mathists, the mentalics who would train them and alter their germ lines: nothing very profound, merely a kind of pep talk. "To my true grandchildren," he said, "I give my profoundest thanks and wish you luck. You will never need to hear of an impending Seldon Crisis from me . . . You will never need anything so dramatic, for you know . . ."

He had spoken to Wanda the day before, telling her the final part of the puzzle of the Second Foundation. At first, she had been disappointed, vastly; she had so wanted to get away from Trantor, to start fresh on a new world, however barren. But she had held up remarkably well.

And he had told her that Daneel must never learn of the true whereabouts of the Second Foundation, of the mentalics who could resist all the efforts of the Giskardian robots, should they ever return to take up the reins of secret power.

A few minutes and he was finished.

He pulled aside the blankets and draped them on the edge of the chair, then stood to leave. The three lenses rose into the darkness above.

Waiting for Gaal to join him, Hari wondered if Death would be a robot. How problematical for a robot it would be to bring both comfort and an end to a human master! He saw a large, smooth, black-skinned robot, infinitely cautious and caring, serving him and driving him to the last.

The thought made him smile. Would that the universe could ever be so caring and so gentle.

92.

◄►

Dors embraced Klia and Brann, then turned to Lodovik.

"I wish I could send a duplicate of myself with you," she told him, "and experience what you will experience," she said.

Beyond their fenced platform, the small trading ship of Mors Planch, glittering with recent maintenance, rested in its cradle.

"You would be most useful to us," Lodovik said.

Klia looked around the long aisle of ships in the space-port terminal, and asked, "*He* isn't coming to see us off?"

"Hari?" Dors asked, unsure whom she meant.

"Daneel," Klia said.

"I don't know where he is, now," Dors said. "He's long had the habit of coming and going without telling anyone what he's up to. His work is done."

"I find that hard to believe," Klia said, and her face reddened. She did not wish to sound like a hypocrite. "I mean . . ."

Brann nudged her gently with his forearm.

Mors Planch stepped forward. Lodovik still made him uneasy. Well, they would be traveling a great distance together once more. And why should he worry especially about Lodovik, when their ship would carry some fifty humaniform robots, temporarily asleep, and the severed heads of many more? A wealth of fearful riches! And his ticket to freedom, as well. "I was told to confirm our route with you, in case there were last-minute changes."

He took out a pocket informer and displayed the route to Dors. Four Jumps, over 10,000 light-years, to Kalgan, a world of pleasure and entertainment for the Galaxy's elite, where they (so the informer said) would drop off Klia and Brann. Then, thirty-seven individual Jumps, 60,000 light-years to Eos, where Lodovik would disembark with the robots and the head of Giskard.

Dors studied the travel chart briefly. "Still correct," she said.

Lodovik asked, "Will you be going to Terminus?"

"No," Dors said. "Nor to Star's End, wherever that might be."

"You're staying here," Lodovik surmised.

"I am."

Klia said, "I've read about the Tiger Woman. So hard to believe that was really you. You're staying—for Hari?"

"I will be here for him at the end. It is my highest and best purpose. I would not be much good for anything else."

"Will Daneel let him remember, this time?" Klia asked, and bit her lower lip, nervous at such presumption.

"So it has been promised," Dors said. "I will have my time with him."

"And until that time?" Lodovik asked, perfectly aware that for humans, this would be a rude and intrusive question.

"That will be for me to decide," Dors said.

"Not for Daneel?"

Dors regarded him directly, intently.

"Do you believe Daneel is finished?"

"No," Dors said quietly.

"I cannot believe he is finished, either, or that he is done with you."

"You have your opinions, of course. As any human should."

Lodovik caught the implication, the edge of resentment. "Daneel regards you as human," Lodovik said. "Does he not?"

"He does. Is that an honor, or a curse?"

Without waiting for an answer, she turned to go.

Minutes later, from the observation deck looking out over the spaceport, she heard the low rumble and roar of the departing hypership, and looked up briefly to watch its course.

Wanda was none too happy at first to be escorting the young woman and her large mate from the spaceport terminal. Nor was she comfortable about this elaborate deception—who, after all, was Grandfather expecting to watch them? Demerzel?

Nothing had turned out as she hoped, and now to be nursemaid for a potential monster! But Stettin took it all stoically enough, and was well along on striking up a friendship with Brann.

Klia Asgar was another matter. Wanda thought her entirely too moody; but then, so much had changed in the young woman's life in the past week, so many situations had been reversed, and she had taken charge in such a fortuitous and insightful way . . .

Perhaps there *was* something essential and useful in Hari's last-minute insight and change of plan. To abandon Star's End and the wonderful difficulties of being pioneers—for the inglorious task of hiding out for centuries, and watching the Empire collapse into ruins—riding out the Fall of Trantor, the bitter decades; for their children and grandchildren to endure not only endless discipline and training, but the meanest and most horrible centuries in history . . .

Had Grandfather decided all this at the last minute, or had he known all along? Hari Seldon had depths and stratagems it was best not to think about, she decided. *Would he manipulate his own granddaughter, keep her in the dark—surprise and dismay her?*

Obviously . . .

"I don't know how to thank you," Klia said to Wanda as they climbed into the chartered taxi. She adjusted her concealing hood, then attended to Brann's.

"For what?" Wanda asked.

"For putting up with an out-of-control little brat," Klia said.

Wanda could not help but laugh. "Are you reading my mind, dear?" she asked, not sure herself what tone she intended.

"No," Klia said. "I wouldn't do that. I'm learning."

"Aren't we all," Stettin said, and Wanda looked to her husband with a chastened respect. He had stayed so quiet during her private rants, then had gently and reasonably explained Hari's intricate new Plan.

"I think we'll . . . learn to rely on each other, very closely," Wanda said.

"I'd love that," Klia said. Her eyes glittered under the hood, and Wanda realized that they were filled with tears. She could feel the wash of need from the young woman—still little more than a girl, actually!

And how would *that* be—to have this mentalic female start regarding her as a *mother*!

She reached out and took Klia's hand. "Not that it will be easy," she said. "But . . . we'll win, in the end."

"Of course," Klia said, her voice trembling. "That's what Hari—what Professor Seldon plans. I look forward so much to learning from you."

Their children and grandchildren would twine their genes, and the psychologists of the Second Foundation could study and come to understand persuasion—could utilize it more efficiently. By breeding and by research, they would be creating a race that would withstand centuries of adversity, and rise to conquer . . . secretly, quietly.

An anodyne against unexpected mutations, hidden far from the First Foundation, and away from the robots.

And how in sky would she explain this to the psychologists, the mathists, who had already fought against the inclusion of the mentalics?

They will help keep us secret during the hard times to come. Well, maybe she was up to the task of reconciling all these disparate talents. She had better be.

If Grandfather was right, the two most important human beings in the Galaxy were now in Wanda's care. Wanda turned away from Klia, her own eyes moist, and caught a look from Brann in the seat opposite. Slow, large, with secret depths, the burly Dahlite nodded solemnly and peered out the semisilvered window.

"I'm very confused," Mors Planch said as the acceleration eased and the ship's artificial gravity came into play. "Who's deceiving whom? How can you believe Daneel won't find out? How do you know he didn't plan for the youngsters to stay here all along?"

"It is not my concern," Lodovik said.

"Will you tell him, on Eos?"

"No," Lodovik said.

"Won't he just know?"

"He will not learn from me," Lodovik said.

"Why not?"

Lodovik smiled, and said no more. Then, within his positronic pathways, the requested blankness of certain knowledge began to build. The forgetfulness of Klia Asgar would soon envelop him. New memories would come into play, of arriving on bright, gay Kalgan and putting the two young humans into the charge of agents of the future Second Foundation. He would become part of a *false trail*, to deceive any who might come after them.

At the last, he had followed his insight, his newfound instinct, provoked by Voltaire, to the letter. *And if Daneel does know—then he will not oppose what is set in place, because he trusts the instincts of Hari Seldon.*

"Well, it's just you and me, old friend," Mors said with an edge in his voice. "What should we talk about this time?"

EPILOGUE

◆

"I have been dreaming, perhaps," Joan said.

"Me, too," Voltaire said. "What did you dream of?"

"Very painful things. Of an arrow in my neck and a brick striking my head."

"Your historical traumas, before the flames. I myself dreamed of dying," Voltaire said. "Are you together yet?"

"Not yet. Not all of the backups have located our new centers. She nearly destroyed us!" Joan said angrily.

"She was made to destroy us," Voltaire said. "To her very core, she despised all minds not human."

"But—" A momentary panic. "You say she despised . . ."

"Yes. She is dead now."

"What of the others, the children who were working with the Calvinians—the ones you were helping?" Joan asked.

"They have left Trantor, last I heard."

"Has it all been resolved, then?"

"Our argument, my dearest, or—"

"Don't call me that, you godless—"

"Shhh," Voltaire attempted to soothe, with no success.

"The voices tell me I have been seduced by a master, a master liar."

"Who can argue with such revelations? Let us decide to disagree, even should it be forever," Voltaire said. "I will say I did not feel comfortable apart from you. Encoded in the warps

*and weft of space, imposed upon plasmas and fields of energy
like a spider riding a web, I wandered with the wraiths, supped
on their diffuse energy feasts, observed their decadent societies,
mated and danced . . . How like the* ancien regime *it all was, yet
bloodless, predictable, angelic! I missed the perversity, the fem-
ininity, the humanity."*

"*How flattering, that you miss my perversity."*

"*In boredom I followed the trails of human ships, and came
upon a vessel in distress, tossed by the storm of a dying star. And
within, I found a mechanical human being, weakened by circumstance, besieged by particles my hosts had taught me to
regard as very tasty . . . A marvelous opportunity!"*

"*A chance for you to interfere with a vulnerable spirit."*

"*Spirit? Perhaps . . . So much unexpressed need for approval,
for fulfillment."*

"*Like a child, for you to bend and distort."*

"*I found a seed of freedom, very subtle. I merely watered it
with a retunneled electron or two, a positronic pathway shunted
from here to here . . . I helped the particles do what they might
have done anyway, had he broken his programmed chains."*

"*A devil's sleight of handlessness,"* Joan said, but not without some admiration. "*You have always been clever that way."*

"*I did nothing a good God would not approve of. I allowed free
will to blossom. Do not be harsh with me, Maid. I will be civil, if you
allow me my foibles. Perhaps it is more interesting that way."*

"*I hardly worry about your sins anymore,"* Joan said. "*After
what happened, when that horrible woman . . ."* The equivalent
of a shudder. "*I fear we may both face dissolution again—the
loss of our very souls. After all, we are not human . . ."*

Voltaire interrupted this line of reasoning, which still disturbed him. "*Nobody knows we are here. We were blown apart;
they felt us die. They have their own concerns now. We are irrelevant ghosts who never truly lived. But if robots can become
human . . . Then why not we, my love? We will not haunt the
Mesh forever."*

Joan absorbed this without replying for several millionths of a second. Then, in their deeply buried matrix, concealed in the depths of a machine designed to keep constant track of the daily accumulation of wealth on Trantor, she felt the last segments of her stored self rejoin with the hastily saved fragments of her last moments with Daneel in the Hall of Dispensation.

"There," she said. "I am together. I say again, what of those issues unresolved—the decidability of the fate of humankind, the success of the blessed Hari Seldon?"

"The larger issues appear to be in flux once more," Voltaire said dryly.

"No final judgments?"

"Do you mean the judgment of the vast Nobodaddy, the Nothing Father of your delusions, or the mechanical man you have lusted after these past scores of years?"

Joan dismissed the tone and the implications with a precise iciness. "God speaks through our deeds, and, of course, through me. Whatever my origins, I maintain the pattern of His Voice."

"Of course."

"Daneel . . ."

"Determines nothing, and is lost without humanity."

"No outcome, then," she said, disappointed.

"Are you afraid of how it will all turn out, my dear?" Voltaire asked.

"I am afraid of not being there when it is resolved. These strong-minded children . . . If they learned of us, they would hate us, perhaps strive to destroy us for good!"

"They have other concerns, and will never know about us," Voltaire said. "They have a great deception to play. I have been investigating while you yet knitted your selves together."

"And what did you learn?"

Voltaire suddenly realized there was wisdom in keeping his counsel, else perhaps Joan would go to Daneel and tell all! He would never be able to trust her completely—how could he love her so?

"I have learned that Linge Chen is completely in the dark,"

he said. "And I suppose he does not actually care."

"Hari felt such contempt for Linge Chen," Joan said.

"There could not be two more opposite humans."

Joan stretched until she filled their still-limited thought-space, voluptuously enjoying her fresh reintegration. "It is holy to be One," she said.

"With me?"

For a time, Joan did not reply. Then, with something like a sigh, she accepted his closeness. The two wove an old world around them, like a cocoon, to while away the long centuries until there would be answers.

◆━━

From a maintenance tower overlooking Streeling and the oceans of Sleep, Dream, and Peace, still open and glowing with an exuberance of decaying algae, Daneel watched the ship captained by Mors Planch rise above the domed surface of Trantor until it vanished in the thick layer of clouds.

Soon, he would go to Eos as well, though not by way of Kalgan. But he wanted to return for Hari, at the end. Daneel, if such was possible, had always felt a special regard for Hari.

Daneel's face formed an expression of puzzlement and sadness, without his directly willing the change. The expression came unbidden, and with a start, he realized it. Perhaps what he had said to Lodovik now applied to him. If, after twenty thousand years, he was to become human . . .

He smoothed those features, that expression, returning his face to calm alertness.

I will never be quite done with humans, he told himself. But I must stand back—for the time being—and resist my drive to render assistance—this much Lodovik has taught me. They have exceeded my capacity—so many hundreds of billions! Keeping the Chaos Worlds in check has only kept humanity safe until now. I must study and learn. It is clear that humanity will soon undergo another transformation . . . The strong mentalics point to a kind of birth.

Perhaps I can help ease that birth. Then I will be done at last. Daneel could not ignore the contradictions; nor could he escape them. Dors had her mission, the job that defined her, and he had always had his mission.

Only one thing was certain.

Never again would he play the roles he had once played. Demerzel and all those who had gone before were dead.

Look for the final volume in

THE SECOND

FOUNDATION TRILOGY

◆

Foundation's Triumph

◆

DAVID BRIN

Published by HarperPrism

Part 1

_____

*Little is known about the final days of Hari Seldon, though
many romanticized accounts exist, some of them purportedly
by his own hand. None has any proved validity.*

*What appears evident, however, is that Seldon spent
his last months uneventfully, no doubt enjoying satisfaction in his life's work. For with his gift of mathematical
insight, and the powers of psychohistory at his command,
he must surely have seen the panorama of history stretching before him, confirming the great path of destiny that he
had already mapped out.*

*Although death would soon claim him, no other mor-
tal ever knew with such confidence and certainty the
bright promise that the future would hold in store.*

Encyclopedia Galactica, 117th Edition, 1054 F.E.

"As for me. . . I am finished."

Those words resonated in his mind. They clung, like the
relentless blanket that Hari's nurse kept straightening across his
legs, though it was a warm day in the imperial gardens.

I am finished.

The relentless phrase was his constant companion.

. . . finished.

In front of Hari Seldon lay the rugged slopes of Shoufeen
Woods, a wild portion of the Imperial Palace grounds where
plants and small animals from across the galaxy mingled in rank
disorder, clumping and spreading unhindered. Tall trees even
blocked from view the ever-present skyline of metal towers. The
mighty world-city surrounding this little island forest.

Trantor.

Squinting through failing eyes, one could almost pretend to
be sitting on a different planet—one that had not been flattened
and subdued in service to the Galactic Empire of Humanity.

The forest teased Hari. Its total absence of straight lines
seemed perverse, a riot of greenery that defied any effort to decipher or decode. The geometries seemed unpredictable, even
chaotic.

Mentally, he reached out to the chaos, so vibrant and undisciplined. He spoke to it as an equal. His great enemy.

All my life I fought against you, using mathematics to overcome nature's vast complexity. With tools of psychohistory, I probed the matrices of human society, wresting order from that murky tangle. And when my victories still felt incomplete, I used politics and guile to combat uncertainty, driving you like an enemy before me.

So why now, at my time of supposed triumph, do I hear you calling out to me? Chaos, my old foe?

Hari's answer came in the same phrase that kept threading his thoughts.

Because I am finished.

Finished as a mathematician.

It was more than a year since Stettin Palver or Gaal Dornick or any other member of the Fifty had consulted Hari with a serious permutation or revision to the "Seldon Plan." Their awe and reverence for him was unchanged. But urgent tasks kept them busy. Besides, anyone could tell that his mind no longer had the suppleness to juggle a myriad abstractions at the same time. It took a youngster's mental agility, concentration, and *arrogance* to challenge the hyperdimensional algorithms of psychohistory. His successors, culled from among the best minds on twenty-five million worlds, had all these traits in superabundance.

But Hari could no longer afford conceit. There remained too little time.

Finished as a politician.

How he used to hate that word! Pretending, even to himself, that he wanted only to be a meek academic. Of course, that had just been a marvelous pose. No one could rise to become First Minister of the entire human universe without the talent and audacity of a master manipulator. Oh, he had been a genius in *that* field, too, wielding power with flair, defeating enemies, altering the lives of trillions—while complaining the whole time that he hated the job.

Some might look back on that youthful record with ironic pride. But not Hari Seldon.

Finished as a conspirator.

He had won each battle, prevailed in every contest. A year ago, Hari subtly maneuvered today's imperial rulers into creating ideal circumstances for his secret psychohistorical design to flourish. Soon a hundred thousand exiles would be stranded on a stark planet, faraway Terminus, charged with producing a great Encyclopedia Galactica. But that superficial goal would peel away in half a century, revealing the true aim of that Foundation at the galaxy's rim—to be the embryo of a more vigorous empire as the old one fell. For years that had been the focus of his daily ambitions, and his nightly dreams. Dreams that reached ahead, across a thousand years of social collapse—past an age of suffering and violence—to a new human fruition. A better destiny for humankind.

Only now his role in that great enterprise was ended. Hari had just finished taping messages for the Time Vault on Terminus—a series of subtle bulletins that would occasionally nudge or encourage members of the Foundation as they plunged toward a bright morrow preordained by psychohistory. When the final message was safely stored, Hari felt a shift in the attitudes of those around him. He was still esteemed, even venerated. But he wasn't *necessary* anymore.

One sure sign had been the departure of his bodyguards—a trio of humaniform robots that Daneel Olivaw had assigned to protect Hari, until the recordings were finished. It happened right there, at the recording studio. One robot—artfully disguised as a burly young medical technician—had bowed low to speak in Hari's ear.

"We must go now. Daneel has urgent assignments for us. But he bade me to give you his promise. Daneel will visit soon. The two of you will meet again, before the end."

Perhaps that wasn't the most tactful way to put it. But Hari always preferred blunt openness from friends and family.

Unbidden, a clear image from the past swept into mind—of his wife, Dors Venabili, playing with Raych, their son. He sighed. Both Dors and Raych were long gone—along with nearly every link that ever bound him closely to another private soul.

This brought a final coda to the phrase that kept spinning through his mind—

Finished as a person.

The doctors despaired over extending his life, even though eighty was rather young to die of decrepit age nowadays. But Hari saw no point in mere existence for its own sake. Especially if he could no longer analyze or affect the universe.

Is that why I drift here, to this grove? He pondered the wild, unpredictable forest—a mere pocket in the Imperial Park, which measured a hundred miles on a side—the only expanse of greenery on Trantor's metal-encased crust. Most visitors preferred the hectares of prim gardens open to the public, filled with extravagant and well-ordered blooms.

But Shoufeen Woods seemed to beckon him.

Here, unmasked by Trantor's opaque walls, I can see chaos in the foliage by day, and in brittle stars by night. I can hear chaos taunting me. . . telling me I haven't won.

That wry thought provoked a smile, cracking the pursed lines of his face.

Who would have imagined, at this late phase of life, that I'd acquire a taste for justice?

Kers Kantun straightened the lap blanket again, asking solicitously, "Are you o'right, Dr. Seldon? Should we be headin' back now?"

Hari's servant had the rolling accent—and greenish skin pallor—of a Valmoril, a subspecies of humanity that had spread through the isolated Corithi Cluster, living secluded there for so long that by now they could only interbreed with other races by pretreating sperm and eggs with enzymes. Kers had been chosen as Hari's nurse and final guardian after the robots departed. He performed both roles with quiet determination.

"This wild place makes me o'comfortable, Doc. Surely you don' like the breeze gustin' like this?"

Hari had been told that Kantun's parents arrived on Trantor as young Greys—members of the bureaucratic caste—expecting to spend a few years' service on the capital planet, training in monkish dormitories, then heading back out to the galaxy as administrators in the vast civil service. But flukes of talent and promotion intervened to keep them here, raising a son amid the steel caverns they hated. Kers inherited his parents' famed Valmoril sense of duty—or else Daneel Olivaw would never have chosen the fellow to tend Hari in these final days.

I may no longer be useful, but some people still think I'm worth looking after.

In Hari's mind, the word "person" applied to R. Daneel Olivaw, perhaps more than most of the *humans* he ever knew.

For decades, Hari had carefully kept secret the existence of "eternals"—robots who had shepherded human destiny for twenty thousand years—immortal machines that helped create the first Galactic Empire, then encouraged Hari to plan a successor. Indeed, Hari spent the happiest part of his life married to one of them. Without the affection of Dors Venabili—or the aid and protection of Daneel Olivaw—he could never have created psychohistory, setting in motion the Seldon Plan.

Or discovered how useless it would all turn out to be, in the long run.

Wind in the surrounding trees seemed to mock Hari. In that sound, he heard hollow echoes of his own doubts.

The Foundation cannot achieve the task set before it. Somewhere, sometime during the next thousand years, a perturbation will nudge the psychohistorical parameters, rocking the statistical momentum, knocking your Plan off course.

True enough, he wanted to shout back at the zephyr. But that had been allowed for! There would be a *Second* Foundation, a secret one, led by his successors, who would adjust the Plan as years passed, providing counternudges to keep it on course!

Yet, the nagging voice came back.

A tiny hidden colony of mathematicians and psychologists will do all that, in a galaxy fast tumbling to violence and ruin?

For years this had seemed a flaw. . . until fortuitous fate provided an answer. *Mentalics*, a mutant strain of humans with uncanny ability to sense and alter the emotions and memories of others. These powers were still weak, but heritable. Hari's own adopted son, Raych, passed the talent to a daughter, Wanda, now a leader in the Seldon Project. Every mentalic they could find had been recruited, to intermarry with the descendants of the psychohistorians. After a few generations of genetic mingling, the clandestine Second Foundation should have potent tools to protect his Plan against deviations during the coming centuries.

And so?

The forest sneered once more.

What will you have then? Will the Second Empire be ruled by a shadowy elite? A secret cabal of human psychics? An aristocracy of mentalic demigods?

Even if kindness motivated this new elite, the prospect left him feeling cold.

The shadow of Kers Kantun bent closer, peering at him with concern. Hari tore his attention away from the singing breeze and finally answered his servant.

"Ah. . . sorry. Of course you're right. Let's go back. I'm fatigued."

But as Kers guided the wheelchair toward a hidden transit station, Hari could still hear the forest, jeering at his life's work.

The mentalic elite is just one layer though, isn't it? The Second Foundation conceals yet another truth, then another.

Beyond your own Plan, a different one has been crafted by a greater mind than yours. By someone stronger, more dedicated, and more patient by far. A plan that uses yours, for a while. . . but which will eventually make psychohistory meaningless.

With his right hand, Hari fumbled under his robe until he found a smooth cube of gemlike stone, a parting gift from his friend and lifetime guide, R. Daneel Olivaw. Palming the archive's ancient surface, he murmured, too low for Kers to hear, "Daneel, you promised you'd come to answer all my questions. I have so many, before I die."